That Tender Light

Copyright © 2011 D. James Then
author@djamesthen.com

ISBN: 978-1-60910-734-5
Library of Congress Control Number: 2011901917

All rights reserved. No part of this publication may be reproduced, stored in a retrieval system, or transmitted in any form or by any means, electronic, mechanical, recording, or otherwise, without the prior written permission of the author.

Printed in the United States of America; Hebron, KY

THAT TENDER LIGHT is a work of fiction. Names, characters, places, incidents, settings, and dialogue are the products of the author's imagination or are used fictitiously. Any resemblance to actual events, locales, persons—living or dead—is entirely coincidental.

Booklocker.com, Inc.
2011

That Tender Light

D. James Then

For:

BARBARA

Nicholas, Jacob, and Margaret

Michael P. Stephens and Judith K. Wright

Joel Brown and Robert DiTommaso, boyhood friends from Lackawanna, NY, who gave their lives during the Vietnam War; May the Lord forever hold these men in the palm of His hand.

✝

> All that's best of dark and bright
> Meet in her aspect and her eyes:
> Thus mellow'd to that tender light
> Which heaven to gaudy day denies.
> —Lord Byron

Book One

August 2010

The truth is rarely pure and never simple.
—Oscar Wilde

One

En route to St. Omer, IN
2:01p.m., Thursday, August 12, 2010

EXITING THE GREATER Cincinnati/Northern Kentucky International Airport, Investigative Reporter Lockwood McGuire turned west onto I-275, crossed the Ohio River, and merged onto I-74 on his way to Indiana via southwest Ohio.

After a nine-month investigation, Lock's gut said he was hours away from solving the baffling and mysterious 25-year absence of reclusive novelist Jack Taylor. He believed Margaret Lee, the ninety-eight-year-old woman he would meet on Friday afternoon, knew what happened to Taylor, and Lock hoped the document he discovered would convince the old girl to tell her story.

Taylor, an American hero and author of eight best-selling novels in the 1970s and 80s, vanished in 1986 at the height of his popularity. No one had seen or heard from him since.

As Lock drove westward this day, the afternoon temperature was in the mid-eighties. However, the humidity was low, an August rarity in the Midwest. Lock considered the air conditioning but decided instead on the rush of clean air flowing in through open windows. It was a refreshing change of pace in his polluted and always-hectic world. He passed a semi and set the cruise control at seventy-five.

St. Omer, Indiana, and his destination—a rural bed and breakfast—was still about an hour away. His colleague on the story, Bridgette Hannah, was already on-site awaiting Lock's arrival and handling local fact-finding. They were to have flown out of LaGuardia together the night before; however, a last-minute phone call kept McGuire writing feverishly at his desk in the newsroom.

Lock smiled. Things were finally coming together.

Back in December when Jake Prescott, executive editor of THE NEW YORK EPOCH, first broached the Taylor assignment, it was eighteen blustery degrees in Manhattan. The temperature from that day to this was one extreme. Lock's interest in the Taylor story was the other. He was against the project initially; now, it consumed him.

As he neared the Ohio/Indiana state line, he remembered his and Prescott's tête-à-tête on a frigid afternoon in 2009, two days before Christmas...

...Why me?"

"Because no one knows what happened to Taylor."

"And you think I'll find out?"

"You always do."

"But, why me?" Lock persisted.

"Knock it off," Prescott said, glaring at his reporter. "I've heard your pointless question six times within five minutes. I won't hear it anymore—not today, not tomorrow, not ever again!"

"Pointless? Pointless, my ass; maybe I'll make it six times sixty," Lock shot back. He was not a happy camper.

"Sounds a bit biblical, bub," Prescott said, shrugging. "The answer's the same, regardless."

"Regardless?"

"Regardless of how much you piss and moan, it's your story, your assignment."

"Piss and moan?"

"Yeah, you challenge everything, all the time."

"I do not."

"Check your response, ace, it actually proves me right."

"No one has ever complained to me."

"Lock, you intimidate editors and reporters by walking into a room. Do you really think anyone has the balls to tell you? The truth is the truth whether spoken or not."

"I should have a say in my assignments, chief!"

Exasperation pushed Prescott's eyebrows upward. "Quite often you do, just not today."

"You're serious. My perspective doesn't count?"

"Let me repeat, frequently it does, but not this time. Incidentally, if or when you find an entitlement clause in your contract, show me!"

"Jake, this Taylor thing is fluff; the union was next."

"Probably in your mind but your union corruption angle is weak, at best. Taylor, on the other hand, is necessary journalism."

"You did say *necessary*?"

"Yes," Prescott replied.

"Really?"

"Yeah, *really;* Taylor's sold 170-million books worldwide. That means millions of readers and millions of reasons to do the story. He was top dog in the late seventies and for most of the eighties. He received a Pulitzer and every other major writing award, except the Nobel for Literature. For good measure, you can toss in his Medal of Honor from Vietnam. Lock, people adore heroes and enjoy watching them from ringside seats. They can't get enough of it."

"A missing novelist is more important than union deceit?"

"I've read your brief on the union. Just because you think a few apples are rotten doesn't mean they are."

"Jesus, Jake. I'm not wrong."

"Perhaps, but I know Taylor is missing. I know people love his books." Prescott paused to use his hands as scales. "Let's see, 170-million books and worldwide acclaim on one hand versus a few thousand interested union members on the other. Geez, it seems like millions and worldwide acclaim wins every time."

"It's been nearly twenty-five years," Lock argued. "He's probably bones in a grave somewhere."

"He might be," Prescott acknowledged. "But what if he isn't?" he quickly added. "Some people, including me, think he disappeared on purpose. If so, then why and where did he go? Does he still write or did he stop altogether? Did he find a new life and chuck the old? What were the circumstances? It's a big story…big stories get my best investigator and that my friend is you."

"Jake, whatever his motives, they have cooled with time. He disappeared in 1986."

"Yes. He returned from London, the first leg of a book tour, and vanished. He skipped out on a series of meetings and interviews, which his reclusiveness says he didn't like anyway, and, like an old song, was dust in the wind."

Irritation filled Lock's expression. He wanted out.

"How will I find anything? He was withdrawn, he hated publicity, and his death would complicate a search. The last time I checked shy dead men don't give interviews."

"However, if he's alive, he just might talk," Prescott countered. "His public would love that. He's an icon on college campuses. Hell, they teach courses about his books and style.

"All of Taylor's novels became profitable movies. Guesstimates say his personal wealth approaches several hundred million. That's a hell of a lot of ginger snaps to leave behind in a cookie jar. The money's in a private trust. I want you to find out why he left, where the money goes, where he is, and what his life's been like for nearly two and a half decades. That's a damn fine story—front page, top fold, maximum exposure."

"Let me get this straight, Jake. You're in the archives saying adios to a retiree, you see a dusty envelope and, voila, Lock McGuire gets a story?"

"Yep," Prescott said, "miracles happen. I want this to be captivating and insightful."

He paused for emphasis.

"And goddamned gripping," the editor added. "Get inside Taylor's head. Sniff the trail like a foxhound. Find out what happened, what changed, why he turned away from a storied career, and what his life is like today. We call that news, my friend, not fluff.

"Recipients of the Medal of Honor rarely drop out. I checked. He displayed remarkable courage and worked hard to become a great novelist. Why toss it all away? It stirs my curiosity; it should arouse yours, Lock. His fans will agree. Remember, that's millions of potential readers."

Lock studied Prescott's gray and bushy eyebrows, which complemented the alabaster sky swirling beyond the windowpane. They had worked together for twenty years. Prescott was sincere, supportive, instinctual, and non-patronizing. However, Lock considered the Taylor story busy work for interns, cubs, or burned-out reporters awaiting their pensions.

"Stiles or Bishop could do this story in a heartbeat," Lock offered.

"However, they're in Albany on assignment. You are here; you are my ace, the best investigative journalist in the country, a bulldog with three Pulitzers. And, if you don't mind," Prescott paused for dramatic effect, "the most persistent son of a bitch alive. Lock, do the fucking story and stop being a pain in my ass."

"Come on, Jake," Lock said. "It's not about awards or persistence; it's about great stories. This one's a scud."

"No, it isn't. You're my best shooter so, to use a pun, *lock and load*. It's your story."

"Why..."

Prescott raised his hand and whispered, "Remember, lad, discretion is the better part of valor."

Lock smiled and nodded in deference to his editor.

"Surely, there's someone else?"

Prescott smiled a tight, frustrated smile.

"Lock, what part of *it's your story* don't you get?" Prescott lowered his voice for emphasis. "If I say no one else, I mean *no one else*. Why debate it? Taylor's life is a blur. My gut says somebody somewhere knows something. Find that person, find Taylor, and find my story."

"Seriously, did Taylor win a Pulitzer?" Lock said, thinking about Prescott's earlier statement.

"Yes, for THE LAST CHAMPION AND THE LAST KING."

"Why do you think he never accepted it?"

"I have no idea."

"Do we know anything?"

"Yes, after London his agent cancelled Taylor's '86 book tour stating his client needed time to recover from a frantic work pace and the recent death of his grandfather."

"So, the agent must have known something," Lock theorized. "I mean logically the statement precludes an accident. He was definitely covering for Taylor."

Prescott nodded. "Taylor was in Manhattan to meet with his publisher and to promote his book before going to Chicago. He had a few interviews scheduled and was considering a new deal, including a book on Vietnam. However, he took his dog, vanished, and never resurfaced. Something happened, something life altering. It's odd."

"The fact that he took his dog indicates premeditation."

Prescott winked.

"You think Taylor could still be alive?"

"He'd be in his mid-sixties," Prescott noted.

"Who's the agent?" Lock asked.

"Walter Levy was; but, he died. Levy, Jr., has the reigns. Background is in the red file on the corner of my desk. Somebody had a notion to do a story in 1991, but it never happened and the file collected dust."

"I can't avoid this, can I?" Lock stated.
"Not a chance. Incidentally, Biddy's working with you."
"Who?"
"Biddy Hannah, she has good instincts and will be a fine investigative reporter. I want her learning from the best."
"Biddy?"
"It's short for Bridgette. She studied journalism at Saint Bonaventure, as Taylor did."
"Jake, am I being punished for some unspoken reason?"
Prescott laughed.
"No, she's an experienced reporter. I figure the St. Bonaventure connection helps. Taylor donated his working drafts and copies of personal papers from each novel to the university. They also have an extensive collection of press clippings and articles."
Lock nodded. "Okay, I'll have her visit the school, possibly something pops."
"Good choice. Shifting gears, how you holding up, Lock?"
Prescott's expression grew serious and Lock immediately knew why. Lock's wife had left him a few months back, at a time when he was working sixteen-hour days and was knee-deep in a story about phony police informants. A quick divorce ended a quicker marriage.
"I've good days and bad. I'm moving forward," Lock noted.
"Thanks for your honesty. You need a change of pace, bud. Do the story and find America's hero. You should get out of here for a few days and try to enjoy the holidays before you work the story. Bridgette will join you in early January, after her vacation. Keep me posted."
"Is this a charity hump?" asked Lock, in a final display of rebellion.
The editor shrugged. "In its purest form, no; it's legit. However, whether you know it or not you run hard. This story provides a tough challenge and a good change of pace."

Lock weighed the comment. "I guess it can't hurt."

He scanned the top of his editor's desk. "No cigarettes?"

Prescott rolled his eyes. "I gave them up a few years ago. Considering your sister's lung cancer, you should, too. Now, leave; I have financial projections to review for 2011."

"On December 23?"

"It's the reason I get the big bucks. But for you, I'd be home drinking scotch."

Lock smiled, bummed a piece of chewing gum, took the assignment sheet and background file, stood up, and started to leave. He paused at the door.

"Can I still have the union guys?"

Prescott smiled. "They won't go away."

"Listen, I know sometimes I'm a pain in the ass."

"Good assessment. The budget code is on the assignment sheet. Get Bridgette involved and do us proud."

"You always get my best," Lock replied.

Prescott pointed at McGuire. "The very reason I picked you, Merry Christmas..."

THE NOISE FROM a passing van pulled Lock back into his warm August afternoon.

Moments later, a road sign indicated he was now in Indiana. However, driving over a rise, he found bumper-to-bumper traffic at least a mile long. In the distance, police lights flashed and a gray sky spoke ominously of rain. A few drops hit the windshield.

He braked, stopped the car, closed the windows, and turned on the air conditioning. He was grateful his appointment with Margaret Lee was not until the next day. Lock picked up his cell.

Two

Bender's B & B, St. Omer, IN
2:45 p.m., Thursday, August 12, 2010

WHEN HER CELL phone rang, Bridgette Hannah thought immediately of Lock McGuire and her heartbeat quickened. She liked him—a lot. He was smart, handsome and a remarkable investigative journalist. The fact that he did not have the slightest idea about her intense attraction to him only deepened her desire. His focus and passion for his work made him naïve to the obvious needs of others; no wonder his ex-wife left him.

"Hello," Bridgette answered after the third ring.

"Hi Biddy, it's Lock."

"Where are you? I thought you'd be here by now."

"I'm caught in a traffic jam near the St. Leon exit. A tractor-trailer hit a guardrail and flipped over. How many people have you interviewed?"

"Approximately twenty," Bridgette replied.

"Anything worthwhile?"

"Yes, a waitress at a local diner remembered Taylor's face when I showed his photograph, although she didn't know who he was. She said he knew Margaret Lee's niece."

"Bingo! That's our first confirmation. Did she seem credible? It was years ago."

"Yes. She said Taylor came into the diner frequently early in the morning for coffee and would write."

"Even better, what makes her so sure?"

"She said she spilled coffee on his papers once and, after cleaning up, asked what he was writing. He told her it was a story about his experiences in Southeast Asia."

"The oft-rumored book about Vietnam," Lock theorized. "I wonder if he ever wrote it."

"I don't know. Anyway, they talked at length when she mentioned that her brother died in Vietnam. Also, she said he always left a twenty-dollar tip."

"Ah, the real reason surfaces, waitresses never forget big tippers," Lock said. "It confirms that he was in the area. That's my girl."

I wish it were so, Bridgette thought. "Hey, can you tell me about the phone call?"

"Phone call?" asked Lock.

"Yes, the one that kept you in the office yesterday, silly."

"Sure, the guy I hired to do background on Margaret Lee called in with his report. You'll recall we didn't find much."

"Well?"

"She's lived on her farm all her life. She was born there. Her husband, William Lee, died in World War II. She never had children, although she did raise a niece, who taught at a local college. Lee's a millionaire, lives with her long-time housekeeper, and keeps to herself. She's never left the country. She's not related to Taylor in any way and, of course, she's nearly one hundred years old."

"Doesn't seem like much to go on, does it?"

"No. For the hell of it, can you do a search on the niece to see if anything pops?"

"I already checked. I didn't find a thing."

"Nothing popped on Lily Veronica Hall?"

"Lily Veronica Hall," Bridgette repeated the name. "Damn, the waitress said he knew Ms. Lee's deceased niece, Ronnie, and said sometimes they dined together. I thought she might be a friend. I did a quick search on Ronnie Lee. That's why I missed it."

"Lee's maiden name is Hall, Biddy. The niece's name is Lily Veronica Hall." He also told her the name of the college.

"They must have called her Ronnie when she was young."

"Check again, would you? It could be important."

"Absolutely," Bridgette said, feeling foolish.

She loathed errors. Luckily, miscues never bothered Lock. It was yet another reason for her deep attraction to him.

"Good," he replied. "I have no way of knowing when the traffic jam will break and I can't get off the Interstate. It's good we're not meeting Margaret Lee until tomorrow. We'll go over everything when I arrive. Let's have supper."

"It's a date," Bridgette said and cringed. Did she sound too agreeable? Was it too soon to tip her hand about her true feelings? She smiled. Hell, would he recognize it, if she did?

"How's the B & B?"

"Comfortable, we're the only guests," Biddy replied.

"Okay, I'll be there when I can."

After they hung up, Bridgette smiled, latched the door, and went to take a hot shower and wash her hair. As the warm water danced upon her lovely skin, she recalled her first meeting with Lock McGuire.

It was early January, after her holiday. Bridgette was in the office one evening checking messages and sorting mail when she found the assignment card. She also read two, one-page summaries, which Lock placed in her mail slot.

As she put conditioner on her hair, she remembered seeing him across the newsroom. He was typing and did not look up when she sat in the chair beside his desk...

...How'd you get the name Biddy?"

Bridgette smiled to hide her anxiety. Prescott warned her to be prepared, saying Lock had an uncanny knack of putting people off balance to gain an edge.

"My brother, who's older by eighteen months couldn't say Bridgette. When he said my name, it came out Biddy. I guess it stuck."

"I figured it was family."

He finally looked over at her.

If the fact that she was a knockout surprised him, it did not show. Lock seemed not to notice.

"Do you like the content of my briefs?" he asked.

She thought for a moment and risked it.

"We've barely met, but it sounds intriguing."

He studied her eyes and smiled.

"We'll get along just fine. Let me restate. Did you read the two summary sheets I placed in your mail slot?"

"I did."

"What's your take?"

"You write well," she replied, still smiling.

"I meant the assignment."

"I know. I'm interested."

"Good, where did you go on vacation?"

"Vermont, I was skiing with friends."

"Are you any good?"

"At friendship, yes, I think so."

"On skis," he corrected, smiling.

"Yes, I've skied since I was a child." She liked his smile.

"I ski some myself."

"That's nice to know."

"But not when a story's pending," Lock stated. "Now, as you shushed in virgin snow, I was busy working. I placed advertisements in select newspapers across the country and, because Taylor won the Medal of Honor, I added military pubs, too. Guess what?"

"What?"

"Are you a smartass, Biddy?"

"Perhaps I'm a little saucy."

A nod indicated he liked her response.

"Well, Miss Mogul, a number of people responded: a few relatives, people who knew Taylor from his hometown, others who worked with him professionally, and a few who served with him in the Army.

"Busy hands are happy hands," she said.

"While you were sipping pinot grigio in a cozy lodge before the flickering firelight, I talked to each respondent, at length. I also read a few of Taylor's books, and several hundred articles and clippings."

She raised her eyebrows, skeptically.

"I speed read," he explained. "Do you want the long or short version?"

"An informative one," Bridgette replied.

Lock smiled.

"Good answer. Taylor was born in Lackawanna, near Buffalo, in 1947. His parents, Edward and Kate Taylor, died in an automobile accident in 1950 when Jack was three—icy roads. His father, an only child, was driving.

"Tomas and Anne Quinlan Gomez, Taylor's maternal grandparents, were legal guardians; however, William and Rebecca Smith Taylor, his paternal grandparents, helped."

McGuire lifted his notebook, leaned back in his chair, placed his feet on his desk, and smiled. He popped a piece of chewing gum into his mouth and continued.

"Gomez and Quinlan practiced medicine until 1975. They met at the University of Buffalo's Medical School. Gomez, a Cuban, remained in the Buffalo area for his wife. They traveled to Cuba annually, especially in the late 1940s and throughout the 1950s. Taylor tagged along. Their last visit was in 1959; they never returned after the Cuban Revolution.

"In addition to Kate, actually Kathleen, Gomez had another daughter—Olivia—Taylor's aunt and his closest living relative. She's eighty-six and resides in a Sisters-of-Charity hospice in East Aurora, New York."

"Did she offer insight?"

"I didn't talk to her; her mental capacity is that of a child of six. We'll visit her."

"Okay."

"As noted, Taylor spent time with his paternal grandparents. Rebecca, his grandmother, wrote for a weekly newspaper—THE LACKAWANNA TRIBUNE. She died at age 57 in 1964, six months before Taylor finished high school. Her husband died in 1961. Apparently, Rebecca's influence was critical in Taylor's development as a writer."

"She was a young woman," Bridgette observed.

"And by all accounts a real dish. Taylor still has extended family in Buffalo and Havana; however, from the calls I've made, they don't know a thing about his disappearance or his status. You'll follow up.

"He attended Catholic schools and played high school sports. As a teenager, he worked at the weekly newspaper with his grandmother. In fact, he wrote a weekly sports column. He was a good student, a fun-loving kid, and a prankster. No one I talked to in his hometown suspected his heroism or his skill as a novelist. He attended St. Bonaventure University, wrote for the student newspaper, and reported news on the campus radio station. He was also a member of the school's rifle team, which placed second in collegiate nationals. His senior thesis predicted the decline of American newspapers in favor of electronic media."

"Astute," Bridgette said. "Newspapers are a dying breed."

"I know, luckily not ours. At the beginning of his thesis, he cited Thomas Merton's 1948 autobiography, THE SEVEN STORY MOUNTAIN. He said the Trappist received his call to the religious life at the Grotto of St. Therese the Little Flower on St. Bonaventure's campus. Taylor hoped for something similar regarding a career in literature.

"I know the spot."

Lock nodded, adding, "He was graduated with honors in 1968 and received the Mark Hellinger Award, given to the top journalism grad. You won that award, too, didn't you?"

She nodded, surprised Lock knew about her background.

He winked and said, "Because of ROTC, Taylor opted for the U.S. Army. He received his commission in February 1969 and became a Green Beret. He trained at Fort Bragg, North Carolina; at Fort Lewis in Washington State; and in the Philippine jungles. Before going to the Philippines, he won the Wolford Cup and quite a few other prestigious international shooting competitions. Biddy, from what I've learned, the man was a hell of a shot from a thousand yards. I imagine the military loved him.

"Beginning in late-1970, he served two tours in Vietnam, with a stint at the U.S. Embassy in Saigon in-between each tour. Unsubstantiated reports say he was a POW during his second tour. I've also heard rumors about sniper duty in Laos, which seems odd."

"Why?"

"Typically, snipers are enlisted men. What's more, tours in Vietnam were usually twelve months; his stint at the embassy was three. The total should be twenty-seven. Army records list him *in country* for nearly thirty months but don't explain the discrepancy. The dots don't connect."

"I take it you've seen his military records?"

"Absolutely," he replied, surprised she would ask.

"Does the Laos angle hold water?"

"I think so, but there's no proof. Several men who knew Taylor said about eight months into his second tour he left Vietnam. He was at a remote outpost and an aide to his commanding general claims Taylor volunteered for a secret sniper assignment in Laos. He could not elaborate."

"Did he offer proof?"

"Hell, no," Lock replied. "We'll dig in and find some. The fact that none of it appears in his official record doesn't mean it didn't happen. The military protects itself."

"Has any of this ever been reported?" Bridgette asked.

"If it has, I cannot find it. Taylor never discussed it publicly. My gut tells me it is important," Lock said, adding, "I've seen many references to the Medal of Honor but nothing about Laos or sniper duty. It's something we will need to explore."

"I wonder what he was doing there. Do you think it could be pertinent to our story?"

Lock paused, opened a cola, and said, "I don't know, but I find it incongruous."

"How so?" asked Bridgette.

"He attended Catholic schools. His grandparents were devout and active in the Church; they supported Catholic initiatives. The Felician Sisters and the Franciscans educated Taylor. He admired Thomas Merton, a Trappist and by-and-large a pacifist.

"Yet, Taylor was fearless under fire according to those who know. Throw in his skill with a rifle and he's the kind of man a government entrusts with sensitive assignments."

"There's nothing in his military record?" Bridgette seemed surprised.

"Nothing substantial," Lock said. "Even his service as a Green Beret is sketchy. Some claim he'd been shot. If so, I can't find it. His Medal of Honor was for action in Tray Ninh Province, in his first tour of duty. Several sources indicate Taylor did not want the Medal, probably because of the attention. My guess, his nomination occurred after he went to Laos, when he wasn't around to stop it."

"Was he really captured?"

"One source said Taylor was held by the Pathet Lao."

"Who?" Bridgette asked.

"The Pathet Lao, communists fighting for control of Laos. Didn't you study history?"

"Who's cheeky, now? I meant your source."

"Sorry."

McGuire looked at his notes and said, "His name's Steve Liston from L.A. He was a medic at the U.S. Embassy in Vientiane. He is now a doctor and I see no reason why he would lie. He said Taylor recuperated there after an escape. Although he saw Taylor a few times, Liston recognized his picture from my advertisement. He alleges Taylor told him that he and two other men escaped during a rainstorm by floating in tributaries and rivers."

"All this in three weeks," Bridgette said. "Impressive."

"Actually, two and a half, I spent Christmas Eve and Christmas with my sister, the same with New Year's."

Bridgette became thoughtful and said, "Okay, so here's the hundred-dollar question. Assuming everything you've told me is true, what, if anything, does your discovery have to do with Taylor's disappearance?"

Lock shrugged and whispered, "Beats the shit out of me."

"Still, it's very thorough," she suggested, supportively.

"Thorough is what I do. We'll figure it out. I'm sure there's relevance; it's up to us to find out what that is. Do you think you can keep up?"

"You're damned right."

"Good, now here's what I need you to do."

He explained aspects of the story he wanted Bridgette to cover. When he finished, he said, "Do you have a boyfriend?"

"Or girlfriend? Is either question appropriate?"

"Yes, I need to know about limits and time constraints."

"In that case, no; however, I do like to sleep daily. It is fundamental to my well being."

"Mine, too, do you smoke?"

"No."

"Good. I've stopped and don't need the temptation. What about dinner?"

"Yes, I do eat." Bridgette was adamant.

"Good, let's go..."

BRIDGETTE DRIED HER hair, applied makeup, selected earrings, and dressed.

Thereafter, she turned to her computer and accessed various research databases. Deeper insight into Lily Veronica Hall might add substance to their Friday meeting with Margaret Lee, the owner Sycamore Glen Farms.

She and Lock had worked the story hard for nearly nine months. Her intuition said it was coming together and they would get their answers the next day.

Excitement poured through Bridgette's lovely body. She was having fun and Lock's appeal was compelling. She wanted to forge a personal relationship and make it much more intimate. She realized she would have to take the first step. That did not bother her, being aggressive was never a problem. It suited her personality and her appreciation of life's joys and benefits.

As she tapped the computer keys, she smiled; it would not be long before she would see Lock McGuire.

She liked the fact that things seemed to be coming together nicely.

The game was afoot.

Three

Sycamore Glen Farms, St. Omer, IN
3:10 p.m., Thursday, August 12, 2010

THE OLD WOMAN shuffled into the cabin's library, slid several books aside, opened a wall safe, and removed a worn manuscript. As she glanced at the title, she ran her fingers over the edges of the curled pages. A love story, a war story, and so much more, she thought. After so many years the time has come.

A moment later, her niece Jenny, entered the room.

"Would you like tea, Missy?"

Margaret Lee smiled inwardly. She would be ninety-nine in December and people still called her *Missy*.

"I would love a cup," she replied. As she moved toward her favorite leather club chair, lightning flashed outside. Through the cabin window, the distant Flatrock River and a nearby orchard briefly turned eerie blue.

"I don't like this storm," Missy said.

"It's supposed to pass in a few hours. Do you want honey and lemon with your tea?"

"Yes, please. Jenny, will you'll stay in the cabin tonight?"

Missy supported herself with a cane as she walked.

"Yes, I'll take the guest room."

"Then, you'll check my email for the background report I've ordered on Lockwood McGuire, the reporter?"

Jenny nodded, as thunder rumbled above the cabin.

"What about Tillie?" The old woman inquired about Jenny's daughter. "She shouldn't be out in the storm."

"She called earlier. She'll stay the night with friends."

"Good, a favor, please, in the top desk drawer is a blue case. Please, bring it to me."

After handing the object to her aunt, Jenny departed.

Missy set the manuscript down, opened the case, studied its contents, counted thirteen white stars on a field of blue, smiled, closed the lid, and put the box into her apron pocket.

She turned on the reading lamp, hooked her cane on an armrest, and sat. She looked out toward the serpentine river and, in lightning's bluish haze, observed a distant waterfall. Nearby, thunder rumbled again.

Missy rested her head and briefly closed her eyes. She had not read the manuscript in more than a year, yet she retained much of it verbatim. Tears rimmed her eyes as she remembered the saddest day of her long life. When she heard footsteps in the hallway, she quickly wiped her eyes and sat upright.

Jenny set the tea service on a coffee table, filled a cup, and blended in the appropriate amounts of honey and lemon.

"I thought we'd have stew for supper."

"Stew sounds delicious," Missy replied.

"I'll be in the kitchen if you need anything," Jenny said. She leaned forward and kissed her aunt's forehead. Then, she added, "I've never read his book but, from what you've told me, it's the proper decision. People will love his story."

"I hope, but who knows from right? I have to say, it remains the dimmest chapter of my life." Missy thought about the secrets she guarded.

The younger woman nodded. "Call, if you need me."

"I shall, sweetheart."

Missy watched her niece go. Then, after sampling the hot tea, as raindrops pinged against the windowpane, she opened the unpublished manuscript.

Taylor wrote it twenty-some years ago. It was his final book. He sent it to Missy several years after he said goodbye to Lily Veronica Hall, Missy's niece and Jenny's cousin.

"I think it's time, Lily," Missy whispered. "I've guarded our secrets too long. Let's shine our light."

Four

Bender's B & B, St. Omer, IN
4:47 p.m., Thursday, August 12, 2010

AFTER A HOT shower, Lock picked up the phone. "Did you find anything on Lily Hall?" He asked when Bridgette answered his call in the next room.

"You made it," she replied.

"Yep, I already showered and shaved; so, anything to report?" He sounded tense.

Bridgette hesitated. *Lock, would it hurt to say hello?* Then, she told herself to relax. She had made up her mind; the coming evening would have more meaning than Lock ever anticipated. She picked up her notes.

"I learned quite a bit. Lily Hall was born in Greensburg, Indiana, on August 14, 1948. She is the daughter of William and Mildred Hall. All are deceased. Lily was educated at Purdue, Dartmouth, and Cornell where she received a Ph.D. in 1970; her focus was English and American Literature."

"I've sent emails to each university; realistically, I don't anticipate responses until Tuesday. My guess, we'll get replies on Wednesday. Hall taught in New York in 1970-71 at a small private college. She joined the faculty at Hannlin College, which is not too far from Lee's farm. She started as a lecturer and became a fully tenured professor in 1981. By the way, Lily Hall wrote three books."

"She did?"

"Yes, the first on Yeats' poetry was published in the mid-70s; her second came in 1979, the subject was pulp writers of the 1930s, 40s and 50s—Hammett, Chandler, Spillane, et al; and her third, entitled HEMINGWAY'S MAGIC, was published in 1981. She authored numerous professional articles."

"Did she write specific to Taylor?" Lockwood inquired.

"Not that I've found, I'll compile a complete bibliography on Monday.

"Good work, Biddy."

"Oh, but wait sweet man, there's more. I've found two revealing articles, which are *must-reads*. They shine new light on everything. I'll bring them with me; let's eat, I'm ravenous."

"Tell me."

"When I see you, I will."

"Okay, do we need reservations?"

"I doubt it; there cannot be more than a few hundred people in a five-mile radius. I doubt there will be lines at any restaurant."

"I saw only two on the way in," Lock replied.

"Did they seem busy?"

"A few cars."

"Well, we better hustle to get a parking spot."

"Biddy, did anyone ever mention your malicious sarcastic streak?"

"It's what makes me who I am."

"Steak at one restaurant, fried chicken or catfish at the other; those are the choices," Lock replied.

"Ravenous women eat steak."

Five

Sycamore Glen Farms, St. Omer, IN
5:48 p.m., Thursday, August 12, 2010

"SUPPER IS READY," Jenny said. "I've decanted wine."
"Good," Missy replied, rubbing her eyes. "I'm hungry."

She checked the wall clock. Several hours had passed as if they were minutes. She removed her glasses, rubbed her eyes, marked her page, set her glasses and the manuscript on the coffee table, lifted her cane, and stood up.

"Do you want help, Missy?" her niece asked.

"I'm five steps slower than I used to be, but I'll make it. Thankfully, my mind is still strong or I'd be a load."

She looked out the window, noting the partly cloudy sky.

"I see our storm is gone."

She turned, walked slowly into the kitchen, sat, and sipped her wine. Then, she sampled the stew.

"It's delicious. I taste curry. Where'd you get the recipe?"

"Amongst the items you asked me to sort. The title on the 3 x 5 card was Caribbean Curry Stew."

"Jack sure knew how to cook, didn't he? Do you still think my decision is the right one?"

"Yes, it's time. Oh, the background report on McGuire you commissioned is on the table, it was in your email."

Missy read it. "A good report, I think McGuire's the one. I agree with you, the time has come to tell the story."

The old woman said grace and lifted her fork.

AFTER HER MEAL, Margaret Lee returned to the library. She reflected briefly on McGuire's phone call from earlier in the week and was ninety-five percent sure about her decision.

Friday's meeting with McGuire would be the final hurdle.

Just then, she heard the whistle of a passing train. It echoed of another time when sorrow seemed too frequent. She had heard that same lonely call on a fateful day in 1987, just after she kissed Lily's cheek. Tears fell from the old woman's eyes.

She removed a crinkled letter from her apron pocket and read it. Jack Taylor wrote the note months after he left Sycamore Glen. It was the last time she ever heard from him. Unexpected and wonderful gifts accompanied his missive. Each gift—like the gold clips in her hair on this very day—was a treasure and Missy did not part with treasures easily.

She reread the final three paragraphs. She knew the words by heart, having read them many times. She did so again, for confidence.

When she finished she closed her eyes and prayed. She asked God to forgive Jack and Lily, and then she asked for her own forgiveness. "Please, dear Lord, don't hold any of it against us; we tried to lead good lives."

She read from Jack's letter, speaking the words verbatim, "Please understand the gifts I have sent are songs from my heart. Please fulfill my request; however, because of Lily, the final decision is yours alone."

She dabbed tears with a lacey yellow handkerchief

"I've decided, Jack," she whispered. "The truth is never pure or simple, but it's always good to speak it."

For most of her 90-plus years, she had never understood why some things, which are so right and proper, turn out as bad as they do. Perhaps, she thought, I can still make honey from old vinegar.

She gazed at the Flatrock River and whispered, "You are a forgiving God, please be gracious with our restless souls."

She slipped the letter into her apron pocket and found her bookmark. Soon, she was reading.

Six

The Steak House, St. Omer, IN
7:16 p.m., Thursday, August 12, 2010

AS THEY SIPPED cocktails, Lock perused the copies of the newspaper articles from Bridgette's research.

"We would have missed their significance had we read these prior to learning about his Indiana connection," he offered.

"They're insightful," she said.

"Very."

"Are you thinking they were more than friends?"

"It's hard not to think that way."

This new information, combined with facts from their investigation, convinced Lock that the story was just a few miles away, at Sycamore Glen Farms. He leaned back in his chair and stared at Bridgette.

"I'll bet a night on the town, Lily Hall's in the mix," Bridgette said.

"I agree. More often than not a woman is."

Bridgette smiled and nodded, and Lock found allure in her big brown eyes, an appeal he had never seen before.

"The right chemistry holds powerful sway over a man and woman." Her eyes never left his as she reached across the table for Lock's hand. It was the first time she had ever risked touching him and his reaction was one of surprise.

"Are you serious?"

She nodded.

"How long?"

"Since before we met. Lock, for an investigative journalist sometimes you miss some pretty strong tells."

He rubbed his chin.

"It seems I do."

She nodded.
"What do we do about it?"
"Do you actually have to ask?"
Bridgette smiled.
"Bridgette, I'm coming out of a bad marriage. I'm a wreck, emotionally."
"I'm not asking for marriage; let's enjoy one day at a time. Perhaps this helps you get back on track."
"You are serious?"
"Very, I've never been more ardent about anything."
"I'm at least ten years older."
"So? I'm more mature than my age."
"Do you think this is prudent?"
"I don't know, but I like the thought of it. I think reality will be equally as good. What do you say?"
"Okay."
"Good, first we'll eat dinner, I'm hungry. You once told me I have to eat to keep up with you. Later, we'll have dessert."
"You know, I'm not big on desserts," he smiled, squeezing her hand.
"Trust me; you'll like what I have in mind."

Seven

Bender's B & B, St. Omer, IN
1:28 a.m., Friday, August 13, 2010

As the soft sound of Bridgette's breathing filled the room, Lock reread the most recent newspaper articles and jotted down several questions. Then, he stood, stretched, and reevaluated Jack Taylor.

The novelist was a loner but Lock's experience said loners seldom made whimsical decisions. Taylor turned away from his successful life for one reason—Lily Hall. Lock carried the logic forward, and based on what he just read, he believed it likely Taylor was still alive. Admittedly, in the intervening period, he could have died; but instinct said *no*.

He remembered an excerpt he saved from Taylor's third novel, THE END OF SORROWS. He opened his laptop and found the file:

By pure chance, he saw Jessie on a sidewalk. He watched from a restaurant's dark interior as she walked by, too afraid to step into the sunlight to say hello. Suddenly, the final moments he spent with her, nearly five years ago to the day, moved through his mind as if happening for the first time.

She wore a red dress and was in his arms again and he whispered he loved her and told her how leaving her was harder than fighting in a war. Her perfume and the fragrance of her shampoo filled the air as it had a lustrum ago. The press of her body against his weakened him and very nearly broke his heart. A lump formed in his throat and he washed it away quickly with a sip of wine.

Reid had never kissed Jessie; never made love to her and never listened to the gentle beat of her heart deep into the night as the sphere turned for them alone. Nevertheless, he knew the pleasure of each intimate caress.

D. James Then

As Quixote with Dulcinea, Reid had tasted Jessie's mouth a thousand times, felt the frequent and impassioned shudder of her body under his, and listened to the rhythmic beats of her heart as he would myriad raindrops from heaven. Too often to recall, he'd fallen asleep pretending his hand was holding hers, captive to the allure of her supple body, her astounding beauty, her remarkable mind, and the rise and fall of her chest as she breathed beside him. It was the rhythm of a prayer.

Sometimes, in the ensuing five years, he wished he had called her to apologize for being stupid and he wondered if she ever thought of or forgave him. However, that afternoon, when she looked directly at him through the restaurant window, he knew the answer.

He sat immobilized with her sweet image a few feet away. Suddenly and magically, their eyes met and Jessie smiled softly, if just for an instant. He knew she did not see him but maybe she sensed his presence. Maybe she remembered his humor. Maybe it was the way he made her laugh. Maybe it was the way he tugged her heart like no other man she had ever known. Whatever the spark, an arc lighted a memory and her love for him was never in question.

Her blue eyes, her casual smile, and the way she nonchalantly brushed her hair in the wind told him she would always care—more deeply than anyone would ever know, more profoundly than she'd ever admit.

He believed, in the recesses of Jessie's heart where she dreamed dreams no one shared, he was always present, just as she was in his. He had glimpsed that secret place twice before: five years ago when he told he would never see her again and once before that on a cruise in the Caribbean, as they entertained customers, she in evening gown, he in tuxedo.

Back then, their eyes met across separate tables for what seemed an eternity and he found an unexpected pathway into a woman's hungry soul. She lowered her guard for him and, from that moment on, she and Reid breathed together, regardless of overt acknowledgement.

That Tender Light

At first, Jessie found it disruptive and treated Reid with restraint; however, because of his good heart, she acquiesced. He knew immediately, she eventually. However, as life moves forward, complications arise. Careers. Emotions. Obligations. Distant drums. Other whispers. Deep realities. They had met at an awkward time. Sans encumbrances, the outcome might have...no, it would have been different.

He watched her walk away. Now, as before, heartrending emotion pumped through Reid's body. He waited for what he thought was an hour, although only minutes passed. He took several deep breaths, dabbed his eyes, paid the bill, and departed, heading west to settle an old score.

Later, as he hunted an old enemy and hid from devils and demons, trucks whined on a rural Oklahoma highway. He made a vow: if he lived through the next few days, and if given another chance, he would find Jessie, take her hand, and never let it go.

FOR A MAN who wrote as beautifully as he did about women, why did Taylor leave Lily Hall? If he loved her, it seemed counterintuitive. There must have been devils and demons. Lock yawned, closed his computer, and curled in next to Bridgette, finding comfort from the warmth of her naked body.

He felt her move into him. She lifted up briefly and checked the time.

"It's nearly 2 a.m., were you working?"

"Just reading, trying to put everything together, trying to make pieces fit," he whispered.

She turned and kissed his forehead.

"I think they will tumble into place tomorrow."

"I hope so."

"I think Margaret Lee knows the whole story."

"Me, too," he whispered, "but will she tell us. I guess I'll have to be my irresistible self."

"Good thinking," she whispered. A moment later, her breathing evened.

However, it was difficult for Lock to sleep. The suddenness of Bridgette was one reason; Jack Taylor was the other. He snuggled closer to Bridgette and there, in the darkness of early morning, he summarized what he knew.

First, Taylor visited Sycamore Glen in 1986.

Second, he came to Indiana because of Lily Hall, who taught literature at a local college.

Third, he believed she and Taylor were lovers.

Fourth, Taylor's disappearance had something to do with the information contained in the articles Bridgette discovered.

Fifth, if the local waitress was correct, Taylor had worked on a story about war and it might have been a ninth novel.

He fluffed his pillow under his head and closed his eyes. Somewhere out on I-74, truck tires purred against the pavement, the sound magnified in the quiet Indiana countryside. He put his arm around Bridgette and held her warm hand.

Soon, he was sleeping; however, recurring and unanswered questions filled Lock's dreams.

Something deep in his subconscious told him something important was missing. Somewhere in his dreams, a voice whispered Margaret Lee's name. Somewhere in that voice hid the answer to the riddle that was Jack Taylor.

WHEN LOCK OPENED his eyes again, he saw sunlight seeping into the room through drapes. It was a new day.

The door was open to the adjoining room. He heard a shower and smelled the scent of Bridgette's strawberry soap.

He went to his bathroom, showered, shaved, brushed his teeth, and put on gym trucks. A few minutes later, he sat on the bed and smiled.

Bridgette Hannah liked him; he could scarcely believe it. He never thought he was anything special, but she changed all that with one glorious night of passion. What a remarkably beautiful woman! She was a gift sent at the right moment in his life.

He rolled onto his back and closed his eyes. He remembered Bridgette's elation that Monday, just two weeks ago, when they got their break...

...You called, Lock?"

Bridgette had just returned from a four-day trip to be with her mother, who was in a Syracuse hospital with pneumonia.

"Yeah," Lock replied. "I think we just broke it."

"Tell me."

"It has to do with an archives engine you found."

"Which one?"

"The one that flagged donations to London's Center for Journalistic Studies," he replied.

"Good."

"Yes, Thursday after you left, I went online and accessed the Center's digital files. We never saw clippings from those publications. On a whim, I entered the proper timeframe, some key words, and Taylor's name. A reference to Indiana popped off the page. I'd never seen it before. That prompted a series of calls and we struck gold."

He was beaming.

"Okay, I can't wait to hear."

She sat beside his desk.

"They were written by Julian Tufts, a retired literary critic for the defunct KNIGHTSBRIDGE LITERARY GAZETTE and KNIGHTSBRIDGE WEEKLY OBSERVER. He was one of the critics who interviewed Taylor in London in 1986 and was very influential in literary circles over there.

"Tufts' interview was similar to all the others we read. Did Taylor plan more books, would he sign a new book deal, who inspired the main character in THE LAST CHAMPION AND THE LAST KING, did his grandfather's death affect his writing, did he still plan to live in St. John, and so on?"

"Lock," Bridgette nearly shouted, "The suspense is killing me. Get on with it!"

McGuire nodded and set his coffee cup on the corner of his desk. He opened his binder and found the page he wanted.

"Here it is. Tufts described a nuance not mentioned by any other reporter in any other article. Perhaps Tufts was the only one who noticed it or maybe Taylor dropped his guard, anyway this is what he wrote:

Toward the end of our conversation, Taylor, relaxed and tanned from many days in the Caribbean sun, responded as he rotated a copper American penny between his fingers. He said he enjoys coming to London because of its history. When asked if his coin was a good luck charm, he smiled and replied 'I hope so; it's from a new friend in Indiana.'

Next up for Taylor is a stopover in New York to sign a new book deal and, despite his reclusive bias, he's agreed to stops in Chicago, Denver, San Francisco, Los Angeles, Atlanta, Washington, Philadelphia, Boston, Miami, and Dallas, his first such schedule in years. Afterward, he'll return to his beloved seaside home in St. John to write more novels.

From this critic's viewpoint, THE LAST CHAMPION AND THE LAST KING is an exhilarating book, beautifully written, and wonderfully entertaining. His character, Christian Arnett, will delight readers. Jack Taylor's good-luck penny seems to have worked its magic, which we hope continues for years to come.

Lock gave Bridgette a document he discovered at a rental car company's archives a day earlier in Oklahoma.

"We did it, Biddy."

Bridgette glanced at the document.

"Tufts' mention of a friend in Indiana fascinated me," Lock continued. To my knowledge, Taylor never visited Indiana. I managed to track Tufts down and talked to him.

"Surprisingly, Tufts retained his old notebooks. When he called back, he confirmed Taylor said 'from a new friend in Indiana.' It was a break, though remote. Who was this friend? Did it tie to a book? Recall he took his dog when he left his hotel in '86, which we agree implied forethought.

"I began to think of ways to confirm a trip to Indiana. If he took a train or plane, or if he rented a car, perhaps I'd find a record. Train manifests don't exist. However, I did find digital flight manifests. I checked all flights into Indiana airports from LaGuardia, Kennedy, and Newark. Taylor wasn't on any. In fact, no one named Taylor was on any flight from the metro area. All who checked would have found the same results and their searches would've ended. However, without the reference to Indiana, they probably wouldn't have thought to check elsewhere."

"I feel a 'but' coming," Bridgette said.

"A Josiah J. Taylor—Jack's full name is Josiah Jonathan Taylor—was booked on a flight from Philadelphia to Cincinnati, six hours after he checked out of his hotel. Six hours is ample time to take a train to Philly. Taylor flew Delta to Cincinnati. He booked passage for a dog, too. His destination is noted on the bottom of the document I just handed to you."

Bridgette checked the document. In the bottom of the rental-car receipt, where the customer designated the destination, someone had written Sycamore Glen Farms, St. Omer, Indiana.

Bridgette was so happy she clapped her hands, stood, and did a delightful little dance.

"Jesus, you amaze me," she said...

Now, Bridgette had amazed Lock and he was damned happy she had.

He heard movement in the adjoining room and Bridgette soon appeared in the doorway wearing only provocative red panties. For a moment, her image stopped his breathing. Lock's heart fluttered with excitement.

"Remember this date, sport, because it's your lucky day." Bridgette quickly perched above him on all fours. Her firm breasts were just inches from his willing lips.

"My lucky day, how?" he whispered.

She smiled, stood up, caressed her breasts teasingly, and removed her panties.

"You get to make love to me a third time and you get to meet Margaret Lee. Hot sex, a mystery solved, and a glorious future, I can't think of anything better."

Eight

Sycamore Glen Farms, St. Omer, IN
8:23 a.m., Friday, August 13, 2010

MARGARET LEE OPENED her eyes and called to her niece.

"Yes, Missy," her niece replied, sitting up on a nearby couch, yawning. "What time is it, anyway?"

"Just after eight o'clock on Friday morning." The old woman laughed. "We have luxurious beds upstairs and we both slept in the library all night."

"The last thing I remember," Jenny said, "Was stopping in to see if you need something?"

"I didn't last night, but a pot of coffee would be good right about now. However, first I want to ask you a question."

"Okay," Jenny said, rubbing sleep from her eyes.

"Do you think God gives people second chances? I mean, if they've done unspeakable things in their lives, does he let them make amends?"

"I believe he does. Why do you ask?"

"That's all Jack ever wanted, you know," she said, cryptically. "That's all I want, too."

"Lily gave Jack hope," Jenny said, "and you; you're an inspiration to us all."

The old woman, still clutching the manuscript, smiled.

"Sometimes I wonder," Missy whispered.

"Lily paid a terrible price," Jenny said. "Fate sets its stage."

The old woman grew pensive.

"And we all play along," Missy added. She turned to her niece. "Can I read to you something Jack wrote in a letter to me?

"Sure."

She removed the letter from her apron and read aloud:

At sunset, heart songs linger beside all country roads.
The music plays at twilight in gray and darkening shadows, as it ushers in the dusking of the day.
The lyrics speak of love lost or found, but of love never forgotten.
For all who hear the songs, an indescribable longing fills their souls with a sense of awe, which is overwhelming.
Whether young or old, those who hear the music believe in the strength of love, in its healing power, in its everlasting compassion.

"That's beautiful," Jenny whispered.

"It is. He was writing about his feelings for Lily. It's all in this manuscript and, if I have my way, the world is going to know. If you'd like, glance through it; however, we'll keep it to ourselves until I determine if McGuire's the one. If I like him, the next few days will be remarkable."

Jenny took the manuscript.

"It's a true story?"

"All of it is true. It's about Laos and his first love, Julia Ormandy. It's about Lily and the peace and passion she brought to him. It's about life and death, love and hate, good and bad. It's his story, the last one he will ever write."

Book Two

August-December 1986

That Tender Light
A Novel by Jack Taylor

My heart upon his warm heart lies
My breath is mixed into his breath
—W. B. Yeats

To My Faithful Readers:

THAT TENDER LIGHT is two stories in one.

Unlike my previous books, this story is a first-person narrative because I experienced everything you will read. It appears in novel form, but it is truth not fiction.

A few years ago, as I sat writing, trying to make sense of my experiences in Laos during the Vietnam War, an extraordinary woman entered my life in a way frighteningly similar to another lovely woman's departure.

Until now, I never revealed my love for either woman, my duty in war, my service as an assassin, my delight in killing, my time as a POW, or my attempted suicide.

This is my final book and I will never resurface. I wrote it in 1988 and sent it to a friend. If she chooses to publish it, the profits, like those from my other books, will help the poor and orphaned in the spirit of Father Nelson Baker, a true man of God from my hometown, Lackawanna, New York. This book is my way of insuring that good comes from evil, which seems a fitting and poignant way to end a career.

Thank you for your unwavering support.

All my best,

Jack Taylor

Chapter 1
That Tender Light

Hawksnest Bay, St. John, U.S. Virgin Islands
8:40 p.m., Thursday, August 14, 1986

JUST BEFORE SUNSET, in that quiet part of day when light lingers and night beckons, the woman emerged from the pines at the northern sweep of the island. Tanned, mysterious, and dressed in white, she was beautiful, with something elegant and erotic in the sway of her hips.

As she strolled along the secluded beach, she skirted the water's edge with the grace of a dancer. Here and there, she toyed with the surf, as it rushed across her bare feet.

When she reached a tidal pool some fifty yards away from my home, she angled away from the water, leaving a trail of delicate footprints in the wet sand.

"She's returned, Sam," I said, looking up from my desk.

My dog became immediately alert. I stopped writing, stood and went to the window to watch, exactly as I had done for the past two weeks. Sam followed and sat beside me in darkening shadows.

As the woman neared the point where the crescent shoreline adjoins the cliff adjacent to my property, she paused to study the scarlet and purple hues of sunset. The sea rolled and shimmered in front of her like a pool of mercury. She glanced briefly in my direction, smiled slightly, and turned back to the sea, the sunset, and her thoughts.

Twilight softened the woman's beauty. Her black, shoulder-length hair floated like strands of fine silk in sea breezes, which molded her flowing white dress perfectly against her lithe body.

I lifted my binoculars to capture her silhouette. She was beautiful in shape and form.

She was thinner than I remembered; her hair lighter and flecked with traces of gold and silver. I placed her age at forty. When she turned to look my way again, I noticed her tanned face, which sloped gently from ear to neck—the chin graceful, the lips full, the eyes somber. Were they blue or green? I guessed blue.

She paced back and forth pensively, arms akimbo. Seconds later, an external nod confirmed an introspective decision. She shrugged and clapped her hands together once, and abruptly seemed carefree.

As she turned and started back across the white sand, I rippled my fingers across the binoculars, as if touching the flesh on her inner thigh. I imagined her skin pressed against mine; my breath mingled with hers.

As the woman walked away, I considered calling to her. However, I rejected the notion. What would I say or do if we did meet? My grandfather and I would fish atop blue water in the morning. Thereafter, I would leave St. John for weeks to promote my new novel, with stops in London, New York, Chicago, and other cities, something I rarely did.

It did not seem like a good way to begin a friendship.

I sighed, knowing my rationale was spurious, at best. Years ago in Laos, a different woman, a woman I loved and hoped to marry, stood on a different shoreline in much the same manner.

I lost her that day because of war and deception, and I worried continually that it would happen again. From that day to this, I feared loving another woman would forever spawn a similar result.

"But, what if I'm wrong," I whispered.

As if hearing me, the woman paused; then, she turned. Through the binoculars, I saw the wind tighten her dress across her breasts. As her nipples hardened, I felt a twinge of regret for invading her privacy.

That Tender Light

Watching her was intrusive the first time and it seemed improper now. At nearly forty, I was beyond the age when a man observes an attractive woman from protective shadows. Yet, I stood there immovable, sensing a loss of something precious, something that was not mine to lose.

A week ago at dusk, I threw caution to the wind and actually summoned the courage to follow the woman.

However, by the time I made my way into the distant pines, she was gone. I assumed she went into one of the secluded homes along the coastline.

The next day, like an obsessed teenager, I went into Cruz Bay where I sat idly outside a cafe hoping to meet her. Sadly for me, I never did.

I never saw her eyes, heard her voice, studied her smile, or watched her hair billow in the breeze. Later, when I returned to my beach house, I felt empty and alone.

Now, I stood mesmerized because only a few times in a man's life does he see a woman and know with certainty how well they would fit together. This was one of those rare occasions.

Approximately a hundred fifty yards away, beyond the tidal pool and quite nearer the pines, she stood on a dune studying the sunset. Then, unexpectedly, she looked directly at my house, directly at my window, directly at me, tilted her head slightly, smiled, and waved.

In the next instant, she disappeared.

"Jesus," I whispered, stepping back, as if punched in the gut. Her simple, spontaneous gesture awakened a sense of déjà vu that was chilling and terrifying.

Julia Ormandy, the woman I loved in Laos, waved in a similar manner, as she stood beside the Mekong. However, her wave was a plea for help, a cry for mercy!

I shook the sensation away, breathed evenly, and set the binoculars aside.

Was the woman's gesture from the beach an invitation? Perhaps, however, before going forward, I had to go back. I needed to exorcise demons and reconcile my past, and the only way I knew how was with a pencil.

Once, I wrote a weaker version of the same story, but I threw it into the Niagara River. I almost threw myself in with it. From that day to this, I never wanted to revisit those terrifying moments again.

However, from the instant I saw the woman walking on the beach, something told me I had to cleanse the past if I wanted a future.

I returned to my desk and, for the second time in my life, I wrote about Laos and Julia Ormandy:

NIAGARA FALLS, NY
FEBRUARY 1975

Remorse crushes hope, deprives sleep, dilutes the spirit, and dulls one's senses. It favors the irrational when it tortures a troubled soul and that night it tormented me again. I stood on Goat Island, beside the Niagara River, wanting death.

"A different outcome this time," an inner voice whispered from deep in my mind.

Probably. Possibly. Potentially.

I honestly did not know. When I first came to the river a few days ago, I lacked the courage to jump into the rapids.

On this night, my tired eyes followed the river's conflicted journey to the precipice, some ninety feet away. There, like the frigid breath of a hidden giant, a mist angled upward and away from the falls. The vapor drifted through leafless trees, crystallizing the landscape. Eventually, it disappeared in a black and starry sky over Canada, leaving a thin coat of icy diamonds in its wake.

"The mist frightens me," I whispered, shivering.

"There's no monster," the inner voice replied, "Do it fast!"

That Tender Light

A loud snap jerked my head sharply to the left. I searched the darkness, wary someone might emerge to challenge me. However, at 3 a.m., only the river moved. I listened intently, hearing just the rapids and the roar of the falls.

"What was that snap?"

"Ice cracking," the voice clarified.

I refocused on the rapids where my life would end in a fluid embrace. Surely, death would stop the guilt and memories. I sat and removed my shoes, placing my feet into the frigid water. Quickly, each leg numbed to the knee.

"Like sleeping," the voice tittered.

I shivered and sniffed the air, smelling something stale. Was it the devil's pant or the stench of hell? I removed Julia's photograph from my coat and, in the moonlight, studied her lovely face.

Treasure gained quickly disappears with equal dispatch.

"Love is much too brittle," I whispered.

Would I see her again on the other side?

When I was a boy, Sister Mary Jerome, a Felician nun, said it happens. She told us a spirit meets loved ones as it crosses dimensions. I shrugged. What did Sister Mary Jerome know? Did anyone alive honestly understand the mystery that waits after death? Nonetheless, I wanted to believe the nun because I wanted to see Julia again.

"It would be wonderful," I whispered.

A mechanical rumble—the growl of a motor—filtered through the trees to my right. I cocked my head, listening. Perhaps, a truck drove the River Road. Quickly, the sound receded.

Julia Ormandy! I closed my eyes, remembering everything about her. I wanted her constantly. I ached for her. If I remembered one of her qualities, they all burst forth to overwhelm me.

Now, after two years, everything merged: her lips on my lips, her skin against my skin, her breath mingled with mine, her laugh consuming mine.

I remembered her scent, as we became one for the first time and, then, every time thereafter. As I moved inside Julia, her brown eyes opened a pathway directly into her heart and her reciprocal passion told me she was mine forever.

Her thick hair, supple body, tanned skin, graceful athleticism, and the magnificent French lilt in her educated voice captured my heart. Her smile warmed me every time I saw it. Heaven's peace resided in Julia's smile. At one time, I did, too. Never had I known anyone as thrilling and, ultimately, nothing as devastating.

My captors in Laos were cruel men. Their pain and torture was physical, but always faded. The pain of losing Julia wormed into my sinew, into my heart, mind, and soul. Every day a piece of me died, until I had nothing left to give.

I opened my eyes and, touching the photograph with a fingertip, I traced Julia's mouth and the slope of her neckline. I remembered my lips there. I remembered every inch of her body and every freckle, and her flesh in my hands. There, in the Laotian heat, forever one, forever turning with a crazy world. Even now, twenty-four months later, that musky scent taunted me constantly.

Then, suddenly, it ended, because of me, because of my stupidity. The Felician Sisters said God hears our prayers. However, when needed most, my God and the God of the Felicians turned a deaf ear.

I slipped the photograph into my pocket, rubbed my eyes, and massaged my temple where scar tissue throbbed terribly in the cold air.

"Blame God all you want," the inner voice whispered, "You know why it happened."

"Go straight to hell."

"Come on, Jack, you liked killing; you made the deal, you did the deed. For every action comes an equal reaction. Did you expect a free pass when you pulled the trigger?"

"You rotten bastard, they lied to me," I shouted.

"Doesn't the futility make it worse?"

It did and the truth scraped my heart raw. If I chose differently, it would have ended differently and Julia would be alive. I told myself that a hundred times a day, maybe two hundred, maybe constantly.

I looked at the night sky, hoping for an answer in the stars. None appeared. I needed Julia now more than I needed her in each of the millions of seconds that measure two years. Yet, when I reached for her, I found fading memories.

The instant our eyes met I fell schoolboy-in-love. I had not planned for that to happen. I was in Laos, in the middle of a war, for one final, deadly mission. After that, I would go home, write books, and lose myself in fiction, in stories, in a world of make-believe.

However, we did fall in love. It happens. It happened. Love lasts forever; however, the absence of love lingers one day longer.

I recalled the spark as my hand caressed Julia's cheek. Two days later, she kissed me and everything tumbled into place. We fit together perfectly in an imperfect world. The room spun. Two hearts beat as one. The world turned.

I glanced at the cold water—my final chapter. I lifted my numbed feet out of river and rolled onto my side. As I prepared to enter the river, the corner of my leather portfolio dug into my ribs. It contained my first draft of the story! I had intended to take it to my watery grave. I believed writing it would neutralize the pain: fire against fire, stone against stone. My grandfather advised against it.

"It's too soon," Tommy said.

The old man favored the restorative powers of priests, doctors, and therapists.

Could men really change what God allowed and then ignored?

Could one man erase another's sins? Did words and prayers hold such power?

I laid my head on the ground.

"You won't do it," the inner voice sneered.

D. James Then

"Would she want me to?"

The voice was silent. I closed my eyes, tucked my cold feet beneath my heavy overcoat, and relived every moment:

Long Tieng, Laos
December 1972

An impromptu visit to a hospital to do a good deed changed my life forever. I did not realize it at the time—rarely does a man have such foresight. However, because of a fateful decision lives would change, men would die, confusion would linger, and hope would erode my sanity an inch at a time for years to come.

The transformation began with an act of charity, an easy task after days of intense training. The sniper rifles were ready, the scopes sited, the maps memorized, the targets studied, the decision to kill rationalized. Only the deed remained.

"What's in the boxes?" I asked, as I approached a single-engine aircraft parked near the Long Tieng runway.

Nick Kunz, my spotter and partner, looked up from a box he sealed and smiled, squinting in the mid-afternoon sunlight.

"Medical supplies...we're taking them to the hospital."

"Hospital?"

"Up at Sam Thong," Nick replied.

"Minutes by air and several hours by ground," I said.

"Yep, flying is easier and faster," said Nick, "and safer."

He tamped down packing tape. "You shot small today, Jackson, really small."

To a sniper, *small* meant tight, concise patterns.

"We're ready," I replied. I motioned toward several cartons and asked, "You scrounge this stuff up, boss?"

"The pilot did."

Nick gestured toward a thin man checking the Helio Courier's oil. I leaned into the aircraft and examined several boxes strapped onto two of five passenger seats. I pointed to a large box on the ground.

That Tender Light

"Where's this one go?"

"Cargo bay," Nick replied.

I stowed it, asking, "What kind of meds?"

"Mostly surgical stuff," the pilot answered, dipping under the wing and wiping his hands with a rag.

"We also have penicillin, morphine, aspirin, blood coagulants, ointments, surgical garments, baby formula, diapers, powder, sutures, syringes, and sanitary pads."

"Jack, meet Maxwell Ruehl," Nick said, "Max, this is Jack Taylor. He's good people."

We shook hands.

"I know a major in Air Force logistics at Udorn," Ruehl elaborated as he pocketed the rag. "His boys flew the supplies up from Thailand. I'll take them north."

"He just gave everything away?"

"Three bottles of single malt helped," Ruehl replied, smiling.

As Nick and the pilot secured the final carton onto an empty aircraft seat, I studied their faces.

"This is definite confirmation."

"Of what?" the pilot asked.

"Nick's been a hustler all his life. You are, too; you two buzzards are birds of a feather."

Nick smiled. "Takes one to know one, these spoils are deceptive altruism, Jackson."

"I see Chubb Dailey's fingerprints all over this," I said.

"You're right. Chubb asked me to help," Ruehl replied.

Elgin "Chubb" Dailey, a pudgy ex-middleweight champ, a retired farm equipment salesman from Elwood, Indiana, and a distant cousin of Wendell Willkie, arrived in Laos in the 1960s, representing the IASS—Interfaith Aid and Support Services—to teach agricultural techniques. Along the way, he helped create schools, hospitals, and medical camps. He also forged a relationship with and then wielded tremendous influence on behalf of U.S. interests, especially with the Royal Laotian Government and its military leaders in their struggles against North Vietnamese and Pathet Lao aggression.

D. James Then

Laos was an active, if not widely publicized, element of war in Southeast Asia and Dailey was in the thick of it. The one-time pugilist influenced clandestine air operations throughout Laos and obtained the supplies various camps, schools, and hospitals needed by whatever means possible. In fact, Nick and I were in Laos because of Dailey.

"Chubb handed me a list en route to Vientiane the other day," Ruehl continued. "He asked me to see what I could do. The IASS hospital at Sam Thong needs supplies to hold them until a restock arrives from the Philippines. I made some calls and," motioning toward the packed aircraft, "you can clearly see the result."

"In life and war, we do what's necessary for the less fortunate," Nick added. "The service echoes through eternity, not the deception. If the end justifies the means, I say to hell with formalities."

"Rules exist to be defied," Ruehl added.

Nick removed several cigars from his shirt pocket and waved them temptingly before my eyes.

"Cubans, Jackson, Max got 'em and a bottle of rare cognac from a British clergyman in Thailand. The man was in need of confidential assistance."

"The poor soul needed penicillin desperately," Ruehl clarified. "Something was burning south of his equator. He sought a private resolution to prevent his bishop from discovering certain bawdy infidelities. The cigars and cognac express the minister's lasting and profound gratitude."

"In other words, one man's pain becomes another man's pleasure," I said, chuckling.

"There you go," the pilot replied.

"The pleasure will be all ours, Jackson," Nick added. "Fly up to Sam Thong and help me unload. Max has promised to have me back by nightfall."

"Guaranteed," Ruehl said, "We don't leave aircraft there overnight. They're easy targets."

I paused; I had hoped to catch some sleep.

That Tender Light

"Come on, Jack," Nick encouraged, "A good deed for some sassy booze and a first-class smoke. In a world of constant shit, it's pure joy, sugar bean."

"You're bribing me," I offered, selecting a stogie.

"You speak the language fluently."

"I hope the booze is as good as you say." I sniffed the tobacco.

"The best, Remy Martin Cognac Louis XIII Grande," the pilot replied.

—

Moments later, the Helio Courier lifted off and we flew toward an orange sun that hung in the sky far to the west of the Long Tieng valley.

As the aircraft banked and ascended, I studied afternoon shadows slanting eastward, wondering if the enemy was near.

In the plane's wake, clouds of red dust formed above the airstrip like swarms of russet insects.

The thought of laughter, cigars, and extremely expensive cognac made life seem idle and uncomplicated.

However, where we would go in a matter of days, a man's life could end quickly. The war we fought, the war that would haunt me for the remainder of my life, lurked just beyond the magnificent Laotian karsts. There, the enemy waited in a war that was so real I could almost reach out and touch it.

Sam Thong, Laos
December 1972

Several hours later, we finished stocking the supply room at the IASS hospital.

"Tell Max and Chubb how much I appreciate everything," Dr. George Ormandy said, standing at the entrance to the supply room. His thin, patrician features seemed out of place in the dirt-floor surroundings. "We're truly grateful," he added.

"I'll pass it along," Nick replied, presenting a robusto to the physician.

The doctor took it with a smile.

"Max is away getting a few things for Chubb. He mentioned you enjoy a good smoke. It's Cuban." Then, motioning toward the stacked shelves, he added, "Max said to contact him, if you need anything else."

The doctor sniffed the cigar, relishing its fragrance.

"Thanks, each of you will be in my prayers. Prayer is my only solace these days," the thin doctor replied, "prayer, my family, and my ability to help defenseless souls."

The doctor tucked the cigar into his breast pocket, shook our hands, and escorted us to the door. As he opened it, excited voices grew louder outside. Through the screen, we saw Hmong tribesmen carrying six wounded children on makeshift litters.

"Dear Christ," the doctor said, opening the door. He shouted down the hallway, "Marie, Julia...get Lu and Ceci!"

I looked over the doctor's shoulder at four young boys and two little girls, their tattered clothing saturated with blood. I noticed leg, arm, and facial lacerations.

The boys and one of two girls were screaming.

The second girl was in shock from a piece of metal protruding from a badly mangled arm.

Nick and I followed the doctor and the Hmong down the hallway and watched the tribesmen place the children on empty beds and gurneys in a small ward.

"What caused this?" I asked.

"Shells exploded," Nick replied, translating the explanation. "A dozen others died due to insurgent activity. It's dangerous."

"What a stupid war."

"It's never far away," he whispered, "and it's getting closer."

The doctor came and stood beside us with pleading eyes, which had lost their innocence long ago.

"Would you help us?" he asked.

Behind the doctor, two women and several men were busy attending to the children.

"Tell us what to do," Nick replied.

"We'll need blood," the doctor said, referring to a small refrigeration unit against a wall. "Wheel it into the ward."

—

After several intense hours, the children were sleeping.

"Thanks," the doctor said, removing a white apron, and wiping his brow. "You helped save six children and earned a few points in heaven."

He turned and glanced toward the ward.

"They'll live." He nodded toward the nearest bed. "I'm worried that little boy there will lose his leg."

He watched a male attendant remove blood-soaked gauze and towels from beside the child's bed. Soon, the doctor sighed and bowed his head.

We could only watch and listen.

"I hate war," the doctor whispered, "with every fiber of my body."

He rubbed his tired eyes.

"It's senseless and will never end. For these children, it is bitterly cruel."

Not waiting for a response, the doctor stood, patted Nick's shoulder, and walked toward the screen door.

"I believe I'll smoke that cigar now," he said.

Nick stretched and followed.

"I'll be with the doc."

"I'm right behind you," I replied as I reached for my hat. "I..."

"Your arm's bleeding," a woman interrupted.

When I turned, I saw a remarkably beautiful face and, for the first time in my life, my knees weakened because of a woman's smile.

"What?"

The warmth in her smile increased and she pointed.

"You're bleeding. Didn't you feel it?"

A faint French inflection enriched her voice.

I checked my forearm, surprised by rivulets of blood.

"You mishandled a scalpel," she said.

Another smile and, yet, another weakening sensation.

"I'm not used to the routine." I replied, shrugging helplessly. "I never felt the puncture."

"You wouldn't, scalpels are extremely sharp. Next time you'll be more careful."

"Honestly, I hope there isn't a next time."

"I, too," she replied. "You and your friend showed promise today. Here, let me have a look see."

She held my arm with her fingertips to examine the wound.

"Not serious, but you need stitches. You're an American, from Long Tieng?"

"Yes."

"Are you a pilot?"

"No."

"Is the war worth fighting?" she asked.

"I don't have the answer. However, as I see it, if people need help, we should help them. These are dangerous times."

She nodded and walked to a nearby cabinet, returned with a service tray, selected a syringe, and filled it.

"A tetanus shot."

"I've had several."

"Then, you know what to expect."

I noticed residue—pieces of lint—on her cheek, apparently from a garment. Instinctively, I brushed it away with my fingertips and, quite unexpectedly and because of the warmth of her skin, I caressed her check and studied her brown eyes.

She turned her cheek into my palm; a lovely smile accompanied a momentary sigh. She was magnificent.

My spontaneous gesture surprised me, as did the sensation of my hand against her warm skin, which was suggestive and exhilarating. She must have agreed because her smile intensified. Staring directly at me, she did not blink and, in that moment, we each discovered something we had only read about in books. Her eyebrows arched expressively.

"My first priority is to stop the bleeding," she stated, breaking our intimate bond. She sterilized my skin, administered the injection, and swabbed the wound with iodine.

That Tender Light

"It burns," I said, instinctively pulling my arm away.

"Then, you'll love this. Now, don't move."

I winced as she sutured the wound. When she noticed my reaction, she giggled.

"What's so damned funny?"

"Your expression, I pegged you as a tough guy."

I blushed, absorbing the warmth of another, deeper smile.

She released her grasp, dabbed the sutured wound with gauze, applied antiseptic cream, and a dressing.

For the first time, I smelled the scent of jasmine perfume.

"Doctor," an orderly interrupted, standing in a doorway.

"Yes," she answered, turning.

"A mother is in labor."

"You're a doctor?" I said.

"Yes, I passed all the exams. I must go," she said, letting her eyes dance briefly with mine. "Babies demand immediate attention. I'll remove the stitches in a few days."

"Should I come back?"

"I'll find you."

"But you don't know my name."

"That's my *second* priority. In time, I will."

"What's yours?" I asked as she walked away.

"Julia," she said, over her shoulder. "Think you can remember that, tough guy?"

Before I could respond, she disappeared through a curtained doorway and I listened to a fading conversation.

In less than five minutes she had dazzled me and later that night, as I slept, I dreamed of Julia's eyebrows arching as I caressed her cheek.

Chapter 2
That Tender Light

Hawksnest Bay, St. John, U.S. Virgin Islands
10:20 p.m., Thursday, August 14, 1986

THUNDER GROWLED TO the west of St. John, breaking my concentration. I placed my pencil beside the initial chapters of my Laos story. Describing Julia was difficult. I felt a pinch of remorse and shivered as I had some thirteen years ago on the banks of the Mekong River, the day everything crumbled.

I breathed deeply, trying to control my emotions.

At least I could handle the memories. At one time, I could not—thus, my visit to the Niagara River. Nevertheless, thinking and writing about Laos drained more from me than I thought it would. I was tired.

I rubbed my eyes, flexed my fingers, massaged my temples, and realized the beach house was dark except for light pooling beneath my desk lamp. I checked the time: 10:20 p.m.

I started to call out for Tommy but remembered my grandfather was playing cards with the Franciscans and would not return until midnight. I stood, stretched my back muscles, and looked at the beach where, in the moonlight, whitecaps foamed atop the incoming tide. The moon's reflection cast a pearled pathway to the distant shoreline, exactly where the woman stood at sunset.

Who was she?

The contours of her lithe body played in my mind, as dormant emotions stirred. I thought about holding her through the night and feeling her heartbeat. I missed female intuition and perception, which I believed were often better than mine. I missed other pleasures, too.

I missed the scent of hair after a rainstorm, a sweet mouth after a glass of red wine, sleepy eyes in the gray light of dawn, and the hollow at the base of an attractive spine.

I missed the feminine sense of humor, and the way women thought, walked, and laughed. I missed their murmurs after passion's release. I wanted to see the radiant glow in a woman's eyes, which told me I had pleased her and she had pleased me. I wanted to see smiles, study eyes, hear whispers, smell perfume, and live life, without fear of retribution or illusion.

I worked my neck and shoulders to loosen tight muscles. Writing aggravated the stiffness I felt, a residual from the beatings I endured in Laos.

I watched the water's sway in the moonlight. The women I preferred were confident, intelligent, and independent. They were comfortable in their skin and instinctively knew they were equal, with nothing to prove. Only a few women like that had ever entered my life, but none in years.

I reconciled myself to the fact that it would never happen again, that heaven would not permit it. Yet, for some muddled reason, the solitary woman walking the beach each evening at sunset changed that perception.

In some ways, she reminded me of Julia and those similarities proved evocative. Was the force pushing me toward the woman on the beach the same that led me to Julia Ormandy?

I stared at the pages of my Laos story.

"Write the story," Tommy whispered one night not long ago. "God doesn't seek retribution, that's the devil's game.

"These sins you think you carry are chains linking you to days that must be forgotten. Write the story, break the chains, and get on with your life. The first attempt was ill timed; you were weak emotionally. You're stronger now and much too young to be alone."

"I'm not so sure, Tommy," I replied. "I have a nagging fear that I still owe for the lives I took, for the bad I did."

"That's human guilt talking. It doesn't work that way."

"How do you know?"

"I just do," he said.

That was Tommy's way; if he believed it, it must be so.

I rubbed my chin; I had not shaved in days. For years, I thought love was far behind me, in days long gone. When I was not writing or restoring old boats or dabbling with paintings or my sketchbook, Tommy and I fished the Stream on our boat, THE ISLAND BELLE, which we fondly called THE BELLE in honor of Tommy's wife Anne, my deceased grandmother.

Until recently, I just assumed I was destined to be alone forever. However, something about the lovely woman on the beach made me reconsider. I hoped so.

Maybe Tommy was right, maybe God had forgiven me for the lives I took, for the euphoria I felt when killing. Perhaps, in His divine goodness, He would grant me another chance.

I stacked the pages of my story in a leather portfolio, which I placed beside my fishing gear by the main entrance. As I closed the windows, my image in the glass resembled a ghost's, a shadow of the man who fought and killed so ferociously in war. I studied my eyes. I had seen so much; but knew so little.

I looked into the night toward the open sea, but saw the last image of the woman instead. Thinking about her made me feel young again and the sweet infatuation pumping through my veins reminded me I was quite virile and very capable of loving a woman.

"Come on, Sam," I whispered, "Let's eat. We're hungry."

My dog's tail wagged. Sam stretched and followed me into the kitchen, where I prepared a simple meal of fruits, breads, and cheeses.

That Tender Light

On the radio, a forecaster reported a quick thunderstorm before midnight followed by blue skies and light winds for the next few days. She mentioned a twenty percent chance of a storm rising in the west and skirting north of St. Thomas about noon the next day.

I chose a bottle of merlot, shut off the lights and went to my private suite, where in the moonlight I listened to Puccini's TURANDOT and shared my meal with my dog.

After we ate, I opened the screen door, stepped onto the balcony, and studied the intermittent lights along St John's northern shore. I finished my wine. Sam followed, ran down the stairs, did his duty, returned quickly, and sat beside me in the darkness.

"Who is she, Sam?"

The dog's head cocked as if he waited to hear the answer. The distant lights flickered like candles and, as I listened to Puccini, I felt her presence nearby. Inescapably, her image rolled through my mind. I stood, thinking, until cool air on my naked chest forced a shiver. In the high hills behind my property, wind whistled in tall pines. Thunder groaned again, this time closer to the island.

The midnight storm would miss to the south and disappear by daybreak. Morning seas should be calm. Far out, a cruise ship skirted the coastline heading out to sea.

I went to bed and, resting on my side with my hands under my pillow, watched the cruise ship until it disappeared. A few moments later, I was asleep with Sam beside me on the floor.

LILY HALL SAT in a small garden not far away, watching the same cruise ship skim moonlit waters.

The amber glow of a reading lamp framed her pretty face as warm wind, sweetened by the fragrances of Bahamian flowers, rippled through her silky hair.

After several moments, her violet-blue eyes turned away from the ship to a birthday card perched on her lap.

"Thirty-eight years old," she whispered. "How did I get here so fast?"

The words felt strangely inappropriate. Age had never bothered Lily. Save for a bad marriage, her life had been full and rewarding.

However, on this day, emotions stirred and then fell in contradictory places.

Lily had a brilliant mind. She was an esteemed professor of English Literature. She owned a successful farm. She possessed timeless beauty, instinctive charm, and an infinite amount of inner resolve. Students adored her, colleagues admired her, friends and family loved her, and men desired her. Lily's *élan vital* made many believe they could own the world, if only they summoned courage to try.

However, earlier in the day, Lily's personal perspective shifted. A simple, hand-made birthday card became a portal to choices made and opportunities missed.

Suddenly, she felt alone and her achievements seemed insignificant. As she perused the card's colorful words, they became symbolic of all the precious moments that had slipped by unnoticed as she built a career and fought her way through an abusive marriage. Busy days became busy months, which became busy years.

Her marriage to a prominent Indianapolis attorney when she was thirty-two lasted six months and was the worst decision of her life. When he hit her, she told him to *fuck off* and moved back to her farm. Three days later, he confronted and threatened her in an alley and, when Lily ignored him and tried to walk away, he beat her, leaving her for dead. Because of his legal connections, a phony alibi attested to by his father, and a lack of witnesses, he avoided conviction.

However, it took Lily years to recover.

Every time she remembered his ingratiating smile outside the courtroom, she cringed. Nonetheless, after their divorce, and despite the beating, he continued to pursue her, showing up at odd moments, wanting sex, or companionship, or forgiveness, or some goddamned thing. His smarmy attitude implied *I could do what I want, whenever I want.* Lily hated his behavior.

Thankfully, he never touched her again and, with the passage of time, seldom came around anymore. However, there were moments she felt him nearby, watching and waiting. For a man used to getting his way, Lily's rebuff must have been a bitter pill.

After her divorce, Lily consciously decided to go it alone. She devoted her life to teaching literature and her farm. However, sometimes, in private moments, she yearned for something else.

Now, in warm night breezes, she finally admitted that, because of her failed marriage and her subsequent reticence, she had encased herself within protective walls.

Perhaps a simple birthday card and a man who watched her on the beach at sunset offered a different path.

"Not all those who wander are lost," she whispered Tolkien's words.

As she studied her reflection in the patio door, distant thunder rumbled. Her eyes were intelligent, her beauty nearing middle age but filled with youthful trim.

"It is what it is," she whispered.

Moving to the railing, she watched lightning streak in the western sky. She listened to the tide and studied random lights along the opposite shoreline, not far from the secluded cove where she walked the beach at sunset. Unexpectedly, a butterfly flew through the dim light and disappeared into the darkness beyond.

Lily smiled.

"When a butterfly enters your life at times of introspection, destiny whispers good fortune," a Buddhist monk stated once in a lecture she attended. Why remember that now? Perhaps it *was* destiny, if such a force existed.

As she turned toward the bedroom, she noticed a copy of Jack Taylor's TOMORROW'S WHISPER on the end table. She lifted the book and read the jacket summary.

She sat in her chair and thought about her gesture at sunset. Her action was uncharacteristic, but at least she understood her motivation.

Earlier in the day, she was at Christ-on-the-Cross School and Orphanage where she taught literature to gifted students each summer. Lily, Sister Danielle, and Tomas Gomez, the Orphanage's doctor, were discussing a timid child who arrived recently from St. Croix.

"Time is the remedy," Dr. Gomez said, as they walked through the school's garden, he on his way to a small clinic, Lily and the nun to their respective classrooms.

"Some children are naturally shy," the doctor continued. "For others, it's a defense. Anna's reservation emanates from fear. It is a prime motivator for young and old alike."

He removed a cigar from his coat pocket and examined it.

"Fear is a unique human emotion," the doctor said, his scratchy voice comforting. "It motivates some; restrains others. It ruins careers, friendships, love, happiness, and the chance to grow up or old with grace; it destroys anything a person can name and more.

"We cannot imagine the things Anna has seen in her life or her interpretation of them. Many parents are heartless bastards." He blushed, saying, "Pardon my choice of words."

"It's okay," Sister Danielle replied. "I know what a bastard is."

"I do, too," Lily said. The image of her former husband flashed through her mind and disappeared.

Dr. Gomez tugged thoughtfully at his white mustache. Then, searching Lily's eyes, he seemed to recall an interesting morsel and smiled.

"Fear challenges young or old alike. Anna's one example, my grandson is another.

"If someone tormented this child physically or emotionally, the solution is trust, patience, and love. If she's naturally shy, guess what, the answer's trust, patience, and love. Build a foundation, Sister Danielle. Something you do incredibly well."

"And, as for your grandson?" the nun inquired.

"He's different," the doctor shrugged. "He frequently watches a beautiful girl on the beach near our home. I know he desires to meet her but he is hesitant. I think past fears prevent him from being proactive. It keeps him from meeting a lovely girl; it keeps Anna from knowing you, Sister Danielle. Sadly, fear is a dominant force in our lives."

Thinking of her abusive past, Lily said, "I understand."

The doctor continued. "Sister, use the kindness I sense in your heart and Anna will respond. Kindness moves mountains. It's love's initial step, designed by God Almighty. First, let her find comfort in your presence. She'll observe and it'll seep in eventually. Don't force it; rather, be there for her. She'll turn to you. How could she not? The rest is a slice of cake."

"You mean piece," the nun said.

Dr. Gomez seemed confused.

"The idiom is a *piece* of cake."

"Of course," he laughed. "I prefer chocolate."

He smiled, clenched his unlit cigar between his teeth, tipped his white Panama, and bid them farewell. They watched him stroll into the clinic.

"He's a character," the nun whispered, as she and Lily walked together. "But, I like his analysis."

Later in the day, before leaving the orphanage, Lily stopped for tea with Teresa—Terri—D'Youville, the founder of the school and orphanage.

Sharing tea had become a daily ritual, a time for dear friends to unwind and compare notes. On this day, they sat in the nun's office, before open windows, watching palms sway in afternoon trades.

"Are you planning a book?"

Lily appeared puzzled.

"Your sabbatical, we've not discussed it," the nun clarified.

Lily smiled. "I've a few articles in mind. Publish or perish, as they say."

"So, you won't play lazy for a whole year?"

Lily's smile widened. "Not I; actually, I've begun to restore the old cabin on my farm, out near the river. You remember it, near the falls where we swim."

Terri nodded.

"I want to preserve it; so much of my family's history is there."

"Lily you're a tomboy, when did you decide this?"

"In the spring," Lily replied, "I worked it all out and proceeded when the college confirmed my sabbatical. And yes, I might write a book about it."

"A modern-day Thoreau, if I remember there's an orchard?"

"Yes. Earlier this summer, I had the foundation and structure repaired. I hired several excellent carpenters to repair the external walls and make a few additions and modifications before winter. I called home yesterday; that specific work is complete. When I return, we will add a porch and replace the roof. Then, the inside work begins."

"Therefore, I guess asking you to stay another week will not work?"

"Terri, three's my limit," Lily noted. "I'll leave a week from Saturday as planned. It's time to go home and hammer more nails."

The nun sipped her tea and changed the subject.

"You always seem to enjoy the children."

"I enjoy their passion." She described Anna, Sister Danielle's timid student. "I wish we could break the barrier." Then, Lily explained the doctor's opinion.

"He's spot on," the nun said. "He's astute in his observations. I'd trust him."

"By the way," Lily added, "I didn't know the doctor had a young grandson." She refilled her teacup. "He seems too old."

"His grandson's not so young, Lily."

Confusion filled Lily's face.

"When he said grandson, I assumed a teenager."

Terri smiled.

"You have no idea who his grandson is, do you?"

"Should I?"

"Sure, you teach literature and you've visited this island for more than a decade. You honestly don't know?"

"No."

"Lily, he's Jack Taylor," the nun said.

"The novelist," Lily replied, her eyes revealed genuine surprise. "He lives nearby?"

"You truly didn't know?"

"No," Lily blushed. "I thought he meant a teenager."

"I'm quite sure Jack's our age. He and his grandfather live near the northern tip of Hawksnest Bay, in a big white house on a cliff above a secluded cove."

"I know the spot," Lily said. She passed it each evening at sunset.

"It's isolated there. As I think about it, theirs is the lone house on that stretch of beach. It's about a mile or so from your condo."

Closer, Lily thought, suddenly realizing *she* was the girl the doctor referenced. *She had to be!* No one else was ever on the beach at sunset.

Had the old man tried to send a message? If so, the favor was both foreign and flattering.

"Does Taylor visit the school?" asked Lily, sipping tea.

"Occasionally Jack tags along with Tomas, although he usually keeps to himself. He's reclusive and works most of the time, unless he and Tomas are fishing. They keep a boat moored at Trunk Bay. Jack is quiet and unassuming, Lily. He is quite funny, once you get to know him. For such a serious writer, he has a wicked sense of humor. You'd never know he's as wealthy as he is."

"I've read all but one of his books," Lily replied. "He has wonderful style, good technical qualities, and superb character development. He uses symmetry extremely well; possibly the best I've ever seen."

The nun turned in her chair and scanned the books behind her desk.

"Have you read TOMORROW'S WHISPER, which was published in 1985?"

"It's the only one I haven't read."

Terri took it off the shelf.

"Take it; consider it part of my birthday present to you."

Now, in the garden, in a soft yellow light, Lily opened Taylor's book and read the opening paragraphs:

As he stood at the water's edge looking out across the English Channel, Robert Morgan considered himself a coward. France and the war were looming. The word coming down from headquarters said they would go soon; that it depended on the weather. The launch time was secret and he was scared, nervous scared. He lit a cigarette and listened to the water's movement, hearing it call his name.

"What are you thinking about, Bobby?"

That Tender Light

"You," he lied to the woman beside him. "I don't want to lose you, Rachel."

Her hand squeezed his arm and she kissed his cheek. Her lips were moist and warm on his cold skin.

"I love you, Bobby...so much."

"I know you do and I love you."

How could he continue the lie?

He wanted to say he did not know what loving someone meant. He wanted to be back in Buffalo working at the COURIER EXPRESS. He wanted to go with friends for beer at Cole's Bar. He wanted to fondle Ruth Ann Dobson behind the public library and never think of war again.

He would have gleefully accepted anything carefree, anything lacking challenge and responsibility. Instead, he was knee-deep in a world war, responsible for leading men into combat at a time when he was so damned scared he could cry, when he would force himself to rise and pretend to be brave with every fretful step.

He studied Rachel's lovely face, her red lips, and her milky-white complexion. Her beauty was classic.

The image of her naked body floated through his mind. He was too much the coward to tell Rachel the truth because he feared he would lose the physical intimacy she afforded him. He used sexual pleasure as a substitute for the moral strength he thought he lacked. His deed was callous and utterly stupid. What made him do it?

"What do you think it will be like," she asked, "out there?"

"Rough," a quick, one-word response noted. He said nothing more.

"You'll come through, won't you, Bobby, for me?"

She kissed him again, tenderly. As their tongues touched and he felt his passion ignite. A faux smile covered his fear.

He knew if he survived the war, it would be for himself, not for anyone else. He must prove he was not a coward, something he would be unsure of until he hit the beach, until he saw action, until he was tested.

How did his life get so complicated?

In nightmares, he cried and cowered in a ditch. He never slept long enough to learn what happened next. If he failed, but survived, he feared his life would be hollow, that anyone he touched would falter, too. Perhaps dying would be better if he were truly a coward. Men do not consider the dead cowards; there is something tragically heroic about a deceased soldier.

"Let's go, silly," Rachel said touching Bobby's elbow, moving his hand to her breast. "We'll have dinner and then I'll give you enough of me to fill the coming months."

She locked her arm in his and they walked to the waiting taxicab. He helped Rachel inside and looked back into the bleak expanse of the English Channel.

Something called his name. His destiny was out there, somewhere in the darkness, in days yet to come. How would he react? He did not know the result, the time, or the place. Nevertheless, a test would come.

He felt a tug and moved inside, into the willing warmth of a woman who thought he loved her. For now, as with every other day, he would silence his fear, hiding it in the passion and physical beauty of an English woman named Rachel Smyth.

Lily smiled, liking the intimacy. She hoped Morgan would prove to have more courage than he realized. Possibly that was Jack Taylor's intent. Maybe we all have a reservoir of courage we know nothing about until we are tested or called.

"How each of us responds is the real question," she whispered, yawning.

She glanced at her wristwatch—nearly midnight.

For the first time, in a day jammed with conflicting emotions, Lily felt sleepy. She stretched and a slight spasm tightened a muscle on her right side, above the small of her back. She massaged the spot until the spasm subsided.

She decided to read more of TOMORROW'S WHISPER in the morning before the driver from the school arrived.

That Tender Light

She walked to the railing and, spreading her legs slightly, let the breeze billow through her white satin robe. She let it rush across her bare calves and thighs, just as she had done many times as a girl on her private porch on warm summer nights in Indiana. Soon, she opened her robe fully, letting the breeze rush across her beautifully naked body. After a while, she tilted her head, as the wind toyed with her long, silky hair.

She saw reflections of her life. Some might have considered it hard: however, only the marriage was difficult. The rest of it? Yes, it took time and effort to earn her degrees and become a college professor and, after her father's death, to keep the farm.

She shrugged. For most of her adult life, Lily believed teaching and farming defined who she was, more so after her divorce. Now, surprisingly, she wondered if something else waited in the wings.

Everything came easy to her, except giving herself to another human being, especially after her marriage ended. Deep in her heart, she believed she would lose her identity and autonomy. Was that true or, like Taylor's character, Robert Morgan, did her fear preclude the possibility of a better life?

Suddenly, she understood her reticence and the anxiety she had sensed for nearly a lifetime. Despite her success, affluence, and independence, Lily remained alone more by choice than for any other reason. She feared losing one life rather than gaining another. She also feared more abuse.

Her thoughts shifted to the man living in a big white house across the cove and his fascination with a solitary woman walking a beach at sunset. What was he like? Was he charming? Was he gentle? Would she like his humor? Could he love her? Could she love him?

She decided to discover a way to meet him.

Lily smiled.

Perhaps her spontaneous gesture was not so silly, after all. She tightened her robe and recalled Walt Whitman's poem TO A STRANGER. She wondered if, in a prior life, she had lived a life of joy with someone. She hoped so.

Why not do so again, why not now, and why not Jack Taylor?

She was a beautiful and passionate woman, warm and thoughtful. Her mind, body, and soul were gifts. Her life and its essence were treasures awaiting discovery.

She switched the light off, went into the bedroom, removed her robe, and, lying naked on the bed, replayed a day replete with sobering emotions.

As was her practice, she prayed in the darkness as the warm sea air moved across her skin and caressed her thighs, stomach, and breasts. Soon, Lily was asleep and somewhere in the darkness, a tired butterfly alighted and slept, too.

Chapter 3
That Tender Light

The Caribbean, North of St. Croix
12:18 p.m., Friday, August 15, 1986

TOMAS GOMEZ STOOD on the bow of THE ISLAND BELLE, poised like a monarch of sea and tide. Behind him, the Caribbean was a pool of liquid azure beneath a wide, blue sky. Now in his eighties, he was remarkably agile.

"This bastard sunlight makes me young again," Tommy yelled. "My legs feel like steel."

"You're a king, Tommy. You own the sea."

He waved, smiled, clenched a cigar between his teeth, paused to light it, and started aft.

"Are you hungry, Jack?" he asked.

"I could eat. How long will it take?"

"Half an hour," Tommy replied.

"Good."

I studied the old man's movements.

Although time had stolen a few steps, my grandfather remained surprisingly agile and nimble. His legs were muscular, his waist narrow, his chest broad, his demeanor impressive, his attitude confident.

Curly gray hair covered his naked chest and his almond skin seemed lighter in the bright sunlight. A faded, red and black tattoo on his left bicep—a combination cross and sword—hinted of a rebellious youth in Havana.

On this day, Tommy wore bleached khaki cut-offs and scruffy deck shoes, which at one time had been as white as the hair on his head.

Now, aged and worn like his old shoes—his best days lay somewhere in the past. However, Tommy still had great utility and therefore much to offer.

We were comfortable in each other's company, as we fished atop deep water for the first time in weeks. Clearly, Tommy enjoyed it.

He accepted the sea and sky gratefully, without condition, and relished the boat's fluid motion, the smell of salt air, and the sunlight against his taut and glistening skin.

I adjusted our course as Tommy hopped over coiled rigging and went below. After I shifted my position, I switched on the autopilot, opened my portfolio, and lifted my pencil. Again, I immersed myself in my Laos story:

LONG TIENG, LAOS
DECEMBER 1972

Two days later, as I departed a late-morning meeting with the guide who would take us into North Vietnam, Julia stood near a cluster of teak trees.

She wore khaki slacks, brown riding boots, and a light blue short-sleeved oxford shirt. A silver cross around her neck sparkled in the bright sunlight.

I patted our guide on the back and bid him farewell.

As I approached, Julia waved, "I came to remove the sutures and to reiterate how much I...ah, we appreciate your help the other day."

"This is a pleasant surprise."

"I hoped it would be," she responded. "You seem preoccupied, is my timing off?"

"No, are the kids okay?"

"Emotionally, they're young enough to forget," she replied. "Physically, they'll be fine. The little boy with the damaged leg is better. He won't lose it."

"I'm glad," I stated, sensing the allure of Julia's supple body.

"I wanted to thank you for the medical supplies, too."

"I can't take the credit. The pilot did everything. I went along to help."

"Nevertheless, I'm glad you did," she said. "May I examine your arm?"

She held my forearm and removed the dressing.

"It's fine. No infection."

Again, the scent of jasmine drifted in the air.

Taking a small kit from her pocket, she extracted the sutures, and applied antiseptic cream and a new bandage.

"Remove the dressing in the morning. It should be fine, thereafter."

She moved so close to me that our bodies touched.

"Now, for the second priority I mentioned the other day, what's your name?"

"Jack Taylor."

"Jack Taylor," she whispered, committing it to memory.

"As I mentioned, mine is Julia, Julia Ormandy," she replied, touching my hand with her warm fingers. For the first time, I understood the deep meaning of a touch.

"You have the same surname as the doctor. Is he..."

"My husband," Julia giggled, finishing my question.

"What's so funny?"

"You are. He's my Uncle George, silly, my father's brother. The other Caucasian woman at the hospital is my Aunt Marie, his wife. She's a registered nurse, as are Lu and Ceci.

"Uncle George is a minister and a physician. My aunt and uncle have served in Laos periodically for nearly twenty years, through the Episcopal Church of Canada and under the auspices of Interfaith Aid and Support Services. My uncle and Chubb Dailey are good friends. They met in the early 1960s."

"How long have you been at Sam Thong?"

"Less than a month, it's temporary. My permanent station is Vientiane, at an IASS pediatric clinic. I've been there for seven months and I leave in five. I've a residency waiting in Toronto. However, my uncle needed help. Every few months he goes to remote villages to immunize the Hmong. I'll cover for him. We were fortunate, another doctor agreed to stay at the clinic in Vientiane until I return. It worked out nicely."

Her fingers tightened spontaneously around mine; the sensation was thrilling.

"Montreal?"

"Please," she replied.

"Your accent?"

Julia smiled.

"You noticed...Quebec, actually. I was born there. We moved to Ontario when I was a child. My family owns thousands of acres of orchards in the middle of nowhere."

"I'm from near Buffalo. You want to get a beer?" I really wondered if she would accept a kiss.

"I drink wine but rarely, I came to see you, to be with you, Jack."

Her eyes embraced mine and her breathing quickened.

"Perhaps a cup of coffee," I suggested.

"Come on, tough guy, isn't there some place we can go, to be alone, just the two of us. I want to spend time with you."

I pointed toward a patch of grass not far away.

"It's as good a place as any."

"Actually, I was thinking of something intimate."

Her eyes teased mine again and I immediately understood. She wanted to do more than just talk.

"My hut is close; we'll be alone. Are you sure about this?"

She smiled and whispered, "That will do nicely. As for being sure, I'm here aren't I?"

—

We moved toward each other slowly in the beginning, talking and laughing, discussing mundane things. The kind of idle chatter hopeful lovers fumble through as they explore each other. In the background, the muted noise of the aircraft on the Long Tieng runway seemed a distant reminder that there was more to the world than just the two of us.

Julia made the first move by placing her fingers on my lips.

"Enough chat," she said, "You talk too much, Jack Taylor."

She kissed my cheek several times and then my lips, lightly at first, then passionately. She tickled my tongue with hers.

"I've something for you."

"What?"

She locked the door. As she returned, she unbuttoned her blouse. A moment later, she stood naked before me. Her olive skin was remarkable, her nipples brown, erect and inviting.

"Why?" I asked.

She smiled, moving into me.

"You have to ask? I felt it and you did, too! Emotion this raw and deep comes along rarely. When it does, a man and a woman should take advantage of it. Only fools let it pass, especially in times like these."

"A woman has never said that to me."

"Actually, I've never said it to anyone, until now. You're the first man, since my pediatrician, to see me naked. You'll soon learn I've never made love before, either. When it hits, it hits hard. I would never have believed it.

"I can't stop thinking about you, Jack, the way you touched me and looked at me. You are the first man to look into my eyes and see my soul. I knew immediately you were different from others who have tried. It was serene and beautiful."

"You're beautiful," I whispered. "I think of you constantly." I kissed her passionately as my hands explored her body. "Is it wise to do this?"

"I don't know. Should we stop?"

"No."

Julia unbuttoned my shirt and then unbuckled my belt. When I was naked, she kissed my neck and chest and then embraced me. She turned her face upward and kissed me hungrily. Her sweet lips and probing tongue—warm, moist, and inviting—created the most thrilling kiss I ever tasted. My head buzzed. As I held her, feeling her naked body against mine, the room swayed. Soon, the entire world would spin completely out of control.

"I should shower," I said, pausing to breathe. "I'm grimy."

"You've a shower?" She seemed surprised. "That's handy."

"Nick and I rigged up a fifty gallon drum."

"Truthfully?"

"Yeah, a few wooden supports, a hose with a shutoff valve, and a pilfered shower head. Ingenious, huh?"

"May I join you?"

"Sure, it's in there."

I pointed toward the rear of the hut.

"It's functional; the sun warms the water; it's a real luxury."

"You'll soon have another," she glanced at the other bed. "Do you expect him?

"No, Nick will be busy most of the day."

Julia kissed me, longer and deeper. More thrills. She arched her eyebrows mischievously.

"Can you check the lock?"

"Sure."

"Then, I'll start the water."

—

A few minutes later, I entered Julia and realized immediately this was her first time. I continued slowly and, seconds later, her brown eyes widened. She smiled and exhaled, easing all tension from her body.

"Fully?" she asked.

"Yes."

"Nothing to it," she whispered. "It gets better?"

"Much."

I moved inside Julia, rhythmically. She relaxed quickly and completely and stared directly into my eyes, her auburn hair layered beautifully upon the white pillow. After a while, enthralled by our fluid movements, she briefly lifted up, held my face in her hands, and kissed me passionately. Again, she tickled my tongue with hers. As our joy grew, her eyes told me she wanted more.

We remained coupled, sweating together in the Laotian heat and, when she climaxed for the first time in her life, she closed her eyes and her body shuddered for several moments.

As she throbbed against me, the silver cross resting in the perspiration between her breasts sparkled like a precious jewel.

Soon, I shuddered, too.

"J'y suis, j'y reste," she whispered. "Here I am, here I remain," she translated. She smiled, looked at me, and added, "For you alone, my love."

"I don't understand French, but I like that."

"My mother was from France," she replied. "My father met her in Europe during the war. She taught me."

"Was," I whispered.

"She died when I was in med school. I miss her."

"I miss you," I replied.

"But, I'm right beside you, Jack."

"You'll leave soon and we'll be apart."

I kissed her cheeks lightly and then, as my lips found hers, the world twisted completely out of control.

She must have felt it spin, too, because she placed my head against her breasts and held me tightly until the sensation passed. Thereafter, the only sound I heard was the gentle beat of Julia's heart, a sound I hoped to hear for the rest of my life.

—

Later, I watched Julia's eyes open.

Sensing my stare, she turned toward me and smiled. She rolled on her side, caressed my cheek, and kissed me.

"Hi, tough guy," she whispered.

"Hi, yourself," I replied.

"Have I started something significant?"

"I believe you have," I replied.

She curled against my chest.

"Tell me something about your life," she whispered.

"Not much to say—I'm from Lackawanna, near Buffalo?"

"The home of Our Lady of Victory Basilica and Father Nelson Baker," she said.

"Yes, how would you know that?"

"I read about him once in a magazine."

"My mother and father died when I was young," I said. "My mother's parents, also physicians, raised me. My mother's mother is from South Buffalo, my grandfather from Cuba.

D. James Then

"My life has been pretty normal. I attended Catholic schools, studied journalism at St. Bonaventure University, joined the army, served in Vietnam, and I'm here for a special assignment. When it's over, I go home."

"What's the assignment?"

I wondered how Julia would react if she knew I volunteered to kill three men from afar. What would she say if she knew the hunt excited me?

"I can't discuss it, Julia."

"Secret stuff?" she asked, checking the time.

I remained silent.

"Whatever it is, you will do it soon?"

"I leave in the morning."

"When will you return?"

"Depends, but not for a while."

"What will you do when you go home?" She changed the subject.

"I would like to write novels, great stories."

"My very own Steinbeck, will that be as easy as it sounds?"

"I don't know; I'll tell you after I've lived the dream."

She kissed me and nibbled my earlobe.

"You know," she added, "My return flight leaves at four. That's a few hours away."

"Nick should be back about four."

"That's advantageous."

Her eyes entertained mine.

"Do you have something in mind?" I asked, kissing her.

She put her hands under the sheet and touched me. She smiled at my response.

"I guess your reaction means yes," she whispered.

"Indeed," I replied.

—

We held each other and eventually Julia leaned over and removed a slip of paper from her slacks. She placed it on a small table beside the bed.

"What's that?"

"It's my address and the clinic's phone number in Vientiane, if I'm not in Sam Thong when you return." She checked her watch: 3:20 p.m. "Will I see you again?"

"When I come back, I promise."

"Good," she said, kissing me. Julia placed my hand against her warm abdomen and traced the outline of my lips with the tip of her tongue.

"You want one more?" she teased after a second kiss.

"Sure."

After we made love a third time, she kissed my neck, cheeks and lips many times.

"What was that for?"

"Forever, I hope," she replied.

She stood and took a quick shower. When she returned, I rolled on my side to watch her dress, impressed by the muscle tone in her long legs.

"You're a dancer," I observed.

"Was," she corrected, "Ballet, almost ten years."

Then, oddly, she started to cry.

"What is it?"

"I never expected this when I left home," she said.

"Expected what?"

"Meeting someone like you," she replied. "I never expected to fall this far this fast; and yet, I have. I like your smile, Jack Taylor. You make me happy inside and out."

"I feel the same."

"Does it seem odd, I mean for it to happen so quickly?"

"I've read it does sometimes."

"Well, for me, it has." She paused and dried her eyes. "Can you be a one-woman man, Steinbeck?"

"If you are the one woman, yes I can."

"Good answer, tough guy," she said. "Is your duty dangerous?"

"Often, yes."

"Are you ever afraid?"

"Often, yes."

"Be careful for me, I want you a thousand more times."
"Just a thousand?"
"Hey, a girl must start somewhere. It's a good number."
She kissed me one last time.
"See you later, tough guy. That kiss must hold you for a while. Remember, I'll be in Sam Thong or Vientiane, most likely the latter. Next time, I'll show you how to hold a scalpel."
"Anything else?"
"You've just had a sample of what's to come. Don't mess this up. You come back to me. Come for tea sometime. We Canadians drink lots of tea."
I smiled.
"I promise I'll find you."
"Of course, you will. Take care of yourself and be safe. Many good days are ahead of us, I sense it."
"And you be safe, too," I replied. "There's a civil war and an attack is never far away."
"If it gets too unstable, we will be evacuated; that's what my uncle tells me. I think he says it so we won't worry. I do anyway."
Julia touched my hand, opened the door, waved, and walked into the sunlit afternoon.

—

Jesus, sweet prince of heaven, I thought after she departed. I was motionless for a long time, thinking of Julia's eyes, feeling her thrusts, remembering the silver sparkle between her breasts. I liked her smile, her humor, and her mind.

I sat on my bed and hugged the pillow. The scent of jasmine told me we had taken a path neither had walked before. When I thought about her kisses, I did not think about communist aggression in and around Long Tieng or Sam Thong, and I managed to forget the men I would kill, the reason why, and the thrill it gave me.

CHAPTER 4
THAT TENDER LIGHT

The Caribbean Sea, North of St. Croix
12:55 p.m., Friday, August 15, 1986

THE OLD MAN brought a tray of fruits and nuts, and sandwiches with tomatoes, ham, and cheese. We ate quietly, enjoying the gentle sway of the boat, tossing scraps of food to Sam and to gulls that dove on THE BELLE.

When we finished, Tommy cleared the meal and went aft. I watched him work the lines and, noticing his steady hands, yelled, "Tommy, you have the hands of a surgeon."

The old man looked up with an appreciative nod.

"Did you say sturgeon?" he shouted, laughing.

"No, *surgeon*, you know as in doctor."

"Indeed," Tommy replied, "Nearly five decades with a scalpel in my hand. Hands of a surgeon, Jesus, you're a big-time comic."

"I have my days."

Tommy laughed again; his white teeth complemented his hair and mustache. However, after he worked the bait and relit his cigar, disappointment replaced laughter. Immediately, I knew the reason. Only a marlin, barracuda, or swordfish—Tommy called them all scags—would lift his spirits. However, we had not had a nibble, which was odd.

Tommy turned away from the poles, climbed the ladder to the helm, sat near Sam, and opened a cooler.

"You want a beer, Jack?"

"Later."

The old man closed the lid and smiled at our dog.

"We need a scag, Sam!" He spread his arms wide apart and said, "A big son of a bitch about this long would brighten our day, huh?"

Our dog, lounging in the shade beneath green deck awning, stood, walked over and curled beside the old man. Tommy rubbed Sam's head affectionately as he drank his beer. Cupping his hand, he filled it and laughed as Sam slurped beer. He hugged our dog.

"I knew there was something I liked about this joker the second I found him on the side of the road. Sam's a boozer."

The dog licked the old man's hand appreciatively. He sat up, cocked his head in anticipation of another mouthful and Tommy, pouring more beer, obliged.

"Tommy, he only likes beer because you give it to him. He's just a big, dumb dog."

"Did you hear him, Sam? He called you big and dumb. Go bite his ass."

Instead, the dog focused on Tommy's hand and the beer can, the tip of his tail wagging. Tommy cupped his hand and again Sam drank his fill.

"Too much and he gets fat. If he gets too big, the vet said it's bad on his joints."

"Ah, bullshit," Tommy responded, feigning resentment. "I don't give Sam much to drink. A little taste can't hurt him or me. Don't forget, I'm a doctor, too. He drinks when I do. We've never been shit-faced. Your grandmother didn't give two nickels if I gave Sam beer. If she didn't, why do you?"

I smiled and laughed, and Tommy laughed, too.

Whenever I cornered Tommy on any issue, he retreated into the inarguable approval of his deceased wife Anne, my grandmother, to bolster his position. We often shared the harmless fiction and thoroughly enjoyed it.

"Maybe you're right," I replied, not pressing the point. Only his happiness mattered. Standing, I flexed my legs and angled THE BELLE through easy swells on a slight south-by-southeast course.

"Nothing's on the lines?"

"Nada," Tommy said. "The scags are on holiday."

We had been on blue water since sunrise when Trunk Bay disappeared in an early morning fog. Now, we were moving slowly in the general direction of Buck Island, which is not far away from the eastern tip of St. Croix.

The day began with great anticipation but turned somber by mid-morning. As the noon hour slipped by, we had yet to hook a fish on either line trailing behind our boat. We were atop deep water, too, some fifteen knots south of St. John, where we fished often and with good success.

As Tommy occupied Sam with chunks of cheddar cheese, a barely-audible rumble rolled over the helm. Surprised by thunder with such a high blue sky, I surveyed the horizon.

"The sun won't last much longer, Tommy. A storm's rising out west. The weather forecast was wrong; we're about to lose our day."

I pointed toward charcoal clouds hugging the horizon.

"The forecaster said the bad weather would go north."

"Nothing surprises me on the water," Tommy replied, standing and looking where I pointed. "Now, I know why we don't catch a scag."

He shaded his eyes with his right hand and studied the distant thunderheads. He used deck binoculars for a better view and immediately saw orange flashes in the clouds. He cocked his head, counting the seconds until thunder passed overhead again. A moment later, a second, deeper grumble rode the edge of a cool wind. Concern furled Tommy's brow.

"Twenty-five knots," he calculated, "less than thirty miles. The air is cooling, do you feel it?"

"I do. The anemometer indicates wind's at fifteen."

"Then, to be safe, we have forty-five minutes before it nails us," Tommy added. "I don't mind rain; lightning scares me. Come around and find a place to drop anchor. Let's ride this out on the shore."

"It doesn't feel good, does it?"

"No," Tommy replied. He removed his ball cap, letting the wind rush across his face and through his white hair.

"By the pace of this wind, the storm will move in fast," he added, stowing the binoculars. "Jesus, it's good to be on the water. Why do we get rain? You know, I wanted to feel the pull of a big bastard by mid-morning; damn it, we won't catch a scag for days."

"We will, this afternoon, after the storm."

"I doubt it. When I was a boy in Cuba, we'd go out on days like this—my father, my uncles, and me—and, if it stormed, we wouldn't catch a scag for days. The big bastards go deep in bad weather and stay there. Lightning scares them."

"I know the feeling."

Tommy smiled and secured his cap firmly on his head.

"In Cuba," he said, "when the weather was hot and good, the four of us would fish all day, hook a few scags, and tell splendid lies. Jesus, we would laugh!

"One day, we hooked a shark and five marlin; six big scags on deck like trophies to our manhood.

"We were as giddy as teenagers who just popped their cherries, and never closer as men...never! My father gave me a cup of rum that day—my first. I tasted it but never had a cupful. Six big bastards and rum to boot...even now, after so many years, I remember the sweetness and the buzz.

"That was my greatest day, until I married Anne. I wish you could have known those men better. They were good, honest, simple, and devout, with big fucking hearts. They'd have loved you as much as I do or more."

Sadness darkened Tommy's expression. He was lonelier than I realized and I tried my best to cheer him up.

"I remember them, Tommy, from our visits when I was a boy. I remember their faces, voices, laughter, the food they ate, the songs they sang, and I know them through you."

That Tender Light

Tommy shrugged.

"But, it's not the same. Our visits to Cuba occurred too long ago. They're like dreams from another time. Those days seem like fiction, like something I read somewhere. I should've forced my family out of Cuba. I had the chance. I wanted them out, but they wouldn't leave. I should have made it happen. Then, the revolution came, which prevented it. I wanted to see them again," he paused, "but after 1959, that never happened."

His voice faded, as he remembered his family. Moments later, anger replaced sadness and his eyes grew serious.

"I hope Castro rots in hell," Tommy said emphatically. "That bearded fuck took my family and my island. To this day, it pisses me off. I'd roust him given the chance."

He laughed loudly when he saw my surprise.

"Tough talk for an old man?"

I nodded, adding, "Didn't you take an oath?"

"So? Because of some words, you think I couldn't end a man's life. I know you think I wouldn't, but I'd put him down. I'd put a blade in his ebony heart and laugh."

Tommy emphasized his conviction with an imaginary thrust.

"My father hated Batista and said Castro was no better. He believed one evil replaced another. For an uneducated man, your great grandfather had reflective instincts. You should have had the privilege of knowing him better.

"Hearing stories does not compare to actually knowing a man. You must be around him frequently to understand him. You must study his face, look into his eyes, hear his voice, see how he works, understand his humor, and watch how he treats a woman. Jack, you can learn much by watching how tender a man is toward a woman, and by learning what makes him laugh." Tommy paused, thoughtfully. "Jesus, where does time go?"

His question, though rhetorical, defined the sorrow etched in his face. He rubbed his chin, pondering his own query.

"Time changes a man's life in many ways," Tommy stated. "I've lost my wife, my daughter, a son-in-law, my parents, my uncles, two brothers, two sisters, and so many others."

Then, studying my face, considering my success as a writer and the life we shared, he added, "I guess time changes a man's life for the better, too. It's just always changing and we never know what's next. If we did know, our lives would be boring or terrifying. Still, sometimes it's hard not knowing what's next."

Our eyes met and, in that instant, we shared a circular intimacy—a simple, complete, and everlasting bond.

"We just never know the choices God gives us," he added.

I nodded. I knew first-hand what he meant and said, "Are they our choices or God's?"

"Probably some of each," Tommy replied. "He gives us the choice and we make the decision. Some are good, some bad."

Tommy turned away and scanned the surface, distracted by a sudden chop in the water. Small whitecaps, pushed by strong winds, surrounded the boat.

"Too much has changed," Tommy said moments later, studying the water but thinking about Cuba and his family.

Tommy had not seen his relatives since 1959. Now, they and his wife, his precious Anne, were dead. Only memories remained, echoes diluted by the unyielding march of time."

"Can we make St. Croix?" he asked, changing the subject.

After a quick mental calculation, I said, "That'd be a stretch and we'd be angling with the storm."

"Trunk Bay?"

"It's a bit far."

"Chocolate Hole Bay, to the south...there's a good pier and harbor," Tommy countered, pointing in the general direction.

"Sure, I'll bring her about."

"We'll have a few drinks at Mama Jo's Saloon. I haven't seen her in a year. You remember her?"

"Sure, tall, big-boned, toothy smile, and large breasts...she likes you."

Tommy smiled roguishly.

"Women usually do! We'll anchor there. I imagine large swells will front the storm. The hills surrounding the bay will protect THE BELLE."

"Listen, Tommy, after we dock, let's examine the fuel system, I think a filter is clogging."

"I'll check. You want me to do it now?" he replied, flicking his cigar into the water.

"No, let's keep moving. Do it later."

"I'll take care of it."

"Can you stow the gear, boss?"

Tommy nodded and went aft. As he reeled in the fishing lines and secured the gear, I put us on the appropriate course. The wind stiffened, the chop increased and thousands of miniature rainbows colored the spray across the bow, as we ran through varying rays of sunlight.

With our course set for Chocolate Hole Bay, I increased speed. The engines rumbled and steadied as THE BELLE gained momentum. Running faster seemed better on the engine. The wind, now directly astern, carried the sweet scent of rain. Not far away, dark clouds transformed the sky from blue to slate gray as we watched.

Tommy took Sam by the collar and led him below, locked the hatch, and came back to the helm wearing a windbreaker. He rested his hand on my naked shoulder and offered me a soft, white sweatshirt. The old man's hand was warm and comforting on my skin, especially in the cool wind. I slipped into the sweatshirt.

"Thanks, that's better. I'm afraid it'll be a few hours before we can fish again."

"More like days, Jack. The big bastards go deep in bad weather."

Tommy stood watching the bow slice through the sea, feeling the speed of the boat in his legs, grateful for his life and the precious time we shared.

"At least we're together, that's more important than a scag."

The old man paused and I sensed a question.

"What's on your mind?"

"You saw the woman on the beach again, didn't you?"

The rise of my eyebrows indicated surprise. I studied Tommy's intelligent face.

"Jesus, you don't miss a beat. How'd you know?"

"You talk in your sleep, boy. Did you go and meet her?"

"No. Why would anything be different today from thirteen years ago? Things turn sour if I love someone."

"Jack, have some respect for God's tender mercy."

"Somehow, I don't think His tender mercy applies to me. Besides, what do I say to a stranger?"

"Start with hello," Tommy replied. "And, go from there."

"That seems too simple."

"Jack, is God giving you a second chance? You should take this woman's hand and never let it go. It might change your life. Have faith not fear."

The rumble of thunder confirmed his words and Tommy nodded as if agreeing.

Chapter 5
That Tender Light

St. John, U.S, Virgin Islands
1:58 p.m., Friday, August 15, 1986

PALMS BOWED OBEDIENTLY as the storm blew in over the small hills that protected Chocolate Hole Bay.

Lightning streaked across an alabaster sky, as we anchored THE ISLAND BELLE in the lee of those dunes in a small, crescent-shaped harbor. She was now safe from the large swells battering the windward side of island.

After securing the boat, with Sam running ahead, we hurried along the pier to Mama Jo's Saloon, some fifty yards up from the water's edge, at the bottom of a small hill, and on the edge of a sugar-sand beach. Cold raindrops snapped against our faces.

"Mother of God," Tommy shouted, scanning an afternoon sky that seemed more like night. "The temperature has dropped twenty degrees. Let's get inside. I'll check the fuel system after the storm passes. I think we'll be here awhile. Right now, I want warmth, whiskey, and a bite to eat."

Tommy looked back at THE BELLE, listing about fifteen degrees in the wind, but struggling nobly.

"She's a good girl," he said, "She'll hold." Tommy pointed east where the sea and sky remained a distinct blue. However, westward from Chocolate Hole Bay, the sky was growing darker by the minute. "Trust me," he said, "The big bastards will go deep and stay away for days."

I smiled and turned the doorknob. Sam entered first.

MAMA JO BRILLEAN, a broad-shouldered black woman, stood at the bar wearing skin-tight white shorts and red halter. She invited us in with an expansive, ivory smile.

"Mind if our dog joins us?"

"Don't mind at all, handsome man," she said, her island accent warm and appealing. She lit a pipe and inhaled. The tobacco's vanilla aroma quickly sweetened the air. "Dogs need comfort, too."

She sipped dark rum from a tumbler and the color of her long fingernails complemented her red halter. Her brown flawless chocolate skin formed the ideal contrast for two large gold hoops dangling in each ear.

Mama Jo, a native of Christiansted, made her livelihood from tourists who snorkeled in and around Chocolate Hole Bay. In good weather, they came by the hundreds to explore coral formations and dive on wrecks in clear water not far from shore.

However, on this day because of the storm, just one couple sat in a corner of the bar drinking beer and listening to Elton John on a booth jukebox.

Briefly, Mama Jo swayed to the rhythm of John's SAD SONGS, then opened her eyes and smiled.

"Dogs don't like storms much," Mama said, as she reached down and patted Sam's massive head, instantly making a new friend.

"Where ya two sea beggars come from on dis bone-bitter day? Are ya hungry? I have three-bean soup on da stove. Grilled cheddar jack sandwiches good wit da soup. How do dat sound to ya?"

She smiled and winked at Tommy.

"Tomas, ya old bone doctor, ya've not seen Mama for months."

"Hello, Mama Jo," he said, grinning. "It's been a while."

"'Bout a year!"

She set her glass on the bar and hugged Tommy, burying his face between her ample breasts. The old man came away smiling and Mama turned toward me.

"My god, is dis da writer man? What's different 'bout ya boy? Let me think."

Then, she laughed and patted her abdomen.

"Ya belly was bigger. Ya've changed for da better, all tanned, and brown as a coffee bean. Come sit with Mama, hide from da storm, have a drink, and tell me lies 'bout da fishes ya didn't catch.

"Rums, whiskies, gins, vodkas, and beers are what I gots. Buy some and help dis lady wid her bidness."

We followed her to the bar.

"One of each," Tommy replied, laughing at his joke.

"I'll have a Kalik. Tommy wants your best whiskey."

I took a handful of pretzels from the bar for Sam and he sat on the floor beside Tommy's stool, chewing gratefully.

After eating soup, Tommy spent the afternoon playing gin rummy at the bar with Mama Jo, waiting for the storm to pass. They told lies and dirty jokes, laughing and teasing each other. Two old friends passing time, when time was the most valued gift they could offer.

I declined an invitation to play cards. Instead, I went to a nearby booth and worked on my story. I reread sections I wrote previously, made several modifications, and wrote more about Laos. It is never easy reliving a past with so many difficult days; however, thus far, I was doing okay:

LONG TIENG, LAOS
DECEMBER 1972

I awoke at 4:10 a.m. and looked across the dimly lit hut. Nick was gone, checking to insure we were mission-ready.

Before dressing, I stood at the window and studied the moon, considering life's peculiarities. Yesterday, I made love to a rare and beautiful woman and, because of some mystical chemistry, a bond formed. However, on this day, I would go into the bush to do what I did best—kill men.

D. James Then

What would tomorrow bring? Tomorrow remained a mystery.

I yawned and rubbed sleep from my eyes. We would be airborne in less than an hour. By mid-morning, we would be north of Phong Sali for a final briefing with our guide Sing Lanh. Sometime after noon, we three would then fly to a makeshift airstrip well east of Sala Phang, in northeastern Laos. There, we would sleep, eat, bathe, and change clothes. Near sunset, we would move out.

I did not know how long we would be off the grid, jargon for radio silence. It might be a week. It could be more, principally if problems arose.

The three of us would be cut off from the outside world, from everything good and clean, fighting on the extreme fringe of war, carrying instant death in a 7.82 mm bullet, trying to force an enemy's obstinate hand.

In addition to radio silence, the mission demanded focus, courage, intensity, vigilance, and excellence. However, ultimate success depended on two uncontrollable factors.

First was the arrival of the targets, which intelligence said would occur by the time we were in position deep inside North Vietnam.

The second was confirming the death of each target.

There was also a third factor, our safe return, which was hoped for but not essential to success.

I rubbed my forehead and replayed Julia's impromptu visit.

Why did she enter my life at such an unusual moment? What moved me to caress her cheek? Why did she respond as she did? I did not know, but I liked the result. I liked her, too.

I picked up my utility kit, walked to the rear of the hut and showered. Before a mission, I never used soap, toothpaste or anything with a scent.

Where we were going, odors gave an advantage to the enemy and an enemy with an edge usually won. In my business, winning meant death.

As I dried myself, my mind drifted back a few weeks to the day when the mission fell into my lap.

That Tender Light

Forward Study and Observation Group
Near the Borders of Laos, Cambodia & South Vietnam

The helicopter emerged from the mist, circled the landing zone, and hovered. Three men, one badly injured, hung from extraction ropes, twisting awkwardly in the downdraft. Upon descent, the two uninjured men freed themselves as the ground crew took the wounded officer, strapped him on a gurney, and rushed him safely away.

As the Med-Evac passed, a corpsman signaled a 'thumbs up.' I returned the gesture and watched the chopper disappear. A moment later, the remainder of Recon Team Arizona landed. As the rotor blades slowed, the ground crew removed the limp body of Bobby Joe Bullard, who died in my arms minutes before landing.

I talked briefly with the ground chief, who said the Med-Evac was heading south to safer environs. As I turned to walk to mission debrief, one of the ground crew passed with a scrub brush and a bucket of water.

I paused to watch the cleanup and shivered when Bullard's diluted blood dripped onto red dirt. The brush's scrape became a somber symphony to Bobbie Joe's last day on earth. I felt flawed and insignificant, and I vowed to kill ten of the enemy to honor his life. It was my only form of retribution. When a sergeant called my name, I looked away, gratefully.

"Boss wants you inside, sir." He motioned toward a Quonset.

My mind tried to release the images of death and bloody water. I dreaded writing Bobbie Joe's parents.

"What's the word on Lt. Thanh?"

"He's lucky, sarge; he'll recover. We lost Bobbie Joe. It's plain miserable out there. Who wants me?"

"The boss."

"Colonel Szantor's here?"

"No, sir, it is General Jacobs."

Noting my surprise, the sergeant said, "He flew in when he heard Arizona was landing. He has two suits with him."

I grimaced. Suits meant civilians, most likely agents.

"Lead the way," I whispered.

Something told me whatever they wanted would not be good, easy, moral, or reasonable.

The stale air inside the sandbagged Quonset was a mixture of mildew, disinfectant, and cigarettes. Thin strands of smoke took the shape of the structure's curved ceiling.

I acknowledged the general and the other men, leaned my M-16 against the doorjamb and removed my field gear. The two civilians stood as I approached a table in the center of the room. Another man, a Laotian, sat off to the side in shadows.

The general smiled nervously, never an encouraging sign, and asked two non-commissioned officers and the Laotian to leave. Jacobs dashed out a butt, removed a fresh pack of Pall Malls from his blouse, opened it, and offered us one.

The suits declined.

"I never acquired the habit, sir," I said.

"They steady my nerves," Jacobs replied.

He lit his smoke and opened a thermos, saying, "Especially with men in the field."

As he poured a cupful of warm chicken broth, his hand trembled. Apparently, the war was gnawing at him.

"Here," he said, giving me the broth, "you probably need it."

"Thank you."

I drank the warm liquid slowly, letting it flow down my throat into my empty stomach. My hunger quickly dulled.

The general—a bull-of-a-man and former collegiate wrestler—turned toward a pale man with a bad comb-over.

"Captain, meet Tom Cline," he said. Then, gesturing toward a shorter man with tightly cropped hair, he added, "and his associate, Chubb Dailey."

Curt nods from the suits acknowledged my presence.

"I heard you had it rough out there," the general said, his Texas drawl thickened by too many cigarettes. "Something like five days of constant rain?"

"Seven, sir," I replied, "two with limited rations."

"I've been there," Jacobs replied, asking, "Bone cold?"

"Aye, sir," I whispered. "We lost Bobbie Joe. Lt. Thanh is heading to a hospital. He'll make it."

"I'm sorry to hear about Bullard. I know his daddy," the general said as he pulled on his smoke, exhaled, and refilled my cup. I noticed more tremors.

After I drank, I placed the cup on the table.

"I'll get right to the point, captain," the general said, as if my cup's placement signaled his cue to begin. "Put this discussion atop the heap and bury it deep once you hear it."

"Yes, sir."

"Jack, my guests have a special assignment...top secret, code word Lineman, and strictly volunteer. Never mention it."

As the general spoke, the stoic expressions of the civilians never altered. Wherever they came from, they grew these bastards cool and collected.

"Sir, I trust this isn't routine study and observation," I said.

"Afraid not, Jack," the general replied and, glancing at Cline, said, "Tom, you have floor."

"Lineman's black, Captain Taylor," Cline stated, "Completely off the grid, with the highest sensitivity. So sensitive, we'll deny it, if asked or confronted."

I caught hints of urgency and desperation in Cline's eyes and made a quick assessment.

"You want me to kill someone."

Cline's eyes widened. Dailey, the shorter of the two men, held his composure.

"What makes you say that, captain?" Cline asked.

"Sir, the only reason men like you come out here with my commanding general is to pitch something. My guess, it's critical and imminent, which suggests two possibilities—either someone needs rescue or must die. Because of the obvious secrecy and, factoring in my shooting skills, I pick the latter. You need a volunteer."

As Cline's eyes shifted to the general, I knew I was right. Dailey remained statuesque.

Perspiration soaked his shirt collar and armpits.

The general's almost imperceptible nod confirmed my assessment.

"I told you he's smart, Tom," Jacobs said to Cline. Then, to me, he added, "They need a long-range shooter, Jack—someone with skill and field experience. Someone with cool and resolve and..."

"Who's killed before," I finished the general's sentence.

"Yeah, that helps."

"Is this because of the many shooting competitions I won back home, sir?"

"It flagged your name."

"Other men—Army, Marines, even Air Force—are skilled shooters," I stated.

"True," Cline replied, "I have a list." He touched his shirt pocket, emphatically. "Your name's first. None of the others is an officer or as accessible. Most important, they lack your clearance level. My orders specify an officer with top secret, code-word credentials."

"And if I decline?"

"We leave," Cline replied evenly. "The burden remains ours and you continue to do whatever it is you do. We'll find someone else; however, you're highly recommended and, honestly, you save us precious time."

I glanced at the general, whose averted eyes gave him away. The son of bitch recommended me, I thought. I looked back at the civilians.

"How far?" I asked.

"How far?" Cline repeated, confused.

"The shot, Tom," the general clarified. "How far is the shot?"

"Possibly half a mile," Cline replied, "Three men, together."

"Christ," I said, "You don't want a shooter, you want a miracle. When must I decide?"

Cline glanced at a clock on the wall.

"You have two minutes," he said. "We need you on board before we provide specifics. I *can* say you will cross borders."

"Can I at least eat a meal, shower, change clothes, write Bullard's parents?"

My displeasure with their urgency was apparent.

"I'll write the letter, Jack," the general whispered.

Dailey placed his hands on the table. He was a man accustomed to getting results and having his way.

"I'll be precise, captain," he began. "If lucky, we have three weeks before the targets are in position. We need an answer now because this is one part of a broad strategy. The sooner you agree, the more time you have to prepare and get into proper position.

"The least problematic but most time-consuming way requires going in on foot, which chews up a few days. Then, once in position, you'll need to take three targets together, which suggests more wait time, unless you get lucky early-on. As I said, the window of opportunity is narrow. We need your answer, now."

Gut check time!

The room became quiet, the mood intense.

My thoughts were self-serving: do the shoot for a ticket home. I would only agree if Jacobs sent me stateside afterward. Suddenly, Bobbie Joe's diluted blood became a flood of futility. I had lost too many men for inexplicable and incomprehensible reasons. I had to get out.

I missed my family. I wanted to fish again with my grandfather and listen to my grandmother play the piano. I wanted to smell fresh sheets and hear neighbor kids laughing. I wanted to write a book, maybe ten books. I wanted to swim, and hike, and sleep in my own bed, and not worry about death lurking behind every tree. I wanted to feel the change of seasons on my skin and smell the cold air after a snowstorm.

Someday, I would put everything in a story and write about fear, and passion, and strong men and beautiful women. I'd write about lust, love, and drinking wine until sunrise, about the magic of a first kiss and the tragedy of a last, about the feel of a clean shirt on my skin or a woman's hand on my chest.

D. James Then

I'd write about meadows playing with the wind and love deeper than any ocean. I'd write pages about the small of a woman's back and her murmurs in the moonlight. I would write about sins and sadness, life and death, and losing one's sanity to the madness of war.

If a few shots set me free and gave my life back, I'd do it. What was the statement Nick Kunz always said: *if the end justified the means.*

I sensed the others waiting for my answer.

"Two conditions," I said. "Kunz goes; if he doesn't go, I don't."

"Done," said Cline. "General Jacobs anticipated your request."

"Nick understands the mission?"

"Enough to agree, Jack," the general said, "not who, when, or where."

"Why not?"

"We hoped you'd tell him," Cline said.

"What's the second condition?" Dailey asked, maintaining his focus.

I glanced at the general, thinking payback time.

"I have a handful of months left in my second tour. I go home afterward; Nick goes, too." I turned to Jacobs, adding, "General, I want out."

Outside, men shouted as a chopper lifted off. Inside, I watched for a hint of the general's decision.

Seconds later, he cleared his throat.

"No turning back, if I agree," Jacobs said.

"No, sir," my heart was pounding, "my word of honor."

That sealed the deal. After several agonizing seconds, General Jacobs nodded. Thereafter, he sipped coffee and lit a fresh smoke.

"You'll go home," he whispered. "I'll draft the orders before you depart. You want a normal life. I'll see to it. The question is: *will the experience you've had here ever leave you?*"

I shrugged. "I hope so."

That Tender Light

Cline sighed, bummed a cigarette, and lit it. Dailey dabbed his brow and neck with a handkerchief, reached into a satchel, and removed a map where the borders of Laos, China, and North Vietnam converged. He spread it on the table, under amber light.

"According to our intell, the three targets will be together in a few weeks," he said.

With a grease pencil, Cline circled a dot on the map of North Vietnam, near its border with Laos and China. Beside it, he wrote *Muong Te*.

"It's a remote village. Not far away is an old French flower plantation, now used by the North Vietnamese as a respite for their top people. It's isolated and peaceful, and considered untouchable because it's so far north of Hanoi."

He placed three, 4 x 5, black and white photos on the map. One was Caucasian; the others were obviously Vietnamese.

"These men will arrive in Muong Te soon for a Christmas holiday. The European is a French ex-patriot, Jean Paul Matiere. His partner," he pointed to a heavy-set man, "is an army colonel, Hoang Van Giang."

"Giang," I repeated the name.

"Perceptive," Dailey interjected. "You obviously recognize the name, Captain Taylor. His uncle, Nguyen Danh Giang, is the North's defense minister, a key player in the war, and was close to Ho Chi Minh. He's tremendously influential."

"Who's the third guy?"

"Si Duc, a key player when it comes to the North's international strategy."

I studied three faces. The Frenchman was in his sixties, the others their forties.

"These are the targets," Cline said. "If you must kill others to get to them, do it. But these three are primary."

He pointed at the Caucasian. "Matiere's a former mid-level French diplomat, an informant and a communist sympathizer. He passed vital info to Giang before the French collapse of Dien Bien Phu.

"He began his association with the North Vietnamese by interrogating French and other political prisoners. Apparently, the money and the authority the North promised were more attractive than a career in the French Diplomatic Corps.

"Use of the plantation is a perk, as very few have access. Matiere speaks Vietnamese fluently. His English is impeccable; we're told with barely an accent."

"He's a perverse fuck," Dailey added, "who likes young girls. Apparently, he cannot get enough of them. He prefers virgins. In the early sixties, he developed a comparable libidinous desire for torture. He visits the plantation near Muong Te twice annually to recharge his batteries, usually with one or more young women in tow."

"And Colonel Giang?"

"He's always with Matiere," Cline replied, tapping the photo with the tip of the pencil. "One does not go far without the other, captain."

"Does Giang share Matiere's predilection for young girls?"

"No, we've never heard that. He might be asexual and a probable drug user, we think opium. Captain, these men are responsible for the interrogation of American POWs in Hanoi and elsewhere in their system. Their interrogation includes torture," Cline said.

"Don't be naïve, ours does, too," I replied, having witnessed it firsthand. "What about the third guy?" I studied the photographs, already beginning to memorize each face.

"He's a real hardliner and against concessions to the U.S. in peace talks."

"Excuse me for asking, Mr. Cline, what advantage is gained by killing these men?"

"A ballsy question, the answer of which is on a need-to-know basis, captain," Cline replied. "You don't need to know."

"Kind of a shitty response, Tom," the general noted.

"If I'm to end their lives, I'd like something to hang it on," I said, trying to be reasonable. "Does this tie to peace talks?"

Cline became thoughtful and Dailey spoke.

That Tender Light

"Consider what I'm about to say pure conjecture."

"Okay."

"The North Vietnamese deny mistreating American POWs," Dailey said. "Taking out the people responsible for the torture tells Hanoi we know more than they think we do. It hits Minister Giang right between the eyes because he raised his nephew. As for Si Duc, he's a prime reason the North has shown intransigence in negotiating a reasonable peace. We hope your actions, coupled with others that will occur, will bring their leadership back to the bargaining table, and quickly. Then, we believe we'll find a way out."

"Si Duc's the target," I stated. "The others are a bonus."

"What makes you say that?" Cline said, smiling a tight, uncomfortable smile.

"If the U.S. gets peace, American POWs will undoubtedly go home and the Administration can focus on other things."

"You seem fairly confident."

"There's no leverage in keeping them. Why don't we just leave?" I asked.

"Never happen, Jack," the general whispered.

"Saving face and peace with honor," I stated. "Do you think this helps, general?"

"I do," Jacobs replied.

"May I ask a question?"

"You can ask," Cline replied. "We might not answer."

"Why not send in Rangers?"

"A bigger force draws undue attention that deep inside North Vietnam," Dailey answered quickly. "And we could lose them. Why risk so many men when several can handle it, with prejudice. Three well-placed shots do the deed.

"A shooter gives us a five-fold advantage. Psychologically, it's chilling. Tactically, we won't have high collateral damage. Strategically, Hanoi's leadership will quickly learn of the deaths and that is where we score major points. Diplomatically, we believe we'll prod them to talk peace. Realistically, they'll know we can get at their top people whenever we want."

"The terrain's a problem, too," Dailey added. "The area surrounding Muong Te isn't readily accessible. A few men moving fast will react better than a larger force. Fewer men minimize the chance of discovery. Choppers seem an obvious way to get you in there. However, the mountains pose problems and, then, there is the noise; it says someone is coming.

"There's another issue, too. Our government does not want attention focused on our efforts in Laos, especially when we want to negotiate a peace and make nice with China.

"The best way to deploy choppers or a larger force is to have them come out of Laos. If discovered, our targets will disappear. In the chess game between countries, an open violation of the 1962 Geneva Accord our country signed acknowledging the neutrality of Laos could have international ramifications. A shooter gets the job done cleanly and quickly, with plausible deniability. The goal: hit and run, just as they do—total surprise and no mistakes."

"I think the world already knows we're here. Anybody with half a brain just has to look and listen. Do the Laotians have the capability to do this?"

"They don't have dependable shooters," Cline replied, "Besides, we don't trust them. They cut and run too easily."

"Can we jump in?"

"Might work," Cline said, "and we've considered it, Jack. However, ground fire might hit the aircraft on the way in. The shooter might be shot or hurt in a jump. A small team going in on foot is best and least problematic."

"And losing a few men," I added, "isn't a big deal."

Cline nodded.

He proceeded to place a series of 8 x 10, colored photographs beside the others; the grain suggested a telephoto lens.

"Look here, Captain," Cline said. "The plantation house sits on a slight rise in the middle of a plateau. As you can see, it's surrounded three hundred sixty degrees by wide meadows.

"Beyond the meadows, steep mountains protect the valley. Air and ground assaults alert the targets and they could get away easily. Here, here, and here."

He pointed to access roads leading into thick forests.

"The facility's heavily guarded if key people are in residence," Cline added. "A shooter, capable of hitting targets from the trees, has two distinct advantages: he sees results instantly and gets away quickly. Pursuit, if attempted, would be difficult. By the time troops cross the fields and reach the forest, shooters will be gone."

"You've considered bombing?" I inquired.

"It's difficult to confirm the targets are dead."

"A sniper's best," Jacobs said. "Go in, hit quickly, confirm the kills, and get out—fast, precise, low-cost, and undetected."

"Who took the photographs?"

"A Vietnamese national named Sing Lanh," Cline replied. "He'll take you in."

"You trust him?"

"With my life, captain," Dailey said. "Matiere has his two daughters; Sing hasn't seen either girl in months. He'll fight for them, you can trust him."

"How do we go in?"

The general leaned over the map, took the grease pencil from Cline's hand, and circled a location in Laos, only inches west of Muong Te on the map.

"On foot, and it starts here, sixty klicks away. Chubb will explain," the general said.

"Captain, have you ever heard of the Ravens?"

"Sure, they're birds."

Dailey smiled.

"Not what I have in mind," he said. "Since the mid-sixties we've had a strong military presence in Laos; unofficial and clandestine, of course. As we said, because of that 1962 Geneva Accord, the U.S. agreed to Laos' neutrality. We agreed never to place military personnel in the country."

"Let me guess, you found a way to do it?"

Cline nodded. "Ravens are forward air controllers secretly assigned in Laos. Officially, they're civilians who provide humanitarian support. Unofficially, they fly military recon out of desolate airstrips cut into mountainsides and hidden in the deepest and densest parts of the country's forests and jungles. Hell, I don't know all the locations."

"Jack," General Jacobs added, "these boys call in air strikes against enemy activity along the Ho Chi Minh Trail or anywhere else they detect activity. They've been effective in stopping enemy incursions."

"They flag targets for fighters or fighter-bombers coming from either Thailand or Nam, which destroy whatever-the-hell the Ravens tell them to destroy," Dailey added. "Now, for this meeting, more information is overkill. Several Ravens will fly you to a location east of Sala Phang, near China."

He pointed to the map.

"From here," he continued, "Sing Lanh will lead you to the plantation. You'll go in under the cover of darkness, passing through China first and at night."

"Is going through China necessary?"

"Sing says the route is a bit longer but easier; he uses a trail his ancestors created a century ago."

"Tough country, Jack, ragged mountains," the general said. "This way avoids much of it. The fact the trail goes through China is incidental; this does not involve the Chinese."

"Unless we're detected," I replied

"I advise against it," the general stated. "As noted earlier, you're on your own and…"

"We'd never be heard from again," I said. "Tell me about our extraction?"

"What about it?"

"Afterward, there's no concern about alerting anybody, we should be picked up."

"Jack's right," the general said, "When they cross the border and are back in Laos, send a chopper."

For a moment, Cline was quiet, which I thought odd.

That Tender Light

"There's always the Pathet Lao, but we should be able to evade them. I'll arrange a lift," Dailey said. "You'll stash a radio and other items and call when you're back in Laos."

I glanced at my M-16.

"That weapon won't do. I prefer a Remington M-40, with a Redfield 3–9 power Accurange Variable Scope mounted, two. Dry stocks, I'll polish each with bee's wax to prevent warping."

"Why two?"

"Shit happens," Jacobs clarified. "He needs a backup."

"I'd like to meet Sing Lanh as soon as possible," I added. "Does he speak English?"

"Reasonably, do you doubt his ability?"

"If my life depends on it, yeah I do...when do you suggest we leave?"

Cline looked at Dailey for the answer.

"Couple hours...you can clean-up, pack, change clothes, and get a hot meal," Dailey said. "You'll go to Vientiane. You'll stay the night and we will move you north to a different facility come morning.

"I'll have Sing available when you arrive. He'll answer questions and have his maps. You'll find him a patient and thorough man, as I'm sure you are, captain."

"Impatience causes death."

I shifted my eyes and watched the general light another cigarette. Now, it begins, I thought. After fifteen minutes of conversation, I had my ticket home: kill and get the hell out.

At that moment, nothing about the mission bothered me; however, in the months and years to come, I would often feel, even though I had not met her yet, that was the day the gods decided Julia Ormandy would never be mine.

—

We spent the night in Vientiane and the next morning, we flew to Long Tieng, also called Lima Site 20A.

Protected by ragged mountains, karsts to natives, we trained daily and prepared the two M-40s we'd take into the bush—one as primary, the other as a backup.

Our weapons were quite accurate up to 1,000 yards, a bit more than half-a-mile.

Sing Lanh arrived that same afternoon and we met with him daily thereafter. Together, we studied the route into Muong Te, discussed when we would travel, eat and sleep, and where we could find potable water. We reviewed Sing's maps and pored over hundreds of photographs.

Sing spoke of hidden caves, ideal for cover. Each day he described various phases of our trek, focusing on the terrain, the vegetation, and animals we might encounter—possibly tigers, but more likely deer, boars, snakes, and wild dogs.

Each night, before sleeping, I polished the stocks of the weapons and loaded ammunition needed for the next day's practice. Then, in total darkness, I field stripped the weapons and reassembled them, until it became second nature.

A few weeks later, on the day I met Julia, we were ready and Sing departed for northeast Laos to make final preparations. Then, on the afternoon that Julia and I made love, we received word to launch.

Soon, we would rendezvous with Sing Lanh. Later, several pilots would take us to a dirt strip near the borders of three countries. From there, we believed we would need the better part of two days to reach the high hills above the old flower plantation at Muong Te, the venue where three unsuspecting men would draw their last breaths.

Chapter 6
That Tender Light

St. John, U.S. Virgin Islands
5:32 p.m., Friday, August 15, 1986

When Mama Jo announced the storm's end, I stopped writing and went back to the bar.

The rain ended, the sunshine reappeared, the wind subsided, and the sea calmed. The transformation seemed magical. The water in the bay was again a shimmering blue and an azure sky stretched to the western horizon, where lazy white clouds drifted aimlessly. In the east, however, the storm tore into the Atlantic, racing toward the African continent beyond.

"Let's see," Mama Jo said, smiling as she did the tally.

My grandfather waited.

"Tomas, ya owe me $84.15. However, I don't want ya money. Honor comes in winning. Bragging rights are da real premium here."

Tommy disagreed and placed four fifties on the bar.

"Fair's fair. Part is for the debt, part for the food and drink, and the remainder is yours."

Mama Jo smiled, folded the bills, and placed them in her halter-top.

"I shall cherish da memory, forever," she said.

As she cleared glasses, the young couple requested their check. I pulled out a stool and sat beside Tommy, who finished his third whiskey. Taking his cue from the departing couple, the old man stood and stretched. He removed three cigars from behind the bar and lit one. He placed a twenty-dollar bill on the bar.

"Tell Mama Jo that's for the smokes," he said. "I'll check The Belle."

He put the other two cigars in his shirt pocket and said, "Come on, Sam, it's time to pay the piper."

He scratched the dog's head and opened the door.

Mama Jo came back and sat beside me, clearly disappointed.

"Dey sits all afternoon," she said, "and only tip me ten dollar. What's a girl to do? Ah, what da hell, it could be nothing."

She laughed, took two glasses, filled each with rum, and added cinnamon liqueur.

"Tell me, ya continue to write books?" she asked.

Through the window, she watched Tommy board THE ISLAND BELLE, which now stood upright in the bright sunlight. Sam jumped and wagged his tail on the deck.

"Yes, I still write."

"I've read each. Tomas sends dem to me."

"Right now, I'm working on..."

I never finished. An explosion near the shoreline rocked the restaurant, shattered its front windows, and knocked us to the floor. For a moment, we were stunned as shards of glass rained upon us.

"What," Mama Jo whispered.

I did not make an immediate connection. Then, suddenly, I thought of a burning cigar, Tommy's three whiskeys, and the fuel system. Had he been careless?

"Tommy, no."

Opening the door, I saw THE ISLAND BELLE immersed in flames; much of its white hull burned by fuel on the water's surface. The explosion nearly split the boat in two.

"Mama, call an emergency team."

The young couple was on the ground, stunned and bleeding; the woman moaned from a wound on her leg.

As I neared the boat, Tommy crawled onto the deck, clearly in trouble. He suddenly seemed feeble.

That Tender Light

Dazed and confused, he had taken the full force of the explosion against his back. Tommy stood awkwardly and wobbled across the burning deck. A broken radius had split the skin of his left arm, which hung limp at his side. Still, on guts alone, he was able to move. The old man's face was as white as snow. Somewhere, Sam barked.

A second, smaller explosion jarred the boat and Tommy turned slightly, struggling to remain upright. As I drew nearer, I saw the charred flesh on Tommy's back. The hair on the back of his head was completely gone. I jumped onto the boat, trying desperately to reach my grandfather.

A third explosion split the boat in half and I fell. Getting to my knees, I saw Tommy standing awkwardly near the helm ladder. The forward section of the boat floated a few yards away, held by the tug of the anchor.

Our eyes met and, instantly, I knew Tommy would die. From his expression, he knew it, too. He shrugged haplessly, mouthed the words *I love you* and tumbled into the water.

I dove in, found him, and pulled him onto the shore. However, by then, he was dead. The blast had devastated much of his upper body. What remained of his hair was charred; most of the flesh on the right side of his neck and on the back of his head had burned and blistered. The tattoo on the old man's arm was gone. Oddly, his face was not marred and seemed angelic.

I kissed his forehead.

"Tommy," I whispered, hugging him, hoping my spirit would rekindle his. I tried to pray but did not remember the words. I put my head on his chest and hugged him as tightly as I did when I was a boy. Then, searing pain consumed me. I gagged, vomited and, quickly, all sensation disappeared. Suddenly, I felt terribly cold.

For the third time in my life, the light of the world, as I knew it, went elsewhere.

AFTER A CALL home, Lily went to the school's garden and sat with Teresa D'Youville beneath two large oak trees.

Off in the distance, a schooner skimmed the waters of Pillsbury Sound, adding a postcard quality to a day dampened earlier by rain.

"Watch the twins, Lily," the nun observed. "They're adorable." A British accent disguised her French heritage.

"They're happy," Lily agreed. She studied the view. "It's wonderful here, Terri. You're lucky to have such beauty in your life."

The nun's smile transformed her round face into a composite of joy and sincerity.

"Yes, I'm blessed," she replied, "as are you with your farm. I must visit soon, perhaps after Christmas."

"We'd love it."

"Do you promise snow?"

"I'll do my best to arrange it."

"Good and I'll hold you to it," Terri said, scanning the horizon. "This land has been in my family more than a century. I guess we have similar heritages."

Then, remembering Lily's phone call, she asked, "How's Missy?"

"She's fine and feisty and opinionated as ever." Lily's face darkened.

"What is it?"

"She thought she saw Hank drive by the house the other day. It bothered her."

"I thought that nonsense was behind you."

"With him, who knows? If he drinks, he becomes obsessed and obnoxious. There is no past, present, or future; there's just *now*, and it's all very real. I haven't seen him in months. Thankfully, the farm hands are there; he won't risk being recognized. He lives between lies and shadows; however, Hank's smart. How could I have been so damned gullible?"

"We all take wrong turns." Still, Terri seemed concerned.

"It's nothing to worry about," Lily said. "I can handle Hank. If he ever touches me again, it will be his last mortal act." She paused. "Let's change the subject. Missy's decided to have a party in Chicago next month in honor of her sister's fiftieth wedding anniversary. She's looking forward to having me home for a year and I am looking forward to it, too. I'm anxious to work on the cabin. I want to finish the restoration."

The nun smiled. "Are you pleased with your visit?"

"Yes, because of the amount of work I did this summer and that which is ahead of me, I wanted extra time to relax. Telephone conversations are fine; however, they cannot replace visits. I do enjoy younger students. It's a nice change of pace from college."

Lily watched the children. "I talked to one of the men helping with my cabin. Much of the outside work is finished, except for the porch. I'm anxious to get started on the interior." Lily yawned. "I'm sorry, I didn't sleep much; I was up late...reading and thinking."

The nun looked at Lily.

"I sense doubt."

"How would you know that?"

The nun shrugged.

"I'm your friend. I can tell when something's on your mind. Just because I'm a nun, doesn't mean I lack a woman's intuition."

"Okay," Lily said, brushing strands of hair from her forehead, "What is it?"

"Are you testing me?"

"Absolutely," Lily said.

"Okay. It's a bad marriage and the fact that you're getting older. That's it, right?"

Lily's eyes revealed both surprise and respect.

"It's not the age as much as the missed opportunity."

The nun adjusted her position and faced Lily.

"Lily, things happen in God's time, not ours. People forget that. Do you remember the first day we met?"

"I could never forget."

The nun giggled.

"I remember your reaction when I said I was a nun."

"Great fun," Lily said, "However, in my defense, nuns weren't around much, if at all, where I grew up in Indiana. I guess we've both come a long way."

"There's a point I want to make, Lily," Terri continued. "The day we met, I knew you were special. All who meet you see it immediately; it is more evident now than ever. You walk into a room and it becomes you. Your passion shines through—in your eyes, in your voice, in the way you carry yourself. Hank is, was, and will always be an idiot, a self-centered, childish, abusive ass.

"We've both traveled far and we've both a long way to go. God is not finished with either of us. I know this because we've too much to add to His creation. We are destined to do wonderful things. God merely works faster with some of us.

"God shapes us to do His work as we fulfill our dreams. We are part of God's plan. You being here, your career, your farm, the orphanage, the school, and the hospital—are parts of His plan."

"And Hank?"

"There was a reason for that, too. Lily, things happen in God's time and by His blueprint, not ours. He never gives us more than we can bear. A change is coming. We are but players on God's stage."

She glanced across the lawn at the children, allowing Lily a moment of reflection and personal introspection.

"You're truly happy aren't you?" Lily asked.

"There's never a day when I'm not."

They had been the best of friends for nearly fifteen years, since graduate school at Cornell. Teresa D'Youville was the only child of a successful importer. Other than her schooling, she had lived her entire life in the Virgin Islands. She returned home to serve as an associate administrator of Christ-on-the-Cross Hospital in Charlotte Amalie.

After her father died, she used her inheritance and the land bequeathed to her to found a school and orphanage as extensions of the hospital. Over time, the school and orphanage grew and the nun assumed more responsibilities. Some ninety children, between the ages of four and eighteen, were in residence. She now served as the hospital's administrator, too, splitting her time between islands.

"What's on your mind, Lily?"

"Have you ever wished for something different?"

"Lord, no," the nun replied. "I don't have the time, besides I've everything I want. Recall, my only need is people to serve."

"At night, when you're alone, don't you ever wonder?"

"Wonder?"

"About a different life," Lily observed, "or doing something new, living some grand adventure."

The nun gestured toward the school and the children.

"This is my adventure, Lily. Each day is new. I have the children, the school, and the hospital. God keeps me exceptionally busy."

The nun studied her friend's expression.

"I haven't fully defined what's bothering you," she said.

"Sometimes, I'd like to be as happy as you are or as happy as others seem; a part of me constantly feels…unsettled."

The nun sat motionless, considering Lily's comment.

"I'm happy because love fills my life. Some find it faster than others do; however, we all find it. You will, too. God won't forget you.

"At the right time, your heart will tell you. Love is in our hearts the day we are born. When it blossoms, your life will change. It will not be a risk, a task, or a difficult choice, and, thankfully, Hank will disappear forever. Patience is the virtue, envy the vice." The nun smiled, adding, "We should not regret missed opportunity; rather, we should embrace that which is yet to come."

Changing the topic, she said, "I'm thirsty, how about a cool drink, Lily?"

"Sure."

"Dominic," the nun called.

A thin, brown-skinned boy came running when he heard his name.

"Yes, Sister."

The nun held the boy's hand and touched his cheek affectionately. His eyes beamed.

"Tell Miss Bess that Dr. Hall and I want sweet tea with ice and lemon."

"Sure." He was off on a run.

"And, tell her I said you can have a big sugar cookie, but only one," Terri shouted.

The boy looked back briefly, smiled, and continued.

As Lily watched the boy she remembered the first time she came to the island, a young college instructor from Indiana helping a friend, not knowing what to expect. The trip was to have been a one-time favor.

Lily spent long days with a handful of children. She worked hard and laughed more than she had in a long time. She shared her passion for the written word with the same ardor her college students admired each semester.

That one-time favor became a fourteen-year labor of love. Annually, in early August, before the fall semester and the harvest, Lily visited St. John and taught an accelerated literature course to promising students.

A slamming door interrupted her thoughts and Lily turned to see the elderly cook rushing toward them.

"Sister Teresa," Bess yelled, noticeably upset.

Lily's first thought was of Dominic. However, after the confused little boy peeked from behind the cook's wide frame, Lily grew concerned.

Lily and the nun stood.

"What is it?" Sister Teresa asked, touching the old woman's arm affectionately.

"Oh, it's terrible. They just called from the hospital."

Bess buried her face in her hands and sobbed. The children watched. The nun moved closer.

"Please tell me what's wrong, Bess," she said calmly. "Take a breath."

The woman wiped her eyes with her apron.

"Dr. Gomez," Bess said.

"What about Dr. Gomez?"

"He's dead. He died at Chocolate Hole Bay."

"God," Terri replied, blessing herself.

"How," Lily inquired.

"An explosion, on his boat," the cook reported.

"His grandson?" asked the nun.

Fear rose in Lily's throat as she waited for the cook's response.

"I don't know," Bess replied. "I just know about Dr. Gomez, not Mr. Jack."

Terri glanced quickly at Lily.

"I hope not," she whispered. "I'm going to the hospital. Lily, stay with the children."

"I shall," Lily replied. "Call me."

She touched her friend's arm for reassurance and stood in a peculiar, sun-filled silence.

Chapter 7
That Tender Light

St. Thomas, U.S. Virgin Islands
2:03 p.m., Monday, August 18, 1986

MY LIFE RESUMED in a private room on the second floor of Christ-on-the-Cross Hospital in Charlotte Amalie, the capital of the U. S. Virgin Islands. I awoke from a deep void as air from a ceiling fan crossed my face and arms, making my skin tingle. At the time, I had no idea where I was.

I sensed I was leaving a long, narrow tunnel. In those initial seconds, I realized I was on my back and that my arms rested upon a clean sheet tucked around my body and stretched tautly over my feet. A feather pillow was beneath my head and sutures bit into my legs and chest.

Footsteps and voices filtered into the room from the hallway. The words were difficult to understand, but not the laughter. The blare of a horn came next and, then, traffic passed beneath an open window. Soon, odors from a busy harbor mixed with the scents of polish and antiseptic.

The newness of it all seeped slowly into my numbed senses. A moment later, like the patina of rare gems, erratic flecks of gold and silver slipped through my eyelids. Perceiving daylight, I opened my eyes cautiously, blinking rapidly to adjust to the sunlight filling the room.

A vase of freshly cut flowers—carnations and roses, with hints of bougainvillea—sat atop a toile chest. The flowers favored Monet. A worn, tufted-leather wing chair stood in the corner and a blue hospital robe hung to its left on a hook. Another wing chair stood opposite the doorway by the wall.

Yellow curtains drifted lazily in a half-opened window.

Music, perhaps Mozart, played softly from somewhere above, the movement poignant.

Vaguely, I remembered a woman sitting nearby, either reading or praying, and another behind in the shadows. Was any of this real? I pressed my thumbnail into my forefinger until it pinched.

"I survived!"

My own voice sounded foreign. I closed my eyes, thankful for the joy of another day on earth. As I had done in Laos, I quickly closed my mind to the pain. However, as seconds passed, the scent of Tommy's burned flesh became agonizingly real. The boat, the explosion, and the resolute expression on his face—a total acceptance of death—frightened me.

Footsteps passed in the hallway. Somewhere, not far away, a man spoke Spanish. Was I wrong? Perhaps it was a bad dream; maybe Tommy was alive! The voice and laughter in the hallway must be his.

Tommy would go on the book tour and everything would be fine. We would enjoy London, see the Palace, tour the art galleries, and attend the opera. Tommy loved opera.

I closed my eyes, trying to remember his handsome face. Instead, I saw Tommy's charred caricature and ruined body, blistered and bleeding on the wet sand, and I saw his china-white death mask.

No, Tommy was dead. He was not nearby speaking Spanish. We would not attend the opera. A living, breathing part of me was gone, forever. Nothing would be as before. Suddenly, I felt hopeless as I relived my futile attempt to save his life.

I moved and a sharp pain burrowed from the center of my chest to the top of my left shoulder. I attempted to massage the discomfort with my right hand, but a restraint prevented movement. Immediately, a tone pulsated nearby, footsteps came hurriedly toward the room, and a short black woman stood beside the bed and smiled.

Her white teeth had the luster of expensive pearls. She wiped my face with a warm cloth. Her skin resembled dark chocolate, her eyelashes fine lace.

"You've decided to rejoin us," she said. "Welcome back, we've prayed for you."

Her accent was of the Islands, clipped and singsong, educated and wonderfully real, and perhaps the finest voice I had ever heard. As she pressed a red button on the wall, I smelled the scent of lilac and felt her soft abdomen, a refreshingly human sensation, pressing against my naked forearm.

"Calling your doctor," she advised. "He wanted notification the moment you awoke. We knew you would, it was a matter of time."

Her smile seemed endless.

"I feel pain in my legs and chest and have an awful headache, too. I'm thirsty."

"Sure."

She placed a straw between my lips and I sipped icy water. A cold sensation went from my throat into my stomach and I remembered a similar sensation with chicken broth during war.

After a mission, when my men had died and I had killed, I placed tremendous value on little things most people took for granted. Things like soap bubbles on my face, or the feel of a clean shirt against my skin, or the way a mother held her child's hand, or the beauty of passing clouds.

Scents, sounds, and images became treasures because I knew life was so extraordinarily fragile, its rim dreadfully thin and precious.

"The water was wonderful, ma'am."

"Sister, please. Sister Ellen Des Jardine."

"Okay. Thanks, sister. Where's Sam?"

"Sam?"

"He's my dog."
"I was told your dog is fine and with your gardener."
"Good."
She checked my leg and chest dressings.
"You've had an ordeal, but you'll recover nicely."
"I hope."
I looked at two IVs, one in each forearm.
"One is nutrition. The other is for pain," the nurse replied.
An elegant diamond cross on a thin gold chain hung from her lovely neck.
"Your injuries were serious; your surgery complicated. The morphine dulls the pain but sometimes causes headaches. We increased the dosage when you stirred earlier."
"I don't remember."
"You wouldn't. Here's something for your headache." She took two pills from a brown bottle. "Swallow. The headache will disappear."
Again, cool water coursed into my stomach.
"Thanks, what happened, sister?"
"Pieces of metal and glass damaged areas near your heart and lungs; your legs, too."
"I remember my grandfather's face on the beach, he's dead?"
She placed her cool hand on mine and kissed my forehead.
"Yes, he's with God."
"I didn't think he made it, a terrible…"
I could not finish the sentence and, soon, she wiped my tears away.
The nun lifted my wrist to check my pulse. The tips of her fingers were warm and preciously smooth. I noticed a simple gold wedding band. I watched muscles ripple in her slender forearm as she pumped air into a blood pressure cuff and, as it grew tighter around my bicep, I felt more and more alive.

She saw me watching.

"Everything's fine," she said, sensing apprehension in my weary eyes.

"Why do you wear a wedding band?"

"It symbolizes my vows," she answered. "We nuns are wed to Christ and the Church," she added, placing the blood pressure cuff on the nightstand.

"I think I knew that. Did I have a visitor, a woman? I recall a woman sitting beside the bed in the darkness, and another woman nearer the door."

"Sister Teresa, our administrator, visited several times. She had a friend with her. She was quite lovely. If you wish, I'll inquire as to her name."

"No need."

I closed my eyes, but reopened them when I heard footsteps.

"How's our patient?"

The voice was American, possibly Boston, but definitely New England.

"His blood pressure has stabilized," Sister Ellen replied.

She moved slightly and I saw a physician standing beside her. He was a short, slender man with auburn hair and fuzzy sideburns.

"Mr. Taylor," she said, "this is Dr. Wilson. He's cared for you since you came to Christ's Hospital."

"Mr. Taylor," the doctor said, patting my right hand. "It was touch and go for a while; shards of glass were close to your aorta. I removed them and others from near the left lung. Your legs took a beating; however, no lasting damage. You're healing quickly. You seem in good shape, are you a runner?"

"Yes."

"It helps. How do you feel?" the doctor asked.

"Tired and I have a headache."

"The morphine," the doctor said. "We'll slow the drip. The headache will dissipate. I'm sorry about your grandfather; I knew him well. He was a fine man, a talented surgeon."

"Thank you, what day is it?"

"Monday, August 18," the doctor said.

"Heart rate?" he asked, checking my pupils.

"Eighty," the nun replied.

"Better. Blood pressure?"

"It is 114 over 76."

The nurse's smile revealed more pearls.

The doctor lifted a chart and scribbled notes.

"Getting better all the time, are you hungry, sir?"

"No. How long have I been here?"

The doctor wrote on the chart again and spoke to the nun.

"He can have juice, broth, gelatin, and sherbet. We'll monitor him through the night; then, we'll adjust." The doctor turned to me and said, "Since Friday."

"Three days?"

"You'll recover fully, probably in two weeks. Honestly, it depends on your body's propensity to heal, which seems high. Were you wounded at some point in your life?"

"Yes, in Vietnam and Laos."

"I thought so."

"How long must I remain here?"

"We'll keep you a few days and, if recovery goes well, we will release you on Wednesday, probably late afternoon. As you begin eating, you'll feel better rather quickly.

"In a few weeks, you'll feel normal. In six weeks, you'll be stronger than ever. You might lose short-term mobility in your left shoulder; however, simple exercise will add strength and running will help. You're a lucky man, Mr. Taylor, you could have died."

"God's grace," Sister Ellen added.

"By the way, where am I?"

"St. Thomas. Christ-on-the-Cross Hospital, Charlotte Amalie," the doctor responded.

I studied his face and asked, "You military?"

"I was, retired Navy. I like the weather and the fishing here."

"My grandfather did, too. Where's his body?"

"Here, at the hospital. We held it for burial."

"He had no chance at all?"

"No, I'm sorry," the doctor said. "He took the blast full force."

I closed my eyes and wept quietly. The nun leaned over, held my hand, and wiped more tears.

"God, will heal your wounds," Sister Ellen whispered. "In time, He'll heal your sadness, too. Please, trust God to ease the pain."

"What you say may be true, but it's difficult to accept."

"It's true," she replied confidently, "just give Him a chance. The pain will dissipate, in His time and way. Try to sleep."

"Have I had any phone calls or press inquiries?"

"No," the doctor replied.

Suddenly, I realized my agent and business manager, Walter Levy, did not know about the accident or Tommy's death. He did not expect us to return from our fishing trip for a week.

"A favor please, doctor?"

"Certainly."

"Please, call my agent and attorney in New York City and explain what happened. Tell him about Tommy and ask him to come to St. John to help me. Tell him no press. Ask him to come in the next day or so."

"I shall."

"Also, call Father O'Hara at St. Patrick's. I'd like to see him, too."

I supplied my agent's name and telephone number and, as I closed my eyes, I heard the doctor say, "Jack Taylor's a brave man, sister, and a war hero. He is a Medal of Honor recipient. Slow the morphine by fifty percent and call me, if needed. Let him sleep. When he awakes give him food, he'll eat."

Funny, I thought, I never felt brave.

The doctor paused before leaving the room.

"Have you read any of his novels?"

"No, I haven't," the nun replied.

"I recommend them; he's also a fine writer."

After the doctor departed, the nurse smoothed the bedding and adjusted the morphine drip. The cool air from the fan slipped across her skin and, opening my eyes briefly, she seemed to enjoy the sensation.

Thinking I was asleep, I heard her whisper, "I wonder what he did to earn the Medal of Honor? Maybe I will read one of his books."

Then, after admiring the flowers and the yellow curtains drifting in the breeze, she went about her duties.

CHAPTER 8
THAT TENDER LIGHT

Hawksnest Bay, St. John, U.S. Virgin Islands
8:11 a.m., Saturday, August 23, 1986

WE BURIED TOMMY beside the grave of his wife Anne, a few hours after sunrise on a breezy Saturday morning. A small group of friends attended the private Catholic service on the sunlit hillside high above our home. Tommy's grave faced in the general direction of Cuba and overlooked nearby islands, and the blue Caribbean.

I stood beside his grave with Sam nearby, smelling the scent of raw earth mixed with salt air, feeling the wind rush against my face, trying desperately to recall everything Tommy meant to me.

Despite the effort, I could only remember his smile, raspy voice, good heart, and strong hands. Tommy was never bashful about displaying affection. In every day we ever shared, he always found a way to say *I love you*. Death could never break our bond. Nonetheless, at that moment, I would have given anything to hear those words again.

"And now, Dear Father," the brogue of the elderly Irish Franciscan filled the air, "We commit the body of your servant, Tomas Angel Gomez, to its resting place in this good earth.

"Lord, we believe Tomas will rise again in great glory. We beseech thee, Divine Savior, guard our brother's soul as it journeys through eternity. We ask this, in the name of the Father, the Son and the Holy Spirit, Amen."

Father Pat, Tommy's closest friend, sprinkled Holy Water on the casket. Then, he placed his hand on the maple box.

"In paradisum deducant te angeli," he said in Latin and stood aside as funeral attendants lowered the casket.

That Tender Light

"May a choir of angels guide you into paradise," I whispered the translation.

Seconds later, the priest and mourners queued, shook my hand, whispered condolences, and departed in groups of two and three. Sister Teresa waited patiently and, as her turn came, she hugged me, holding my hands in hers.

"He was the finest of men," she whispered. "He loved you and he loved the children. We'll miss him; you're both in our prayers."

"Your kids meant the world to Tommy. Thank you for visiting me in the hospital after the accident."

Her smile seemed warmer than the sunlight.

"You needed prayer and a human presence. Tomas was kind," she stated. "You are, too. Don't let your grief destroy you; don't fall victim to its gloom. You must continue to write, therein rests God's compassion."

"I will. As for right now, it hurts."

She hugged me again.

"Come see me, if you must talk." She squeezed my hands, kissed my cheek, and departed. After a few paces, she reiterated her invitation. "Remember, come for a visit."

Walter Levy stood waiting with his wife a few paces behind and to the left.

"Jack, we should go, too," he stated, stepping forward to be close.

"I'll be along presently, Walter. I need some time."

"You're okay here alone?"

Okay? No, I was not okay and never would be again.

"Yes, I'll follow, I promise."

"Sure, we'll be in the residence."

I watched them depart, stared at the casket, and soon spoke.

"All things come to pass, Tommy. I need to tell you something and I hope you will hear me.

"As a prisoner in Laos, you kept me alive. I wanted to submit to their demands because I was tired, hungry, humiliated, and afraid—afraid of dying, afraid I would never see you, afraid I would never taste freedom again.

"You were always there for me as a boy and you were with me in Laos. After the beatings, I'd hear your voice and remember the things you taught me and I knew, if I gave in, I'd be empty for the remainder of my life. I took the pain and torture and, because I did, I got out alive and retained my dignity. I even became a writer. You always said desperate acts of courage move a life. Now, I know what that means.

"All I am, and ever will be, I owe to you and each of my grandparents. None of this—the money, the success, or the independence—would have happened if not for each of you. Tommy, you will live in my heart, forever. Where I go, you'll go and Tommy, I love you, too."

I put my face in my hands and sobbed, releasing the emotion I had suppressed since the explosion at Chocolate Hole Bay. Certain things in life I did not understand and Tommy's death was among them. After I wiped my face, I ran my fingers through my hair and gazed at the casket.

"Goodbye, Tommy."

I touched my dog's head.

"Let's go, Sam."

Sam whined, stood, and walked with me.

AFTER PERHAPS TWENTY paces, the woman from the beach emerged from the shadows of a stately kapok tree. In the sunshine, in a simple red dress, wearing matching pink earrings and a strand of pink pearls, she stood radiant and beautiful and was a welcome sight.

She waved timidly and started to leave.

"Please, don't go," I said.

She smiled and waited.

As I approached, she extended her right hand and, as I took it, our union became instantly electric. Sparks seemed to leap from her heart into mine. She held my hand a moment longer than expected before letting go.

"I'm sorry for your loss. Dr. Gomez was a kind man."

"Thank you." I studied her splendid face. "I've seen you on our beach."

"Yes."

"Tommy never told me he knew you." I dabbed my eyes with a handkerchief. "Forgive me, these past few days have been...well, difficult."

"You're okay."

She stooped and patted Sam's head.

"Who's this big guy?"

A soft mid-western lilt filled her voice.

"Sam's been with Tommy and me since 1980."

"Hello, Sam," she said.

Sam rubbed his head against her outstretched hand. Her pink fingernails were exquisite against Sam's blond coat.

"He's beautiful."

"Tommy found him on St. Thomas when Sam was a pup. He's family."

"He's magnificent."

"The old man spoiled him."

"Dogs are supposed to be spoiled," she replied. "He seems attached to you."

"That, he is."

She stood and studied my eyes. I could tell she liked me. However, I did not know she felt a deep connection or that she wondered how such a thing could exist, considering we had never met.

"I hope my presence isn't an imposition. I had time before the launch departs for St. Thomas. I wanted to extend my sympathy because I knew and respected your grandfather."

"I'm pleased you did. Tommy was special. By the way, my name's Jack Taylor."

"I know, I've read your novels. They're wonderful."

"Thank you." I studied her face, becoming captive to her violet-blue eyes. "And, you are?"

"Lily Veronica Hall." She studied my reaction. Her smile thrilled me and she knew it.

Lily Veronica Hall! The name floated through my mind with all the brilliance of poetry and seemed to repeat a thousand times in but an instant. I would cherish the moment forever. Lily was everything I hoped for, and more.

Lily's face was tan, lightly freckled, and accented by large dimples, which doubled her beauty when she smiled.

I knew I could lose myself forever in the depths of her incredible eyes and in them never again know pain or sorrow. Her perfume whispered of eternity, the warmth radiating from her supple body frightened me.

In her mind, she discovered compassion, strength, intensity, and commitment. She later told me that my smile calmed an indescribable yearning that had bubbled within for most of her adult life. For an instant, absolute peace swept through her body and she welcomed its solace. In that moment, and for the first time in her life, Lily felt complete, fulfilled, and truly special. The emptiness and remorse from her marriage slipped away forever.

"It's wonderful to meet you, Lily," I said, willing her to want me, hoping she read my thoughts.

"The pleasure's mine."

I wanted my breath to mingle with hers, my heart to beat upon her heart. Deep inside, the intense desire seemed proper and beautiful. Had she asked, I would have gone with her immediately, and stayed with her forever. To my surprise, she once told me she experienced the same sensation and comparable sentiment.

That Tender Light

"You knew I was watching from my beach house?"

"I thought you might be; I wasn't sure," she replied.

"If I invaded your privacy, I'm sorry."

Lily blushed slightly and toyed with the handle of her purse until the momentary embarrassment passed. She added, "You didn't do anything wrong."

The edges of her black hair fluttered lightly in the warm breezes. Far beyond her shoulders, an indigo sea rolled and shimmered in morning sunlight.

Her crooked smile, her slightly uneven teeth, and her dimples formed a masterpiece.

Her presence eased the pain of Tommy's death and the fear of a thousand empty tomorrows. I wanted to feel her nearby for the remainder of my life.

"Where did you meet Tommy?"

"At the orphanage school."

"Sister Teresa's?"

"Yes, I visit annually, in August. Terri—Sister Teresa—and I are dear friends. We were roommates at Cornell. I come for my holiday and during my visits, I teach advanced students of various ages."

"And what do you teach, Lily?"

"Literature...I talked to your grandfather sometimes, when he visited the clinic."

"Tommy never mentioned it."

"He might not have known I was on the beach. We knew each other casually."

"Tommy always knew more than he let on; that was his way," I said, thinking about the illuminating conversation we had on THE ISLAND BELLE.

Lily smiled and noticed the scar above my left temple.

"I guess it's a small island," she added.

One with many surprises, I thought.

"Why did you wave a few days ago?"

"You know, I've actually thought about that," she replied, shrugging. "I knew you lived there and I enjoy your books. I guess it was a way to say hello. I took a chance; was it silly?"

"No, but it was definitely a surprise, but a welcome one."

I chose not to mention the similarity to a heartbreaking day in Laos, a long time ago.

"How many years?"

"Pardon," she said.

"Visiting the island," I clarified.

"Fourteen."

"I don't recall seeing you before; I think I'd remember."

"I've always stayed at the school," she said. "This time I used a friend's sister's vacation home here in Hawksnest Bay. It's lovely, isolated, and near the water. The other beaches on the island are often crowded. I like solitude when I walk. I find being near the water is therapeutic."

"It is."

I remembered a trail of footprints in the wet sand.

The blare of a ship's air horn drifted across the island, interrupting our conversation. Briefly, an awkward silence descended as warm winds and countless seconds passed. Finally, Lily glanced at her watch and pointed toward a waiting taxi.

"I should go; the ferry leaves soon. I'm going home."

"May I ask a question?"

"Sure," she responded.

"When I was in the hospital, after the accident, Sister Teresa sat in my room, with another woman. That was you?"

"Yes."

"Why?"

"She wanted to pray for your recovery. She is my friend. I went with her because I knew your grandfather. We were both concerned."

"Thank you for being there and supporting her."

"Well," she offered, "my driver. My flight leaves a few minutes before eleven. If I miss the launch at Cruz Bay, I'll miss my flight. I must go home."

She touched my hand lightly with hers. The sensation was again electric and memorable.

"You have my sympathy," she whispered, "and my wishes for good fortune. In time, you will heal. We all do. Time, too, is therapeutic. I know from experience."

At that moment, I wondered how it would have changed my life and hers had we met in another time. Was it too late to find out?

As she turned to leave, I remembered Tommy's advice about risking everything for a chance to love someone.

"Don't go," I said. "I mean, I'll drive you to the airport. I've someone to see on St. Thomas, an aunt, Tommy's daughter. She doesn't know about his death."

"She wasn't with the others?" Lily seemed confused.

"She couldn't be; she doesn't live far from the airport. It's on my way and you won't need a cab. Let me buy you a cup of coffee." My eyes pleaded for acceptance.

"Will it be difficult for her?"

"I don't think so. Olivia's a six-year-old child in the body of a sixty-something disabled woman. I believe she will understand, but I doubt she'll be hurt. Tommy wanted her nearby when we moved from Buffalo. She is my responsibility now. She's with the Sisters of Charity and I have to make sure she's happy to honor Tommy."

I awaited Lily's answer.

"Please, may I take you to the airport," I said.

Her smile actually saddened me, because I would not see it after she left the island.

"Sure, but we won't have much time."

"Then, let's make the most of time we have. Any luggage?"

"A few pieces," she answered.

I took her arm lightly, walked her to the waiting car, and tipped the driver, who transferred Lily's bags and departed. I opened the jeep's passenger door and Sam jumped onto the rear seat, leaned his head over the side, and whined. He looked at Tommy's grave, as if saying farewell. Lily turned and stroked my dog's chin.

"He's grieving," she whispered.

"He might suffer more than I. We both need time. When does your plane leave, Lily?"

I watched her open her purse. An exquisite diamond bracelet accented her tanned left wrist, but her slender, artistic fingers bore no rings.

"My flight departs at 10:45," she said, checking the ticket.

"We have a few hours," I replied, glancing at my watch. "Enough time to check in and have a cup of coffee."

"Actually, I prefer tea when I fly."

AN HOUR AND forty minutes later, Lily lifted a wedge of lemon and squeezed a few drops into her second cup of tea, sipped it, and watched passengers queue for the commuter flight to Miami.

The time had been tighter than we anticipated. Tourists disembarking from several cruise ships snarled traffic around Charlotte Amalie's busy harbor, but we still had time for coffee and tea.

For most of the drive, we discussed Tommy, his Cuban heritage, and Lily's annual visits to the orphanage. Now, sitting in the airport, simultaneously thrilled and frightened by each other's presence, we searched for something to say to break an uncomfortable silence.

"Do you like flying?" she asked.

"I don't mind it." I smiled when I discovered a small black spot in the iris of her left eye...beauty's imperfection. She smiled, too, wondering which of her secrets I had discovered.

That Tender Light

"I've done so much of it in my life. When I was a boy, we flew to Havana. I've flown often since, quite a bit in the military and, of course, for business."

"Actually, I fear flying," Lily said, matter-of-factly. "But I enjoy new places."

"How do you get beyond the fear?"

"I take a deep breath, and get on the plane and go. I have found if I occupy my mind, with books mostly, I don't think about it. Of course, tea helps...must be the antioxidants." She smiled, adding, "I also say every prayer I know."

I chuckled, saying, "The real defense surfaces."

"Hey, don't knock it. Raw courage is a remarkable character trait in a frightened woman, it demands respect."

"I'm not mocking you, Lily, honestly...why the fear?"

"The smaller planes are too confining and, as for the larger ones, it seems counterintuitive that machines so heavy can fly as high and as fast as they do."

"Now that I think about it, Tommy wasn't too fond of flying, either. Sam on the other hand, loves it. Where is home, Lily?"

"St. Omer, Indiana; in addition to teaching, I own a farm."

"A farm?"

"Yes," she replied, "half a dozen Guernsey cows, some chickens and several horses, but no pigs. I won't have pigs. Primarily, though, we grow corn and beans—soybeans."

"And where do you teach?"

"At Hannlin College, I'm with the English Department. I've actually used excerpts from your books to illustrate aspects of symmetry and character development."

"I'm flattered."

"Jack, you have extraordinary talent. I particularly enjoy your character introspection and balance. Each is rare by modern standards."

I fidgeted with a spoon, feeling uncomfortable.

"Caught in the act by a true professional, it takes great effort to achieve the effect I want. I like rhythm and a certain lyrical sense. The symmetry helps develop a story. The same is true with introspection. Symmetry, when used properly, adds a powerful element of surprise. I'm sure you understand the construct."

"I do."

Her eyes were happy. She opened her purse and removed a business card. "If you're ever in Indiana, perhaps you could talk to my students."

I studied it, noticed Ph.D. after her name, and slipped the card into my shirt pocket.

"I'd enjoy that. Is there a man in your life?"

The question surfaced so unexpectedly that I blushed. Embarrassed, I looked away. Lily sipped her tea, amused, but clearly pleased by my interest.

For a moment the sparkle in her eyes dimmed and, just as quickly, rekindled.

"No one serious; I was married once. However, it didn't work out."

"So, you own a farm, have a doctorate, and teach. Are there other mountains to climb?"

"A few, I'm refurbishing a cabin on my property, which was our original farmhouse built in the 1860s. I've some reading to do and several articles to write. I am fortunate to have a year's sabbatical; it's my first. Is there a new book?"

"Yes, my eighth is entitled THE LAST CHAMPION AND THE LAST KING and it will be published in a few weeks."

"What's the storyline?"

"A mercenary dying in Spain evaluates his life in Africa and the loves he lost. It covers the rich history of African struggles."

"Are you considering another?" she asked.

"Yes."

That Tender Light

After a few seconds, she seemed disappointed I did not say more. I wanted to but, at that moment, did not know how to explain or describe the things I did and experienced.

"Where is your farm?"

"St. Omer is sixty miles southeast of Indianapolis and about the same from Cincinnati. It's authentic farm country, rural, and always peaceful. It's been in my family since before the Civil War."

I smiled, wondering about the sensation of kissing her soft lips. I did not know it, but she longed for that same kiss.

"How many acres do you own?"

Before Lily could answer, an agent made an announcement:

"Ladies and Gentlemen, attention please, this is the final call for Flight 1745, departing for Miami. Please board immediately through Gate 6. This is our final call for Flight 1745 to Miami. Please, board now."

"I should go, Jack," Lily said, becoming noticeably tense.

"You'll be fine, remember those prayers."

She smiled and lifted her purse.

"Now, it's off to Indiana," she said. "Thanks for the tea. I enjoyed meeting you and Sam. Your grandfather will be in my prayers."

We walked to the gate.

"Thanks again for attending Tommy's service," I said.

"I'm happy I did and pleased I met you. Your next book, can you tell me anything about it?"

I studied her face, hoping to memorize her beauty. She was a sweet person, perhaps the sweetest I would ever meet.

"It's about Vietnam and Laos, my experiences in the early 1970s. It's about a woman I loved when I was there. It's about things I did and saw—some were ghastly."

"Do you continue to see the woman?"

The meaning of her question was apparent.

"No; however, I've a story to tell. I tried to write it once before, but it was too soon. This new version I started a few days before Tommy's death. I've been so out of it since the accident that I haven't found the desire to write."

"You'll rebound in the coming days," she said, confidently.

She turned and I noticed a playful expression. To my surprise, she pressed a coin into my right palm.

"A penny for good fortune," she said. "Make a wish for the book's success. It's always good luck when you receive a new penny." Her smile touched my heart. "Pay it back when you can," she added. "Don't be a stranger. People like us need the best of dark and bright."

"Lord Byron?"

She nodded, was silent for a moment and then, to my surprise, she kissed my cheek. The fragrance of her perfume sweetened the air as she moved away.

"A lovely fragrance, what is it?"

"Chanel Number Five...I'm happy to have met you, Jack Taylor. Remember, when you're in Indiana, I'd be thrilled by a visit."

"You are beautiful, Lily," I whispered, surprised I said those words. "I hope you don't mind my comment."

"Of course not," she replied. "I want to be beautiful."

"Well, you are."

Her blue eyes sparkled.

"Travel well, Lily Veronica. Enjoy your day."

She kissed my cheek again and briefly touched my left hand with her fingertips. She let them linger before reluctantly pulling them away. She turned, walked down the ramp, and, before boarding the aircraft, looked my way.

"More than five hundred," she shouted over the prop noise.

That Tender Light

"Five hundred," I repeated.

"Acres...you asked about my farm; five hundred and fifty acres. It's a bit of heaven on earth. Come see it, sometime."

She laughed, waved, and entered the aircraft.

I watched the gate attendant close and lock the door, hoping the sensation of Lily's kiss and the warmth of her fingertips would never disappear.

I removed her card from my pocket and studied her name. Lily Veronica Hall. The card carried the scent of her perfume. I slipped it into my pocket, sorry that I had not returned the kiss.

As Lily's aircraft rolled toward the runway, I walked to my jeep, as my heart pounded with uncommon emotion.

I looked at the shiny, new penny. I had said goodbye to two people that day. One I loved and was gone forever. The other I hoped to love and the sensation of her kiss had already begun to pull me to Indiana even before her plane was airborne.

CHAPTER 9
THAT TENDER LIGHT

St. John, U.S. Virgin Islands
7:02 p.m., Saturday, August 23, 1986

LATER THAT EVENING, inspired by my time with Lily, I went into my study, turned on the desk lamp, and opened my portfolio, which Mama Jo had couriered to my home.

When I was convalescing, I believed I would not finish the story. However, after talking to Lily, seeing the expectation in her eyes, feeling her respect for my work, and sensing the excellence she demanded, I felt compelled to write again.

If for no other reason, I wanted Lily to understand what happened in Vietnam and Laos. If she knew and accepted it, conceivably everything would be fine. Suddenly, I wished I had been a better man. Seconds later, I was again in Southeast Asia:

Airborne, Over Laos
December 1972

The mills of the gods grind slowly but exceedingly fine, I thought, as I finished dressing. I gathered my gear and walked toward two Cessna Bird Dogs standing in the darkness several hundred yards away.

Off to the east, a fine line of pink light edged along the mountaintops, announcing the advance of dawn.

The breeze against my face hinted of cool end-of-year mornings of my youth in Western New York when autumn stole some of the hawk from the coming winter. Back then, I slung the morning Buffalo Courier Express from an old blue Schwinn.

I never dreamed a woman as remarkable as Julia Ormandy would enter my life, never considered war, never thought of Southeast Asia, and never envisioned killing men and liking it.

That Tender Light

Of course, I never thought my own kind would deceive me or that I would execute men to get out of a war that rotted the marrow of my bones.

What I was about to do was not honorable, but selfish. What would the Felician Sisters who taught me at Transfiguration Elementary say?

They would be against killing.

It is a sin, they would say.

Is it a sin, if it is in a war?

That is different, but it is best not to go to war.

Nevertheless, I was in a war and I wanted to get out it and, if killing did that, I would do it. For that perspective, the good sisters had no answer. I was on my own.

"Are we ready?"

"Locked and loaded, Jackson," Nick replied, standing in the darkness near the aircraft.

I looked at the two pilots. They nodded and tossed their cigarettes aside. "On your order, captain," one said.

"Let's go."

—

The two aircraft lifted off effortlessly before sunrise. Intuitively, I checked the time: 5:02 a.m. The Bird Dogs banked sharply to the left simultaneously; then, easily right, beginning their ascent to 9,000 feet. Nick was in the lead Cessna some fifty feet above and slightly ahead of my aircraft.

I leaned forward to study his plane's dull-green underside. I rubbed my eyes and smiled. Nick was probably asleep. My resourceful friend from Kentucky routinely napped on any aircraft like a baby in a warm blanket.

The eastern horizon was a splendid sight, far out on its edge, shafts of sunlight angled toward the earth like columns of translucent gold. Nothing—not man or war, or good or bad—stopped the sunrise.

Far in the west, darkness still held purchase over western Laos, northern Thailand, Burma, and the Bay of Bengal beyond. Thousands of stars and a bright moon hung in the sky.

D. James Then

We were hardly fifteen minutes into our flight time when my pilot motioned downward with his thumb. "Sam Thong," he yelled above the engine noise. "Do you think anybody's awake down there?"

"A few people, I doubt many at this hour," I replied.

"Ever been to Sam Thong?"

"Once," I shouted, sensing Julia's cheek in my palm.

"They do a fine job down there," the pilot replied.

I studied the landscape trailing beneath and behind the aircraft. In the middle of the lush countryside, puddles on Sam Thong's dirt runway reflected light like large pieces of a shattered mirror.

"Did it rain?"

"About two this morning, it didn't last long," he said.

Clusters of huts and buildings sat on either side of the runway. One building, the hospital, stood out as larger and longer. We were too high to see movement.

Was Julia awake? Was she an early riser? Was she with patients?

I had so much to learn about her. I smiled. I had seen her body, moved inside her, watched her eyes flutter as she slept, and knew how her lips curled into an easy half-smile when she saw me watching. For now, those images would suffice. In days to come, they would give me strength.

Our incredibly moving union was gripping and unexpected, and quite possibly numinous. I leaned against the headrest and closed my eyes. Heavenly father, I prayed, let me see her again; please, keep her safe.

As fate often dictates when lives touch, Julia awoke precisely as our aircraft flew over Sam Thong. Through a parted curtain in the window beside her bed, she looked into the light gray sky. Somewhere above she heard the drone of single-engine aircraft.

That afternoon, she would remember stars and the moon in the morning sky; however, by then, the sound of aircraft had slipped her memory.

That Tender Light

Before settling back onto her cot, she checked the time: 5:18 a.m. She pulled a blanket over her chilly shoulders and briefly remembered my hands on her body, touching her as no man ever had. As she drifted off, she prayed for my safety; a prayer sleep prevented her from completing. Later, as she drank her morning tea, Julia would wonder if God ever heard or answered unfinished prayers.

—

"We'll be over Phong Sali in forty, our first stop in fifty," the pilot shouted. After adjusting controls, he glanced at the M-40 and said, "Wherever you're going, better you than me."

"It's best to keep it that way."

The plane shuttered in a wind current and jostled my head against the headrest.

"Sorry," the pilot shouted, "Hard to anticipate the updrafts, there's a hell of a lot of them in and around these karsts. The winds can be strong at times."

"Not a damned thing you can do about it." I said and settled in my seat. The jostling reminded me of the last jump Nick and I made in survivor training...

...Jesus," I yelled when Nick Kunz finally opened his eyes.

"What?"

"I thought I'd have to toss your sleepy ass out of the plane."

Nick rubbed his round face, yawned, and removed his helmet. He scratched his shaved head and smiled sheepishly.

"It's my nature, Jackson," Nick shouted, replacing his helmet and fastening the chinstrap. "I sleep when I can; I figure I'll need it, eventually."

We had known each other for nearly six months and, as we trained, I came to understand that my new friend possessed deep resolve and unending inner strength. Unlike other trainees, Nick never lost his composure. He was bold and fearless. Regardless of what our instructors said or wanted, no matter how demeaning, Nick accepted it with detachment and excelled. He was unflappable and dominant at every turn.

D. James Then

Our instructors ran us ragged, worked us bone tired, forced us to eat bugs and snakes and roots, and dehumanized us at every turn. We survived screams, interrogations, water boarding, slaps, punches, and various other forms of inhumane treatment. Through it all, Nick remained bemused and decidedly calm. He was a tough son of a bitch.

"Does anything ever bother you?"

Nick looked at me, his usual detachment evident in his brown eyes.

"Why would you say that?"

"You've an unyielding reservoir of patience for whatever they throw at us; it's actually quite enviable."

His expression darkened as he considered something from his past. He shrugged and replied, "I saw my mother raped, sodomized, and beaten to death when I was twelve years old," he said matter-of-factly. "I killed the bastard—a local cop and organizer who drank too much. Shot him dead with his own gun, first in his groin, then in his forehead. After that experience, what could life hand me that would be worse?"

Nick motioned around the aircraft but his sweeping gesture encompassed everything we experienced in our training, would encounter in war, or would face in life.

"This stuff they throw at us? Compared to what my mom endured, it is pure bullshit. It'll never bother me, sugar bean, not ever, not on your sorry sinful soul."

A few moments later, Nick was sleeping...

...Mind if I light one up," the pilot shouted, pulling me away from old memories.

"Go ahead."

The pilot flicked a Zippo and struck a blue flame.

"Want one?"

"I never acquired the habit."

The pilot banked slightly right, following the lead aircraft.

"I've smoked since junior high school; it's why I'm so thin."

"Where was that?"

That Tender Light

"Pella, Iowa, what about you?"

"Lackawanna, New York."

"Near Buffalo, right?" he asked. "Steel mills are there?"

"Yeah, miles of 'em."

"My dad told me about them, he's in sales," the pilot said.

I soon closed my eyes. The cigarette smoke brought thoughts of Sing Lanh and our first day in Long Tieng...

...Nick and I entered the hut not knowing what to expect. We were meeting Sing for the first time. We found a diminutive man, thin and wiry, muscle and bone, and with a brown-eyed intensity that bore to the center of our souls. Sing, about forty years old and five and a half feet tall, lit a filtered cigarette with a wooden match. He blew smoke on the flame and smiled.

"Little man doesn't have an ounce of fat on him," Nick whispered, "He can't weigh but a hundred pounds."

"Actually, one twenty-eight, sirs." Sing's eyes were cheerful.

"He understands English, Jackson."

"And Vietnamese, Lao, Hmong, and Chinese, too," Chubb Dailey added, walking into the hut behind us.

"These men you mentioned, Chubb?" asked Sing.

"Yes," Dailey said. "I can only stay a minute." He placed his hand on Sing's shoulder. "Gentlemen, meet my friend Sing Lanh. Believe me, he walks the talk; you can trust him. He'll answer your questions. I'm sure he has some for you. He'll guide you to Muong Te. Do what he says. He's been over the route numerous times. He'll get you in unnoticed and, barring any mishap, he'll get you out." He looked at Sing. "How long will it take to walk in?"

"Fifty-five or sixty hours," Sing said, "from drop point."

An aircraft engine started in the background.

"That would be my ride, boys," Dailey added, "IASS in Vientiane has loaned us a physician and we're going down to bring her back. She'll fill in at the hospital. We need a backup because our regular doc is going into remote villages to examine children and provide care."

D. James Then

Before Dailey departed, he turned to Kunz, saying, "Don't let Sing's size fool you, Kunz, he's one tough cookie. You will learn to trust him, as I do."

Sing's nervous smile revealed a lower jaw missing several teeth. He noticed my interest in a large scar curving from his left earlobe to the center of his neck.

"You see cut," Sing said.

"Hard not to," I replied.

"Matiere did this," Sing said. "He takes daughters and leaves me for dead."

"And your back," I said, noticing Sing's awkward posture.

"From beatings, I stoop when I tire, is no problem." Determination filled Sing's brown eyes. "Have much to do," he added, "Back pain can't stop me."

He reached out and shook our hands. His grip was strong; his hands calloused and large, despite his slight stature. Outside, Dailey's aircraft tore down the runway and lifted skyward.

"You wonder if you trust little man," Sing acknowledged, looking first at me and then at Nick. "You bet," he paused, his voice soft and without pretense. "Teaching me to trust you is important, too. Which is shooter?"

I nodded.

"Chubb say you the best. I pray this is so, is very long shot. Now, we work."

Sing moved toward the table.

"We sit, okay? I have little sleep in two days and am tired."

"Would you like to rest now?"

"No, later; too much to do and say."

Nick pulled a chair away from the table and Sing eased his small frame onto it.

"Are you hungry or thirsty?"

"Water, please, I require not much food," Sing replied.

I poured a cupful of water from a pitcher on a nearby table. As he drank, Sing held the cup with both hands, as if guarding a treasure. His fingers were badly misshapen.

Over the cup's brim, he noticed us studying his hands.

That Tender Light

"Crooked fingers from Matiere," he whispered.

"Is he a cruel bastard?" asked Nick.

Sing nodded, set the cup aside, and took a few pulls on his cigarette. When he spoke, his staccato observations proved not only economical, but also informative.

"Sirs, my family live in North many decades," he began, "Farmers and hunters. Borders mean little. China, Laos and Vietnam just names, they are part of same land. Names say who rule land, but land is permanent. Names change, yes. Land never changes. Forests stay same, yes. Springs stay the same. Rivers and mountains stay same, yes. Land lasts longer than governments. I know way.

"Borders mean nothing to me, mean nothing to ancestors. We love land, not border, not government. Roots grow in soil, watered by human sweat. Government destroys spirit, but not land. I'm Hmong; I'm Lao; I'm Vietnamese; I'm Chinese—all in blood, all in land."

He patted the center of his chest, adding, "My family lives for years in area fifty kilometers wide and deep. They hunt and harvest, laugh and cry, make babies and work land. I am born near Muong Te. I live in China, in Laos, in Vietnam. The French train my father agriculture at Dien Bien Phu. Father teaches me. I work land at Muong Te. I know farming, indeed.

"My life changes after Dien Bien Phu. Better, yes. I marry have two sons and two daughters. Years pass. Matiere wants girls and takes them."

Tears formed in Sing's eyes as he continued.

"No one stops him; no one cares. Who knows where girls are, now gone maybe. My wife," he paused and touched his heart again, "she die, heart saddened and break. I fight when Matiere takes daughters. His men beat and cut me, stomp hands, leave me as dead." He touched his scar. "My wife and boys fix this. I tougher than Matiere think. I will find my daughters. I will not rest. I have family north of Phong Sali. There, I meet Chubb and join his fight. I not fear Pathet Lao. I help Chubb; he helps me.

"Sirs, I like Chubb. When he says Muong Te and Matiere, I say I take you. I pull the trigger to kill Matiere, no problem, yes."

Sing paused and reached into his pocket, removing a series of hand-drawn maps, bound in waxed paper and tied with packing string. He untied the bundle and opened each map carefully. Surprisingly, the maps provided intricate detail.

On that very day, and in those that followed, Sing took us through each section of the trail, using his maps and photographs to illustrate perspective.

He provided descriptions of the landscape, the times he recommended we travel, and the locations for rest. He patiently answered our questions.

Sing learned our expectations, too. We taught him hand signals, discussed camouflage, and illustrated how to move with stealth and economy.

"We go in here," Sing said a few days later, referencing a point near the Chinese border. "Best at sunset; Muong Te plantation is two days. Going through China at night is good."

"How far is Muong Te from the launch point?" Nick asked.

"Sixty kilometers," Sing replied.

I did a quick mental calculation: about forty miles. That was nowhere near fifty-five or sixty hours.

"Averaging a mile an hour, not including sleep time, puts us in position the morning of day two," I said. "We'll move faster."

"Very doable," Nick whispered. "But, let's keep it at fifty-five, as Sing says. If we beat it, that's to our favor."

"We come out here," Sing said, pointing to a spot northeast of the plantation. "Big mountains, thick forests; warm and wet. We move in and out of mountain passes on trails used by my people. This way is best."

We continued working for several hours and afterward, Sing went to our hut where he used our makeshift shower. When he removed his shirt, we saw a series of scars on his back.

"Matiere do that, too?" Nick seemed visibly concerned.

"His men did."

"Same thing," I replied.

That Tender Light

"A tough man we have here," Nick said. "I trust him."
"As do I," I replied...

...Our final destination's coming up," the pilot shouted. "The other boys are already on the ground."

I checked the time. It had taken nearly thirty-five minutes to fly from our first stop north of Phong Sali.

"How close to China?"

"A few kilometers," the pilot replied.

Minutes later when we landed, Sing and Nick stood waiting.

Sing led us to a small, unnamed village east of Sala Phang where we ate a light meal of fish, pork and rice, and studied Sing's maps one final time before sleeping for a few hours.

We awoke before sunset, ate rice, washed with clean water, and changed into odorless commonplace clothes.

Before we entered the lush forest at the edge of a mountain range, we watched the sun setting in the west. Then, without anyone giving a command, we turned and began our journey, with Sing taking the lead. I was third in line.

CHAPTER 10
THAT TENDER LIGHT

London, England
6:27 p.m., Thursday, September 18, 1986

THE AFTERNOON'S CHILLY drizzle became evening's cold mist. I nursed a scotch in the Lowndes Hotel's Mimosa Grille in Knightsbridge after a last-minute interview with critic Julian Tufts. I sat at the bar ostensibly watching pedestrians avoid puddles and splashes from passing traffic.

Honestly, the rain, traffic, and damp streets held no interest. I focused on Lily's pretty smile as I idly rotated her penny in the fingers of my left hand.

The good-luck coin made her a constant presence in my mind. Despite thousands of miles, she felt very close and very real. A month had passed from the day I buried Tommy and drove Lily to the airport. Yet, it felt like only hours.

The sensation of her impromptu kiss lingered on my cheek. Her warm voice continued to resonate. The handful of thoughts we shared implied something greater than a casual encounter should have implied.

I was smitten and, after she left St. John, I called her often. However, I always hung up before the first ring. What would I say? How would she respond? Would she remember me? Would someone else answer? Did she even care?

My indecisiveness made me a fool and I vowed that each aborted call would be the last. Yet, within hours, I would dial again, only to hang up, again!

However, after I arrived in London, I had been too busy to call. Thereafter, I decided to let it pass, to forget Lily, to get on with my life. Yet, despite my conviction, Lily surfaced in my mind daily and now, with the book tour over, she reclaimed a permanent spot in my thoughts.

I watched traffic pass. Was a relationship possible? I hoped it would be; I wanted another chance to love a woman. I sipped my drink. Tommy would have urged a call; no, he would have raised hell and forced it.

"Easier said than done, Tommy," I whispered, especially with my baggage.

Losing Julia Ormandy had pinched tender nerves.

"Could I have another shot?"

Julia was the only woman I ever loved and that experience nearly destroyed me.

I considered Elisa Sheridan, the artist I knew on St. Thomas. Together off and on for eight years, she was my last physical relationship. She was sexy, talented, beautiful, passionate, and compassionate. She loved me. However, I chose not to love her. I was afraid and it finally ended.

Jesus, I thought, what a way to live! I set my empty glass on the bar and motioned for another drink.

Other women shared parts of my life, but only briefly and, after Elisa, never another. I remembered names, faces, soft nights, and easy days, but little else. Relationships blurred, the sum of which was an insignificant total of human interaction. Damn it to hell, if I were destined to be alone why then did Lily feel so different? I studied the penny, remembering her smile, her kiss, the violet shades in her eyes, the way she stood on the beach, and her dress taking the shape of her body in the wind.

For the past day or so, thoughts of Lily filled every waking moment and they surfaced in my dreams, too. She stood central to everything I did, said, or thought. We had each waited a lifetime for the other to appear. Something magical happened on the day we met; the excitement persisted and the magic, too.

Some indescribable force ripped away past restraints and pulled me toward Indiana.

The more I fought it, the stronger the tug. One glimpse of Lily's eyes, one touch of her hand would tell me.

The bartender refreshed my drink, adding a twist of lemon. He placed a bowl of peanuts nearby.

"Want a menu, mate?"

"Sure. Say, am I able to call the concierge with your phone?"

The bartender nodded and soon placed a menu and the telephone beside my drink.

"Touch one four," the bartender advised. "Give a nod when you're ready. The salmon is excellent. Our filet's superior and the bangers and mash are popular, as are the fish and chips."

The bartender went to serve two women who entered the Grille. I surveyed the woman nearest to me, a redhead, and admired the pure texture of her skin and the smart curve of her calf.

I smiled briefly when she noticed me. A slight shrug said I apologized for staring. She smiled when our eyes met a second time and nodded receptively to an advance. Instead, I turned away and dialed the concierge.

"Bellman," a voice responded.

"I'm sorry, I wanted the concierge."

I saw my reflection in the mirror behind the bar. For an instant, I was in Laos, on the morning of my last mission. I quickly diverted my eyes and the memory faded.

"You dialed correctly. Ms. Abrams is away, briefly. I am covering. May I assist you?"

I touched the spot on my cheek where Lily kissed me.

"This is Jack Taylor in 221B. I'll be in my suite by," I checked my watch, "7:45 p.m. Please have Ms. Abrams call. I want to schedule a flight."

"Indeed, sir. She'll ring promptly as requested."

"Thanks."

I ordered the salmon and ignored the redhead's glances, focusing instead on a farm in Indiana.

THE TELEPHONE RANG at the specified time.
"Hello."
"Mr. Taylor, it's the concierge."
A pleasant female voice filled my ear.
"Thanks for returning my call."
"You desire travel arrangements, sir."
"It's for a U.S. flight, for the day after tomorrow?"
"Not a problem," she replied.

I explained my wish to arrive in St. Omer, Indiana, as early as possible on Saturday morning and said a flight from New York to either Indianapolis or Cincinnati would suffice.

"Please use Josiah J. Taylor for the booking," I said, adding, "I'll have Sam, excuse me, my dog with me in New York. Put him on the flight, too."

"Sam's a grand name for a dog. May I have his breed and approximate weight?"

I supplied the information.

"I grew up with Labrador Retrievers. None of this presents a problem. Do you have a payment preference or shall I add the additional charges to your invoice? Everything is paid by your London representative, sir."

Conscious of my privacy and Walter Levy's penchant for snooping, I replied, "I prefer this to remain confidential."

"A credit card will suffice, sir."

I considered her suggestion. My credit card statements went through Levy's office, too. Walter would find out eventually, but why serve it up.

"I have cash and traveler's checks, I'll prepay. I want this to be strictly confidential."

"As you wish, sir, I'll use my personal card if you prefer and you can reimburse me."

"Please reserve a rental car, too."

"I shall, but you'll need to supply a credit card when you pick it up. I know for a fact you can pay with cash when you return the vehicle. If you do, they will not run the card."

"I appreciate that, Ms. Abrams."

"Is there anything else, sir?"

"No."

"Splendid, I'll ring back presently."

"Thanks. Oh, before you go, my message light is on."

"The operator can assist, I'll transfer."

"Thanks."

"Mr. Taylor?"

"Yes?"

"I enjoy your books. You are a splendid writer. My mum loves your stories. I cannot wait to read the newest. I read the capsule in yesterday's newspaper. It's a thrill simply talking to you."

"What's your mother's and your first name, Ms. Abrams?"

"Mine is Eloise; mum's is Sharon."

"I'll have autographed copies for each of you."

"Truly?" she asked.

"Absolutely."

"Gracious of you, sir!"

"Good, remember my request is confidential."

"You've my word, sir. I shall deliver the tickets personally. As for confidentiality, I will be on maternity leave soon. No one will know; a moment, please, for the operator and my best to you."

"You, too."

A second later, the operator came on line.

"Yes, Mr. Taylor?"

"I have a message."

"A moment please, sir. Do you prefer delivery?"

"No, just read it."

"Certainly," she paused. "Mr. Levy requests a call today."

"Thanks. By the way, what time is it in Manhattan?"

"A few minutes before 3 p.m.," she replied, "exactly five hours difference."

Walter would be in the office, awaiting the call.

"Please connect me." I gave her the number and waited for the connection. Soon, I heard ringing.

"You're connected, sir."

"Walter, Jack here."

"Jack! How's the tour?"

"Fine, I just had the final interview. It seems I have a very popular book. I have signed books all over London. The advance work has been thorough and reviews are favorable."

"That's an understatement; they're extraordinary! How are you holding up?"

I understood his two-pronged question. Part was genuine interest in the book's success; part was concern for my well-being after the accident and Tommy's death.

"I'm fine, physically and emotionally. I continue to walk every morning to rebuild the strength in my legs. People love the book." Then, thinking of Lily, I said, "I'm moving forward."

"That's splendid."

A slight pause stopped the conversation.

"Jack, I'm flying to Atlanta tonight and I'll be in meetings all day tomorrow. I wanted to brief you before you depart London. I won't see you until late Friday."

"Okay."

"I've great news. I've scheduled a meeting with Gerard Burns at Genesis. He is interested. Steve Harenda at Scrib's wants three books but I think we can get five from Burns. I'm talking multi-millions, Jack. He wants to meet you and discuss storylines."

He paused, adding, "It's working out as you predicted."

"How do you mean?" I asked.

"You wanted to use the time between London and Chicago to negotiate a new deal, and we'll do better than anticipated. Of course, Harenda doesn't know I've talked to Burns. Let's play one off the other and see what happens. We'll have nearly five days in the city, which should be enough time. Per your suggestion, I'm glad we did London first. The momentum coming out of England has generated keen interest and excitement.

"The Burns meeting is Tuesday afternoon; Harenda is Wednesday morning. You'll have the weekend to lose the jet lag. Oh, I almost forgot, in addition to your scheduled appearances on networks and book signings in Manhattan, I've lined up interviews with THE EPOCH, other metro newspapers, key periodicals, and a few radio talk shows. Folks are excited; they rarely see you. This keeps building momentum. By the way, we'd like you to join us at our place in the Village. We have plenty of room."

I hesitated. Because of Lily, my pending schedule slipped my mind. I would have to skip everything. It would create a stir, which was manageable in the short term.

"Jack, did you hear me?"

"Yes and its all good, Walter. I'll grin and bear it. However, I'll stay in the hotel as planned. I am deep into something and want time alone to focus on it."

"Joanna's counting on your visit."

I considered mentioning Lily but quickly decided against it. Levy would never understand; he would argue against canceling everything, specifically the publishers, after working hard to schedule the meetings.

"Walter, honestly, I don't want interruptions this weekend," I replied. What I wanted was to kiss Lily and make love to her, the thought of which seemed thrilling. "By the way, is Sam in the city?"

That Tender Light

"He's at the Town Kennel."
"Good, I'd like him in my suite when I arrive."
"Not a problem, I'll see to it. Joanna will be disappointed."
"I've made up my mind."
"Okay, she'll get over it. This new idea you're working on, it has possibilities?"
"It might be my best story ever. Let's have a drink together Friday night, when you return from Atlanta. Call me when you land."
"You sound encouraged."
I noticed Lily's penny on the nightstand, picked it up, and balanced it on my forefinger.
"Yes, I am. Give my regrets to Joanna."
"I'll have Sam groomed and ready."
After we said goodbye, I dialed the operator.
"Yes."
"Hold my calls, I'll check later and send a bellman up."
"Certainly, Mr. Taylor," the operator replied.
I changed into a comfortable pair of gym trunks and an old St. Bonaventure tee shirt. I poured a glass of water and opened my portfolio. Again, I was in the midst of my mission into North Vietnam via Laos and China:

Muong Te, North Vietnam
December 1972

Our trek from Laos, through China and into North Vietnam, was gratefully uneventful. The route Sing chose, though long and arduous, was as unoccupied as he had predicted.

Occasionally, we heard the chatters and growls of dholes, which are fox-like mammals. We thought we heard a tiger and twice we passed rat snakes. Once a regal python, at least 20 feet long slithered by, not too far away. We also encountered several red-shanked doucs, amongst the most colorful of all primates.

D. James Then

However, as Sing advised, we never saw or heard another human being and, thus, we moved very fast. As we neared hour twenty-three, and as night approached, Sing signaled a stop. We pulled together in a tight circle, talking mouth-to-ear.

"What is it?" I asked.

"Muong Te Plantation twelve hundred meters," Sing whispered, indicating the correct direction with his eyes.

"Good cover?"

He nodded, adding, "Place for sleeping, too. I take many photographs there; forest ends, then fields, soon many plantation buildings."

Suddenly, a branch snapped to our right and we hugged the ground instinctively. Someone or something moved nearby in thick undergrowth. When we heard another snap, followed quickly by a third, I held up two fingers, pointing to my eyes and ears. My signal was clear: watch and listen.

After ten minutes, without hearing another sound, I crawled close to Sing, saying, "Where did you take photographs?"

"Five hundred paces," he whispered.

Twigs snapped again, followed by squeals and grunts. Animals rooted nearby.

"Boar," Sing whispered.

Soon thereafter, casual voices came from somewhere behind the wild pigs and immediately the animals quieted.

"Hunters," Sing whispered.

I spread my fingers wide and motioned toward the ground with my palm. Instinctively, we settled at differing angles. Soon, two North Vietnamese regulars came up a small hill to our right, seventy-five feet away. I watched the men survey the terrain. They were hunting animals, not humans, and did not know we were nearby. Movement suddenly rustled branches fifty yards forward. A soldier pointed his weapon and fired.

"Aye," he yelled, pursuing his prey. The other man laughed, drank from a bottle, and followed. Several minutes later, after I signaled the *all clear*, we crawled forward; Nick was beside Sing and I was a body-length behind.

That Tender Light

Sing was the first to crawl into a reasonably hidden natural recess. He turned efficiently and rolled silently into an opening amidst elephant grass and ferns to a spot where a gentle slope leveled. Nick slid in on his back and sat upright. I came in last and, after settling, lifted the facial webbing of my Ghillie suit. I wiped my face with my hands to cool my skin. The others did the same and Sing sipped water.

Nick moved beside me. "Charlie was hammered."

"Shit-faced," I replied. "Let's do this and get out."

"Forty miles in less than twenty-four hours is hauling ass," Nick said, adding, "I'm whipped." He sipped from his canteen.

"Good job, Sing," Nick said. He removed a small tin of peanut butter from his belt, opened it, and placed a smear into his mouth. Sing took some and I ate the remainder. Nick buried the tin. He settled onto the ground in a spot where soft moss supported his sore back.

"Feels wonderful," he whispered, "We only have a few minutes of daylight left. It's too dark to mark positions." He closed his eyes. "You take first watch, Jackson."

I smiled and removed one of Sing's maps, studied it in the waning light, and quickly established our location.

"Here's the stream we crossed and this is our position. The plantation is there." I pointed southeast.

"Follow," Sing said and we crawled to the top of a moss-covered knoll. Sing moved a branch slowly.

"See," he said, pointing.

Using the rifle's scope, I scanned a renaissance château with side buildings in the center of wide meadows overgrown with wild grass and flowers.

"One thousand one hundred meters to the château," I said, marking the distance. "Can we get closer?"

"Yes."

I studied the plantation, counting ten men. Only two carried weapons, probably the hunters. They had missed their prey. I turned and studied the tree line to the left and right. I saw several better shooting positions. I handed Sing my binoculars.

"You see Matiere?"
Sing studied the compound.
"No," he said, "Ten men important, big shots come."
"They're getting ready, something's happening."
"Hunting for meat is good sign," Sing added.
I nodded toward the two soldiers with weapons.
"They had no idea we were close. They're careless."
"The whiskey," Sing whispered.
"This far north they have a false sense of security. They think they're invincible."
"Strength is weakness," Sing replied.
"Exactly, we have the advantage."
I used the scope and surveyed the compound again, methodically checking the windows in each building. As I moved to the main building's upper floor, a curtain moved and a light came on. I held steady and thought I saw someone I recognized. A second later, the man's image disappeared and the light went out.
"Did you notice that man?"
"Yes."
"You ever see him before?"
"Did not see him long enough," Sing replied.
"He seems familiar to me."
"Many Asians look similar," he said.
I nodded and when I heard grunts to my left, I quickly located the position.
Two wild pigs were routing in the field for bulbs, now more courageous without hunters stalking them.
"Boar," Sing said, "a local favorite. They not bother us. If they smell us, they go away. They only attack if cornered."
"Then, I suggest a wide berth," I whispered as we crawled back. As Sing nodded and yawned, I said, "Get some sleep."
—

I sat alone listening and watching. I considered the men I would kill. I wanted to be closer than eleven hundred meters, which was problematic.

That Tender Light

When killing three men together, the shorter the distance the better the margin of error.

I closed my eyes briefly and, within seconds, I heard the voice of Sister Mary Jerome, the Felician nun who taught my eighth grade class.

"Killing to get out of a war is immoral, Jack. How did you get here? You should never have let it get this far."

"Hindsight is visionary, Sister. These bastards torture our men."

"And the bastards on your side don't? Justice is God's purview, Jack. I did not teach this. Would Merton approve?"

"It's war, Sister, war's evil. We suspend real life and do what we must, to win."

"Rationalize however you wish," the nun scoffed. "You weren't born for this! Why does it please you, so? You were born to be an instrument of the divine, not the wicked."

"My country called, Sister."

"Be truthful," the nun said. "Your selfishness called; be careful of what you wish?"

"Why?"

"Be truthful, truth brings honesty. Come on Jack, you remember what Merton said."

I nodded. "We must only make choices which enable us to fulfill the deepest capacities of our real selves."

"Is pulling a trigger the real you?"

I blinked myself awake, knowing the answer.

Soon, I crawled over to the spot where Sing and I had studied the compound. A light glowed in a window in the guard's building at the compound's edge. In an upper window, I saw a young woman.

"I was born to write," I whispered.

As I dozed again, I heard Sister Mary Jerome's voice say, "Tell me, Jack, where does killing fit with writing?"

—

I fell into a deep sleep and the devil smiled at me.

"Your soul for your freedom," he whispered; his breath smelled rancid. "Then, everything you want will be yours."

D. James Then

Suddenly, I opened my eyes, relieved to find sunlight filtering in through the treetops. The devil, real or imagined, vanished when a hand slipped over my mouth.

Nick looked at me.

"Visitors," he whispered softly into my left ear. I felt his warm breath against my skin and his hand smelled of dry grass and leaves.

He removed his hand and whispered, "Hunters, two hundred yards south; four of 'em."

"Searching for us?"

"No, they're after the pigs. Sing is watching. You were dreaming and mumbling, bud."

Before I could answer, a shot rang out, followed quickly by two more. An animal squealed and, soon, elated voices shouted. Nick and I crawled to Sing, who held up four fingers and pointed. Quickly, two more shots rang out, as did another squeal. We heard shouts of exhilaration.

"Four men shoot two big boys," Sing whispered. "They prepare big feast tonight which means..."

"Our targets have arrived," Nick said.

Sing smiled. "I think, yes; check courtyard."

Two Citroën sedans stood in the shade.

"Matiere and the others?"

"Yes, my guess Matiere and Giang come in one, Si Duc in the other. They arrive in the night; I see automobiles at sunrise."

I thought of the young girl at the window; was she waiting for Matiere?

"Good, we should find better shooting positions."

"I already have two," Nick said, pointing southwest. "One is at 510, the other at 450; both are doable but I like the former. It's a better shot, no obstructions and the sunlight is indirect."

—

Jean Paul Matiere went to the window when he heard the retort of rifles. Looking out, he saw four guards walking beside a cart carrying the dead animals. He smiled. The evening meal would be delightful!

That Tender Light

An early riser, Matiere sipped an espresso and scanned a copy of a TIME MAGAZINE he received in Hanoi. As usual, the reporting on the war or the treatment of American POWs was inaccurate and uninformative. Selfishly, he wished reporters would do a better job.

Skimming the pages, he considered—and then quickly rejected—the notion of his usual morning walk. He had worked hard these past few months. Skipping his regimen would make little difference in the scheme of things. Besides, his duties had tired him and, during the past month, he had not slept as much as he preferred.

Matiere's normal routine called for a brisk walk in the morning. He walked again at sunset after his dinner, his only meal of the day. The long walks kept him fit and, for a man in his sixties, the more he walked the better he felt and the better his sexual prowess.

He lit a panatela and studied the blue sky. The warm and pleasant breeze coming through the open window reminded him of France. A smile creased his thin lips; he loved Muong Te plantation, a glorious spot to rekindle sagging spirits.

His mind soon turned to the Americans he interrogated.

They were smug, with their bravado and brash attitude, specifically one formidable admiral. He would break him, just as he broke them all, it was a matter of time. No one could withstand his methods. The South Koreans lasted the longest; those mean little bastards were tough. Still, he broke them, too.

Matiere chuckled.

His North Vietnamese superiors considered him a sadistic bastard. Probably, he was. However, they never tired of results or the information he provided, especially concerning the American chain of command and the personal information he gleaned, the kind they favored dearly. His little friends delighted in terror-filled American eyes when electrodes pinched certain vulnerable body parts.

"Juste mon genie," he whispered, repeating, "juste mon genie."

D. James Then

He enjoyed his cigar for a few moments. If he were a sadistic bastard, he had a peculiar genius for it. A thief is always a hero in someone's eyes! He received handsome payment for his service. He had fine wines and much freedom, and an unending supply of the young women he favored. Ah, this latest one, she was magnificent, utterly wonderful.

He leaned against the windowsill and surveyed the tree-lined road winding through the valley toward the forest beyond. The way it meandered to and from the compound reminded him of rural Bordeaux, near his childhood town of St. Emilion. Ah, St. Emilion...his days there were wonderful!

Nothing was as superb as the French countryside. However, the Muong Te plantation came close. He felt protected in Bordeaux as boy and he felt protected at Muong Te as a man. Peaceful and far from the drudgery of war, it was an idyllic spot. Perhaps, he'd live here after they won the war and, as Ho Chi Minh predicted, they would defeat the Americans.

The way Americans fought was absurd. How can a country win a war with rules as stupid as the American leaders imposed on their men? Rules of engagement, they called them. In war you kill first, think later. Nothing else mattered.

Winning is the only goal in life! He taught his good friend Colonel Giang how to win. When the portly fellow awoke, they would continue their talk on the art of interrogation. He smiled satisfactorily. That mean little son of bitch learned extremely well and quickly realized the strongest men crumbled easily.

Men would say anything to stop the torture; the trick was to get them to tell the truth. His and Giang's discussions over the next few days would focus on techniques required to extract accurate information essential to further their cause.

Giang would have money for him, too. Thus far, he had pocketed hundreds of thousands of U.S. dollars from the drug trade Giang's and his little side operation supported, and they had just increased the price, which meant an even bigger take. If he could not torture Americans, he would soften their minds with drugs. What fools they were!

That Tender Light

The mantel clock chimed and he instinctively checked the time: 7:30 a.m.

Movement on the bed pulled Matiere away from the window and he gazed appreciatively upon the naked body of a sleeping seventeen-year-old girl. The sheet had slipped from her shoulders, exposing her surprisingly ample Oriental breasts with their pert little nipples. She rolled on her stomach, exposing her luscious backside.

What a great ass, he thought.

Suddenly, lust supplanted thoughts of war and torture.

Matiere walked to the bed, dropping his robe to the floor.

The sleeping child was perhaps the best he ever had, and he had many. She liked it rough, and his size or proclivities did not frighten her. Quite the contrary, she welcomed them. Had he met his match? He considered their moist night, perhaps she was the reason he felt so drained.

He leaned over and kissed the girl's neck and back to awaken her, and, by doing so, became fully aroused. When she opened her eyes, his hands curved gently over her backside and toyed playfully with private places. He felt her delightful shiver. She instinctively spread her legs and giggled. She was already moist when he probed her vagina—truly, a gift from heaven

He mounted her from behind and, for indeterminable minutes, raw and dominant passion enslaved him, a passion the young woman shared with abandon. Two souls joined in a blissful and tortuous journey, unaware of anything else.

Had they known Matiere's last day on earth was fast approaching, their ardor would have been more intense. Soon, the Frenchman, Giang, Si Duc, and others would die horrible deaths.

A RINGING TELEPHONE interrupted my concentration.

"Hello."

"This is Eloise Abrams, sir. I'm afraid I've encountered a problem.

"Which is?"

"Availability is nil from the New York Metropolitan area to either Cincinnati or Indianapolis on Saturday morning; the entire day is booked."

"Seriously?"

"I'm afraid so." She said.

"Is Louisville a possibility?"

"I considered flights to Kentucky, but no luck. I can route you through Chicago to Indianapolis, but you'd arrive late Saturday evening and you requested morning."

"Then, there's no other option?"

"I can arrange a train from Grand Central Station to Philadelphia and from there you'll fly directly to Cincinnati. You would arrive about 11 a.m., local time. Indiana is on U.S. Central Time, one hour difference."

"Make it Philly."

"I shall have it all ready in the morning. Mr. Taylor?"

"Yes."

"Thank you for the books and for the one hundred pound note. The money wasn't necessary."

"That's to thank you for keeping a confidence. Please, purchase something for your baby. It's our secret."

"Indeed...good night, sir."

"Good evening, Eloise. Have a wonderful life."

I looked in the mirror, remembered my grandfather's position, and whispered, "I hope you were right Tommy."

CHAPTER 11
THAT TENDER LIGHT

Sycamore Glen Farms, St. Omer, IN
10:03 a.m., Saturday, September 20, 1986

LILY STOOD AT the kitchen window admiring the blue sky. She scanned the rolling countryside until her eyes found a distant patch of woods.

There, in a century-old orchard, a log cabin stood atop a rise not far from the Flatrock River. It was Lily's favorite spot on the farm and the reason for her sabbatical. Restoration was underway and going well.

She heard the rumble of tractors in fields to the south—farmhands working the soil. To her right, a quarter mile away, a red-tailed hawk rode high currents. Overhead, the sun ruled a near-cloudless sky.

So many of the farm's nuances calmed her. The soil's scent at planting time. The gentle sway of wild flowers in summer breezes. The loud snap of tree limbs in winter. The constant advance of wildlife. Colorful blossoms in springtime. A bird's song at sunrise or an owl's hoot at dusk. The sound of the river. Ice forming on the pond. A tractor rumbling in twilight. Rain gurgling in the gutters. Rabbits scurrying or woodchucks feeding at sunset. The abundant silence of new snow. The lure of a passing train on the big trestle. Autumn's gold and russet. Pheasants on the wing with colors ablaze. Her aunt tinkling the piano. Her parents' muffled voices in the kitchen as they shared coffee and the remains of the day. The vivid pink and purple hues of a summer sunset. The lighted farmhouse at night. These, and myriad images and sensations, shaped Lily as wind molds the earth, slowly and with purpose.

Lily breathed in fresh air.

The day held promise. She loved Sycamore Glen. Her grit, humor, commonsense, keen intuition, love of literature, and business acumen came from her land. The farm was Lily's foundation, the source of her enduring resolve. Because of it, Lily believed she could do anything, at anytime.

The land anchored Lily, and was a constant source of renewal. Whenever a day took a spotty turn or problems arose, like those in her failed marriage, she would walk down the dirt road, past the barn and adjacent pond, toward the cabin, the orchard, and the river beyond. Along the way, the farm's understated beauty erased the day's grime and a natural catharsis invariably renewed her spirit, regardless of the season.

Lily heard movement down the hall and checked the time: a few minutes past ten. Missy—her Aunt Margaret—was ready for her trip to Chicago. Lily placed her coffee cup on the counter and fixed a thermos of hot tea for Missy's trip, slicing and wrapping wedges of lemon in aluminum foil. As did Lily, Margaret Lee preferred tea with lemon whenever she traveled.

A moment later, Missy stepped into the kitchen.

"Are you ready?" Lily asked, kissing her aunt's cheek.

"Yes, dear, I am. I want to get on with that anniversary party. It'll be fun."

Lily lifted the thermos and they went outside via the front porch steps. There, her cousin Peter Bender and their housekeeper Ruth Grace waited in a polished green station wagon. Lily helped Missy into the back seat, fastened the seatbelt around her aunt's waist, and closed the door. She leaned in through the open window and caressed Missy's cheek.

"You behave yourself, young lady."

Then, turning toward Ruth, seated in the front seat, Lily teased, "No bars in Old Town."

Ruth Grace, a prim fixture at the farm for more than thirty years, feigned anger, smiled, and said, "You ruined my fun, Lily Veronica. Now, I'll have to close a few, just for spite."

"Ruthie," Bender asked, "have you ever tasted beer, whiskey or any alcohol?"

The housekeeper looked at Bender and said, "In my day, Peter my boy, in my day."

"Well, I'll be damned." Bender laughed and started the car.

"Seems like a good day for a drive, Pete. You take care of my girls. You'll be with them in Chicago for a month, can you take it?"

Bender smiled at Lily.

"Sure, I can. They all love me." He rubbed his shoulder. "You're in for rain, Lil, my shoulder aches."

"Rain, you're kidding, right? There are no clouds."

"Bet you a buck."

"You're on. When do you think you'll be in Elmhurst?"

"I'll guess four or five this afternoon. Purdue is playing a home game, so we might hit some traffic. We'll stop after Lafayette for a bite at the usual diner. Then, I expect clear sailing into Chicago."

"You'll pick me up at Midway?"

"Yes. October 8 at 10:40 a.m., U.S. Air Flight 1492, just like Columbus."

Lily smiled, brushing Peter's cheek with her fingertips. They had always been close in a casual and affectionate way, even if he was fourteen years her senior. She remembered writing him little-girl letters when he was in Korea. He always wrote back and Lily waited impatiently for his letters, only satisfied that he was alive when she held an envelope in her hand.

She winked at her cousin.

"You're a good man, Sally was lucky to have you."

"I was lucky to have her, Lily."

Their eyes met and held for a moment as each remembered Peter's wife, whom they buried last summer in the family plot behind the cabin near the river.

"I miss her," Lily whispered.

"I do, too, more than you could ever imagine. It's hard letting go. I would have done anything for her; you, too."

"I know."

"Lily!"

"Yes," she said, turning to her aunt.

"You'll be here at noon, right?"

"I've errands to run and won't be back until one. Why?"

"Damn, Matt Porter's coming later this morning to pick up quilts I made for the bazaar. They're in my room, on my cedar chest."

"Not a problem. I'll drop them off."

"Thanks, sweetheart, I promised Matt."

"Consider it done. Travel well and enjoy your day."

Lily smiled. She had chosen the exact words Jack Taylor spoke before her flight departed St. Thomas for Miami. At that moment, she wanted him more than ever.

As Bender put the car in gear, Lily stepped back, and watched the station wagon roll down the driveway. She waved goodbye and stood there until her family disappeared beyond the covered bridge.

So much time, she thought as she entered the house, two and a half weeks before I go to Chicago. No classes. No student papers. No faculty meetings. Just my cabin and my books! Just what I want to do, when I want to do it!

"I could get used to this," she whispered.

As she locked the front door, she wondered when she would hear from Jack Taylor. She shrugged, smiling. She would, in time. She knew it.

A moment later, seated at a cherry desk in her library, she skimmed a card file and dialed.

"Porter's Funeral Home."

"Millie?"

"Yes."

"Lily Hall."

"Oh my, is everything okay, Lily?"

Lily chuckled. "This isn't a call for services, Millie."

The woman on the other end giggled.

"Habit, I guess. How can I help?"

"Missy made quilts for the church. I think Matt intends to pick them up around noon. No one will be here. I'm running errands. I'll drop them off and save Matt a trip."

"Oh, Lily, you just missed him. He's taking a body to Rushville. He'll make stops for the bazaar on the way back. Will you hold while I try to reach him on the two-way?"

"Sure."

Millie Porter placed the call on hold and Sebileus' FINLANDIA filtered into Lily's ear.

"He's not answering," Millie said, forty-five seconds later.

"Then, I'll put a note on the back door and place the quilts where he'll be sure to find them."

"Ruth or Missy won't be there?"

"They're off to Chicago."

"Then, it might be best to leave them."

"If Matt calls, tell him about my note."

"Certainly, but I'm sure he'll find everything. Nice talking to you Lily."

Lily said goodbye, hung up, and wrote the note. She went upstairs, pulled her hair into a ponytail, and decided against makeup. After a quick shower, she changed into jeans, a blue sweatshirt, and white tennis shoes. Downstairs, she placed Missy's quilts in a box and, on her way out, placed it on the back porch. She taped the note to the door.

D. James Then

At 10:50 a.m., Lily exited the farm's driveway in an old red '68 Ford pickup and turned right. After navigating a few back roads, she turned onto Old Michigan Road, comfortable with the feel of the truck in her hands as it gained speed on the open highway. She did not notice the automobile following about a quarter mile behind.

THIRTY-FIVE MINUTES LATER after the dust settled back onto the road in front of the farmhouse, a Ford sedan turned into the driveway. A big yellow dog sat in the passenger seat with its head out the side window, enjoying the rush of warm air on its face.

My heart raced. I had traveled thousands of miles to get to this point in time and the final few yards were the longest, most difficult of my life.

"What will I say, Sam, what if she's uncomfortable seeing me? What if I was wrong, what if she's with a man? Jesus, talk about embarrassing."

I stopped the car briefly, considered returning to New York. The message I left for my agent had a Monday delivery. I could stop it. No one would ever know I left the city. I rested my head on the steering wheel, chiding myself for not calling in advance.

No! I touched the penny in my shirt pocket and summoned the necessary courage. There would not be another man!

I parked near the farmhouse and climbed the front porch steps. Sam followed timidly and I gazed at him suspiciously.

"What's with you? You're a dog; you're supposed to display courage at all times."

I patted Sam's head and he sat near the front door.

I pressed the doorbell and chimes sounded inside. I waited. When no one responded, I pressed it again, hearing more chimes. I knocked several times. No one answered.

"Just my luck, she's not home, Sam."

I heard machinery in fields behind the farmhouse, walked to the railing, and leaned out. Shading my eyes from the bright sunlight, I studied two tractors.

"Lily is not there, Sam."

I walked to the rear of the house, thinking there might be a garden, hoping she'd be there. I walked a narrow stone path accented by pink and white veronica. Not seeing anyone, I climbed the back stairs, walked across a small porch, and knocked again, and again no response!

As I turned, I saw a note taped to the lower windowpane, removed it, and read the message:

Hi, Matt:

I've gone to my eye doctor and bookstore in Batesville. Sorry, I missed you. I tried to save you a trip. When I called, Millie said you were in Rushville with a body and would come directly here. The quilts are beside the glider. I hope they sell high. Missy hopes so, too.

Regards,
Lily Hall

Holding the note and seeing her name brought me closer to Lily. I taped the note back onto the window and went to the rental. Sam ran on ahead, braver now, and relieved himself in the grass. I wondered who Matt was and why a body? I knew I had missed Lily by minutes.

"The story of my life, let's go, Sam."

I turned the Ford around and drove away, deciding to stop at Bender's Bed & Breakfast, which I passed earlier. I remembered an exit for Batesville on I-74, but possibly, I would find a faster way.

CHAPTER 12
THAT TENDER LIGHT

Town Square, Batesville, IN
1:07 p.m., Saturday, September 20, 1986

SEVERAL HOURS LATER Lily closed the optometrist's door surprised by a chill in the air. Off to the west, a distinct line of gray clouds announced the leading edge of a storm. Rain *is* on the way, she thought. She shivered, vowing never again to doubt Peter's trick shoulder.

She smelled leaves burning nearby. Lily loved the scent; always had. She descended the stairs, waited for vehicles to pass, crossed the street, and walked down a tree-lined sidewalk past the Batesville Public Library toward a community parking lot and her pickup.

Several pedestrians smiled as they passed. Lily waited for a traffic light, crossed the street, turned into the lot, and walked directly to her pickup. As she reached for the handle, a nearby clock tower chimed AMAZING GRACE. Out of habit, she checked her watch: 1:07 p.m.

She was behind schedule and, if it rained, she would not work on the cabin. Silas, her carpenter, and his sons would be gone. If so, Lily decided she would read.

She opened the pickup's door, placed her package on the passenger's seat, and slipped in behind the steering wheel. The worn leather seats felt cool through her jeans.

She started the engine, let it idle, rolled down the window, and was preparing to back up when she noticed paper tucked under the driver-side wiper blade.

Immediately she assumed a parking ticket and quickly checked for posted restrictions. She found none; then, why a ticket? She opened the door and, standing on the running board, lifted the wiper.

That Tender Light

To her surprise, she retrieved a gray linen envelope. Turning it over, she saw her name printed concisely. The paper's fine texture piqued Lily's curiosity. She sat behind the wheel, opened the envelope, and removed two folded, but matching sheets of stationery.

Sitting there in a '68 Ford pickup truck in softening afternoon light, she immediately recognized a poem by William Butler Yeats and spoke the words aloud:

> I whispered, 'I am too young,'
> And then, 'I am old enough';
> Wherefore I threw a penny
> To find out if I might love.
> 'Go and love, go and love, young man,
> If the lady be young and fair.'
> Ah, penny, brown penny, brown penny
> I am looped in the loops of her hair.

"Jack Taylor," she whispered. After a quick search of the parking lot, she unfolded the second sheet:

Dear Lily:

I have thought about you constantly since our meeting in St. John. We could have dinner tonight. You could talk about your farm and I could tell you how I'd like to lose myself forever in the depths of your blue eyes. I believe that would be a delightful experience. By the way, here's your penny back, until the next time.

Jack Taylor

PS: If your answer is yes, I'm in the library across the street. If no, drive away. However, please understand, I want to see you again. I've traveled four thousand miles for that pleasure.

Lily held the penny and burst into laughter. Surprise, delight, apprehension, and happiness swept through her body. She turned and looked through the truck's rear window toward the library.

"Lily."

Through the driver's side window, I saw Lily's lovely face and her magnificent eyes. Her hair was longer than I remembered and she had lost weight, but her smile was the same, the substance of dreams and wishes.

She opened the window.

"Do I know you?" she asked, touching my hand.

I found a trace of nervousness in her beautifully crooked smile. Her eyes were a darker and a more expansive blue in the shadows of the truck's interior.

"Your note said you were in the library," she teased. "I don't see any books."

"I was there, honestly. They have my books. It's a very good library."

"You didn't allow me time to drive away," she teased.

"Would you have done that?"

"No. Have you been waiting long?"

"Many years," I answered.

"You're a patient man," she whispered, smiling.

I nodded.

"Patience is one of my virtues, but not today. When I saw you walk by, I couldn't wait, it's been too long."

"It's been too long for what?" she asked.

"For this," I replied, and leaning inside the pickup, I kissed her, gently at first, and then passionately. She returned my kiss and probed my tongue lightly with hers. Her mouth tasted vaguely of mint and the fresh, early-autumn air. Her kiss held the promise of a lifetime of gentle afternoons and tender nights. The tips of her fingers warmed my cheeks.

I kissed her again and looked into her eyes.

"I've wanted to kiss you seemingly forever."

"Was it worth the wait?"

With my thumbs, I wiped away tears that formed at the edges of her eyes.

I was sorry I did not kiss her on St. Thomas, but was enormously happy I did so now. I wanted that privilege in each of my remaining days.

"Yes…don't cry, Lily."

"I've been waiting, too. I knew you would come. I knew it! This makes me incredibly happy."

I understood the complexity of her simple words, which defined two lifetimes of waiting, searching, and hoping.

"So, how about dinner, I've barely eaten today. I should feed Sam, too."

She looked around.

"Your dog's with you?"

"Sure, he usually is; he's sleeping in the car down the street. Hungry?"

"Yes, but I'll cook. This day belongs to you and me; let's not share it with anyone else."

I kissed her check.

"I came because I was lonely."

"I know." she whispered, nodding. "Now, everything seems perfect. Hey, I have a question," she said, changing the subject.

"Shoot."

"I'm wondering how you knew this was my pickup. Have you been snooping?"

I nodded, saying, "Easily answered, I was trained to study and observe by the Green Berets."

"I'm not buying it," Lily replied, with a slight headshake.

"Okay, the truth. The front vanity plate says Sycamore Glen Farms and your note indicated Batesville's bookstore."

I pointed down the street.

"It's the only bookstore in town. I asked Chris, the nice woman behind the counter, and told her I was a friend. She said I just missed you. Then, she told me your truck was here. I figured you had to be nearby. It became obvious, even for me. I had you pegged. Smart, huh?"

"Damn proud of yourself, aren't you?"

I smiled.

"Hey, why would Matt be with a body?"

"What?"

"Your note said Matt was with a body in Rushville. What's up with that?"

Lily giggled.

"He's a mortician."

"Now, I understand."

"You are both insightful and nosey. Let's go to my farm?"

"You bet."

A minute or so later, I followed Lily back to Sycamore Glen. I noticed a gray sedan on the road behind us, but paid it no mind.

Chapter 13
That Tender Light

Sycamore Glen Farms, St Omer, IN
2:09 p.m., Saturday, September 20, 1986

SCATTERED RAINDROPS FELL as Lily drove into the barn behind the farmhouse. I pulled in beside her, slung my travel bag over my shoulder, closed and latched the barn doors, and held Lily's hand as we walked toward the house. When she unlocked the door, Sam hurried inside.
"You think he remembers me?"
"He might, although right now he's thinking food. He's allowed in?"
"Sure."
"Give him a few days, Lily, and he'll know you well enough to last a lifetime."
Lily set her things on the countertop, stooped, and patted Sam's head, as he sat near the sink.
"I think Sam and I will get along just fine," she said. "I don't have dog food."
"We'll make due. A few pieces of bread and fruit should hold him for a while."
Lily stood upright.
"Bread's in the top drawer next to the stove. Apples are in the fridge, in the crisper."
"You have a big house."
"It's been in our family for more than a hundred years, since 1882," she said. "As the family grew, it replaced the original cabin, which is nearer the river. Over time, my ancestors added rooms, as have I. The kitchen is part of the original structure."
"I like it."
She took my things.

"We live modestly, but comfortably. I'll put these in the library, next to my desk."

She walked down a short hallway, returning seconds later.

"How long can you stay?"

"I'm supposed to be in Chicago late next week...a book tour."

She smiled and gave me a pie tin.

"For Sam," she said.

I took several slices of wheat bread, broke them into bite-sized pieces, chopped an apple, and fed Sam.

"I'm going to Chicago, too, the week of October 5. My father's sister is having her fiftieth wedding anniversary. My aunt, cousin, and housekeeper left a few hours ago for a month's visit and to prepare for a party."

"You're here alone?"

"Yes, good timing."

She came to me, touched my cheek lightly, and rested her head on my shoulder. I smelled her perfume and felt her warm body against mine. She took my hand and placed it on her chest above her rapidly beating heart. The contour of her breast thrilled me. She smiled and kissed me tenderly.

"After Chicago, do you return to St. John?"

"No, I'll visit a few cities and others will be added, if it's a best seller. Usually it takes two months to promote a book."

"And, what happens then?"

"I have the rest of my life to figure that out."

"How's the book doing?"

"Good."

"Is it a bestseller?"

"I think so; the publisher expects sales in the millions."

"You decided to visit me, on a whim, in-between tour stops?"

"Yeah, although right now no one knows I'm here."

"Why?"

"It's personal," I replied. "I decided to visit you in London, but didn't tell anyone. I'm supposed to be in New York."

"For business, obviously?"

"Yes, my agent and publisher want a new book deal. They are anxious for me to sign."

"Why not tell the truth?" asked Lily. "It's usually the best practice."

"They'd want to know more than I want to reveal, at least for now. Besides, they'll learn I've gone when my message is delivered Monday morning."

"Will they be angry?"

"Conceivably, but they'll get over it."

"Do you do this kind of thing often?"

"I never have before. I wanted to visit without obligations, objections, or outside interference. Nothing else matters to me right now."

"I'm flattered," she said. "But, won't your sales suffer. People might think something has happened to you."

"Something has happened to me."

"You know what I mean."

"I do. My message advises them not to worry. I said I'm fine and I would call. I explained something personal needed my direct attention. Knowing my agent, he'll use my injuries from the explosion or my work pace as the reasons. People will think what they want. As for the tour, the publisher's marketers do a fine job and my reputation is sound. The books would probably sell at the same pace without personal appearances. I'll get back on the book tour soon enough."

I kissed her neck and cheek, smelling her perfume.

"I keep my personal life private and separate, I always have. Believe me, coming here is the smartest thing I've done in years. I don't like interviews. I don't need a book deal. I want a better life, which means you and me."

"And book sales won't suffer?"

I considered her question.

"It might help. If people think something has happened to me, the book will get more coverage than all interviews combined. Trust me, my visit here will get out eventually; these things have a life of their own."

"But, isn't a great deal of money involved?"

"Sure, but I already have more money than I'll ever need. What I don't have is what I truly want."

"Which is?"

"You know the answer. It's the reason I'm here."

She kissed me softly.

"Yes, I do. I knew I'd see you again," she whispered. "I never doubted it."

She kissed my cheek and pulled away to find a mixing bowl in the cupboard.

"This wasn't an easy decision for me," I admitted. "When I finally made up my mind, everything crystallized."

I chuckled.

"What's so funny?"

"Since St. John, I've attempted to call you at least a hundred times, but I hung up before any call went through."

I moved behind her, my arms encircling her waist, and kissed her cheek.

"Why?"

I hesitated.

"Come on, I want to know," she whispered.

"I was afraid you wouldn't take the call, that you wouldn't remember me."

"Silly boy," she said. "The important thing is you're here and we should see where it leads."

"I'd like that. Short term, this is our business only."

"Okay, you open a bottle of wine and I'll turn up the furnace, it's chilly."

"Where's the wine?' I asked.

She pointed toward a doorway.

"The dining room is down the hallway, beyond which is a small alcove with a wine rack. You choose."

She kicked off her tennis shoes and opened the refrigerator.

"Do you mind music?"

"No," she replied, "Whatever you select is fine."

As Lily blended eggs, an aria filtered through the farmhouse—poignant and apropos.

"Somebody likes opera," I said, returning with a bottle of Merlot and two wine glasses.

"My aunt, she dabbles in the arts and classics."

"I love them, regardless."

"Regardless of what?" she asked, taking a glass.

"Regardless of wine and cheese or beer and burgers."

"I prefer omelets this afternoon," she replied.

"Omelets are good."

I filled the glasses and we each sipped wine.

"The piece is lovely. What is it?" she asked.

"VISSI D'ARTE, VISSI D'AMORE...literally I lived for art, I lived for love, from TOSCA."

"Puccini?"

"Well done."

"Lucky guess, I'm just a Hoosier farm girl at heart. Do you know what she's singing?"

"Is this a test, professor?"

"Absolutely," she replied, enjoying our banter as much as the music and the wine.

"Okay, the short interpretation. Tosca is lamenting to God. She's being forced to give herself to Scarpia, a man she loathes, to save Cavaradossi, a man she loves with all her heart and soul."

"That's pretty heavy." Lily said, making a silly face.

"Life is a tangled web, huh? Let me add, Tosca never intends to become Scarpia's lover. In fact, as he kisses her, she plunges a dagger into his heart."

"Ouch," Lily said, flinching.

"And," I said, "whispers one of the more famous lines in all of opera, IT IS THUS THAT TOSCA KISSES."

"Not terribly romantic, is she?"

"I agree. Anyway, in the third act, as Scarpia's men advance to arrest her, Tosca throws herself off a parapet because she has lost Cavaradossi and murdered Scarpia. All of this, of course, to the noticeable sobs of opera aficionados."

"Does the heroine always die in an opera?"

"Lily, it's part of the allure; it's what opera lovers crave. Hidden love. Unrequited love. Forbidden love. Mistaken love. Passionate love. Just like everyday life, huh?"

I took her wine glass, placed it on the kitchen table beside mine, drew her close, and kissed her.

"Have you ever been to the opera, Lily?"

"I've never had a reason."

"We shall go one day where it is best, in Italy."

"I'd like that."

She studied my eyes and rubbed her nose against mine.

"You want me to put the omelets on hold?"

"That seems appropriate."

She placed the bowl in the refrigerator and took my hand.

"Let's go upstairs," she whispered.

"That seems appropriate, too."

LILY'S BEDROOM WAS warm, the ambient light intimate. It was large, comfortable, and decorated in soft shades of green and burgundy. The fragrance of her perfume lingered.

I noticed an antique dresser, a queen-sized bed, and a huge bay window revealing a distant river. Far off, patches of thick woods stood shrouded in a thick September mist.

That Tender Light

The only book in the room was one of mine, HUNTER'S CHALLENGE, resting spine up on Lily's nightstand. She saw surprise in my eyes as I placed my travel bag on the floor.

"I like that particular book," she said, bending to remove her socks. "I'm re-reading it and considering a critique of your use of symmetry for THE JOURNAL OF MODERN AMERICAN LITERATURE. I trust that's okay with you?"

She moved against me and I kissed her cheek.

"Will you spell my name correctly?"

"Sure," she whispered.

"This is magnificent, Lily."

"It is; I love how you write," she replied.

"I mean being here with you."

"That, too," she whispered.

Nervously, we moved in concert with Puccini's music. She kissed me again—softly, sweetly, passionately. Her mouth hungered for mine and her perfume hinted of distinct and secret pleasures.

"I haven't done this in a while," I admitted, cupping the sides of her breasts lightly with the palms of my hands.

"Neither have I, but I think we'll find our way. We shouldn't have much trouble, if the parts work."

"I believe they will."

"Then, we'll be fine."

Lily kissed me, letting her tongue play with mine.

She pulled my sweater up over my head and removed my tee shirt. She studied my tan.

"Do you spend a lot of time in the Caribbean sun?"

"I do."

She noticed a purple scar under my left pectoral and another a few inches away, slanting downward to the left. Several older, longer, but lighter, scars sloped toward my backbone near the middle of my right ribcage. As she touched each one hesitantly, questions formed in her eyes.

Putting her hand in mine, I brushed her fingertips across the left side of my chest.

"These two are from the accident at Chocolate Hole Bay."

"And these?" she asked.

She touched the older scars, feeling their coarse texture. I delighted in the warmth of her fingertips and the scrape of her nails against my skin. Lily looked into my eyes and, seeing the scar by my left temple, she touched it briefly, her eyes inquisitive.

"The two on my right side and those on my back are," I paused, "from Laos, when I was a prisoner of war, from beatings. At the time, they hurt like hell," I added.

I brushed my fingers over the scar near my temple.

"This one's from a knife fight. Fortunately, I won."

She kissed the spot and her breath was hot on my skin.

"I'm happy you did," Lily whispered, nibbling my earlobe.

I removed her sweatshirt and she unclasped her bra. Then, she unbuttoned her jeans, removing them and her panties with one fluid motion.

She pushed her clothes aside with her bare foot and stepped back allowing me to see her fully naked.

I absorbed her beauty with a sweeping glance. In the soft light of a private afternoon, I thought Lily a masterpiece. I moved to her, put my hands on her naked hips, and pulled her against my body, my hands molded to the curve of her backside.

Feeling our flesh touching was sensuous, and strangely and wonderfully familiar. I kissed her pink nipples, which quickly hardened. As I held Lily, she loosened my belt buckle and held me, feeling every inch, cupping me fully as I grew.

She turned her mouth to mine and kissed me eagerly.

"I have dreamed of this moment."

"As, have I," I whispered.

After I removed my clothes, I carried Lily to the bed, placing her easily on her back. I kissed her eyes, lips, breasts, and abdomen many times. Then, I spread her legs gently, appreciating the allure and vulnerability of her naked body, fascinated by the contours of her breasts and the appeal of her abdomen.

I knelt and tenderly kissed the inside of her thighs. When I probed her softly with my tongue, Lily sighed and whispered my name affectionately. She moved in a way to suggest she desired more. My tongue probed more deeply, tentatively at first and then with refined tenderness. The sweetness of her luscious body was mine completely. Her beauty consumed me. After several moments of intense pleasure, Lily shuttered and whispered my name—a deep, husky plea for more and forever.

I held her until the pleasure subsided and she sighed.

"It's been a long time, but worth the wait."

I smiled at her, lifted my glass from the nightstand and we each sipped wine. After I replaced the glass, Lily cradled me against her breasts and I toyed with her nipples.

I moved my fingers lightly in circular motions around each areola, while she enjoyed the pleasure of release radiating throughout her body.

Moments later, she motioned for me to lie beside her. She kissed my lips lightly and then longingly, excited by the taste of wine and the peppery scent of our lovemaking.

"Lay back," she whispered, her expression was intense. She turned and placed the tip of an index finger in the wine, pulled my foreskin back easily, and tickled me with her wet finger. She giggled as I shuttered from her touch. Her lips encircled me and she rocked gently.

"You don't have to," I whispered.

She paused and smiled, her blue eyes were powerful.

"I know," she replied, "I want to."

In the ensuing moments, intense and unbelievable pleasure floated through my body.

"Come inside me," Lily whispered.

She moved beneath me, guiding me with her fingertips, as our eyes connected and there, in the half-light of a rainy Saturday afternoon, we made love for the first time with a vast silver-gray sky as our backdrop.

I moved slowly until she was moist enough to take me fully. Gently, I went deeper as our excitement mounted. Instantly, any residuals from Lily's marriage and her fear of losing her identity disappeared, as we became one inseparable force.

We remained coupled for a long time, sustained and warmed in a gratifyingly fluid motion, until Lily felt a warm surge and heard me sigh. In the next instant, she shuttered a second time, forcing her pelvis hard against mine to expand her pleasure.

I felt strong contractions as I pressed deeply into her.

Using her fingernails, she scratched my back lightly from neck to tailbone to enhance my elation and our intimacy.

Moments later, after our bodies calmed, I rolled onto my side and held Lily in my arms. I kissed her cheek and her lips, and we were quiet for a while.

"You were right," she whispered.

"I was right?" I asked, connecting freckles on her bicep lightly with the tip of my tongue.

"It's been too long," she whispered.

Lily became thoughtful.

"I love you," she said. "I've been waiting for you my entire life. Do you think it's odd to know so quickly with such assurance?"

"No, I don't."

It had happened to me once before and now, as if dreamlike, it clearly was happening again.

"I've needed you here with me," she added.

"Well, I'm here now and I'm yours."

"I know," she whispered, placing her warm hand in mine.

Rivulets of tears rolled down her cheeks and I wiped them away with my thumbs.

"You'll never leave me, will you?" she asked.

"Only if you ask, I'll be yours until the day I die."

She hugged me, crying softly against my chest.

"We must make up for so many wasted years."

"Not wasted," I replied. "They were a prelude."

Just then, thunder rumbled in the west and heavier raindrops tapped the windowpane. We spoke about rain and things my grandmother told me when I was a boy.

The sound soon faded into a steady, lighter rhythm. We felt comfortable in the silence, satisfied to hold each other in the waning light of a wet afternoon, realizing our passion revealed more than words could ever explain.

"I love how you hold me," she whispered some time later.

"Knowing how to hug is an art."

"Yes, I think it is," she agreed.

We talked about our lives for a while and then we were quiet, happy to hold each other. Soon, her breathing deepened and steadied. I held Lily as she slept. I watched the rise and fall of her naked breasts, thrilled by her delicate eyelashes, already thankful for moments like this we would share in years to come.

Chapter 14
That Tender Light

Sycamore Glen Farms, St Omer, IN
7:53 a.m., Sunday, October 5, 1986

If magic exists in the world, its threads wove the next two weeks together into a tapestry that was remarkably dreamlike. We were inseparable; an idle moment never passed. It seemed we breathed together.

The hours blurred into a maze of sunlit days and romantic nights, of gentle laughter and constant conversation, of warm breezes and long walks, of quiet intimacy and passionate exploration, of clear choices and bold decisions, of hard work and tender play, of war and supposed heroism.

Never once did we argue, or disagree, or wish we were elsewhere. If fact, in everything we did and said, we were constantly aware that, because of our rare discovery of love, we needed to live life in full to make up for years of joy misplaced and dreams broken.

It is cliché, but *love was lovelier* the second time around.

That year the weather was unusually warm and we spent many hours working on Lily's cabin.

More than anything, that work brought us together. At the start of our extraordinary journey, we did not know what to expect. However, we soon found that each day was better than the previous and we believed our union was predestined.

On the morning of our fifteenth day, Sam jumped onto the bed and licked Lily's face. Sitting beside her, he stared into her eyes, panting and smiling as big dogs do.

She opened her eyes and laughed.

"Gee, he's a pushy guy."

That Tender Light

I stood beside the bed.

"Do you always sleep this late?"

Lily turned and checked the time.

"It's barely eight o'clock. How long have you been awake?"

"Since five, I took Sam outside and edited some sections of my story. He wants you up."

"Meaning, you want me up," she clarified.

"Well, yeah, that too."

I leaned and kissed her.

"These past weeks have been magnificent," she whispered, touching my cheek.

"I don't see why it would ever change. As beginnings go, it's been wonderful."

Lily threw off the covers, exposing her fully naked body. Her beauty bowled me over. Sam watched Lily sit up and run her fingers through her hair.

"He's staring at my breasts."

"He thinks you're beautiful."

Lily stood and slipped into her yellow robe, tying it emphatically at the waist.

"I am beautiful," she said, starting for the bathroom door. "Did you make coffee?"

"Sure."

"Good."

She paused to look out the window at an endless blue sky.

"I think you and the puppy should take me to breakfast."

"He's not a puppy, Lily."

She paused, looked at me, and smiled.

"How little you know, Jack Taylor. All dogs are puppies and all men are little boys. One just has to know where to look and what buttons to push."

"I suppose then, by your logic, all women are little girls?"

"Only when we want to have our way with little boys," she replied. "What about breakfast?"

"It's a date, but I've yet to shower."
"Then, get busy bud; we're burning a good day bad."

THE HOT SHOWER pulsated against my spine and the backs of my legs, relieving the pain and stiffness I still endured each morning from the beatings in Laos.

I stretched my hamstrings and did a series of ankle lifts, working the muscles of my calves. I exited the spray and washed myself thoroughly, watching the soap thicken against my skin. Slowly I turned and washed my hair with shampoo and shaved, using shampoo foam as lather, a habit from the army.

Turning into the hot spray, I rested my head on my forearms as I leaned against the shower wall. I had Lily and, for the first time in many years, I was thoroughly happy. I closed my eyes, enjoying the warmth, as it relieved the ache in my muscles.

I heard the shower door slide open and Lily move in beside me. She adjusted the second showerhead's temperature to match mine and, soon, additional spray beat against my skin.

"I thought you went for coffee?"
"I drank some," she said. "Why waste water?"
I started to turn, but her hand stopped me.
"Stay there," she whispered.

She moved in behind me, blocked the hot spray with her body, and poured warm oil between my shoulder blades. As the oil crept down my spine, Lily's hands began working the tense muscles, moving slowly from the small of my back to my shoulder muscles and then back down. She did this repeatedly, aware of the effect her fingers had on my libido.

When she finished, she stepped aside and hot water beaded against my oiled skin. After she soaped my back, she moved again and the water rinsed the foam and oil away.

"Did you like that," she whispered, nibbling my earlobe. She moved her hands to my penis and caressed me.

As I turned to face her, she kissed me passionately and, as she pressed into me, she felt my erection against her abdomen. I looked into her blue eyes.

"Here and now?"

"I thought you'd never ask," she replied.

Lily lifted one leg around my hip and, as we became one, her eyes widened. Quickly, the heat from our bodies merged as warm water played a symphony upon our skin.

WE ATE BREAKFAST at STORIES, a small diner in Greensburg, Indiana. After a server named Betty poured coffee and departed, Lily whispered, "I love you." Her happiness was unmistakable.

"And, thee I love," I replied, sipping my coffee. "Betty serves a good cup of Joe. Do you come here often?"

"Occasionally would be a better choice of words."

She smiled at me.

"What?"

"Someday, I'll know all about you, from the time you were a boy to now," Lily replied. "And, you'll know about me."

"Do you think you can handle it?"

"Sure."

Her remarkable blue eyes owned me.

"Is the restaurant always this crowded?"

She nodded.

"I could write here."

"It's so busy, how could you concentrate?"

"Lily, sometimes the best place for a person to be alone is in the middle of a crowd. Places like this have no pretense; people mind their own business. Often, I take character nuances from people who sit nearby."

Lily seemed surprised.

"I thought you made it up. May I ask a question?"
"Sure," I replied.
"Why haven't you written about your time as a prisoner of war or about the Medal of Honor before now?"
"I did once but tossed it away."
"You did?"
"I didn't want the story. The same goes for the Medal; others deserved it just as much or more than I did. Besides, I was there to serve and did." I paused. "Tommy convinced me to give the story another shot; he said it would help my psyche and that people needed to know what America's men experienced in that war."

Betty placed toast and a fresh pot of coffee on the table.
After we ordered, Lily asked, "How's Jerry, Betty?"
"Better, he's walking, which is good news."
"Tell him I said hello. Tell him Missy and I think of him."
"I sure will. Thanks for everything, Ronnie."
"It's nothing; we wanted to help."
"The gesture is appreciated." Betty placed her hand on Lily's, smiled, and went to place our order.
"Ronnie, what's that about?"
"It's a derivative of Veronica. That's what I was called when I was young and in grade school. Some still use it. You, however, cannot."
"So, I take it you know her well?"
"Yes, we were in school together. Her husband is a musician; he plays stringed instruments, actually quite well. He studied at the Curtis Institute in Philadelphia. He was with The Indianapolis Symphony and taught students locally. Jerry was in a serious accident recently. His legs and arms were broken and, for a while, he was in critical condition because of damage to his heart. It's been tough on them. His heart stopped once."
"How'd you help?"

"Missy and I covered their mortgage for a year. Their income is a little tight because of Jerry's disability compensation. It is important to give back, especially when you have more than you need. Betty's had a rough go in her life. We wanted to help. FYI, her brother died in Vietnam. Her mother suffered terribly; she was never the same."

"That war shattered many lives, Lily. Some men never adjusted." I paused, thinking about her good deed. "Tommy said kindness and charity link people directly to God."

Lily said, "Your grandfather had good instincts."

I studied her lovely face.

"Tommy was right about many things, mainly you."

"Me," she seemed surprised.

"He knew I wanted to meet you. He told me if I ever had the chance to take your hand, do it, and never let it go."

"I like him more."

I watched Lily butter her toast and then cover it with strawberry jam. Soon, Betty placed our orders on the table.

For Lily, she served eggs over easy, sausage, ham, and home fries; I had oatmeal and fruit.

"You're going to eat all of that?"

Lily looked surprised.

"No, I ordered it for display," she replied, giggling, and testing the eggs. "Of course I'll eat it, I'm hungry. Want some, Hemingway?"

Suddenly, a sense of déjà vu came over me; Julia used to call me Steinbeck.

"No, the oatmeal will do."

I noticed her expression change as she thought of something.

"May I ask a question and promise you won't laugh."

"Sure."

She became pensive and seemed hesitant.

"What is it?"

"Where would we live? I mean I teach and have a farm in Indiana; you write novels and live in paradise. Not your basic hop, skip, or jump to the next town over, is it?"

"Is this a trick question, Lily?"

"No, why would it be?" she answered.

"First, isn't living together presumptuous?"

"If it's to be the eventual outcome, I treat it as a fact."

"I'm old school, shouldn't I ask you to marry me."

"Marriage isn't necessary but it would be wonderful and would make me happy."

"So?"

"Yes." She replied.

"Hell of a proposal, huh?"

"It did the job," she replied.

She put her fingers to her lips and touched mine.

"Sealed with a kiss," she whispered.

I smiled, sampled my oatmeal, added raisins, sprinkled brown sugar, and said, "We live in both places, as we choose. Consider St. John in the summer and during holidays. The remaining time, we'll spend at the farm. Sam could wander o'er hill and dale. He is a natural hunter; it will be a good experience for him. Maybe he'll meet a babe."

"Sam can fend for himself, I suspect. What about you?"

"I've met a babe."

"You know what I mean."

I ate my oatmeal. "I'll just need someplace quiet to work; can you think of a cozy nook?"

Lily's face glowed.

"My cabin!"

"Now, you're thinking!" I winked at her.

"You've considered this all along."

"The professor uncovers a heretofore unknown fact. Did you like the babe comment?"

"It served its purpose."

Chapter 15
That Tender Light

Sycamore Glen Farms, St Omer, IN
7:07 p.m., Monday, October 6, 1986

I WAS REVIEWING and tightening my Laos story for most of the afternoon, as I had done on and off for days. I was deep in thought and getting anxious to work. I had not written anything new since London. I did not hear Lily enter the library or slide a chair next to mine. However, her hand on my thigh broke my focus. I smiled and kissed Lily's forehead, smelling shampoo.

"You've showered."

"I was working at the cabin, sealing the new logs we put in. I needed a shower; I shaved my legs, too. I also took a nap. I'm versatile."

"I was so busy I didn't hear you come in."

"You were working, so I was quiet."

The warmth of her fingertips was reassuring. Sam, hearing movement looked up, watched Lily, and settled back into a blissful, sigh-filled sleep.

"I think he's used to me and the house."

Her fingertips rippled lightly atop my thigh.

"You write in long hand," she whispered, yawning.

I smelled toothpaste. Her eyes seemed sleepy and again I noticed the black fleck adrift in Lily's iris. Her right cheek retained wrinkles from her pillow. I kissed her. She was beautiful, with or without wrinkles.

"Dickens wrote in longhand, Shakespeare, and others."

Her elbow jabbed me.

"They didn't have typewriters, you goof."

"I know. Actually, I feel the story better with a pencil, besides lugging a typewriter is a pain."

"A pain, where?"

"It hurts my back. A retired English teacher on St. John proofs and types my manuscripts, and sends them off. She then sends the original draft and copies of notes to my university for its archives. My agent manages everything thereafter, while I move on."

"He does a good job?"

"Absolutely, and he's compensated handsomely."

"A lot of money?" asked Lily.

"Yes, especially with residuals. If he's managed his money as well as he has mine, Walter Levy doesn't have a care in the world."

"Do you?"

I studied her appealing eyes.

"Not financially; however, before you, I felt awfully dry emotionally. That feeling's gone."

She whispered, "Will you be my love forever?"

"I have to say it?"

"It helps; besides, a girl likes to hear it."

"Then, forever it is."

She glanced at the manuscript. "Do you have a title?"

"Not yet, but I'm considering A SECOND SIP. Someone once told me a second sip of wine is always sweeter."

"Like second chances," Lily replied. "We should take advantage of them, if they come along."

I nodded. "Until I decide, it's my Laos story."

Lily's yellow robe, open to a point below her collarbone, revealed the upper slope of her breasts. Her warm, inviting body, just inches from mine, ended my concentration. I put my pencil down, giving her my full attention.

"You're pretty after you sleep."

She smiled, squeezing my forearm. Not long ago, I believed I would never love another woman. However, on a peaceful farm, an old story ended and a new one began.

"Will it be a novel?"

"It sounds like one."

"Sounds?"

"Yeah, I hear a story as I write it, as if it's an audio track. When it sounds right, it tells me I have something special. Most people, as they read, hear their voices narrating the story. For me, my voice tells me if I have something special."

She giggled. "Does it send a telegram; make a phone call; use a messenger?"

"Stunning, intelligent, sexy, and a wiseass; why is that?"

"Because," she smiled, "I can say what I want, when I want. Seriously, you hear the story?"

"Lily, my books start with a peculiar voice, it's what guides me. When it's working, I don't write the words, rather they flow through me onto the paper. I'm the conduit, an interested participant hearing a story unfold, as anxious as the next person to learn what happens next."

"Does this occur with everything you write?"

"With eight books it has."

"Then, you've started books you've not finished?"

"I cannot count the times. Everything begins with a voice, which often isn't sustainable. Much of what I write loses force quickly; however, now and then, I find a jewel."

"Do you plan a story from start to finish?"

"No, I start with an idea. Something stirs me to write a passage. If I have something good, I'll fashion a storyline, but not every detail, which is tedious and stifles creativity.

"After the storyline, I write a detailed ending because I want to know how the story will end. I liken it to taking a trip without a destination. I hate to meander.

"When a story flows, its rhythm drives me. If I force words on paper, I stop because the piece lacks context. However, I do try to keep everything I write. Sometimes specific passages or dialogue find new life in different settings."

"You keep everything you write, good or bad?"

"Yes, except the draft I told you I threw away. Keeping everything helps me with writer's block. I never know what might move dialogue or develop a scene.

"The voice of a good story is an extremely compelling force with no patience for normal things in life, like eating or sleeping. When I hear it, sometimes I write fifteen hours a day with few, if any, interruptions. When I stop, I'm surprised by the time I've consumed. Hours move like minutes. The book on your nightstand, for example, took less than two months to write. My most recent book took only four. For me, writing is enormously intense."

"You don't stop for research or to clarify certain points?"

"No, that comes after I've written the story; I'll go back and make corrections. I have an extensive reference library and several research assistants in my agent's office help, if needed."

She pressed into me, her body warm and appealing.

"How do you develop ideas for your stories?"

"Mostly, it's through observation. Experience plays a role. When I'm not writing, I read fiction and nonfiction, quite a bit actually. I love to watch and listen to people. Inspiration emanates from many sources."

"The creative process varies by author. My data suggests all truly successful writers have active imaginations, a knack for seeing life slightly askew." Lily said.

"Things rummage around in here and gel," I tapped my head.

"Odd steps beget great journeys," she whispered.

"I'm interested in life's juxtaposition. The reasons people move together or pull apart, how death brings life, how dreams fight reality, why hate crushes love or vice versa, why good smothers evil, and so on; life askew, yes."

Another jab from Lily forced a smile.

"My new book, THE LAST CHAMPION, tells the story of a man willing to risk his life for the freedom of various peoples, yet he can't bring himself to love another human being. That is viable friction, and a good story needs friction.

"Tommy and I met a mercenary with those peculiarities in Africa while on Safari. Tommy recognized the man's imperfection and encouraged the book.

"The exploration of personal conflict offers great potential, regardless if it's overcome. The fact that it strengthens or weakens a person's character offers great potential. With such a storyline, I can create symmetry and introspection, and find a moral compass."

She took a bite of the cornbread I made earlier in the day and chewed thoughtfully

"Just so I understand correctly," she said, "if a story has a voice, if it offers friction and juxtaposition, if you can create symmetry and introspection, then it might become a novel."

"That's it. By the way, you're the only person who knows about this current story. I haven't told Walter; although he's under the impression I'm working on something." I rippled the corners of the manuscript and searched Lily's eyes. "This one's more personal than my other books."

"Why?"

"I address my flaws and failings."

"Flaws?"

"We all have them, Lily."

She kissed my cheek and put her head on my shoulder.

"Are you worried that I'll blab?"

"No, I believe if something's important, you say so. Good or bad, no loose ends."

"No loose ends," she repeated, her fingers played against my neck. "I'll remember."

"You enjoy teasing me. Why?"

"Because you're a *teaseable* person and I know I can."

"And what gives you that perspective?"

"Because I hooked you the moment we met. No loose ends, remember."

Her fingers brushed the hair behind my left ear.

"I'd like to read your manuscript."

When she tickled my earlobe with her tongue, excitement swept through my body.

"I'll leave finished pages on the desk. I'll give you a brief overview, if you want."

She rubbed my leg.

"You decide."

"It's autobiographical, with poetic license thrown into the mix. It's based on what I did in Laos, but Vietnam's in there in the form of flashbacks."

"I take it war's the theme?"

"More like how choices and stupidity shape a life."

She must have detected an edge in my voice.

"Bad choices?" she asked.

"Bad enough."

"Your scars tell part of the story, huh?"

"Yes, but some scars aren't visible."

I kissed her neck and squeezed Lily's hand. I looked directly into her eyes.

"How much do you know about my military service, Lily?"

"You told me you received the Medal of Honor, which isn't awarded without cause."

"Or pain," I added, "or fear. Fear plays a big role."

I stopped, wondering what I should reveal.

"What?" she asked, as I paused.

"This book touches upon things I did and felt during war. Things I have never discussed with anyone, except Tommy. He knew quite a bit."

"Okay."

She waited, as I controlled obvious anxiety.

That Tender Light

"Lily, I'm sorry to say, at one time I took comfort in killing the enemy. I made myself very proficient. I'm not proud of it. In fact, I now detest it. I killed to get out of the war and for revenge. Today, that man is gone. He dried up and blew away. However, that he once existed cannot be denied."

I looked for signs of contempt or condemnation; however, her expression never changed.

"If you're worried I'll disapprove, you're wrong," she offered. "I'm a big girl and I know good men do bad things in a war. You made it out. You have carved a great life; you bring joy to millions. What matters most to me is the man I know today not the man you once were. I never met the previous version."

"You never will," I whispered. "However, memories remain and I have things to say. It's not nearly as bad as it once was but thoughts ramble about and frighten me occasionally. I've actually feared finding someone like you."

"Why?"

"Divine retribution, reprisal, payback, you name it."

She caressed my cheek.

"I don't think so."

"I wonder."

She knew I had something to say.

"There's more?" she asked softly.

"On my last mission I agreed to kill three men to help move the peace process along. Killing for peace was absurd but I saw it as a selfish way out of war."

"Did it help the peace process?"

"I think Nixon's bombing of Hanoi did most of it. He tried to carve the semblance of a peace and our POWs came home. Nevertheless, South Vietnam collapsed. However, for me, there is more to it than my mission. I was deceived. When I learned that, I killed the man who double-crossed me. By doing so, I set wheels in motion and lost someone very dear."

"You lost someone?"

"Yes, I've often wondered if her death was part of my punishment, part of my penance for my actions and reactions. Frankly, I worry it will happen again. I live in constant fear that it will rear its ugly head."

She seemed confused.

"Lily, a man who killed and hated as I did, never walks away without paying tribute. Mine was a woman named Julia Ormandy. Still, I wonder if that was total payment."

"I'm not following, Jack."

"I'm concerned it will happen again."

She understood.

"You're worried you'll lose me?"

"It's crossed my mind, yeah."

"You shouldn't. The God I worship forgives people."

"I hope you're right." I touched my manuscript. "I support many charities, seeking absolution. I try hard to give back."

Through the window, the headlights of two sedans, one gray and one brown, moved slowly past the house. The lights quickly disappeared, as each car entered the covered bridge.

"Thinking back, I find no rationalization for what I did other than fear and hate. Either you conquer it or it conquers you. I became the best at what I did, and killing was involved. I was a prisoner of war, Lily. I killed there, too, to escape. They were cruel bastards."

"Tell me."

"It's never been reported. It happened in Laos; I'd been in North Vietnam and was working my way back."

Lily seemed confused.

"Lily, my final mission remains classified and probably will for years. This book will describe it, despite the Army's wishes. I was tortured. The enemy tried to break me but didn't. They would have; I escaped before that happened."

"But, did you have a choice?"

"Sure, I was raised a Catholic. I could have said no from the start. However, as my men died, my hatred expanded and crystallized. My only motivation was getting even. Eventually, some internal switch tripped and nothing else mattered. After my final mission, after my capture, my goal was to take the pain and find a way to escape by any means possible, killing included.

"As they beat me, I'd tune out. Don't ask me how. I did and it insolated me. I became oblivious to the pain but I had to get out. If it meant killing men or women, so be it. I didn't break. I almost did, but I survived because of my training and because of what Tommy taught me as a boy."

"Which was?"

"He taught me that whenever I felt sorrow or disappointment, I was to fix my mind on a singular topic and focus on it from top to bottom. He was smart enough to know that if I did that, I wouldn't have time to let bad thoughts steal my mind."

She squeezed my hand.

"You miss him, huh?"

"Tommy meant the world to me."

"Why do you call him Tommy?"

"Instead of gramps or grandpa?"

"Yeah."

"I learned from my grandmother that his parents called him Tommy when he was a boy in Havana, actually Tomasito. Tommy fit. He never complained or corrected me. I wish we could have said goodbye differently."

"Sometimes life doesn't turn out as we plan. Sometimes no matter how hard we try, whatever our dreams; the outcome is bad. I was married to an abusive man. I never dreamed he could be like that. We just never know, Jack."

I kissed her neck.

"The fact that I've killed men doesn't bother you?"

"Different person, different time," she stated. "The man I know loves me and is a poet." She gestured at the manuscript. "Is this the story you were working on when your boat exploded; the one you mentioned at the airport?"

"You remember?"

Her eyes sparkled and she said, "Of course, I remember."

"I wrote a draft a long time ago. Back then, Tommy advised against it and, as usual, he was correct. It was premature. I actually write about that. Tommy didn't want me to write the earlier version, but he quickly encouraged this more recent one."

"Why?"

"He wanted me to get over my fear, to get on with my life. He wanted me to meet you and he knew my past was holding me back."

Lily adjusted her upper body against mine.

"Don't novelists dislike people reading their material?"

"An old wives tale."

"When can I start?"

"Being an old wife?"

She poked me, "Reading the manuscript."

"You decide."

She sipped my coffee.

"You make strong coffee, Hemingway."

"I like strong coffee."

She smiled.

"Another point to remember," she whispered. Lily looked at the window. "It's raining; weather report says it'll stay through the night."

"Do you want to do anything special?"

"This is as special as it gets," she replied.

She held my face in her hands and kissed me tenderly.

I caressed her abdomen, feeling firm stomach muscles. She looked into my eyes.

"I love you," Lily said.

"Pretty good for two people who hardly know each other," I replied.

"Yeah, it's incredible. I hoped we would; I didn't know for sure." She kissed me again, and whispered, "Today, from where I sit, my world looks special."

"I love you, too, Lily."

"It starts somewhere, doesn't it," she whispered.

"It's in the choices we make."

"Le premier pas coûte le plus."

"You speak French?" I was genuinely surprised; Julia spoke French fluently.

"Some."

"Something about a step?"

"Yes. The first step costs the most," she explained.

"And because it does, many miss so much: a great love, a deep friendship, a grand achievement, and more. Tommy always said no risk, no reward."

"Mostly, I think fear restrains us," Lily replied, paraphrasing the old man's observation at the orphanage. "I think fear's the reason."

"God, you sound like Tommy."

She smiled and moved her lips to my ear.

"I know exactly when I fell in love with you, Jack, if you want to know," she whispered, her warm breath taunted me.

"You've pegged the exact moment?"

"Sure, it's when I touched your hand at the airport, just before my flight departed."

"I remember you were nervous. You surprised me with a kiss. I thought you were the prettiest woman I'd ever seen."

"Thought?"

"Sure," I smiled, "and you will always be."

"Good recovery, I like nimble."

"Tell me more."

"I figured it all out one night during a thunderstorm."
"More rain."
"I'm going for more coffee first, you want a refill?
"One more cup."
While Lily was in the kitchen, I stacked my papers and placed them in my portfolio. I moved to a nearby sofa and Sam followed, settling by my feet. Lily returned with two steaming cups. After she set them down, she nibbled cornbread and tossed a chunk to Sam, who caught it in mid-air.
"He's nimble, too."
"Runs in the family...you were saying?"
"This tastes delicious."
"I'm full of surprises."
"Hmmm, I like surprises."
She curled against me, her bare feet tucked under her bottom. Again, the slopes of her breasts tempted me.
"After I returned home," she explained, chewing cornbread, "I went full bore into the cabin's restoration, approving plans, ordering supplies, pulling nails, and more."
"And, you're getting paid a professor's salary for a full year? Not a bad way to make a living, Dr. Hall, perhaps I should teach."
She smiled.
"I don't think so. Teachers teach, writers write."
"Will we get back to this love thing?"
Lily became thoughtful.
"One evening, as I listened to the wind, I realized the moment I touched your hand I fell in love for the first and only time in my life. It had to be love. I've thought about you every minute of every day from that moment. You're at the center of everything I do or say. Why so quickly? A touch, a smile, a discussion, a cup of tea, and an innocent kiss on the cheek, how does love grow from that?"

That Tender Light

"You forgot the penny. The penny played a truly critical and important role."

"Okay, toss in the penny. It's head-over-heels in love."

"It is for me, too."

"Are you sure?" Her expression was sincere.

"I feel it, breathe it, and think it."

"I, too; I knew you'd visit. You had to come to me."

"Pretty sure of yourself aren't you, doctor?"

"Perhaps…"

"It's our rhythm."

"Rhythm is important."

"The penny did it," I said.

"It was a part of my master plan."

She remembered pressing a new penny into my palm and surprising me with a kiss, sensing delight she never expected. She saw the same expression when I looked through the pickup's window, the same when she stood naked before me in her bedroom.

"Well, you should be proud because everything aligned."

Lily finished the cornbread and sipped coffee.

"Can I get you anything else?" she asked, putting her hand on my thigh.

"Only you, forever."

Lily smiled, fluttering her eyelids.

"Moi?"

"More French, how utterly Continental," I teased.

As she opened her robe, I shooed Sam into the kitchen. He complied and moments later, we moved to the singular rhythm created solely by the power that moves the universe. We were one in spirit, captive to each other's passion.

LATER, AFTER WE nibbled fruit, cheese, and fresh bread we sat in Lily's library in worn leather chairs directly across from each other.

"This is a great room," I said, yawning.

"I like the view." Lily replied. "This was the dining room in the original farmhouse. I remodeled not long ago, added a new dining room and a suite for Missy with a full bath and closets. I wanted this room for a library."

"You love your farm."

"I can't think of anywhere else I'd rather be. My roots are here and it's an easy drive to Hannlin. This is my home, Jack. It's who I am. The farm got me through Hank's injuries. I took long walks daily."

I waited, sensing more.

"He broke ribs, kicked me in the back and stomach, damaged my kidneys, and blackened my eyes. There were other bruises, but thankfully nothing lasting. It took months before I felt normal again, physically."

"And emotionally?"

"Oddly, that never bothered me as much. Getting away from him was therapy by itself. I never dwelled on it; more that I made a dreadfully bad choice."

"Never?"

"No, never and I'm grateful for it. I do regret the choice."

"Does he ever pester you?"

"He pops up occasionally, trying to gain an edge. He hated that he could never control me. I told him if he ever laid a hand on me again, I'd be the last woman he ever touched."

I studied Lily's face and knew she was serious.

"Good for you," I whispered.

I studied the bookshelves and changed a prickly topic.

"Have you read these books?"

"Most of them."

"Do you speed read?"

"No, but I read fast. The only problem is sometimes I mix fact with fiction. I catch myself thinking I actually did some of the things I've read."

"Our president does the same thing. Sometimes he confuses his acting roles with reality. Who's your favorite?"

"President?"

"No, silly...author."

She smiled.

"Yeats and Byron for poetry and I'm partial to Hemingway and Shakespeare."

"Why?"

"Yeats for sheer beauty, Bryon for his passion, Hemingway for his directness, and Shakespeare for the way he collars a phrase. I like the earthy style of pulp writers, too. Raymond Chandler is a favorite."

I saw something play in her eyes.

"Go ahead," I said

"You're as good as they are, you know."

Her comparison made me uneasy.

"I don't think of myself that way."

"I do and you are," she continued. "You write with elegance and authority. Your characters are splendid. The reader feels what your characters feel. You don't mince or waste words, a characteristic of an exceptional writer. The way you use the language is descriptive and elevated. Your stories are rich, emotional and artistic, and the source of your magic. Hemingway, Fitzgerald, Faulkner, Shakespeare, Dickens, Chandler—they had it; as, you do."

"Possibly, the only thing I have in common with Hemingway and the others is success. I don't have comparable bodies of work. They were more prolific than I am. For me, a book is a hard proposition. As for magic, I've never heard that."

"You write books and aren't familiar with the magic," Lily said. "A writer's magic brings people back for more. The public loves a great writer because he or she unlocks emotions they themselves feel but cannot express.

"Authors of literature, great storytellers weave profound emotion into their stories. They provide everlasting gifts. People crave stories that transcend generations. The public clamors for special books. When one comes along, it's magic! You have it whether you know it or not; whether you agree or not."

She then quoted Lowell's ALADDIN: "When I was a beggarly boy and lived in a cellar damp, I had not a friend or toy, but I had Aladdin's lamp." She smiled at me. "It's magic, Jack."

I was fascinated and I detected a sample of her skill as a teacher. Her students were lucky to have her.

"I write what I hear, Lily. If I don't hear it, I don't write it. The words go straight from my heart onto the paper."

"Again, that's magical," she reiterated.

"Maybe."

"There's no maybe involved."

I yawned.

"Are you that tired?"

"Flat-out bushed."

"Let's go upstairs," she whispered. "You take care of puppy."

I watched her exit, drawn again to sashay of her hips, the graceful movement of her hands. After she departed, I looked at Sam. "She says I'm a good writer. Now, that's the magic."

CHAPTER 16
THAT TENDER LIGHT

Sycamore Glen Farms, St Omer, IN
5:19 a.m., Wednesday, October 8, 1986

WHEN I AWOKE in the semi-light of pre-dawn, I heard Lily breathing and felt the warmth of her body. I turned slightly to face her.

She lay on her pillow facing me with her hands resting near her face. In the moonlight, I studied her trimmed nails. Her lips seemed gray in the soft light, the hair on her arms resembled minute flecks of silver thread. As always, Lily's face was beautiful when she slept.

When I touched her check, she murmured and settled deeper into the pillow. I slipped out of bed and stood at the window. A bright moon and stars filled the sky. It would be a clear day.

I watched an automobile pass on the road in front of the farmhouse and found a tee shirt. I went down stairs, started the coffee, and made a few pieces of toast for Sam, who was always hungry.

After fifteen minutes of stretching my stiff muscles, I poured a cup of coffee and went into the library. I turned on the desk lamp. I wanted to write because we would leave for Chicago later that day. Soon, I was absorbed in my story:

Muong Te, North Vietnam
December 1972

Nick said, "Pedestrians," the morning of our fourth day.

I lifted the rifle and, through the scope, saw four men exit the compound. They were laughing. They paused while the tallest man, Matiere, stooped to tie a shoe. When he stood, he took the north road accompanied by three bodyguards.

After fifty paces, the road curved east and away from the compound. I focused on the back of each man's head.

"The Frenchman's the tallest."

"I see him," Nick replied, using the scope of our second rifle.

"Sing, do you see Giang or Si Duc?"

Sing, using binoculars, studied the compound.

"No, Giang or Si Duc not present, Jack."

"They're in the house," Nick whispered. "We must kill the three men together."

"Confirmed, we won't take one without the others."

"We wait, more?" asked Sing.

I watched Matiere and his men turn eastward.

"Tall son of bitch and he seems younger than his age and in good shape. Sing check the compound, are you sure Giang or Si Duc haven't exited?"

"Yes."

"They're in the compound, Jack," Nick whispered, "We saw each man two days ago."

Sing whispered, "Is true."

"Hard not to recognize the lard ass," Nick added, "Giang has put on weight."

"Bigger target, we'll be patient. I feel this is our day."

"Patient like earth," Sing whispered.

I looked at him, a question obvious in my eyes.

"Earth always patient; turns and changes in its time."

—

The Frenchman and his guards were sweating. Ever since his childhood in St. Emilion, Matiere walked twelve miles a day. He enjoyed a brisk hike on sunny mornings, after his coffee, notably under a blue sky with warm air. He liked to work his muscles and get his heart pumping. He usually walked for an hour and a half, forty-five minutes in either direction. He walked six miles total, twice daily, and rarely missed his routine.

They had been at it for about eighty minutes and his guards were doing well. Matiere smiled, listening for heavy breathing. There was none.

That Tender Light

Much better, he thought. When these particular guards first joined his detail, they could barely keep up; however, in six months, their conditioning had improved markedly. As they neared the compound, Matiere studied them. He believed they could do better. He decided to test them that evening, pleased by the challenge. A mild form of torment, he mused.

When they rounded the narrow dirt road leading to the compound, Matiere heard voices. He paused to light a cigar. He hoped his associate Colonel Giang had finally decided to walk with him. Getting in shape would benefit him greatly. Lean dogs run longer, Matiere always advised.

A moment later Giang exited the compound, with Si Duc, and waved. Matiere liked each man and most specially Giang. As a younger man, Giang had studied in Paris, he spoke passable French, read fine books, and enjoyed good wine.

They had a common bond. Giang enjoyed art and sculpture, and possessed a noble interest in poetry. Matiere was pleased. Giang's level of sophistication was far above that of the typical officer he encountered.

He was also entrepreneurial; they were making money on their drug gambit, which further endeared him to Matiere. To top it off, the colonel played a decent game of chess and usually brought Matiere the international newspapers. Overall, they had a fine relationship.

Matiere waited for the two men to join him. If Giang and Si Duc decided to walk, Matiere would be accommodating.

"Hello, my friend," Giang said. "We'll join you."

"Good to see you up already," Matiere replied cordially.

Giang smiled as he approached, preparing some bit of humor when the left side of his head disappeared. When the Frenchman turned instinctively toward the trees, a bullet penetrated his oft-exercised heart.

Matiere dropped to the ground. The last drops of blood nourishing his dying brain enabled him to observe Si Duc and two bodyguards fall beside him, each dead from devastating head wounds.

For several seconds, blood oozed from Matiere's chest onto the dusty road. After his heart stopped pumping, the dry road quickly absorbed his syrupy blood.

Matiere's third bodyguard, trying to crawl to a stone fence, died from a neck wound. The colonel's assistant, who was beside Giang when he collapsed, stood stunned and frozen. His inability to react made him the seventh victim.

A young woman, who had been standing on the porch, ran toward the road.

"Sing, is that your daughter?"

"No," Sing replied, watching the girl. She fell on her knees beside Matiere, crying. They were the last movements she ever made. She fell dead across the Frenchman as a bullet removed the top of her head.

"Why that child?" asked Sing.

"She was there," I replied, coldly.

In less than twenty seconds, eight people were down.

"The three we came for are dead," Nick whispered the confirmation.

"Shouldn't we see more guards?"

"I see one by the fence, toward the gate," Nick replied.

I found movement, waited, and when a man lifted his head, I squeezed the trigger.

"Nine down," Nick said.

"Let's get the hell out of here," I whispered.

"Good," Sing replied. He clearly was uncomfortable.

A moment later, we moved swiftly across Sing's patient earth, our movements so quiet we did not disturb a muntjac deer, standing fifty yards away with its nose up, trying to catch dangerous scents in the air.

—

The odor of human excrement and the copper scent of blood thickened the air by the time anyone ventured near the dead. The first human movement came at the door of the guards' quarters. A daring young lieutenant stepped cautiously into the sunlight, scanning the tree line with binoculars.

That Tender Light

He heard voices nearby and turned toward several staff members standing beneath the porte-cochere of the main building. As the young guard went to the bodies, a woman began to wail. The crazy old cook by the sound of her hideous voice, he thought.

"Go up to the house and silence that annoying woman," he shouted to someone inside the guardhouse. Then, after listening to a reply, the officer quickly added, "The person who did this is gone, you dumb ass. Otherwise, I, too, would be dead. Go to the house and quiet that old cow now, before I shoot you. Don't make me say it again."

Immediately, a young soldier scurried to the main house.

The lieutenant watched briefly and walked warily to the killing field to check each body. Matiere, Giang, Si Duc, and the others were dead. When he crouched to examine Matiere's face, the old man's eyes seemed frozen on some horrible last image. Blowflies were busy planting eggs at the edges of the Frenchman's eye sockets. The lieutenant turned away and gagged. As a diversion, he watched pink flowers bow in light breezes, as if paying homage to the deceased.

It did not help. He gagged again and vomited into the flowers. The officer wiped his mouth with his handkerchief and drank cheap whiskey from a pocket flask. He looked at the bodies again, noticed more flies, gagged, and took another gulp. He wiped his mouth and put the flask away.

"We will never find the bastards who did this," he whispered.

A few seconds later, a soldier joined the officer on the road.

"We have radioed, sir," the man said.

"Good, how long before anyone arrives to assist us?" the lieutenant asked.

"Perhaps an hour," the man replied. "We've been ordered to pursue."

"Pursue...pursue what, a ghost?"

The officer laughed, his superiors were crazier than the loony old bitch whining up near the house.

Didn't they know the man who did this was long gone?

Didn't they know that he and his men lacked the skill to track an assassin, that they were inferior in every way? However, to his subordinate, he said, "Yes, we will pursue. Tell Nguyen to radio our compliance."

As the lieutenant lifted his binoculars to scan the trees, a second young woman joined him, pointing to what she believed was the shooter's position.

"There," she said, pointing.

The officer checked the location. His instinct told him he must be smarter than the shooter to catch him and he knew he was not. For the first time in his young life, the cocky officer understood the meaning of true incompetence.

"He's gone," he whispered. Probably for good, he thought and hoped. A moment later, filled with fear, he and several others began the long trek across the meadow.

—

We were four miles away, moving quietly though the humid air, leaving no trail to follow.

We quickly and efficiently negotiated the dense forest, walking whenever possible in narrow streams to conceal footprints. Following Sing's lead, we moved into and out of tight passes and canyons.

We went over, under, and around a variety of rock formations, sometimes barely able to squeeze through the space provided. Occasionally, we checked our back trail. Then, we were up and running again, confident no one could ever follow us.

At twilight, as we neared China, we paused to rest in a thicket of pine.

"If anyone tried to follow, we lost him hours ago," Nick said.

Sing looked skyward.

"No stars, rain will fall," he said. He stood and pointed to a narrow gulley about a quarter mile away.

"A cave," he said. "We rest, is dry there."

"We may not feel it because we're running on adrenalin," I said, "but our bodies are tired and we should eat, too."

That Tender Light

After a cautious descent through sparse foliage, Sing knelt beside a boulder, where several yellow bushes grew, the ground was thick with dead leaves the color of new copper. As he removed a series of rocks piled beside the boulder, lighting streaked like sparks from a farrier's grind and soon thunder rolled across the narrow valley.

"I put rocks here," he said. "I alone know this cave."

"Nobody has touched them?"

"For sure empty," Sing replied. "We sleep. No one find us."

We bellied into the cave. The area inside was dry and empty, and wide enough for three men to rest comfortably. Sing, the last man in, smoothed away impressions and prints with the palms of his hands. As he restacked rocks at the entrance, Nick and I removed penlights from our belts.

"No concern for tracks," Sing said, "Rain will wash them away, but caution is good."

"You both look like hell," I whispered, holding my light to examine their faces.

Sing turned and smiled, his nicotine-stained teeth, seemed white in the dim light.

"You boys hungry?" asked Nick.

Sing gave a 'thumbs up.'

"Good, let's see what we have."

We quickly pooled our rations.

"Six tins of peanut butter, two of crackers and cheese, one each of dried apricots and raisins, and three chocolate bars; also, tins of almonds. This is a feast for a king," Nick said.

He rationed the food and we ate quietly in the glow of the penlights, captive to our private thoughts. We did not talk about the eight men and one woman I killed. After drinking water, I yawned, placed my head against the earth, and slept.

Sometime later, in the deepest part of my sleep, I dreamed Julia and I were on a beach and nearby a gray horse grazed in tall grass at the edge of white sand. The man attending the horse was the same man who was with Dailey and Cline near Bet Het, but why him?

D. James Then

The beach was empty; the blue water placid. The air was warm from a high, hot sun and palm trees swayed in ocean breezes. The horizon seemed a million miles away. The heat from the sand permeated our blanket and felt good against our bodies. Heat waves rose in all directions.

Julia wore a two-piece, blue bathing suit—her tanned skin appealing, her smile inviting. She was beautiful. However, I wore dusty fatigues. An M-16 rested on the blanket near my scuffed jungle boots.

"Tray Ninh Province was the specific tour of duty," Julia said. "Please, tell me. You'll get the Medal."

I kissed her cheek and smiled.

"It's not important."

"It is to me," she said. "You promised."

I heard the water lapping against the shore as I organized my thoughts. I wondered if I should tell her. Her smile encouraged the story.

"Everything happened in slow motion, Julia. The platoon leader and an enemy scout fired simultaneously. They both were dead. When we saw the scout, we knew something big was imminent. I was the only officer; my duty was to assume command.

"We were in the wrong place at the wrong time. Thinking back, it seems bizarre. Christ, after it happened, I couldn't remember a thing. I only knew that I survived and my men did, too. Most of it surfaced several days later; however, nuances pop up continually."

"But, you did well?"

"I didn't turn and run. Is that doing well?"

I glanced at the horse and the attendant. What was the meaning of a pale horse? Did I see that man at Muong Te?

"Your training took over."

"Actually, fear took over."

I examined Julia's cheek, her brown eyes, her soft eyelashes, and the fleshy slope of her breasts. She was magnificent. I loved her deeply.

That Tender Light

I placed a hand on her dancer's thigh, saying, "My commanding officer recommends the Medal of Honor, but I don't want it. He said what I think doesn't matter."

She pressed into me.

"He's right you know."

"Not for being lucky and scared. Where's the honor? I did not want my men to die; I did not want to die. A survival instinct took over and I reacted."

She felt me growing.

"Like you're reacting now?"

She kissed my lips lightly. She laughed and poked my ribs with her elbow. I winced. I had knife wounds along my ribcage, where stitches pulled at dry skin. Julia did not see my grimace.

She watched the horse roaming in the grass.

"That horse is handsome; the man is creepy," she said. "How many men did you have that day?"

"A dozen, no, I should be specific. Actually, fifteen men were with me; we were in the northwest sector of Tray Ninh Province, with orders to protect battalion's flank, as part of Operation Bold Union. It was my second time out and I was terrified."

"Bold Union, why that name?" she asked.

The gray horse nickered and grazed, its tail swishing flies and its coat shiny in the bright sunlight. The attendant waited to brush its tail.

"I have no idea but it was part of Vietnamization, Nixon's attempt to let the South fight its own war. He was backing out. After the enemy scout died, we moved up a rise toward a little-used dirt road, hidden by trees and weeds. A private out on point signaled an enemy advance six hundred yards away. I doubt they knew their scout was dead, but they soon would. Two of us crawled forward and estimated that about a hundred fifty men were attempting to flank battalion...

...Get command on the horn," I whispered to my sergeant.

He made the call and handed me the phone.

D. James Then

"Bold Union leader, this is Bold Union Three, we have bogies on Road Six. One five zero strong, company strength, two klicks from your six."

"Deal with it," the colonel replied. "They are hammering us in a frontal assault."

"Any air support, sir."

"Negative, you are on our own, three, Bold Union out."

I turned to my sergeant, clearly shaken, and requested claymores.

"We have eight," the sarge replied. He looked over at a private who was nearby and whispered some advice. "Steady sir, we're all scared, but the men don't need to see your nerves. We have the advantage because Charlie won't know we're here until he's in position to die."

"Thanks," I replied and took a deep breath. "I hope Charlie likes surprises, because he's about to get one right up his pecker. Split the men on either side of the road behind us.

"You and the private stay here on the south side. I'll go on the north. We position the claymores in the weeds about ten yards apart. Parallel to the road and use a daisy chain so they explode together inwardly on the road.

"I also want two grenades from each man. Pass the word, nobody fires, I mean nobody dares breathe until I bang the drum, understood?"

"Aye, sir," the sergeant replied, with a nod.

"Good, when I flip the switch, the order is shoot-to-kill. Give me four claymores."

I crawled across the road, hidden by a slight rise. The sergeant and the private stayed even with me on the opposite side. My hands shook as I anchored and aimed the anti-personnel mines, and wired them together.

I started heaving uncontrollably. With the enemy and possible death a moment away, I gagged my guts out. I popped a stick of gum in my mouth.

Chewing stopped the heaves; however, all the while in my mind, I hear the Lord's Prayer repeatedly.

That Tender Light

It's my voice, but it's as if I'm listening to a radio. I believed I would die right there on a dirt road. Luckily, Charlie didn't see me and I slid back into the weeds next to my men.

"You possess two gigantic balls, captain."

"You scared, Vince?"

"You bet your ass, sir, but I'll get over it when sparks fly."

"You've seen action?" I asked.

"Yes, sir, here and in Korea," the sarge said. "Have you, sir?"

"Second time and I'm scared shitless...worse than the first. When Charlie enters the kill zone, pop goes the weasel. Take out whoever remains standing. When I give the signal, you and the others hustle your hairy asses out of here. Get behind those anthills fifty yards back. I'll be coming fast; you stop and I'll run over your ass."

"You should know I did the forty in less than five seconds in high school, sir," he whispered. "Think you can beat it?

"Is that some kind of record?

"Sure, at my school," he replied, smiling.

"Well, don't cry when I flame it." I patted his shoulder.

"I'd be honored, sir," he replied.

As Charlie came steadily toward us, I counted one hundred fifty-seven men.

As I tried to even my breathing, I heard a thrush singing. The strangest things enter your mind in combat; I remember hoping the bird would survive.

"Easy, sarge," I whispered, "Everything's cool."

"Cool as a spring breeze," he replied. "It's party time."

We both readied our weapons. A few seconds later, Charlie moved between the claymores and the explosions killed about seventy men immediately. I lifted my M-16 and pulled the trigger. My men fired, too.

Enemy soldiers fell were they stood.

"Now," I yelled, and started throwing grenades. I heard men screaming and I watched them die in slow motion.

After the last grenade, I crawled onto the road, fired my M-16, and killed perhaps six more.

I popped in a new clip and, as I turned to leave, I found a soldier struggling on the side the road, trying to stand. He had flesh wounds in both thighs.

"What's your name, boss?"

"Edwin Williams," he replied.

"I'll get you out of here, Williams," I said, "You got anything left in those legs?"

"I'll give you everything," he said, shouting, "Behind you, sir!"

I turned and spiked four men coming up fast on our position.

"Do you see more?"

"No, sir; if you don't mind, you're good."

"Save your breath, I'm lucky...

...In my dream, Julia rolled on her side and kissed me.

"The man by the horse disappeared," she said. "It's odd."

She said we should swim. She removed her bathing suit. I admired her naked body as I removed my fatigues. After we made love on the blanket, the horse moved closer, staring at Julia's moist skin.

Why had the man I saw in the window at Muong Te been standing beside the pale horse? Where did he go?

Then, horrified, I awoke as I remembered the meaning of a pale horse. I opened my eyes, disoriented. I did not know where I was until I smelled the cave and noticed light filtering through the rocks at the entrance. Soon, everything came into focus and I was grateful the darkness hid my terror.

—

The thump of the H-34 Choctaw's blades broke the twilight calm. It arrived about an hour after we recovered the radio, and some twenty hours after we departed the cave. The chopper came in over trees, about a hundred yards to the right of the designated rendezvous point. Using a flashlight we buried on our way in, Nick signaled our exact location.

The chopper flashed an acknowledgement and touched down. We quickly hopped aboard and the Choctaw lifted off.

"Lineman, Lineman One, over," the co-pilot radioed.

"Roger, Lineman One."

"Liners in the basket," the co-pilot responded.

"Roger that Lineman One, Lineman out."

"Good to see, you," the co-pilot yelled. He was one of the men who flew us north.

"It's good to be seen," Nick replied.

I glanced at Sing's drawn face.

"You look tired."

"Yes, worried about daughters," he replied. "I find one day."

"I hope so."

Sing seemed puzzled.

"What is it?"

"If woman at plantation was daughter, would you kill her?"

"No," I replied, closing my eyes.

Five minutes later when the chopper shook hard the first time, I thought of air currents. When it shook again, only harder, I sensed trouble and opened my eyes. When the Choctaw lurched violently to the left, I knew we were going down.

"What's happening," Nick shouted, awakening.

In the dim glow of red interior lights, Sing's face distorted with fear. "We're going down," I yelled, "secure belts."

In the forward cabin, the pilot and co-pilot fought futilely to control the chopper's descent.

"Mayday, mayday," the pilot yelled into his mouthpiece, "Lineman One going down." He gave a location.

As ground fire riddled the fuselage, Nick grabbed his right leg above the knee.

"Someone's zeroed in on us pretty fucking good," he shouted. "I'm hit."

Tracers flashed in the night sky and thick smoke filled the chopper's interior.

"We're going down," the co-pilot yelled. "Repeat, we are going down."

"I can't hold it," the pilot yelled. "Brace for impact."

Kunz' face was chalk-white. Pale horse coming, I thought.

"Sing, hold his head," I shouted, pointing to Nick.

Sing tried but could not move.

It the midst of a wild spin, the air rushing into the chopper was amazingly fresh and eliminated interior smoke.

"Sing, be ready to extract Nick when we hit."

For only the second time in my life, everything turned in slow motion. In the sky above, I saw the moon and thousands of stars. Then, looking where I thought the ground should be, I saw rice paddies and patches of jungle coming at us fast.

"Fifty feet," the pilot yelled and a second later the chopper hit hard, listing immediately to its right.

Water from the paddy splashed inside, the chopper groaned, pitched more to the right and then everything was quiet. Immediately, the air filled with the odor of fuel and burning metal. Sing was stunned, Nick unconscious.

I shook Sing and he gathered his senses. We took Kunz by his armpits, pulled him from the wreckage, and started running.

"The pilots," I said.

"I think both dead," Sing shouted.

We were nearly sixty feet from the chopper when an explosion threw us face down into the rice paddy, and I lost my grip. A moment later, in the flash of a second explosion, I saw Sing running toward distant trees.

I reached for Nick but could not find him. As I shouted his name, a third explosion rocked me backward into the paddy. I was in the mud but managed to get to my feet. I turned and followed Sing.

When I reached the trees, I rolled onto the ground and sat upright. I shook from fear but quickly adrenalin took over. I looked back at the burning chopper, trying to see Nick. I heard voices and instinctively ran in the opposite direction.

After about a mile, pain in my legs forced me to stop. I discovered deep and bloody scratches from thorns. My ankle hurt, too. It was swollen but not broken. I fell to my knees, swallowed my fear, and listened for pursuers—no human sounds! The smell of burning fuel drifted in the air from the smoldering helicopter.

That Tender Light

I stood and ran, hoping Nick made it out. Moving through the trees, I prayed 102 Psalm:

Hear my prayer O Lord,
Let my cry come to thee!
Do not hide thy face from me,
On this day of my distress!
Incline thy ear to me,
Answer quickly when I call!

Minutes later, my shirt snagged on a branch and suspended me several feet above the ground. Using my knife, I cut the shirt away and fell to the ground. I came up fast, slipped the knife back into my boot scabbard, and removed my sidearm.

Moonlight filtered through the treetops. Something snapped to my left.

"Here, sir," Sing whispered. I saw his silhouette and crawled over to him.

"You okay?"

"Yes," my friend replied, "Very scared."

"Did you see, Nick?"

"No, you think dead."

"I don't know. They shot him. Do you have a weapon?"

"A knife," Sing replied.

"I have my .45 with four clips and a knife. Do you know where we are?"

"No, but we must go west, now we go south," Sing said.

"You take the lead."

However, as we stood to leave, a sharp pain burned at the base of my left ear. The image in my eyes went from black to green to orange to yellow to white to nothing at all.

Chapter 17
That Tender Light

Sycamore Glen Farms, St. Omer, IN
9:14 a.m., Tuesday, October 14, 1986

TWO DAYS AFTER we returned from our trip to Chicago, we bounced along in Lily's pickup heading for the cabin out near the Flatrock River. Lily wanted to sketch a new kitchen and measure for antique cabinets she hoped to purchase from a dealer in Madison, Indiana.

As we parked the pickup near the orchard, a blue heron stood in the weeds on the opposite riverbank. The bird studied us for several moments, stretched its neck, and flew down river some three feet above the water. Two thrusts of its mighty wings took the bird fifty feet away.

"I guess he felt crowded."

"Mr. Blue has lived here forever," Lily said.

"Mr. Blue?"

"Yeah, he's a fixture around here."

A light wind rippled the leaves of sycamores, maples and several magnificent oaks. The blue sky was precious. The warm air, devoid of humidity, still hinted of summer.

Lily took it all in with a sweeping glance.

"The leaves are turning, the colors will be splendid."

We wound our way through pear and apple trees, still heavy with half their fruit. Water dripped from leaves from a light overnight rain. Here and there, we sidestepped puddles and when the path turned sharply right, Lily's cabin came into view.

It stood on a small rise centered in a meadow where wild wheat rippled like waves of gold in tender breezes. Patches of red and orange wild flowers added color and, to the left of the cabin, a sentinel blue spruce stood tall and straight.

She saw me studying the tree.

"My great grandfather's brother James planted it waist high, according to his diary. This is where life in America began for my family," Lily said, taking my hand as we took the path to the cabin.

"Originally, there were three rooms," she said. "The main floor was one large room, forty by twenty feet. The upstairs had two bedrooms, with a center staircase."

She pointed to small orange flags.

"See here and there, this will be a wraparound porch. In the back, I've added a wing with a large study and kitchen on the main floor, and another room upstairs. Two full baths, too—one downstairs, another up. We'll also have a fireplace in the master bedroom and…"

I put my fingers to her lips, stopping her in mid-sentence.

"What?"

"Lily, you told me this the first time I saw the cabin, a few days after I arrived."

"I know. I wanted to tell you again. It's important to me," she said. "I can envision it here in the winter with snow all around. It'll be lovely."

"It's wonderful," I said, touching her elbow.

She looked at me, surprised.

"You really think so?"

I nodded and kissed her.

"Right now, the kitchen is my big concern. Water ruined the original hickory cabinets. Luckily, a dealer in Madison might have replacements. I want to check the measurements."

"I'll help you."

"You said you wanted to write after breakfast. There's a wrought iron bench yonder in the sunlight." She pointed to a grove of cedar trees. "It's such a lovely day and it's quiet there. Lucky for you there's no table for a typewriter."

"I'll help you and write later."

"No, you write now. Afterward, we'll spend the remainder of the day together and take a drive."

I nodded and watched Lily bound up the front steps and enter the cabin. When I moved to the bench, I reread the last few passages and, then, I was busy with pencil in hand:

Northern Laos
February 1973

I opened my swollen eyes as I heard my name.

I was on my stomach; my hands under my chin for support. I listened intently.

Several minutes passed—nothing, not another sound!

"I know I heard it."

I rolled on my side and sat up, listening. Was it a dream?

Perspiration rolled down my forehead and crossed the bridge of my nose, dripping slowly onto my naked chest. The drops fell slowly, a second apart; the sensation was a moment of reality in an otherwise ill-defined world.

"Who spoke my name?" I cocked my head attentively. "Did I dream it?"

I half-expected the voice to contradict me. I wiped perspiration from my nose and forehead with dirty fingers. I sniffed the sour-sweet air, a mixture of dirt, sweat, and my own excrement, wishing I could cover the metal pot in the corner. I gathered a few handfuls of dirt and tossed them into the pot, hoping to mask the stench.

I felt my face again; my beard was thick. Once, in college, I grew a beard on a whim. From what I remembered, the growth meant four or five weeks. Was it February? I did not know. My confinement had distorted all concept of time.

"Jesus Christ, five weeks. Has it been that long?"

If I withstood their torture for five weeks, I lasted thirty-five times longer than I thought I would. Why didn't I hear the voice again? I felt helpless and angry, and I hated the disorientation.

That Tender Light

"Son of a bitch!"

I touched my face again. If my beard was five weeks old, I had been in solitary confinement more than a month. Where are Nick and Sing? Were they alive? Maybe it has been more than five weeks, I thought, scratching my chin. I tried to remember the exact number of days but it was useless.

I stood and extended both arms parallel to the dirt floor. I opened my hands, palms down, and rotated my arms slowly three hundred times, working the joints and shoulder muscles. My shoulders hurt terribly from the torture and I found the rotating motion eased my pain. I was determined to keep my muscles toned and strong for my escape. As I worked my arms, I listened for the voice—nothing!

Standing in the darkness, I felt cuts and welts on my back—wounds that forced me to sleep on my stomach. I touched my puffy eyes. If I survived, I would have scars on my body for the remainder of my life; however, I would live with scars if it meant getting out alive!

After I finished rotating my arms, I was sweating heavily and I used the perspiration as a lubricant to knead the pain from my aching shoulders.

From my first day of captivity, I refused to provide any information to my captors and paid heavily for my silence. I told them my name and explained I was a U.S. civilian in Laos, teaching farmers and villagers about water conservation and planting techniques. I said all the men in the helicopter were en route to Phong Sali to meet with and teach farmers. Why a weapon, they asked. For safety from thieves, I said. It was silly.

I told them they made a mistake shooting the helicopter down. I knew they considered me American military and thought my story absurd. Hell, it sounded absurd to me as I said it. Nothing I could do or say would change their minds. The bastards hated me, they hated my silence and strength, and they tortured me repeatedly for it. I smiled in the near-total darkness. I had not given them a goddamned thing. They could all rot in hell.

D. James Then

Mostly they whipped bamboo across my upper spine or against the back of my calves and thighs. The tips of the bamboo, wrapped tightly with strips of cloth, were often soaked in brine. The sting was excruciating and it lasted long after the beatings stopped.

If I was lucky, I passed out. The enemy hated that. They would revive me, and then continue with hours of endless questions. Why was I in Laos? Did I work for the CIA? Did I call in airstrikes? How many men had I killed? What did I know of bombings on the Ho Chi Minh trail? Did I train their enemies? What did I know about secret listening posts? What did I know about military strategy? They went on and on, like a broken fucking record! Truthfully, they knew more than I did.

When they were not beating me, they sat with me in my cell for hours, forcing me to kneel on the hard ground with my feet tied together. Sometimes, they tied my hands behind my back and, using a rope they slung over a rafter, hoisted my arms up and away from my spine and shoulders.

They would leave me hanging for hours. The angle of my arms brutalized my joints and shoulder muscles. It restricted blood flow. Any sudden movement brought agonizing shards of pain to my shoulders, upper arms, and knees. Often, because of intense pain, I would pass out. When my captors eventually released the rope, the pain from blood flowing back into my arms was like heated venom and they would laugh at my agony.

Sometimes my captors lied to me and told me things they claimed I revealed to them. Once, I almost believed them, thinking I had succumbed to their torture. My captors said I discussed Chubb Dailey, bombings, the CIA, and the Ravens. They said I committed atrocities. They revealed locations of secret radar installations and described reconnaissance flights over Sam Neua. That is when I knew they spewed total bullshit. I did not have a clue about any of those things, and did not care. I hated them and hoped, given the chance, to kill them because hope was my only sustaining force.

That Tender Light

I stood there, sweating. I extended my right arm as a guide to avoid hitting the wall. Slowly, I began to circle the cell, walking for exercise. I increased my speed by one full step, after every fifty laps. The movement warmed my sore thighs and relieved the pain in my calves. Ten steps in each circle equaled about thirty feet, three hundred and fifty times meant about two miles.

Walking kept my legs in shape and I wanted strong legs to run in the jungle or swim in the rivers after my escape, and I knew I would escape. I just did not know how or when; however, when the time came, I would be prepared.

As I walked, I prayed. I said the Rosary and the Lord's Prayer. Sometimes I would recite the Beatitudes or the Memorare:

Remember, O most gracious Virgin Mary, that never was it known that anyone who fled to thy protection, implored thy help, or sought thine intercession was left unaided.

My grandmother taught me that prayer. Prayers I could not remember weeks ago now came to me easily. A killer who prayed seemed unreal; still, I did it.

After I prayed, I made up stories. I constructed plots and spoke the dialogue. It kept my mind sharp because I wanted whatever edge I could create to defeat the bastards who held me captive. I wanted them to consider me weak; it would be easier to kill them and escape.

After the stories, I did pushups until my shoulders gave out. Some days I did only three or four, on others, as many as thirty. Thirty-one was my best.

Afterwards, on my cot, with my arms feeling useful again, I sensed I could endure another day. It gave me hope and I needed hope to survive.

Sometimes, I would put my face near the base of the door to peer into a thin line of light. I fantasized about sunsets and landscapes, about bright skies and warm fires, about Julia and long walks. I spent time in that light with my grandparents, too.

D. James Then

I remembered trips to Cuba to visit relatives. I remembered picnics in the summer at Chestnut Ridge Park near Buffalo, and the sight of my grandparents sleeping in the soft shadows while I read books and drank pink lemonade.

I remembered annual trips to the Catskills to fish for trout and to Yankee Stadium, after the fishing ended. My grandfather loved the Yankees; he loved to watch Mantle, and Berra, and Martin, and Ford.

In the summers, in Buffalo, when my grandfather was away from the hospital, we would sit in the bleachers at the stadium and watch the Buffalo Bisons, with Luke Easter and other future or past major leaguers, play Triple 'A' Ball.

We would go to all the games when the Havana Cuba Sugar Kings came to town. Sometimes, if a ballplayer knew the language, my grandfather would go down to the dugout and speak in Cuban Spanish with the player and each man would laugh. I would laugh, too, because I understood many words.

I remembered working at the newspaper with my father's mother, before she died. She loved the newspaper, loved the sound of well-written words. She inspired me to write.

She taught me grammar and explained the styles of great American writers like Hemingway and Fitzgerald and Faulkner and Cooper and Steinbeck. She depicted great books as special and different. She encouraged me and told me I could write stories equally as good.

My desire to write stirred my imagination in that hellhole. It took me to my grandparents, to my friends, to things I loved like sunshine or the scent of printer's ink or the sounds of a baseball game or icy glasses of Coca-Cola on lazy autumn afternoons in Havana or Buffalo.

Julia was a constant, too. I spent one day with her! Yet, I sensed her skin, saw her smile, smelled her body, and felt its enthusiastic passion. My arms and my heart ached for her.

"Goddamn it!"

Had I really been in solitary confinement for five weeks or possibly more?

That Tender Light

My only connection to the outside world was my imagination, the thin line of light beneath my door, and my interrogators, who were brutal sadistic bastards.

Since I had been in solitary, I'd seen full daylight only once. They had allowed me to bathe in a stream in cool early morning air. I hated them for taking that pleasure away and I would kill them for it.

If I didn't listen to them, they beat me.

If I didn't respond to their questions, they withheld my meals.

If I didn't bow to their authority, they threatened to kill me.

If I didn't stay strong, I would not last.

If I didn't last, I could not kill them and escape.

If I didn't get away, I might never know freedom again, see my grandparents, or touch, hold and love Julia.

In addition to prayers and stories, I resorted to other mental games to maintain my sanity. I forced myself to remember everyone I had ever known whose name began with each consecutive letter of the alphabet. Thus far, I had made it through every letter many times, except 'Z'. I'd only known a Zoë in college.

When I could no longer remember names, I focused on foods, or places, or anything else I could think of, like math and history. I would do that until I fell asleep. Sleep meant freedom.

I listened for the voice again. I sat with my back against the wall. I closed my eyes and drifted off to sleep. Minutes later, like a heavyweight's jab, the voice hit me again.

"Jack, can you hear me?"

"Nick?"

I heard a thud and a scrapping below my cot, and quickly pulled the bamboo frame away from the wall.

"I'm here."

I felt along the wall and found an opening the size of a fist.

"Is that you, Nick?"

"You found the hole," he said.

"Yes, how long did it take you to break through?"

"I think five days," he said and I heard him crying.

"I broke through a few minutes ago and passed out," he added. "I didn't want this big of a hole. If these dipshits find it, they'll kill me."

I probed the hole with my fingertips. The wall was two or three inches thick. I put three fingers through the opening.

"When did you do this?"

"At night, when they slept, I worked through with a small piece of metal I found outside and hid under my tongue. I knew someone was next to me, I hoped it was you. It gave me hope, Jack," he said, sobbing.

Instantly, the hole became a secret passage out of solitary confinement.

I cupped my hands around the hole to muffle my voice.

"Nick, are you okay? I've heard terrible screams. Did the bastards beat you?"

"Like granny's rug, Jackson. I hurt all over; I keep passing out. The bullet is still in my leg. I keep squeezing pus and shit out of it. I don't want to die in a pigsty. They beat me because I refused to make a propaganda film. I won't do it. They want me to say the U.S. has troops in Laos. If I make the statement, they promise food and a soft bed. I'm so hungry sometimes I wonder how I stay alive. Sometimes, it's so damned tempting. We need to get out, you hear me, Jack? We must get out."

"I know. Did they mention Muong Te?"

"Not a fucking word, I doubt they know."

Our fingers touched. The simple gesture, humane and heartwarming, was an act of love, a gesture of courage in a world defined by savagery.

"We're moving," Nick said.

"You sure?"

"Yeah, I faked passing out and the guards left me on the floor. They smoked cigarettes in the doorway. The bastards still don't realize I understand their language.

"Where are we going?"

"I think toward Sam Neua."

"When?"

"Tomorrow or the day after."

"You *don't* think they know about Muong Te?"

"They think we're pilots who fight them; they also mentioned heavy bombing in Hanoi."

I remembered Chubb Dailey said our mission was part of a broad strategy. I would not put it past Nixon to resume bombing the piss out of the North to force its hand.

"Do you know why we're moving?"

"I'm not sure," Nick replied. "A guard mentioned camp thirty-one, said he helped build a tower there."

"What is camp thirty-one?"

"I don't know but if it's what I think, we've been there before.

"Is it near a river?"

"Yes, I think."

I remembered the water system in Laos; most, if not all, rivers fed into the Mekong.

"I was held in a cage near a river."

"Me, too," Nick replied.

"The cages were rusty."

Nick made the connection.

"Wire cages near a river."

"Exactly, we might get out. The Mekong flows past Vientiane, right?"

"Yes, but we're probably hundreds of klicks away."

There, in the darkness, I began to conceive a simple escape plan: get out, float in the river at night, drift with the current, hide during the day, and figure the rest out along the way. Risky for sure but, for me, survival became more difficult with each passing hour of captivity.

Fight or die, I thought. I chose to fight. I would fight the bastards and anyone else in my way for several reasons: I wanted to live and be free. I wanted to feel Julia and I wanted to go home. I vowed to kill anyone who tried to stop me.

"Do you think they'll move us?"

"Yeah, I do."

"They must never know we've talked. They cannot find this hole. We have to plug it."

"How?" asked Nick.

"Can you pee?"

"I think so."

"Find some loose dirt or clay. Soak it in urine, make putty, and plug the hole from your end. I'll do the same from this side. Smooth it with your fingers to match the wall's surface. Throw some dry dirt on top to make it blend in and hide it. They must not find this hole."

"They won't," Nick said.

"Stay focused."

"I'm going home," Nick said. "I'll smother any shithead who tries to stop me, Jackson."

I scooped a handful of dry earth, held it in my palm, and forced myself to urinate. Then, I formed the clay into putty. I filled the hole, using the side of my palm as a trowel, smoothing the surface. I took a handful of dry clay, rubbed it between my fingers until it formed a fine powder, and covered the spot.

I repositioned my cot against the wall. I was sweating profusely, as my pulse pounded in my temples. A shiver curled down my spine when I sat. Maybe I would see Julia and my grandparents again.

Maybe, my grandfather and I would fish.

Maybe we would drink beer, smoke cigars in the evening, and discuss the nightlife in Havana.

Maybe, I would make love to Julia a fourth time, and a fifth, and many more times. If we could escape, we could float away and get out.

I lay on my side and said the Lord's Prayer until sleep consumed me. The lives I had taken had yet to bother me.

LILY SURPRISED ME when she set a blanket on the bench.

I stopped, rubbed my eyes, and stretched.

Lily made a silly face as she sat beside me.

"I don't care what you look like, you're beautiful."

"I thought we'd pick apples on the way back; I'll bake a pie. Would you like that?"

"Sounds delicious, do you have your measurements?"

She leaned forward and kissed me.

"That sounds too personal to answer," she whispered, kissing me again. Like the day, her smile was perfect.

"Why the blanket?"

"You have to ask?"

She stood and spread it on the grass near the bench. Then, she unbuttoned her shirt.

"I thought you had intelligence training."

I stood and helped her, saying, "I'm well trained in both intelligence and exploration."

"Then it's time to practice one of those skills, Hemingway. Hurry now, my heart is on fire."

A moment later, an uncommon and steadfast connection linked us together. A few feet away, Mr. Blue turned his head and politely looked away.

Chapter 18
That Tender Light

Sycamore Glen Farms, St. Omer, IN
6:11 p.m., Thursday, October 16, 1986

I RETURNED FROM a late afternoon run and found Lily reading on the front porch with Sam by her side. She wore jeans and a Hannlin sweatshirt, her hair pulled back in ponytail, her face lovely without makeup. Using a disposable camera she used to record progress on the cabin, I snapped a photo of Lily and Sam. As I leaned down to kiss her, I smelled soap and knew she had bathed.

She smiled and accepted my kiss.

"Yuck, your upper lip is sweaty," she said, pushing me away. "You need a shave, buster."

"What are you reading?" I wiped my face with a towel.

"Poetry, Francis Bourdillon."

"The night has a thousand eyes, and the day but one," I said. "Is that correct?"

"LIGHT is his poem, yes." She looked at me thoughtfully.

"We accomplished quite a bit at the cabin today."

"A few more days and the roof will be finished. The kitchen is gutted and the floor repaired—a good day's work."

"Are you enjoying yourself?" asked Lily.

"Lily, building is like riding a bicycle, you never forget. When I was a boy, my father's father remodeled for spare money and he taught me a few things. By the way, Silas' son told me he would begin the porch tomorrow. I'll help with the structural braces and the floor. It should move fast."

We heard the distant sound of machinery in the fields.

"They're harvesting beans," she said. Her eyes grew wide and she pointed. "Look, Jack, three deer...they're splendid."

I looked where she pointed.

That Tender Light

A large buck and two doe ate at the field's edge, probably spillage from the harvest of beans.

"The wildlife is another reason I love my farm."

"Let's take a drive after my shower; we'll stop somewhere for a steak dinner," I said.

"The deer remind you of venison?" She smiled at me and my heart ached. "Just teasing, dinner sounds wonderful."

"Good."

"Now, go take your shower."

"Are you getting rid of me?"

"Yes, I want to read."

As she leaned forward to kiss me, Lily winced. She lost her book and it tumbled onto the porch.

"Are you okay?"

She arched her back, winced again, and quickly rubbed a spot to near the small of her back, on the right side.

"I think I pulled something."

"A muscle?"

"Yes, for the past month or so, I get an occasional catch and a sharp pain takes my breath away, and it really hurts. I had a physical when I returned from St. John. My doctor said I probably did it working on the cabin."

I picked up her book, straightened the pages, and placed it on a table. I asked to her roll on her stomach.

"Show me."

She lifted her shirt and touched the spot.

"Right here," she said, touching the area above and to the right of the base of her spine.

With the palm of my right hand, I pressed lightly on Lily's cool skin. When I probed deeper with my fingertips, I heard her sigh.

"Does it hurt?"

"Yes."

"The muscle is tight; there's a knot. I'll be right back."

I took Sam into the house, fed him, and rummaged through my luggage. After, I sat beside Lily, told her to turn slightly and lift her sweatshirt. I poured a few drops of liquid on her skin and then massaged the knot with my fingertips. As I worked the muscle, a peppermint-like fragrance filled the air. A few moments later, the knot disappeared completely.

"God, that feels and smells so good. What is that?"

"Oil of Agarwood...a Cistercian priest in Laos gave me a few vials to help soothe the pain in my legs. He called it the oil of truth. He said it relieves pain, heals the body, and expands the heart. I order it from Thailand. I use it frequently on my legs for its restorative powers. The priest used it on the lepers he treated. He told me Adam took a shoot from the tree when he left the Garden of Eden. You think there's a sexual connotation?"

Lily sat up and adjusted her position.

"I think we should find out."

"But you said I was sweaty."

"I'll shower again," she replied, removing her sweatshirt. She was braless and I caressed her breasts as we kissed.

"And the deer?"

"They could care less," she replied.

"What about the boys doing the harvest?

"They're too far away, besides it's difficult to see through the dark screens."

She laughed and pulled me close. An instant later, the rocking porch glider eliminated the sound of tractors working in distant fields. The deer continued eating and, after they had their fill, they walked away as twilight thickened into darkness.

In The morning, a brisk wind moved through the sycamore trees and scattered leaves randomly on the lawn.

That Tender Light

   The air chilled overnight and autumn seemed to be losing its foothold against the coming winter.

   I had not slept well. Maybe it was thoughts of Laos, the steak we ate, or the bottle of cabernet we drank. Whatever the reason, I tossed and turned, only to awaken early and in a dark mood.

   My back ached and my head throbbed. I waited for aspirin to ease my discomfort. I did not want Lily to see my gloomy disposition. I stood at the kitchen window, sipped coffee, and watched Sam sniff the trail of a nocturnal animal. I took deep breaths to eliminate my anxiety.

   After a while, I turned to refill my coffee cup and, on the table, I saw Lily's book of poetry from the night before. I flipped through the pages, found a Bourdillon poem I had never read, and whispered the words aloud:

THE DEBT UNPAYABLE

What have I given,
Bold sailor on the sea?
In earth or heaven,
That you should die for me?
What can I give,
O soldier, leal and brave,
Long as I live,
To pay the life you gave?

What tithe or part
Can I return to thee,
O stricken heart,
That thou shouldst break for me?
The wind of Death
For you has slain life's flowers,
It withereth
(God grant) all weeds in ours

D. James Then

"What tithe or part can I return to thee," I whispered.

I often wondered the same for the lives I had taken. I had killed too many people, had seen too many others die. As I closed the book, I shivered. Slain flowers and withered weeds rummaged around in my mind and I worried the debt incurred was *a debt unpayable*. Thankfully, writing helped ease my anxiety and I wanted to finish my story for Lily:

Northern Laos
February 1973

The sting of bamboo came hard across the bottoms of my bare feet and I sat up, groaning. The bastards were at me again. Instead of lashing out, I accepted the pain stoically. If I fought back, they would beat me senseless. I sat motionless, without speaking.

Fury and hatred etched the expression of the diminutive guard holding the cane. Behind him, through the open door, I saw sunlight. Nick was right. We would move. Why else would this prick hit me?

A second blow bit worse than the first.

"Up now, fucking Joe, you go!"

Sensing a third blow, I rolled quickly onto the floor, stood upright, and bowed obediently.

"Please, no more."

"Out, now!" the guard ordered, pointing at the doorway.

He dug the cane's tip into the small of my back as I shuffled toward the doorway. Once outside, I sucked in clean air, vowing not to let the guard know how much my arches hurt. I breathed deeply, relaxed slightly, and moved my feet apart to steal a peek at my footprints in the dusty ground.

No blood, the bottoms of my feet had not split. Open wounds infected quickly, which made running impossible. If I found a way to escape, I would need healthy feet. I wiggled my toes. In time, the pain would subside; my feet would be okay. I thanked God for that.

That Tender Light

I studied the blue sky briefly, savoring the fresh air on my face. Despite my confinement, my eyes adjusted quickly to the light. Morning, I guessed, seven o'clock.

Not far away, several dogs barked at the scent of sizzling meat. Suddenly, I realized how hungry I was. Squinting, I turned toward a pit fire where a small lamb roasted on a skewer. Two hounds stood beside the cook, who threw them pieces of seared fat.

The guard's cane bit into my back again and I moved forward. I remembered the hole I plugged the night before, considered looking back, and decided against it. A glance would cause suspicion. I hoped the makeshift patch dried. Please, dear God, don't let this fuck find it!

"Move!" the guard shouted, again.

His cane dug into the area above my kidneys and drops of urine trickled down my left leg. The involuntary reaction was the result of frequent beatings. I quickly contracted pelvic muscles because guards humiliated prisoners if or when they soiled themselves.

"Go, fucking Joe," his voice demanded, the cane dug deeper.

I bowed and quickened my pace and my dutiful response worked. As we continued onward, I concluded the guard had no reason to return to the cell. No one would see the patch. Triumph, like hope, came in small batches.

"Go!"

Pointing with the cane, the guard directed me toward a spot where Nick Kunz and six Laotian prisoners waited beside an idling truck. Nick—his face badly bruised—wore a khaki shirt and ill-fitting, black shorts. A soiled dressing covered his injured and swollen leg.

As I stood waiting, a second guard struck us violently across the backs of our thighs. I fell to my knees and this time the intolerable pain brought tears to my eyes. I fought hard not to pass out. Surprised by the sudden blow, I lost control of my bladder and peed myself.

The guard saw it and immediately laughed. He told the other guards, who delighted in my misfortune. As their laughter subsided, two guards grabbed me by my armpits and dragged me behind the mud-splattered truck. They dropped me near the tailgate, where sour-sweet exhaust fumes made me gag.

A moment later, another man fell beside me. I turned and saw Nick. The left side of his face was twice its normal size; one eye was swollen shut. A deep gash, infected and crusted with dried blood, angled upward from his inflamed left cheek, crossed his nose, and stopped at the mid-point of his forehead.

Nick had the thousand-yard stare of a man who saw death. However, he sucked in air through his mouth, focused on my face, and smiled with puffy lips. He winked with his good eye.

"I filled that fucking hole," he whispered.

"You okay?"

"If my mom took it, sugar bean, I can, too. Remember, we're moving," Nick said. His voice was barely audible; my reply was an imperceptible nod.

"You cocksucker!" an American voice shouted.

Surprised, I turned slightly and watched guards usher two men into the dusty yard.

A black man reached out to help a Laotian, who had fallen. However, the butt of a rifle stopped him.

"It's Sing," I whispered.

When the guard struck Sing, the American broke away and went to the Sing's side. The guard took the rifle and hit the black man squarely in the chest, again with the butt end. I heard bones crack and the prisoner slumped to his knees.

"You motherfucker," he sobbed, half crying, "You chicken-shit, motherfucker!"

The guard pointed his weapon at the black man's head.

"No," the guard squealed, "No, no, no."

He ordered two of his comrades to drag Sing away. Then, he pulled the black man to his feet and, as he stood, the guard hit the man flush in the face, breaking his nose. The American fell to his knees again and blood poured from his nostrils.

"I no motherfucker," the guard said, laughing, "You a motherfucker."

He forced the black man to his feet, kicked him twice in the groin, and pointed to the waiting truck. The guard remained a few paces behind, his rifle ready if the prisoner bolted. As he neared the truck, the black man turned suddenly, and screamed, "Asshole, motherfucker."

"No," someone shouted. The guard fired his weapon directly into the black man's face. Half his head disappeared and, as his body hit the ground, his left foot twitched awkwardly.

"You dead, now," the guard screamed and fired three rounds into the dead man's chest. The prisoner's foot stopped twitching and a fat guard threw the body on a nearby bonfire.

The guards made the remaining nine prisoners queue. I was first in line, Nick second. As I prepared to enter the truck, I felt Kunz' finger touch my back.

"You see my face, Jack. I look like Chuvalo after fifteen rounds with Ali in '66."

"You should've ducked," I replied.

Nick managed a sad chuckle.

"I did."

"You're a tougher man than I," I whispered.

"You're tough enough, Jackson."

"Sometimes, I wonder if we'll survive."

"I know I will," Nick said. "One way or another, I'll find a river and the water will cleanse my wounds. I'm going into those rapids and, if anyone tries to stop me, I'll kill him."

Nick began to sing softly a hymn by Boberg and Hine:

When through the woods and forest glades I wander,
And hear the birds sing sweetly in the trees.
When I look down, from lofty mountain grandeur
And see the brook, and feel the gentle breeze.

"No talk," a guard shouted, as his pockmarked face flushed red with anger. He looked at Nick. "What say? Answer me!"

"I love your mother and I'll make her smile the day I kill your rotten ass," Nick replied, barely audible.

"What he said?"

Nick was lucky the man's English was poor.

"He will do as you say," a Laotian prisoner did the translation.

"Idiot American," the guard said.

As he slapped Nick's swollen face, a nervous laugh covered the guard's lack of English. He moved his rifle and rammed the barrel into Nick's festering leg wound.

I heard something pop.

Immediately, the air filled with the sickening scent of pus. To Nick's credit, he remained upright, though clearly suffering.

The filthy rifle barrel pushed against my ribs.

"Truck, now," the guard yelled. His face so close, I smelled sour, cigarette breath.

I climbed into the truck, took a seat, and watched Nick hobble in behind me, helped by Sing and the others. Nick sat, placed his head against the boards, closed his eyes, and moaned. I looked at Sing.

"You okay, Jack?" he asked.

I nodded.

The guards slammed the tailgate and locked it. The driver shifted into the proper gear and the truck jerked forward.

"Who was the black guy?"

"Don't know," Sing replied.

"Jack," Nick whispered, "I need some help here; my leg's in bad shape. It's bleeding, I feel it."

"It's not blood, the infection broke," I replied. "Ugly white fluid is running down your leg. We have to remove the bullet."

"You can get it out later; I need help with my knee. I think it's dislocated. Hold me down so I can pop it back in."

As I moved aside to allow Nick space, I found a small crack between the sideboards and leaned hard against it to let daylight seep into the truck's dark interior. I saw Nick's disfigured knee and rivulets of pus and blood.

"Jesus," I whispered, "Gangrene?"

Sing indicated no with a shake of his head and said, "But is not good."

I felt the truck turn and, through the crack, I looked at the spot where we stood moments ago. Blood pooled on the ground where the black man died. The two hounds walked over and lapped it tentatively, before returning to the pit and scraps of lamb. Several guards stood near a blazing fire watching the black man's body disappear in the flames.

"I wonder who he was," I said. "Did anyone know him?"

No one answered.

"Jack, come on," Nick pleaded. "My fucking knee hurts."

"What should we do?"

Nick looked at the Laotians.

"A few men should hold my lower leg to immobilize it," he said. "When I twist, you and Sing turn my upper leg fast. The knee should pop into place. I might pass out. If you can, bind the knee to secure it. Something is torn really bad."

Sing spoke to the others.

"They understand," he said.

The Laotians held Nick's lower leg tightly.

"Okay, Nick, go for it," I said.

Again, Nick sang words from How Great Thou Art:

When Christ shall come, with shout of acclamation,
And take me home, what joy shall fill my heart.
Then I shall bow, in humble adoration,
And then proclaim: "My God, how great Thou art!"

He twisted sharply and we all heard a noticeable snap. Nick groaned twice, exhaled, and passed out.

"We must wrap it," I said.

"Here," Sing said, pointing to the bottoms of his trousers. "Tear off, make strips, tie together, and wrap."

I quickly tore off the bottom of one of Sing's pant legs.

Sing tore the other. We tied inch-wide strips together and, using a figure eight motion, Sing wrapped the knee tightly.

When he finished, I removed the soiled dressing from Nick's leg wound.

"Jesus, Sing," I asked, "Can you get at the bullet?"

Several men tore the legs off their trousers as Sing reached over and squeezed the infection. After wiping excess pus, Sing probed the wound and, using his narrow fingers, removed the bullet. He and I squeezed out the remainder of the infection, and wiped it away with strips of cloth.

"Good," a prisoner said.

The man took several pieces of charcoal from the truck's floor and, using the base of his hand against a sideboard, ground the charcoal into a powder, and poured it into the leg wound. The man whispered to Sing.

"It will clean wound," Sing translated.

He gave some to Sing and me and indicated we should use it on our hands. Another man tore his shirt off below the waist and used it to bind Nick's wound. Sing and I lifted Kunz onto our laps and cradled him against our bodies to immobilize him. I held Nick's head in my lap, feeling the truck's motion against my legs and in the small of my back. After a while, I lowered my head and cried quietly. I started to pray the prayers my grandmother taught me, those I said so many times in my cell.

I prayed for Nick, for the other men, and for the dead American. I prayed to see Julia, to hold her, to love her, to feel her warmth, to hear her voice, and to see her smile.

I prayed repeatedly for freedom, hoping God would end the madness. I prayed for life without war and I asked God to take me home, no matter the price.

As the truck rumbled through northeastern Laos, I fell into an uneasy sleep and dreamed of a time when my grandparents and I visited my grandfather's family in Cuba.

In my dream, we attended Sunday Mass at the Catedral de la Habana. Then, we ate lunch with my aunts and uncles, scooping grilled fish and poultry from blue ceramic bowls. I saw my grandfather playing a mandolin and heard him sing songs with his father in Spanish, songs I did not fully understand.

That Tender Light

Women played cards with my grandmother and I heard their colorful skirts swish as they walked by, smiling and tousling my hair. Some kissed me.

Everybody was drinking beer or rum punch. I remembered friendly jokes and great laughter. We sat near the water and, far out, boats entered and exited the harbor. To the north and east, I saw open water and whitecaps atop big waves.

Later, in my dream, I sat with my grandparents in the rear of a taxi, with my face pressed against the window as we returned to our hotel.

I saw a beggar for the first time. I watched with interest as the man, dressed in tattered black clothes with rags for shoes, poked through garbage cans searching for scraps of food.

When the taxi stopped, I turned and saw my grandfather take a hundred-dollar bill from his billfold. He then asked me for one dollar. I took a bill from my pocket and watched with selfish horror as my grandfather exited the taxi and gave the money to the beggar. I felt cheated, violated, and humiliated.

"Why did you give that tramp our money?" I was indignant when Tommy returned to the taxi.

"Because we have it and he needs it," he replied softly, lighting a thin cigar.

My grandmother smiled.

"To those who have much, much is expected," she stated.

"One day, Jack," Tommy said, "the kindness will come back to you and me, and it will be much greater than what we have given that beggar. It's the way God works. One good dead begets a greater one."

Just then, my head snapped against the sideboards as the truck hit a rut. I rubbed my tired eyes and massaged the back of my head. I leaned hard on the loose board, letting light in through the crack.

I surveyed the faces of my fellow prisoners. I saw terror and shame and I felt as dirty and helpless as that beggar I saw in Havana. I wondered if providence would ever repay Tommy's and my kindness. If so, I hoped it would come quickly.

Soon thereafter, he truck stopped and the rhythmic sway disappeared. I opened my eyes, leaned against the boards to admit light and studied the other men. I saw pain, fatigue and, worst of all, acceptance. I heard voices outside and tried to determine what would happen next. I could hear but not understand a muffled conversation near the tailgate.
"Sing, can you understand them?"
"We eat, we stand in the sun," Sing replied.
"Same old song and dance," Nick whispered, "some little dick exerting authority."
"You're awake."
"Off and on, for a while," Nick replied. He supported his weight with his elbow. Sing placed a hand on Nick's forehead.
"Is cool," he said, adding, "I take out bullet."
"You do good work," Nick whispered. "My fever broke?"
Sing nodded.
The cab doors opened and closed quickly and a guard shouted an order. Soon, footsteps came toward the tailgate.
I shifted my weight to ease the pressure in the small of my back and peered through the crack in the sideboard. From this sliver of a vantage point, the foliage surrounding the yard appeared impenetrable. I looked skyward; the sun was straight above. Noon, I thought, or one o'clock. We had been in the truck five or six hours. At roughly thirty miles per hour, we could have covered one hundred eighty miles. Hell, for all I knew, we were going in circles.
I tried to stand, felt dizzy, and sat. The top of my head pounded and, when I swallowed, my throat was raw and swollen. The others looked as bad as I felt.
"Heat prostration's setting in. We need fresh air, food and water, and fast."
Nick nodded.
I touched my cracked lips and, wetting them with the tip of my tongue, tasted salt and blood. I looked at my hands in the narrow strand of light. They were shaking. I'd never seen trembling before.

That Tender Light

Two Laotians helped Nick sit upright. I leaned forward, placed my head between my knees, and breathed deeply. I rubbed my temples to force the lightheadedness away.

If I didn't get water, I knew I would die, we all would. Why didn't the pricks give us water? For that injustice, I vowed to kill a guard, or two, or three, or more. It made no difference to me; someone would die.

"You sick bastards," I whispered.

"Easy, Jackson," Nick said, patting my shoulder.

When my dizziness passed, I sat upright and rested my head against the backboards. To my surprise, something poked my neck. I turned and felt the object with my fingers.

Christ, a loose nail! Adrenaline pumped through my body. I wiggled the nail quickly, gave it a tug, and removed it. I held it between my thumb and forefinger, examining it as a jeweler appraises a gemstone. A three-inch-long nail was a victory! I felt its point, quickly realizing I could kill with it.

Chains rattling near the truck forced me to refocus on the guards, who were about to open the tailgate. I wet the nail with pasty saliva, leaned forward, and slipped it, dull edge first, into my rectum. I rocked gently on my butt; it did not hurt. In fact, I discovered the gentle rocking motion diluted the pain in my lower back. It eased the soreness in my neck and shoulder muscles, too.

I moved from side-to-side finding more relief, hardly noticing the nail's presence. If I could find a good-sized rock, I'd have two weapons. Better yet, a protruding nail held tightly in my fist could easily kill a man; surely, it could blind him.

I continued rocking gently, smelling a pungent combination of pus, fear, urine, excrement, and perspiration. I put my ear against the crack in the sideboards and listened for the sound of rushing water. Nothing.

I looked at Nick and asked, "Can you sit up, boss?"

"Yeah."

"Listen to me; they'll be in on us in a minute. Your number one goal is to protect your leg—nothing stupid.

Let your leg mend because when we get out of this rat hole, you will need every ounce of strength. Understood?"

Nick sat up and winked.

"I'm there, Jackson. Nothing stupid, I promise."

"Good. How's the leg?"

"It hurts. I'm not nearly as warm as before."

Nick's hand moved to the front of his shorts.

"Ah Christ, I pissed myself."

"When you were sleeping, it'll dry."

"I feel like a dumb kid," Nick said, "Do you hear water?"

"Nothing; however, I did see thick jungle through the crack in the boards."

"When we step out look for a tower," Nick whispered. "It points the way."

Someone banged a club or rifle butt hard against the truck's side and we all jumped.

"Here we go," I whispered.

"Eyes forward, hands on knees," an unfamiliar and authoritative voice shouted. The good English surprised me.

Chains rattled again and the tailgate swung open. Each prisoner squinted as bright sunlight replaced darkness. Fresh air poured into the truck bed and the breeze sliding across my arms and face gave me another small victory, another reason for hope.

With my peripheral vision, I saw several buildings and small huts with wire sides. The jungle surrounding the yard was a wall of dense foliage.

I almost cried; however, I swallowed hard and forced a big lump of sorrow deep into my chest, in a spot where I kept all fear tightly in check. Get even, I thought. If I still had emotions, I had not lost my mind.

Another fresh breeze drifted into the truck.

"Jack," Nick whispered, "You hear water?"

"No, I don't," I replied. "I think the beatings have damaged my ears."

"We're close. I think I hear it. Find the tower."

That Tender Light

I nodded. I wanted Nick to be right because I wanted to be free. I would die before I took more torture. If survival meant short-term compliance and submission, I'd gladly do it. Time would become my greatest ally. Study their routines. Examine the alternatives. Give an inch. Take a foot. Stall. Buy time. Do anything to survive and then, strike when least expected. Weakness becomes strength.

"Stay alert," I said to Nick and Sing, "It all stops here."

A guard pushed two buckets between the two benches. Despite hunger and agonizing thirst, no one moved toward either bucket. We waited for permission, knowing if we did not that the guards would beat us.

Risking eye movement, I studied the lead guard. The little man seemed disappointed when no one moved. Clearly, the guard wanted to hit someone.

Fuck you, I thought; fuck you straight into hell! You will soon die. I studied the faces of my fellow prisoners. They, too, were resolute. To a man, they kept their eyes in a squint to avoid temptation.

Finally, after several agonizing minutes, the lead guard tapped the floorboard with a club. He pointed to the two men seated at the beginning of each row.

"You first, one bowl water and one bowl rice, pass down."

He extended a stack of wooden bowls and ordered them passed down the line. Respectively, each man scooped a bowlful of water and one of rice and then slid the buckets to the next man. The process repeated until each prisoner received his portion. As I waited, I watched the others consume their rations slowly, finding pleasure in food and water. When my turn came, I ate and drank slowly to enjoy the moment.

"Now," the lead guard shouted and motioned to us to get out of the truck.

Four guards, standing nearby and holding AK-47s, took several steps backward. When I stood up, I looked across the compound. Not far away, perhaps twenty feet, three more armed men stood watching us.

D. James Then

"Lead guy is bastard," Sing whispered.

I was the last man out of the truck and I placed my tender feet onto the warm earth gingerly, making sure my legs would support my weight. I was stiff from the confinement but stood reasonably well. The water and rice helped.

I looked around the camp tentatively, half expecting to see the Cuban beggar standing in the weeds. However, the tramp remained hidden in my memory and in my dreams, and I wondered if he would ever step forward to repay his debt.

—

The lead guard demanded we stand at attention near the tailgate. Then, abruptly, he walked away. We stood obediently in the intense sunlight for at least an hour.

The remaining seven guards watched quietly from the shade of nearby trees; their weapons ready. Clearly, they would kill any man who disobeyed. They smoked cigarettes, laughed, pointed, and sipped water.

Several times, they laughed at Nick's bandaged and bloodied leg, and occasionally, they fired off a round to scare us into doing something stupid.

They poured tantalizing cupfuls of water onto the patchy grass tempting us to break formation. They laughed as they tempted us. Their action was yet another form of torture devised to antagonize and torment.

I chose to ignore the guards, their actions, and the heat by concentrating on cloud formations in the distant sky. Using the sun's position to determine direction, I concluded the clouds floated eastward, like huge tuffs of cotton, on the edge of high currents—nature's beauty incongruent to war's brutality. Perhaps God was nearby.

I studied cloud shapes, colors, and positions in the sky.

Later, the lead guard returned wearing clean clothes. He had showered and gazed at the dirty prisoners with noticeable contempt.

He raised an arm and pointed toward a row of huts, built in a semi-circle around a small courtyard.

That Tender Light

"Go," he shouted, smacking the first prisoner with a cane to get him moving. As the other prisoners shuffled past, the lead guard lit a cigarette. With his attention distracted, I poked Nick in the small of his back.

"South is to the right," I whispered without moving my lips.

"Here," another guard yelled in the distance, indicating a spot near the huts.

Again, we stood at attention in the sunlight. The lead guard went before each prisoner. He walked down the line slowly, grunting arrogantly and, when he stood before me, he blew smoke into my face. I showed no reaction and the guard sneered. He looked over at Nick, standing before a hut to my right. Then, turning back to me, in surprisingly good English, he asked, "What did you say to him before?"

He pointed at Nick and, again, exhaled in my face.

"That the sky was beautiful," I lied. I hoped my stoic expression disguised the cold, hard contempt imbedded in my heart for this guard and all the others.

"If only you could fly," the guard whispered.

Unexpectedly, he slapped my cheek. I stood my ground, quickly internalizing the discomfort. Not far away, Nick sucked in air but did not move. Nick, I thought, not one fucking word.

"Quiet," the guard said.

He slapped me again and the second blow wobbled me.

"No more talking," he shouted. "You talk, you hurt."

I studied the man's round face, dark eyes, and comical nose. He is a pompous bully, I thought, who enjoys tormenting helpless men. I smiled inwardly; the man before me would crumble quickly. Bullies always do. I would kill him.

I knew I had to take my mind off the intense desire to fight back. To do so, I concentrated on the warm earth under my bare feet. Somewhere directly beneath me, thousands of miles away on the extreme opposite side of the earth, people stood free. If I were capable of burrowing through the earth, I would eventually resurface as a liberated man. The idea was ridiculous but certainly comforting.

Instead, I vowed to escape another way and, before I did, I would kill the prick standing before me. I could already feel the joy it would bring.

I moved my feet slightly, keeping my rectum contracted to hold the nail firmly in my body. At the right moment, I would bury the three-inch spike deep into the bastard's eye.

One second at a time, one minute at a time, one hour at a time, and one day at a time—I vowed to survive and win.

"You turn right," a different guard said, shouting.

All prisoners complied.

I studied the structures. They were three-sided, roofed, wire cages large enough to hold one man. Next to the cage I would occupy, stood another with metal restraints, wired to a generator. They hung freely and moved idly in the breeze. I knew immediately it was a torture box. I fought off panic. I clenched my fists to control the tremors in my hands. Get a grip; you must stay focused to escape!

"Enter," the lead guard demanded.

I looked at my dirty feet. I had been without shoes since the first day. The guards routinely removed shoes to thwart escape. If Nick was correct and a stream was nearby, I would not need shoes in the water. Quickly, I looked up; fearful the guards would read my mind. Do not give them a hint, I reasoned. Stay strong for Julia, for your grandparents, for your sanity.

"In," a guard shouted and hit me across my back.

My daydreaming put me half a step behind the other men. Jesus, get everything out of your mind! Get it out, now! Stay focused.

I entered the cage quickly and, when I turned around to face the guard, I noticed the clouds were gone, drifting freely in the upper winds somewhere far away. Escape was now my singular focus. The Cuban beggar's image reappeared in my mind. Pay it back, I pleaded, pay it back now!

Chapter 19
THAT TENDER LIGHT

Sycamore Glen Farms, St. Omer, IN
1:07 p.m., Saturday, October 18 1986

AFTER I FINISHED writing and Lily returned from the cabin, we rode horses, ending up on the distant southern edge of the farm. We were in patchy woods now, the wind was light, the air still warm from a sun-filled afternoon. We maneuvered our horses into an area adjacent to a stream and dismounted. Out on a nearby highway, an old blue truck rumbled by and soon the sound of its motor disappeared. The thought that the truck might have stopped crossed my mind but then Lily's voice distracted me.

"It's over here," she said, taking my hand. We walked and found a large, moss-covered boulder sitting on the crown of the small hill.

"There," she said, handing a flashlight to me. "Roll those two rocks away."

I stooped and pushed the rocks aside, suddenly sensing déjà vu. The entrance of this cave was eerily similar to the one we occupied after the Muong Te assassinations.

"Are you okay?"

"Yes," I replied and looked inside. "The cave's big enough to hold seven or eight people."

"My ancestors hid fleeing slaves here during the Civil War. According to our family bible, slave hunters never found the escapees or this hiding place."

"What if there were more than eight?"

"There's another cave behind the falls near the cabin. Seldom, at least according to the annotations in the bible, did escaping slaves travel in groups larger than four."

I replaced the rocks, stood up, and hugged Lily.

"I love showing you these things," she said. "They're part of me. I came here often as a girl, still do, if the mood strikes. I sit and read. These woods are special to me, I feel safe here. I sat here the day of my divorce and I sat here the day my mother died, spent the whole afternoon, crying and thinking, and praying, too.

"My father found me and stayed with me until dark. I asked why my mother had to die so young, wondering how I'd go on without her. I thought I couldn't and I wanted to die, too. My life seemed over. I hated God for taking my mother away. I hated Him for allowing such pain.

"My dad listened. He was quiet for the longest time. It must have been unbearable for him, losing his wife. He kissed my cheek and whispered words I'll never forget. He said, 'Lily, God's not vengeful, He transcends time and feeling, and wants only the best for us. What happens to us either strengthens or defeats us.' He said when we fall we must get up. Your mother wants you to get up. She didn't believe in failure."

"Good advice."

Her face beamed with sincerity.

"Then, I ask you to do the same for me," she said.

"What do you mean?"

"You didn't know; however, I watched as you read my book of poetry the other day. I didn't hear your thoughts but I sensed them. What happened to you, whatever you did, it's over. It'll never happen again. I want you to get up, as my father said. Get on with your life, with me in it. When you think differently, I don't have all of you. Do I make sense?"

"Yes," I replied, "I hope God isn't vengeful; however, when a man has done the things I've done, providence seems to find a way to even the score."

She grinned, adding, "Whatever happens, I'll always love you. I want you to take solace in my love, find peace in that."

I kissed her, hoping she was correct.

"Now, let's go back to the house. You can edit what you wrote today, while I call a man about cabinets."

As she made her call, I wrote:

Vientiane, Laos
February 1973

They met at 2 p.m. in the lobby bar at the Khun Bu Lom Hotel, a five-minute walk from the IASS clinic.

Because of the time of day, the usually busy room was nearly empty. The air was noticeably cooler inside than out. The surrounding gardens and the building's thick walls blocked the day's heat, muted the persistence of passing traffic, and stifled the din of the commercial district.

As she walked through the entrance, Julia saw Elgin Dailey sitting with another man in an alcove, drinking coffee. A six-bladed wooden fan swung above the table like a metronome pacing the easy rhythm of the day.

Dailey looked up and waved casually when he saw Julia. He put his cup down and whispered something to his associate who turned toward Julia and immediately smiled. As she approached, each man stood.

"Thank you for meeting me," she said, nervously extending her hand.

Dailey shook it and positioned a chair. As Julia sat, the scent of jasmine drifted over the table. A multi-colored butterfly clip held Julia's auburn hair in an attractive single braid. She wore a white blouse and yellow skirt and, except for a gold watch on her left wrist, had no jewelry. Her manicured fingernails bore clear polish. A rich tan deepened her flawless almond skin. Despite the ambient light, her intense brown eyes sparkled.

Subliminally, she sensed Dailey's associate study her notable physical qualities. She had endured male scrutiny throughout her life. Men were often foolish in Julia's company. The only man who had not played a fool was the reason for her visit.

"Tom Cline," Dailey's associate said, extending his hand. Julia accepted it, making her grip slightly tighter than his. A bit of doubt quickly cracked Cline's confident veneer.

"Please sit, have you eaten lunch?"

"Yes," she replied, "at the clinic."

"Julia," Dailey began, "Tom is a U.S. liaison officer. Tom, not long ago Julia helped us at our hospital in Sam Thong. Julia is Doc Ormandy's niece. She's with Interfaith Aid and Support Services in Vientiane, which has been her permanent station since she arrived in May.

"When Julia requested a meeting, I thought you should attend," he added.

Cline, infatuated by Julia's appeal, added, "I'll help in any way, if I can."

"Thank you," Julia replied, sensing a lie.

A waiter stopped long enough for Julia to order a cup of tea. She positioned her hands hesitantly on the table, placing one atop the other. After the waiter departed, she looked at Cline furtively and spoke directly to Dailey.

"I came for a clear understanding of Jack Taylor's status," she began, her soft voice direct, her intelligent eyes focused. "Despite repeated requests in the past weeks, nobody's told me a damned thing. If anyone knows anything, it's you, Elgin."

"We normally don't discuss these things, Julia."

"This goes beyond normal. I'm not a child. I know how the world works. I helped you, now you help me. Where is he? Is he alive? Surely, you know something."

"How do you know, Jack Taylor?" asked Cline.

She studied his eyes, fully aware of his intent to dodge her question.

"I don't see where that is any of your business, Mr. Cline," she replied, a furrow crossed her brow; however, she soon eased her intensity. She smiled slightly. "Since I'm the one asking I'll say this much: I met Jack at Sam Thong, he helped us save six wounded children, and we became friends, more than friends, actually. We care for each other deeply."

That Tender Light

"I see," Cline replied.

"Respectfully, sir, whether you do or don't is unimportant to me. Jack's safe return is. His work was dangerous and confidential because he alluded to it.

"He indicated he might be gone several weeks. Several have turned into eight and, despite repeated inquiries, no one tells me a damned thing. I talked to my uncle but he doesn't know. Surely, with your clandestine activities and network, you know something."

"Jesus, Julia," Dailey said, checking the room.

"We're the only ones here, Elgin; the bar is empty. I know more than you think. People talk, rumors spread, and I listen. Right now, discretion isn't as important as candor."

"About Jack Taylor's status, there's nothing we can tell you," Cline said truthfully; however, he immediately added a semi-truth. "I'll say this, he was involved in a supply mission in the northeast sector of Laos, up near Phong Sali—the helicopter was shot down."

"Sweet Mother of God," Julia whispered.

Dailey looked at Cline, raising his eyebrows skeptically.

"Chubb, it doesn't make any difference if she knows a chopper went down," he said to Dailey. Looking at Julia, he added, "Insurgents control a portion of the territory up there."

"It's a volatile area, changes occur daily," Chubb added.

"What was he doing?"

"Delivering food and medicines," Cline continued, adding flesh to his lie.

She studied Clines eyes.

"Somehow, I think not," she replied. "That debate is for another day. Did you search for him?"

"Of course, we sent a rescue crew and they found the crash site. Ground fire riddled the downed helicopter. The pilot and co-pilot died in the crash; their charred remains were in the wreckage. The body of a third crew member—not Jack—was in a nearby paddy. No other bodies were found and, unfortunately, no clues either."

"Then, Jack might be attempting to return."

"Yes, it's the optimistic view."

"And the pessimistic?" she asked.

"He might be dead or captured," Cline stated.

She swallowed hard.

"Christ, you don't hold back, do you?"

"Why would I, Dr. Ormandy? As I said, the insurgents hold various sectors of Laos. They're terribly unconventional in their treatment of prisoners."

"However, there's a chance, I mean, he could be alive?" Julia clearly needed hope.

"A reasonable possibility, yes, but no one knows. He could be lost or finding his way back. However, the more likely scenario is, if alive, he's been captured."

"Or, he's dead," she whispered, stating one possibility.

"Let's hope for a more positive outcome, Julia," Dailey added. Chubb wisely chose not to say that death might be a better alternative than capture by the Pathet Lao.

"Dear God," she whispered, shivering. Julia breathed deeply to prevent more tears. She sipped her tea, and nervously added half a teaspoon of sugar, even though she rarely used it. Her cup trembled noticeably as she drank.

She looked at Chubb Dailey.

"Elgin, I ask a favor."

"Yes, Julia, if I can."

"Promise you'll contact me if you learn anything—good or bad. I'll keep a confidence." She sighed, adding, "God, if I knew where to look, I'd go myself."

"Not a wise move, Julia," Dailey replied.

"No," Cline added, quickly. "With heavy insurgent activity, it's not a good place for man or woman, especially an attractive Canadian doctor. They kill men readily. They do unspeakable things to Caucasian women. If they ever ask questions, it's long after they've acted."

"If they ever ask," Dailey whispered.

"So, I'm forced to sit and wait?"

That Tender Light

"As we all must," Dailey said. "If I hear, I'll contact you immediately."

Cline nodded

"Thank you, I'll keep this conversation confidential," Julia said. She drank more tea, stood, and, leaning over, placed her lips beside Chubb Dailey's ear.

"I love him," Julia whispered. "Bring him back to me."

"I assumed as much," Dailey replied.

However, he knew they would make no effort to find Jack Taylor and the others. That was the arrangement; if alive, they were on their own.

She placed her hand on his shoulder, patted it twice, nodded at Cline, and, without speaking, departed. The two watched her leave, hearing the fan circling above. Soon, she disappeared into the flow of humanity outside the hotel.

—

A block from the Khun Bu Lom Hotel, as traffic honked, pedestrians hurried and pedicabs sped by, Julia braced herself against the wall of a building and inwardly watched an anticipated life pour through her mind.

In it, she and Jack were happy, there was a wedding day, children, and much more. She saw a man and woman grow old together and she heard laughter and songs and hungered for days filled with love and intimacy.

She saw Jack writing books, the long walks they would take and trips to Europe to see London and Paris and Rome. She felt pieces of a life-yet-to-be slip through her fingers. After a while, she placed her head in her hands and sobbed.

People passing noticed her sorrow; however, no one offered help. Finally, when she could breathe normally, she walked slowly to the clinic and her patients, wanting a miracle.

ABOUT FOUR THAT afternoon, we dined, alfresco, in a garden court of Château Madesimo on a hilltop overlooking Madison, Indiana. Earlier, Lily purchased kitchen cabinets and we decided to sit and enjoy the waning sunlight.

Below, on the Ohio River, sailboats circled lazily atop the shimmering water. Every now and then, tug horns blared as barges heaped with coal moved toward power plants up river. In the distance, on the Kentucky shore, men fished with young children. High above, a passenger jet flew steadily southwest.

I studied Lily's face. Sunlight flushed her cheeks and highlighted flecks of gold and silver in her hair.

"What are you thinking, Lily?"

"I'm remembering the warmth of my skin against yours as you hold me, the firm and soft spots of your body, the way you breathe, sigh, and whisper my name. I want to hear and feel those things forever and I just asked God to let me be the instrument that smoothes the harshness of memories you carry. Does that answer your question?"

"Yes." I glanced at the river saying, "Since I've been with you, everything has clearer meaning and deeper emphasis."

"I'm just a woman who loves you, Jack," Lily whispered.

"You are much more than *just a woman*, Lily. We fit together in a very special way and I think that's rare."

She touched my hand.

"I agree; you've given my life new meaning."

Lily smiled and the color of her blue eyes seemed to merge with the sky above, making the universe seamless.

"Just remember, if we fall, we must get up," she added.

She handed her menu to our waiter and watched as he poured Madesimo Chianti.

"Your lunch will be here presently," the waiter advised, departing.

"Thank you," Lily replied.

She lifted a loose strand of hair and tucked it behind her right ear; the simple movement was both appealing and confident.

I looked down the hill at Madison's main street.

"This is a neat little town."

"My aunt and I come annually for the art festival. I met Jonas Littleton on one of those visits. I was browsing in his antique shop and found my library desk and credenza."

"He seems a decent sort."

"And his prices are fair," Lily added. "Antique dealers often over price and under deliver; Jonas operates differently."

"He stocks quality and his price is reasonable. I'm happy he called. I like the cabinets. Angus Hall's carvings won't be on the doors but at least I'll still have hickory."

"I can replicate the carvings."

"You know how?"

"Sure, hidden talents, remember?"

Lily smiled and scrunched her face at me.

After sharing an antipasto, we ate veal served with vine-grown tomatoes over angel hair pasta tossed in warm olive oil flavored with basil and oregano, and Romano cheese. The bread was fresh and delicious

"When I was young," Lily said, chewing thoughtfully, "Hollywood filmed a movie in Madison, based on a novel by James Jones.

"Frank Sinatra, Dean Martin, and Shirley MacLaine starred, also Martha Hyer and a few others. My mother was still alive. She, Missy, and I drove down to watch. We wanted to see Sinatra, and we did. We were thrilled. We saw Dean Martin, too."

"Thrilled?"

"Beyond belief," she added. "I stood close to him on one occasion; his eyes were *unbelievably* blue. He winked at me, Jack. I love Sinatra's music. The movie was an adaptation of Jones' second novel: SOME CAME RUNNING."

I sipped my wine and said, "A fine writer; he wrote FROM HERE TO ETERNITY and THE THIN RED LINE."

"He died in the late seventies, if I remember correctly," Lily stated.

"I actually met him in 1975, Lily, about a year after his A TOUCH OF DANGER. We talked at a cocktail party I attended, hosted by several publishers for new authors and agents. Jones was an interesting man. FROM HERE TO ETERNITY and THIN RED LINE are perhaps the great American war novels."

"Norman Mailer would argue they aren't," she replied, smiling.

"I know. His NAKED AND THE DEAD is a truly fine book. I prefer Jones' stories."

"Have you met Mailer?"

"No, never met Norman. I would like to talk to him; however, our paths have never crossed. I stopped going to parties, I don't fit in." I sipped my wine. "The less I have to do with small talk and those kinds of gatherings, the happier I am. I like my life as it is. Hell, I have to force myself to do a book tour."

"Privacy means a lot to you, doesn't it?"

"It's something I seldom, if ever, relinquish." Then, remembering how suddenly I left New York, I added, "I should call Walter, to let him know everything's okay."

She nodded.

"Did Jones make an impression?"

"Yeah, a good one, I can't say I met him long enough to say more, Lily. I liked him and I do like the way he helped aspiring writers with his literary retreat in Illinois. You know, he told me it took him six years to write ETERNITY.

"Six years is a long time?"

"Especially because of all the typos," I replied, laughing. "He used a typewriter."

"Aren't you the brazen one," she said, lifting her wine glass and winking like Sinatra.

I smiled at her, saying, "It takes one to know one."

WHEN WE RETURNED from Madison, we drove to the cabin in the red pickup. It was dark but, with flashlights, we saw that Lily's carpenters had finished the roof and, surprisingly, they had completed the porch floor. They also constructed part of the railing.

After our inspection, we went inside and clicked on the lights. A carpenter's radio came on, too. Lily showed me Angus' carving on one of the damaged cabinet doors—an intricate bouquet of flowers.

"Do you think you can replicate this?"

I examined the carving, saying, "Sure, I need palm carving tools. The wood is hard. If one of your carpenters doesn't have a set, I'll buy one. I think I can match it."

"Where did you learn to carve?"

"In the hospital, after Laos, it helped pass the time. I did sketches, too."

She smiled and her expression filled with mischief.

"You never asked me to see your sketches, isn't that a standard line?" she asked, pursing her lips.

I put my arm around Lily and kissed her cheek.

"I've never used it. I'll sketch you, if you want."

"With or without clothes?"

"It makes no difference; I love you either way, perhaps one of each."

"One day soon," she promised, returning my kiss.

By chance, on the radio in the background, Sinatra sang MOONLIGHT IN VERMONT and I pulled Lily close.

"Do you know how to dance, Miss Lily?"

"I do, if you're asking."

"Indeed."

I took her in my arms and, in the glow of a few light bulbs—to the voice Lily loved—we danced together for the first time in a world we alone occupied. As I held her, all my worries disappeared.

Lily said, "You are my music."

At that moment, our love for each other was as high as canyon to sky and, as I glanced out the window, the wild wheat seemed to sway in the moonlight to the music. As we held each other, the world and the universe aligned and I knew I would never love another woman. I had found the love of my life, the woman who would take away the remnants of too many grim days.

As we swayed to the music, Lily's kisses moved across my neck and cheek.

"Want to go back to the farmhouse?" I whispered.

"Why not right here, right now," she replied. "Dancing always does it for me."

"Then, we must dance more often," I said.

Soon Lily sang with Sinatra, *"pennies in a stream, falling leaves of Sycamore..."*

"Ah," I whispered in her ear, "more talk of pennies."

BACK IN THE farmhouse, Lily fell asleep reading on the sofa. I covered her with one of Missy's quilts and stood watching the rise and fall of her chest.

"Never, did I ever believe this would happen again."

I kissed the tips of my fingers, placed them gently against Lily's cheek and she moved slightly.

"I love you," I whispered and then, quite unexpectedly, I trembled uncontrollably. Frightened, I went onto the porch with Sam. Memories of war inundated me and I was edgy.

I stood and breathed deeply, trying to calm myself, and watched the lights of an airplane far off in the night sky.

As I scanned the stars in the heavens above, a lone car drove by slowly, out on the highway.

"You know, Sam," I said, sensing my dog nearby, "most people think when they look up at the night sky they see a million stars.

That Tender Light

"It's a fallacy, bud; we only see several thousand stars at any given moment. Still, some of those, because of the speed of light, no longer exist.

"Memories work the same way. We tend to remember things which no longer exist and, like the light from dead stars, they seem real when they're actually illusions."

I glanced toward the living room where Lily slept and I remembered the chilling words from Matthew's Gospel—all things must pass.

"One day she will be gone, as will I, and I don't want it to end. I want these moments, these days, and this love, to last forever. But it won't and that scares me."

Sam, sensing my uneasiness, moved against my leg.

Then, for the first time since I was a prisoner in Laos, I bowed my head and asked God to clean the slate, to forgive me, to allow me to hold onto Lily, forever.

As I walked back into the farmhouse, I hoped my prayers were not wasted. I hoped, as Lily believed, I stood forgiven.

I checked Lily and went into the library. My story called:

Northern Laos
February 1973

Sometime after midnight, on the second night, I timed two guards as they walked the compound, coming together and then parting near the front of my cage. I did it ten times and their fastest rotation was forty-five seconds to make it once around the outer circumference of the courtyard. I chose forty seconds to be conservative.

On the eleventh pass, as the guards disappeared from view, I began counting one one-thousand-one, one one-thousand-two, as I levered the nail back and forth trying to snap a link in the wire fence. If I could break one, I'd do another, and another, and I could get out. When my count reached forty seconds, I stopped, lay on my side, and feigned sleep.

D. James Then

After the guards passed, I worked the wire again. Sometime after the guards' fourteenth or fifteenth pass, Nick spoke to me.

"Jackson," he said.

"Go ahead, you have thirty seconds."

"Are you timing them?"

"Yes."

"Me, too. I've been in this camp before, I know it."

"I don't recognize it," I replied.

"I do. Tomorrow, in daylight, look behind your hut through the bamboo. I saw the tower. You check, too. It will be at your one o'clock somewhere behind you. We go out there."

"You sure?"

"Yeah, we go down a path beneath the tower, about forty feet to a good-sized stream. I carried lumber for them and saw guards take the path to bathe. It leads to a river."

"Got it."

I fell to the cage floor, faking sleep. After the guards passed, I resumed bending the wire, believing it would snap eventually. In the morning, I would search for the tower.

—

A light, unexpected rain began falling a few hours after sunrise and intensified throughout the next day. By mid-afternoon, when Julia was entering the clinic in Vientiane, a severe thunderstorm stalled directly over the prison camp. Rain and high winds lashed the cages and surrounding jungle relentlessly.

The guards ignored the prisoners, leaving us exposed to and suffering in elemental cruelty, subjected to a brand of natural agony far beyond anything they might have concocted.

We all shivered in the cold and shuddered from the lightning. It was only a matter of time before death claimed one or more of us.

I, however, appreciated the storm because it gave me time to work on my escape. I ignored the cold, the wind, the rain, and the thunder and lightning, and actually welcomed the coming darkness.

That Tender Light

My captor's negligence became a cloak under which I worked frantically to break the links of wire on one side of my cage. My previous attempts had failed because I could not devote enough time to flex the wire fast enough to snap it.

The storm changed my fortunes.

Starting at the bottom and again using my treasured nail as a lever, I bent the wire back and forth rapidly. In less than an hour, I had snapped two links. Six or seven more and I could squeeze through the opening. I knew my choice was now or never because, after the rain stopped and the storm cleared, the guards would discover the broken links. They would break my arms and legs, and, quite possibly, kill me.

"How you doing, Jackson?" asked Nick through the downpour.

"I've snapped two," I replied. "My fingers hurt like hell but the nail's working."

My plan was to get out, go to the hut where the guards stowed tools and somehow free Nick, Sing and the others. A pickaxe, crowbar, or steel rod would do the job. Then, we would find the stream and the river.

A door slammed suddenly and I stopped. I heard voices and laughter. Give me half a chance here, I thought. The door slammed again.

"Guard's coming," Nick warned.

I peered through the silver downpour. In the blue tint of lightning, I saw a guard coming across the compound carrying a wooden bucket—our evening meal! It would be rice with either fatty pork or boiled fish heads, usually the latter. Because of my intense focus, I had lost track of time.

Clearly, from his expression, the guard wanted no part of the storm. Oddly, I empathized with him.

I watched him walk to the farthest cage, push a bowl of food into it, and work his way down the line. As he moved from cage to cage, the rain slowed and then stopped completely. Moonlight peeked through a break in the clouds and everything was quiet.

D. James Then

Fingers of white mist drifted along the ground near the edge of the jungle. I studied the breaks I made in the wire links and looked at the guard. Why come now, you stupid bastard?

I moved to the front of the cage, using my body to hide my handiwork. As I did so, I heard the guards keys jangle and decided to kill the prick. I would get out faster. Then, I'd kill the other guards with the dead man's weapon.

I positioned the nail in my right fist, pointed-end out, tight between my second and third fingers. I held my clenched fist behind my back and watched the guard fill Nick's bowl. As he finished, the moonlight disappeared and rain began to fall, now heavier than before.

Be grateful for little favors, I thought, breathing easier. If the guard shouted when I punched him, the noise from the rain would muffle his cries. The guard ambled toward my cage and ducked instinctively as lightning struck somewhere nearby.

"Aye," he shouted, nearly tripping.

He laughed as a portion of my food sloshed from the bucket onto the muddy ground. The guard looked at the food and dumped whatever remained into my bowl. Then, he opened the feeding door and slid the bowl into my cage.

"Huh," he grumbled as he extended his arm to place the food on the cage floor. Lightning flashed again and the guard cowered. In that instant, with his attention diverted, I grabbed his outstretched arm and pulled him hard against the wire.

I drove the protruding nail into guard's left eye. I pulled it back, heard a sucking sound, and punched the guard twice in the right eye with equal force. He died immediately.

I held onto the man's arm, keeping him propped up, and stole a quick glance at the guard hut. No movement, no one was aware of my deed. I shifted the dead man's body slightly to the right, propped it against the cage, put my free hand through the feeding door, and found his keys. When I had them, I let the man fall to the ground. Seconds later, I was out.

Easy, I thought.

"Jack," Nick shouted.

That Tender Light

Another guard turned the corner and I reacted instinctively. I tightened my fist and, using the nail, punched the second guard in the temple several times. Again, a sucking sound signaled another death. I pushed him into the empty cage and closed the door. I freed Nick who, in turn, pulled the first guard into his cage. Nick picked up an AK-47 and tossed one to me.

"I'll go kill the guards," I said, "You free the others."

As Nick worked his way from hut to hut, I ran across the prison yard and peered through a window in the guard shack and saw five men playing cards and smoking cigarettes.

I crept to the door, unlocked the weapon's safety, and kicked in the door. As thunder rumbled in the sky, I fired short bursts, quickly killing all five.

I did a fast calculation: seven guards down. Only the lead guard remained. Where was that son of bitch? I turned and went back to Nick and the others.

"Seven of eight are dead. Let's get moving."

Sing spoke to the others and I assumed he told them they were on their own. Seconds later, the four Laotians disappeared in the darkness, their footprints hidden beneath puddles of water. We never saw them again.

"What did you say?" asked Nick.

"If you caught, you die," Sing replied.

"Which way do we go?"

"Jack, stay low and follow me," Nick replied, taking lead.

"I never found the tower," I said.

"I did," Nick said. "Quiet, I heard noise back this way when the rain stopped, a door slammed."

"You sure it's this way?"

"Yeah, the stream's down a gentle slope. With the rain, the water will be running high and fast."

"We follow stream to river," Sing said from behind. "I think Nam Ou. There are canyons, much growth, sometimes is busy."

"Okay," I replied, adrenaline pumping. We would need to be careful. My legs felt strong; my heart beat rapidly. Deep inside the thrill of killing warmed me, as it always did.

Lightning flashed again, revealing the outline of a tower.

"There," Nick said, pointing.

As we moved across the compound, I saw the lead guard exit an outhouse. He held an umbrella in one hand and adjusted his trousers with the other.

I did not hesitate. I jumped and shoved the barrel of my weapon deep into the man's left eye socket. I hit the son of a bitch repeatedly with the butt end of the weapon making his head a bloody pulp.

After a few more thrusts, Nick grabbed my arm.

"You can't make him any more dead, Jack," he whispered.

"He was taking a dump," I shouted. "We're suffering in the cold and this prick was taking his evening dump?"

"Stream here," Sing said, as he moved down the slope.

I followed Nick and a minute later, we found Sing standing beside fast-flowing, ink-like water. We moved downstream and disappeared into the night, three men seeking freedom. After walking several hundred feet, we stood at the edge of a thirty-foot cliff, watching water pour into a dark void. We heard but did not see the river below.

"I need a few seconds to breathe," Nick said. "You think anyone's following?"

"I doubt it. We killed them all. We're good until someone finds the bodies."

"My legs hurt," Sing said, breathing heavily.

"Mine, too," I added, "I slipped on every rock I stepped on. How deep you think it is down there?"

"I hope deep enough," Sing replied.

"Can you swim?"

"Good enough. I go first."

He jumped into the void.

A moment later, we heard his voice in the darkness.

"Come," Sing shouted, "is deep."

Nick and I went over together and soon the rapidly moving water carried us away. I had no sense of direction, I just knew the current was swift and the movement felt euphoric.

That Tender Light

I grabbed onto a large tree branch and, as I floated along, my feet occasionally touched soft river bottom. However, for the most part, I drifted along suspended in water.

I was hungry and tired, my wrist hurt, the bottoms of my feet ached, and I swallowed too much sand and sediment. Nevertheless, we were moving toward freedom.

It might have been one hour or five but when the rain stopped, the moon broke through the clouds, and thousands of stars laced the night sky. As our eyes adjusted in the moonlight, I saw weeds and tree limbs floating in the current.

Sing, in front some twenty feet away, grabbed several limbs, pulled them together, and hid his upper body. Nick and I did the same. On several occasions, we thought we heard a motor running in the water behind us but a boat never appeared.

"I think I jammed my wrist," Nick said, bobbing in the muddy water. "Are you cold?"

"I'm freezing."

"I lost my weapon when we went over the falls."

"Me, too," I said. "Can you hang in there?"

"For a while," Nick replied.

Perhaps, half an hour passed before Sing angled toward the shore. He crawled from the water and worked his way in behind a series of huge boulders, something was terribly wrong.

We hit the shoreline twenty yards away, in a towering canyon, and came out fast, feeling chilled to the core of our bones. We flopped next to Sing, who moaned in the darkness.

"Leeches," he whispered.

"Where?" asked Nick.

"All over," Sing said, shivering and removing his shirt.

Bloated black parasites covered Sing's back.

"Jesus," I whispered.

Sing removed the remainder of his clothes and suddenly, Nick and I realized the bloodsuckers covered our bodies, too. Nick dropped his shorts and hissed as he saw leeches on his genitals.

D. James Then

He pleaded, "How do I get them off?"

Sing picked up a sharp piece of shale.

"Like this," he said and began scraping leeches off his skin.

I tossed a piece of shale to Nick, found a piece for myself, and stripped. We cleared our genitals first; then, we removed the leeches as best we could from our legs and upper bodies. I scraped Sing's back and legs. Sing did the same for Nick.

Afterwards, they removed leeches from my back and legs. By the time we finished, the sun was rising. We were weak, tired, and hungry. Suck marks covered most of our bodies.

Nick stomped on the parasites.

"They make me gag," he said. "How do we keep them off?"

He watched Sing apply mud to his bites to draw down any swelling.

"If we do not protect ourselves in water, we won't."

"So, what do we do?"

"I think of something," Sing said.

We moved into the undergrowth to sleep and, as we did, the dark mud on our skin dried and became a light brown.

Chapter 20
That Tender Light

Sycamore Glen Farms, St. Omer, IN
3:09 a.m., Monday, October 20, 1986

IN THE BLACK of early morning, I moved next to Lily, spooning my body against hers with my arm around her naked waist. The fragrance of her bath powder insulated me from the all the wrongs of the world.

Lily awoke with my touch and noted the time: 3:09 a.m. So early in the day, we alone seemed to occupy the world. Instinctively, she moved close to me and for a while, the warmth of our bodies merged and we became one source of energy. We were in love and aware that we moved each other in ways neither could have accomplished alone.

"That was nice. Why were you awake?" she asked, when her heartbeat calmed.

Her question came on the edge of a husky whisper as moonlight slipped through the window and angled across the bed, creating various shades of pearl gray. She glanced toward the window and saw a clear sky with a bright moon and many stars.

"Did you hear me?"

"Yes," I replied.

"What's bothering you?"

"Sometimes," I began, "My past haunts me and I can't sleep. I try to comprehend things that happened."

She put her hand over mine.

"Are they bad things?"

"They're not good, Lily."

I heard her sigh and whispered, "I could a tale unfold, whose lightest word would harrow up thy soul, freeze thy young blood."

"Shakespeare's HAMLET...now, you're testing me."
"If the shoe fits..."
"What you dreamed, did it actually happen?" she asked, adjusting her pillow.
"Yes."
"You want to talk about it?"
I remained quiet for several seconds.
"Lily, do you really want to know?"
"Yes."
I considered her request.
"The bad dreams usually relate to war," I began. "Things I saw and did flow into one river of awareness. Often, they lack rhyme or reason. Sometimes they replay reality. It just depends."
"Is this from when you were imprisoned?"
"Not this time."
"But, it hurts?"
"It doesn't hurt; it defies logic. The person in my dreams is not the man I am today. I want to reach out, shake him, and say get the hell out of there. However, I can't change the past." I paused, adding, "Old scars, ragged memories."
"Does talking help?"
I searched for the right words.
"I've only discussed these things with Tommy."
"I'm a big girl."
She turned toward me, kissed my forehead, and cuddled tighter against my chest. I kissed her cheek.
"Please," she whispered.
"It began as shadow duty," I whispered. "Everyone in the unit pulled the duty occasionally, mainly for missions near the DMZ or over North Vietnam. This was before I went to Laos. We were aboard a chopper shadowing a C-47, which was gathering radio intelligence."
"Shadow duty?"

"Shadowing was a precautionary measure used during airborne intelligence missions, in case the aircraft went down. We were not especially sophisticated. Our orders were simple: retrieve or destroy classified documents and destroy all equipment before the enemy got to it."

"What about the men?"

"We were to save them, too, if we could. However, the classified stuff came first. It sounds absurd but, in retrospect, so was much of that war.

"On this particular day, we'd been airborne since dawn. The mission should've been easy because SAMs—surface-to-air missiles—had never been observed in that sector, despite its proximity to the Trail."

"Trail?"

"Ho Chi Minh Trail, originating in North Vietnam, it passed through Laos and then swung back into South Vietnam at various exit points. The C-47 carried linguists, radio operators, and intelligence analysts. They intercepted radio communications and relayed analyses to a ground commander, who used the coordinates for air strikes against enemy movement on the Trail.

"Early into the mission, around seven or eight in the morning, the C-47 lurched badly to the left. The pilot set it down in a small clearing, in an area that seemed deserted.

"We were half a mile out, with the sun at our back. We dove and hit the deck hard. The pilot—a kid from Pickens, South Carolina—landed near the crash site.

"We expected intense ground fire but surprisingly all was quiet; the war seemed foreign. The C-47 sat reasonably intact but, when we entered, we found all on board were dead, except two, and they were missing.

"Fourteen men had been aboard, Lily. We found twelve bodies. It was a mess and a damned tragic loss of incredibly good young men.

"In the brief time it took us to get to the crash site, the enemy managed to get in and take away the only two of the nine survivors who could walk. However, we knew seven others had survived the crash."

"But you mentioned twelve bodies?"

"Yes, nine men survived the crash but seven had injuries preventing them from exiting the aircraft. Charlie put a bullet into the backs of their skulls, execution style. They did not shoot the five who actually died in the crash. That's how we determined two survived without major injuries. They were the only men missing; the seven who could not leave were killed. It happened on both sides."

"It did?"

"Yes. Anyway, three of us stood guard while others melted the equipment."

"I don't understand."

"Handheld, flare-like devices, which emitted intense heat, they destroyed the equipment. We took codebooks, radio frequency guides, and any classified documents we found. We took dog tags, too.

"We'd been on sight only minutes when two enemy soldiers emerged from the jungle, to the left of the plane. They exited a series of tunnels used to move troops undetected. They took our men there. They returned for equipment and anything else salvageable. They didn't know we were shadowing the mission."

I paused and my arm tightened around Lily's waist.

"We killed them and I went into the tunnel for our men. I crawled thirty yards in the dark, moving cautiously toward muffled voices. I came to an underground room, about ten feet square. In smoky gray light from kerosene lanterns, I saw two blindfolded Americans guarded by two of the enemy. Their backs were to me and they had no idea I was there. I shot each one.

"After I freed our men, I realized I'd killed two young girls, barely teenagers. As we exited the tunnel, we encountered three more enemy coming from another direction. I killed each quickly because, in that war, you died if you stopped to think."

I paused. The bedroom was tranquil. Outside, the wind knocked sycamore branches against the farmhouse. Through a heating vent, I heard the furnace creaking and popping. I placed my hand on Lily's hip.

"I looked into their eyes before I shot them. Staring actually freezes people," I said. "A moment ago, I saw their faces in my dream. One was an old man, the second a young boy, and the third another teenage girl. Panic, confusion and a plea for mercy filled their eyes. They were afraid and vulnerable.

"Lily, I killed a boy, three girls and an old man—possibly their grandfather—all of us caught in a senseless war. Our men died as needlessly, too. I wonder why it had to happen, and why I was the man to do it."

Lily stroked my cheek.

"I cannot answer your question," she whispered, "I'm not qualified. However, if you hadn't killed them wouldn't they have killed you? If they had, you wouldn't be here with me. It sounds trite but it's true. You wouldn't have written your books or enriched so many lives."

"Maybe, maybe not."

We were quiet for a while.

"You must understand something," I whispered. "I loved it. I never could get enough. The rush associated with killing was addictive. Then, almost instantly, something changed and that light went out.

"Lily, I saw too many men die and suddenly I wanted it to stop, at least my part of it. My grandparents deserved the boy they reared to become a better man.

"Agreeing to do what I did in North Vietnam was a way out the madness. I fear I sold my soul that day. Now, I wish I'd never lifted a weapon." I paused. "Don't hate me."

"I'd never hate you. I didn't know you then," she said. "I don't believe what men do in war for their country or to save their lives is wrong. War itself is wrong, it's the real sin."

"And if a man realizes he likes it, what then?"

Lily did not answer.

"So many lives," I continued, "I've seen too much death in my time. I used to think I understood. As I grow older, I don't understand a damned thing. It was senseless for our men to die. My killing those people was senseless.

"What I did in Laos, too? What good came of it? Maybe it helped the peace effort, maybe not. I used to get high on killing. Our men didn't want to die, those kids and that old man didn't want to die, and I didn't want to kill them. Yet, it all happened. Does God ever forgive men like me? Deep in my bones, I don't think so."

She turned and kissed me.

"I believe God forgives but only if men or women forgive themselves." She kissed me, adding, "Once, I attended a lecture given by a Jesuit priest. He said man is so naive in his follies that God forgives him immediately for his transgressions, the same way we forgive a child for doing wrong. I believe God punishes those who start wars and not those who are forced to fight them."

I kissed the side of Lily's neck.

"I hope so, Lily. However, from time to time, I wonder if God comes after bums like me with a vengeance because we destroyed His creations."

"I sense you're wrong, Jack."

She caressed my face with the palm of her hand and this time my tears wet her fingertips. Lily held me and later, when my breathing evened, she relaxed her grip.

"I know this," I whispered, "I love you. And I want our love to last."

"It must," she replied. Moments later, Lily was asleep in the pearl gray of that early morning.

However, sleep never truly came for me and hours later, uncomfortably awake, I decided to work on my story:

Northern Laos
February 1973

I jumped off a cliff as I scrambled to get away from leeches. However, as I drifted in the night air, thousands of yellow eyes peered up at me from the jungle below.

Hundreds of men waited patiently as I floated downward, smug in the realization they would soon torment me. I could already feel the beatings they would exact.

My legs, back and arms ached terribly in anticipation and I felt blood trickle down the backs of my thighs. Suddenly, sucking leeches seemed more than bearable.

Drifting downward, I saw a rat perched on the shoulder of each man. The yellow, beady rodent eyes followed my descent with savory anticipation.

Before I hit the ground, I managed to glance eastward toward the horizon and was surprised to see sections of my hometown. I saw steel mills and the orange haze emanating from the blast furnaces as slag poured into Lake Erie. I smelled the sour-sweet sulfured air common to Lackawanna's First Ward. I cocked my head; I heard something. What was it? A saw whined as it sliced bar after bar of cold steel in the storage beds along Route 5.

Several blocks from the mills, a neon sign blinked at the Park Grill. We went there after playing softball in the field along the railroad tracks on the edge of Bethlehem Park, where I grew up. Many of my friends—Sonny, Beans, Doc, Carney, Joe, and Bob—were there, playing gin rummy and drinking Genesee beer, telling lies and laughing, as they always did.

D. James Then

I yelled to get their attention, to tell them to go to Canada and hide from the war. They did not respond. I looked more closely. Joe and Bob were ghosts in uniform and holding orders. I was too late! Each had already been to war and, oddly, I knew each man died.

Pete De Porte leaned on the bar, his left arm missing. Tetch Muzzuci lay beside a pool table in a hospital bed, bandaged from head to toe. Pat Brener shook like hell in the shadows.

The war reached beyond Laos and Vietnam. The decisions of the powerful hurt the common. Good boys died and for what? A fucking tragedy contrived and conceived by stupid men! Our mothers and fathers did not raise us to die in war—in a war that crept into the safe, little Italian neighborhood where I grew up in the shadows of steel mills, thousands of miles away.

I turned to my left and noticed my grandmother park her new Ford and walk into Our Lady of Victory Hospital, over in the city's Second Ward. Across the street, I saw Our Lady of Victory Basilica and Father Baker's orphanage.

Why didn't my grandmother see me? Why didn't she save me? Why didn't she stop the madness?

I turned right. Trains pulled coke and coal past a pond we called BARE ASS BEACH. We skinny-dipped there on hot summer days and lied about screwing Italian girls who would later become our wives. The train turned east and then south and crossed a three-tiered trestle where Red Collins fell some thirty feet into Smokes Creek, dizzy as hell from Pall Malls we stole from Socco's Grocery Store.

I felt homesick for my rusty old city, with its little houses, crooked fences, and neat little tomato and pepper gardens. Nothing ever looked so good. However, the rugged Laotian karsts soon blocked my view and I focused on insurgents and their rats awaiting my descent.

"I hate this," I thought.

I reached for my .45. I had it and a knife. Then, inexplicably, I saw myself fall feet first into a rice paddy, burrowing nearly up to my waist in mud.

That Tender Light

For a moment, I felt paralyzed, believing I had cracked my spine. I checked my hands and face for blood—nothing! I wiggled my toes in my jump boots. Soon, I realized fear had immobilized me.

I forced myself to breathe slowly and relax, to let my body go limp. My grandfather taught me the technique once when we were ice fishing on Lake Erie, when I was a boy. The ice cracked beneath us and we plunged into the slushy water. I was frantic as I struggled on the surface—my clothes wet, my boots heavy. I believed the weight would pull me under.

"Stop fighting, Jack," Tommy's calm voice said from somewhere behind. "Force yourself to relax, let your body go limp. You will float. As you do, swim to thicker ice and crawl out. You will be fine."

Sure enough, it worked.

I heard the old man's voice again, comforting, calming, always in control.

"Force yourself to relax."

I did and crawled quickly away. Covered with mud, I hid in the darkness, while the guards with their rats searched for me. For the time being, the mud was ersatz armor, the darkness my mother protector. However, it ended abruptly when a soldier stepped on my chest. The pressure made me grunt.

In the next instant, I opened my eyes.

Nick looked at me.

"You okay, Jackson?"

"Yeah, I was dreaming. What time is it?"

"Twilight...it'll be dark soon."

"You hear or see anyone?"

"A boat passed half hour ago," Sing said. "They look for us."

He held mangoes and jackfruit.

"God provides," he said. "You must eat."

I broke the fruit apart and ate it.

"How long have we been here?"

"Probably twelve hours," Nick said. "We'll move out in total darkness."

"Should we walk some?"

"Risky and hard," Sing said, "especially, if they look for us. We stay put until dark. Nam Ou is busy in daytime, trust no one."

"How far did we come?"

"Sing thinks we drifted nearly ten miles," Nick replied.

Sing looked at me.

"They have no idea we here. Best we avoid people."

"And you still believe this river is the Nam Ou?"

"Yes! It flows to Mekong and Luang Prabang. Places there are safe for us. We hide in day or people report us for money."

I noticed perspiration had created stripes in the dried mud on their skin.

"You've been working."

"Come see," Sing said.

Together we crawled away.

A few yards from the edge of the Ou, hidden by trees and thick grass, Sing showed me three floats he and Nick had fashioned from branches, vines, and palm fronds. In the center of each was a makeshift basket, space enough for a man to curl, concealed from view.

"It stop leeches," Sing whispered. "No one see us in dark."

"This little man's a genius; they'll act like sieves," Nick said.

Later, we floated in the darkness, staying ten yards apart, using branches as rudders. The floats enabled us to drift with our bodies below and heads above the surface, hidden in the center of leafy limbs, concealed in mesh-like baskets.

Nick heard the motor first. We had been in the water for several hours when a rumble came up river. Nick hissed softly to alert us and we quickly maneuvered to the shore. Soon, voices came across the water in the darkness and then we saw a yellow beam of light skim the surface, moving methodically back and forth, five hundred yards forward. The light paused on pieces of floating debris large enough to conceal men. We heard several shots.

"They're searching," I whispered, angling beside Nick.

That Tender Light

"You bet your ass."

"There," Sing advised, "fast."

He maneuvered us to a spot about twenty yards away beneath dense overhanging branches. Soon, we hid in thick weeds. As the boat chugged by, a man on the bow turned toward me and I saw his face in the moonlight. He was the same man I saw in the window at Muong Te and the same man who sat in the shadows in the Quonset near Ben Het. If our mission was about helping the peace process, why was a man associated with Tom Cline and Chubb Dailey on a boat, helping bad guys search for us?

"Did they see us?" asked Nick.

"No," Sing replied. "But something is odd."

I looked at him, saying, "The guy standing on the bow?"

Sing nodded.

"What about him?" Nick asked.

"He was with Cline and Dailey in Ben Het."

"He works for Cline, not Chubb," Sing clarified.

"Son of a bitch," Nick whispered.

"Exactly," I stated. "Cline is playing us and we need to find out why."

"We get out of this, I'm with you, Jackson," Nick added. Sing's nod said he was with me, too.

"First things, first," I replied. From my expression, Nick already knew Cline was a dead man. For some reason he sent us on this mission and, now, wanted us dead. It made no sense.

We crawled to a small rise and lay beneath aquilaria trees, which blossomed yellowish-green flowers. There, we listened to night sounds. Twenty minutes after the boat disappeared, we worked our way back to the river and slipped into the water, drifting away in the current as a light rain fell. The face of the man on the boat drifted with me. I would never forget it.

—

The next morning, the sun was warm and the air sweet; however, movement in the weeds made me open my eyes and listen cautiously. What was it?

D. James Then

For a moment, everything was quiet. Soon, I heard movement again. Not too far away the tall grass bent unnaturally. Someone, or something, was hunting us.

I nudged Nick and tapped Sing's shoulder.

"We have company!" I mouthed.

Nick crawled quickly to his left, as I moved to the right. Instinctively, Sing eased backward, barely noticeable in the tall grass. He removed a sharp piece of shale from his shirt; Nick did the same.

Once in position, I pressed myself low to the ground. My heart beat rapidly and I felt a pounding in my ears. I smelled the sweet, rich earth beneath my chin and noticed a colony of red ants working only inches away. They seemed unaware of my presence.

I took in a slow, deep breath to steady myself and searched for something to use as a weapon. Damn it! I wished I had the weapon I lost when we jumped into the Nam Ou. I turned slightly and felt a rock beneath my left leg. I took it from the dirt and held it in my right hand. I fisted my nail firmly into my left hand and waited.

I was nervous and afraid. Instinct told me to run; however, I held my position. Running usually meant death. Raw determination calmed me. Whether I lived or died, I vowed never to go into another cage or prison pen. Not again! No one would ever torture me or hurt my loved ones. Not ever! I wanted to live but I was prepared to die. I looked quickly at Nick and Sing. Similar resolve registered in their expressions.

Sing held up two fingers, indicating two people.

The grass moved, this time much closer. Tentative steps parted the grass and I heard heavy breathing. The footsteps paused, then, came again, cautiously. Something definitely sniffed a scent. My muscles tensed as I waited to attack.

Seconds passed, perspiration rolled off my eyebrows and the ants found their way up my elbow and crawled onto my forearm. I shivered as they tickled my skin and I blew on them, hoping they would scatter.

That Tender Light

Any minute, I thought, hearing louder movements. I was afraid but alert, agonized by the ants, ready to pounce, ready to kill when a large-headed animal abruptly poked its head through the tall grass.

I jumped back.

"It's a tiger," Nick shouted.

I kneeled, prepared to attack.

"Is not harmful, it's a dog, a chow," Sing said.

I lowered my arm. The dog walked toward me tentatively, sniffed my face, whined, and sat, panting."

"I'll be damned," I whispered, letting all tension ease from my anxious body.

The animal sniffed my hands several times, howled, went down on its belly, rested his head on my thigh, and licked the back of my wrist.

"Chu Li," a young voice shouted from within the grass, "Chu Li, where are you?"

The dog barked twice when it heard its name and began wagging its tail enthusiastically.

A young girl, perhaps ten, stepped through the tall grass, holding a burlap bag against her chest. She stood next to the dog and patted its head. The dog turned, sat up, looked at the girl, and licked her cheek. The child did not seem frightened by our appearance. A moment later, Nick sat on his heels in the grass and a soft smile crossed the child's face.

"You dirty," she said, pointing at his face, her English was a pleasant and complete surprise.

"Don't be afraid," I said, holding out my hand in a gesture of friendship. "Can you help us?"

Hearing more movement, she noticed Sing in the shadows.

"Oh my, three," she whispered.

For an instant, I believed she might turn and run; however, she stood her ground.

"You understand English, help us, please." I repeated.

"I think so," the girl replied softly. Then, raising her arm, she waved frantically.

"Pa," she yelled, "Come see Chu Li's men."

"We're coming, Ami," a male voice shouted back. The accent was Australian.

An older man, tall and wide of frame, limped through the thick grass, supporting his weight on a polished cane fashioned from the limb of a teak tree. Surprise registered in his wrinkled face. The little girl put her hand in his and half a dozen other children, clutching burlap bags, popped out from behind him, clearly anxious to see the cause of all the excitement. He smiled as he gazed on three dirty and desperate men.

"My name is Daniel Webster," he whispered, "but not of devil or dictionary fame. I'm a Cistercian priest from Australia. You must be the men our insurgent brethren are hunting."

He turned and whispered something to an older boy, who took off running.

Speaking to us, the tall cleric added, "You needn't worry, we'll hide and protect you. The children will be silent as church mice. Are you able to walk?"

"Yes," Nick replied. "Where are we?"

"Not far from Nong Khiaw, a lovely village. Please, follow me, and quickly. One never knows who's rummaging about."

The old priest watched me brush ants from my forearm and smiled.

"Let's get you out of here before those ants do lasting damage, if bitten by enough of them, the little scats can kill. I've ordered a meal and we'll get you a bath. Then, if God wills, you'll get to safety."

I shivered, removed the last ant, and followed the priest. Nick and Sing were already with the children.

—

The old cleric, now in obvious pain, shuffled into the room. His face ashen, he looked every bit of his seventy-eight years. He had mentioned his age as we reached the school.

He held a red lacquered cigarette case in his hands and offered us one. Nick and I declined. Sing took several with matches and placed them in his pocket for later.

That Tender Light

The priest looked at the open case.

"Do you mind if I burn one?" he asked.

"Not at all," Nick whispered.

"What happened?" I asked, referring to the priest's discomfort.

"I've a benign tumor near my spine with a mind of its own; sometimes it presses on the vertebrae, which makes walking a nightmare. A doctor at the Australian embassy told me it is growing in a spot that makes an operation dangerous. Therefore, I live with the pain, which crops up at the most inopportune times. If not removed, it will cripple me, but I'm too old. When it bites, I look like the ancient cuss I am. Oil of Agarwood with a drop of peppermint eases the pain. You've been beaten. It'll soothe you, too. I'll provide some to you."

He glanced at our appearance and smiled. We were wearing clothes the priest had taken from an old trunk.

"The good Sisters asked me to toss those clothes long ago. The fact I didn't affirms Ecclesiastes—to everything there is a season, and a time to every purpose under the heaven."

He struck a match, put it to the tip of his cigarette, and inhaled deeply. He exhaled, smiled, blew out the match, and tossed it into a nearby ashtray.

"My youngest sister sends me smokes from Melbourne; she usually mails a few dozen cartons twice annually. They often come in handy, especially if I need to pitch a trade. She sends them to me like clockwork, ever since I've lived in Laos, which is nearly half a century, now. I've served in this facility as its rector for forty of those years." He again examined our sartorial appeal. "I say you fellows look smashing." His smoke-filled voice reminded me of a rasp honing dry wood. "I trust you feel better after a good scrub," he continued. "The clothes aren't the best... clean and functional, though, hey?"

"They'll do, thanks," I replied.

"Was the meal adequate? Bread, rice, and fruit always suffice. You don't want rich food after your ordeal, just enough to stem the hunger and rebuild the spirit.

"Richer foods can come later. Titeu, our nurse, tells me she's provided salve for your leech bites. You must apply it. Nasty little buggers...you're lucky you removed them. Can kill a man, they can."

He looked at me mischievously, "Similar to those ants." He chuckled and pulled a chair from against the wall. As he sat, he sighed. "Sitting relieves some of the pressure," he whispered. His face quickly regained its color. "You should know men are searching for you. It's only a matter of time before they return. I'd say a day or two. They were here yesterday morning, but departed after a quick inspection."

He perceived our concern.

"Not, to worry," he quickly added. "You won't stay in any of these buildings. We'll move you shortly up the hill, where it's much safer. I have already sent word to the Australian Embassy in Vientiane, confidentially and discreetly, of course. We have codes you know. They'll take up your cause."

"Is this an orphanage?" asked Nick.

"No, 'tis a school. Our children are not orphans; they belong to our sick. We serve those afflicted with leprosy. We will hide you shortly in the anteroom to our leprosarium, which is on the hill above the school buildings. Actually, the sisters will take you. The way my back feels, I think it best I stay here."

He motioned toward the window and a series of pale buildings half a mile away.

"You'll be safe. Most locals are superstitious concerning leprosy. We have never seen anyone venture near the leprosarium—not even the Pathet Lao. It is taboo.

"As I said, our children are not orphans. They're the offspring of lepers; we care for them because their parents cannot. However, though not orphans, our children are indeed outcasts. God has placed them in our hands and in our care. We educate them and give them a reasonably good life. All will finish our version of secondary school and some will go on to university in Bangkok or Vientiane. They're adorable."

He wiped his sweaty brow and changed the subject.

"Back to where you will stay; once you are inside the leprosarium you'll be safe. We must wait for my embassy's directions; I'm sure someone will come for you."

Noticing Sing's obvious concern, the priest spoke with compassion.

"Sing, is it?"

"Yes."

"Sing, does leprosy scare you? You seem afraid."

Sing nodded.

"Trust me, you've nothing to fear," the priest stated. "Let me give you an orientation. Leprosy or Hansen's disease is a chronic illness caused by bacteria. Mycobacterium leprae is the scientific name, a term I doubt you will ever use or retain. It replicates quite slowly. Its incubation is about five years but symptoms may take as many as twenty years to appear.

"Leprosy, while contagious, isn't highly infectious. Transmission occurs via droplets, from the nose and mouth, during close and frequent contacts with untreated cases. It's the reason we separate the children from their parents. Leprosy affects the skin and nerves and, if untreated, can inflict progressive and permanent damage to the skin, nerves, limbs, and eyes.

"Fortunately, a momentary encounter does one no harm. So, Sing, you have nothing to fear. Where we hide you, you do not come in direct contact with lepers. We'll take you to an anteroom where the children go to visit their parents.

"We sterilize it with antiseptic and we'll supply surgical masks to impede any possible inhalation, if you prefer. Considering your plight, and knowing discovery is a probability in the school or the rectory, you have no other choice.

"You'll be safe inside. We'll feed you. The sisters are readying for the journey as I speak. As I said, the leprosarium is up on the hillside." He paused and added, "God must favor you. It seems more than dumb luck we were near the river. You are only about a hundred kilometers from Luang Prabang. With luck, you will be there soon. From there, you'll go to Vientiane."

He paused and smiled.

"This is beautiful country, with great mountains. Too bad you're on the lamb and miss most of the beauty."

"We have been busy," I replied. "We were surprised by the child's English."

The priest smiled.

"I take full responsibility," he replied. "They learn the language from a young age. It will help them as adults."

"What were you doing by the river?" Nick asked.

"This time of year, the children and I hunt paper mulberry shoots, which grow wild in fertile soil, quite abundantly. We collect and nurture the shoots and sell them to farmers all over Laos who, in turn, cultivate them. Its fruit is sweet. Its bark has a particularly strong fibrous composition especially useful when producing high-quality paper.

"The paper mulberry's tender leaves and twigs are often used to feed deer. Venison is a delicacy. Many in Laos raise deer. I guess you could say we were being capitalists, when our little Ami and Chu Li, as she calls him, happened upon you. Our dog's name is Charlie, after Prince Charles; it has unusually big ears for a chow. Chu Li is the best Ami can do.

Now, an important question, do any of you play chess?"

―

A nun took us up the hill in a cart pulled by oxen. She steered the cart behind the building to an entrance obscured by lattices of vines and apricot flowers.

"I'll secure the door, when I leave," she said. She told us her name was Sister Henrietta, originally from New Zealand.

"A small room's off the entrance with a pot to relieve oneself," she said, handing a sack to each of us. She pointed to a small window. "If anyone besides Father or a nun tries to enter, go through the door on the far side of the anteroom and into the ward. Go to the first room on the left and wrap your face, hands, and feet with gauze from the sacks. Each contains a vial of duck's blood—it seems human; pour it on the gauze around your mouth and fingertips. It's a quick disguise."

That Tender Light

She smiled and shrugged apologetically.

"It's the best we can do."

She asked us to bow our heads and said a prayer in Latin. Then, she smiled warmly and kissed our foreheads.

"My mother always kissed my brothers, sisters, and me for good luck as we left the house. It can't hurt."

"Thank you," Nick whispered.

"I pray God protects you," Sister Henrietta whispered. "I'll return in the morning with more food when we come to feed the sick. Please, don't be afraid, our patients are good people. They need as much protection as you do. They'll be silent if someone's about, you should, too."

She closed the door and we heard her lock it from the outside.

Sing immediately wedged a chair against the doorknob for added protection.

Afterward, we dosed on padded wooden benches, feeling warm and protected by the faint smell of ammonia in the air.

Chapter 21
That Tender Light

Sycamore Glen Farms, St. Omer, IN
11:11 a.m., Tuesday, October 21, 1986

I WAS WRITING in the library and heard the phone ringing in the hallway.

"I'll get it, Jack," Lily yelled from upstairs.

Since my concentration snapped, I stood and went into the kitchen to refill my coffee cup.

I was about to return to my story when I heard Lily coming down the stairs. She kissed my cheek, smiling.

"An important call?"

"Yes and an unexpected one. The department chair has had an emergency appendectomy. He selected me to represent him and the English Department at meetings with Hannlin's president and its board. We recently submitted a proposal to expand the department and it's been deemed worthy of decisional review."

"When will you leave?"

"This evening and I'll only be away for a few days. I'll stay at my apartment."

"Do you want company?"

"Yes, but I'm afraid it wouldn't really work. The meetings usually run most of the day. Because I'm filling in for the department head, I'll cast his vote on various other issues that arise regarding Hannlin's long-term goals. I expect the next three days will be extremely busy and fairly intense."

"Okay, what time will you leave?"

"About four this afternoon," Lily replied. "I'll be back for sure late Friday afternoon. Right now, I need to run into town, pick up a few things and then I'll come back and pack. I'm actually looking forward to the opportunity."

That Tender Light

"Well then, I'll stay here and write."

She walked over, kissed me, and went back upstairs.

I nodded, sipped my coffee, and went into the library. I was nearing the end of my story:

Vientiane, Laos
February 1973

When she heard the bell jingle above the clinic's outer door, Julia glanced at the time. It was a few minutes after 6 p.m. She paused, stretched her back, and refocused, asking the nurse beside her to remove the infant's diaper.

Julia began her day before sunrise and she had been on her feet ever since. She briefly rotated her head to ease the strain in her neck. More than anything, she wanted to sit and read, sip a cup of tea, and then sleep. She smiled at the baby. She assumed the child would be the day's final patient. However, recalling the bell, if someone needed her, she would stay.

She heard a man's voice in the outer room but, as the baby cried, Julia became intent on eliminating the child's irritation. She examined the baby's rash, cleansed it, and told the nurse which antiseptic cream she wanted. A moment later, as she applied the salve, the baby's cries turned to deep sobs and then disappeared into quiet contentment.

"Much better, isn't it sweetheart," Julia whispered, tickling the little girl's chin with her knuckle. She kissed the child's forehead. She looked at the nurse and said, "Not terribly difficult, huh?"

The nurse smiled.

A moment later, an assistant entered the small examination room.

"Doctor Ormandy?"

"Yes, Syha, do have we another patient?"

"No, a man's here for you... sent by Elgin Dailey."

Jack Taylor!

Julia looked away. She did not want anyone to see her fear.

Jesus, please let him be alive!

She took a deep breath and when she turned to respond to her assistant, Julia's expression was again professional.

"Tell him I'll be along presently, Syha," Julia replied. "I must finish here."

"Certainly, doctor," the assistant answered.

He cannot be dead, Julia thought, as she applied more cream. She quickly diapered the infant and removed her surgical gloves.

"Take the baby to her mother," Julia said to the nurse. "Give her a supply of diapers, a bar of cleansing soap, and enough antiseptic cream for two weeks. Explain how she must wash the rash using only that soap and warm water and tell her to apply the antiseptic cream three times a day. Explain that her baby is fine and the rash will disappear."

She watched the nurse cradle the child in her arms and depart. Then, after Julia washed her hands, she took a deep breath, forcing calm throughout her body.

"May I help you, sir?" she asked, entering the waiting room. She held out her hand, "Julia Ormandy."

The man shook it and said his name was Max Ruehl.

She turned to her assistant.

"Syha, may I have a moment alone with the gentleman."

When the door closed, Julia said, "You've a message for me from Elgin?"

"I do, doctor."

He handed her a small yellow envelope.

Julia held her breath, as she removed a folded piece of notebook paper.

She sat on a child's chair, read the missive, and tears slid down her cheeks.

"Good news, I hope," the man said softly.

She breathed deeply to maintain control.

"The best," she replied, reading the note again. Dailey's simple message read: *Julia, he is safe, and is en route to Vientiane.*

That Tender Light

Julia stood and smiled, no longer embarrassed by her tears. She leaned forward and, quite unexpectedly, kissed Ruehl's cheek. He felt her warm tears against his skin.

"In ancient times the messenger kept his life. Here, good news also earns a kiss. Please, extend my gratitude to Elgin."

"I will," Ruehl said, instinctively touching his cheek as he left.

Julia read the note again, held it against her rapidly beating heart; she bowed her head. Thank you, she thought, thank you for answering my prayers.

—

Two days later, at 5:04 a.m., I stood at the window, thinking I heard thunder. I parted the heavy drapes slightly and looked into the darkness. Stars filled the sky and, at the bottom of the hill, candles flickered through the windows of a small chapel. Beyond the school, a circle of eight lanterns stood in an open field, which I thought peculiar.

Behind me, Nick and Sing slept soundly on wooden benches. We had not heard a sound in the adjacent ward since we arrived, although I guessed the lepers knew of our presence.

Yesterday, at sunset, when Sister Henrietta and another nun brought our food, she delivered a note from Father Webster. The message: *contact made, be ready.*

I noticed a human form slip past a school window.

"Nick, Sing," I whispered, "Movement below. They're looking for us."

An instant later, a key slid into the outer lock.

"It's Sister Henrietta," a voice whispered through the heavy wood, quickly easing our tension. "You must hurry; they've come for you from the Embassy!"

Sing removed the chair and, when the door opened, the nun stood with two men.

"We've a chopper below, sir; follow me," the voice was Australian. "My men are guarding the school. Double-time it, lads!"

I looked at the nun, who smiled at me.

"Father Webster?" I inquired.
"With the children, his back...you must go."
"Thank you and thank him for everything."
She watched us run down the hill toward the helicopter.

Within minutes, the chopper disappeared into the night sky and as it banked to the left and headed for Luang Prabang, I saw Sister Henrietta and another nun, dousing the lanterns in the field beside the school.

I put my head back and closed my eyes.

I thought about holding Julia and I wanted to see my grandparents.

CHAPTER 22
THAT TENDER LIGHT

Sycamore Glen Farms St. Omer, IN
7:18 p.m., Wednesday, October 22, 1986

LILY AND I spoke that evening.

"So how was your first day as acting department chair?"

"Boring," she giggled. "No, not true, our work is important for the faculty and students; it will shape the college for the future. I miss you. I can't wait to see you."

"I feel the same way."

"We have something important going on, don't we?"

"Yes, I think we do."

"I can't talk long; we're getting ready for dinner with the president and the board."

"Not a problem, you do what you must do for the sake of good old Hannlin and I'll go back to writing my story."

"Do you like what you're hearing?" She asked, giggling.

"It sounds pretty good and the end is near. I'm hoping to have it finished by the time you return."

"You are that close?"

"Yes, be good, I love you."

"I love you, too. Jack, you're the best."

As I wrote, I was unaware that in a few hours our lives would change forever:

Fuchu Air Station, Japan
February 1973

Tom Cline stood when his office door opened. His guest's expression was serious, his eyes intense, and Cline knew immediately that the news was not good. He hated bad news. Lately, there had been far too much of it. He wished he had retired a few years ago. He pointed to chairs near the window.

D. James Then

In the distance, Mount Fujiyama stood prominently against a magnificent sky in afternoon sunlight. In nearby rice paddies, workers spread fertilizer. The scene was picturesque, despite the odor.

"What have you learned?" Cline asked, pouring coffee.

"Taylor and the others are alive," the man said, lifting a cup.

"Damn it," Cline said, "I had it all arranged and delivered the money. Why?"

His man shrugged and sniffed the air. "This is not a reference to our friends in nearby paddies, but shit happens."

Cline shook his head. "That's not good enough. Do you think Dailey or General Jacobs knows about me?"

"Not yet, how could they?"

Cline rubbed his tired eyes. "Still, I wonder. Nothing would surprise me. How did they get out?"

"I went to the camp. Somehow, one man, my guess either Kunz or Taylor, managed to overpower and kill a guard by driving a stick or something through the man's eye. The dumbass guard had keys on him. They all escaped. They killed the guards and left, probably floating in the Nam Ou, although I cannot be sure. I helped search from a patrol boat."

"And?"

"Nothing...not a trace. It's a busy river but no sightings."

Cline did not hide his dissatisfaction. He hated fuckups.

"They are stupid and idiotic...I never should have approached those clowns."

"I might have insight," the guest added, "A source in Luang Prabang reported a helicopter lifting off several hours before dawn yesterday morning from an Australian compound. Two hours later, after sunrise, the copter returned.

"You're thinking Taylor and the others?"

"Yes, I am."

"Then, they'll go to Vientiane," Cline whispered, "You hustle back there and learn what you can. I'll follow tomorrow. Let's kill these fools and be done with it."

—

That Tender Light

We went to the American Embassy in Vientiane, where we recuperated and were debriefed. General Jacobs visited and told me about the Peace Accord and said I would receive the Medal of Honor. I told the general I never wanted the Medal. He said, "It's a done deal. You're going to San Diego."

By his expression, I knew any argument was futile.

"Sir, a favor please," I said. "I've met someone, a Canadian doctor who's with IASS. She and I are in love."

The general was surprised.

"I'll be damned," he replied. "Good for you."

"She doesn't leave Vientiane for a few months. I'd like some time with her before I go; I have thirty days leave coming, sir."

Telling him I also wanted to find and kill Cline was never a consideration. When Cline turned up dead, if they ever found his body, I did not want the general's suspicion focused on me.

"Jack, I can get you ten days, maybe two weeks; however, per orders, you go stateside. The Army likes Medal recipients back on home soil. If you were still in Vietnam, you'd have to leave immediately. I think I can swing an exception. I'll just say you need time to recuperate before travelling."

"Thank you, sir."

"God speed, Jack."

—

I watched the general's automobile disappear around a corner and took a cab to join Nick and Sing at a restaurant a few blocks from That Dam, a stupa very near the center of Vientiane.

"Did you find him?"

Nick sipped whiskey and nodded.

"He's in a suite at the Cheaux Hotel," Sing whispered.

"Is anyone with him?"

"Never after 4 p.m.," Sing added.

"Nick, what about the guy on the boat?"

"I talked to Max Ruehl. He says the guy is Cline's assistant and bodyguard."

"Do you think he suspects anything?"

"Max? I doubt it; in fact, I led the conversation in such a way that he was the one who brought it up."
"Good."
I looked at each man, asking, "Any reservations?"
"No," Sing replied. I already knew Nick's answer.
"Do we do this today?"
They nodded simultaneously.
"I say, yes," Nick whispered. "Cline's man usually leaves Cline's suite about 4 p.m. and meets a woman a few miles away. They typically spend the night and he returns in the morning."

Just as Nick had described, Cline's assistant, departed the hotel at 3:55 p.m. Sing followed him, returned forty minutes later and said, "He's with the woman."

"Let's rock and roll, Jackson," Nick encouraged.

Sing drove us to the side of the hotel on Rue Toulan and waited as Nick and I walked through a secondary entrance and took the stairs to the second floor.

"His is Room 204," Nick said and went to get into position.

Seconds later, I walked down the hallway. Nick stood on one side of the door; I was on the other. He nodded and I knocked four times.

"Just a moment," Cline said from somewhere inside.

When the door opened, I quickly pushed into the room. Cline was holding a knife and nicked me several times, one cut was near my temple. When Nick tackled him, Cline's knife and a revolver flittered across the wooden floor. Nick's chokehold quickly rendered Cline unconscious.

We taped his mouth, hands and feet, rolled him in bedding, and hustled him to the automobile, where Sing waited. We were in and out in less than five minutes.

No one saw us. We drove southeast out of the city, heading toward Xieng Khuan, an area devoted to religious sculptures. However, along the way, Sing took a side road. Religious icons would not help Cline.

After several kilometers, we stopped in an isolated and wooded area, not far from the Mekong River. We stood Cline up, taped him against a tree, and revived him with cold water. We wanted answers. He broke fast and at times whimpered like a child. The third needle under a fingernail did the job.

"It all has to do with money, what else?" he groaned. "Jesus, are you stupid?"

"Money?"

"Yeah, money and drugs and you three stupid asses and Dailey never realized you were being played."

"What about that peace process bullshit you laid on Jack and me in the jungle?" Nick asked.

"That was real. They were viable targets; however, Si Duc had nothing to do with drugs. It helped; Nixon got his accord."

"Why drugs?"

"Winning takes money and tactics that governments don't always fund. A French agent I knew had a connection to Giang and Matiere."

"*Knew*, I take it he has conveniently disappeared."

"You learn quickly, Taylor. Matiere wanted to retire well, he wanted a nest egg; I don't know about Giang or give a shit. We funneled money to them and they routed drugs to us via drops along the Ho Chi Minh Trail. We picked the stuff up, turned it around, and made a tidy profit. Everyone made money, lots of it."

Nick punched Cline hard in the face, breaking his nose.

"You piece of dirt, you sold drugs to fund your bullshit activities."

Cline spit blood and I noticed he lost several teeth. His comb-over was hanging hideously over his left ear. The skin of his white scalp had many liver spots.

"Yeah, pretty slick, huh?" he offered.

I choked him hard, saying, "Why did you send your man to Muong Te; you knew we were going there? Why risk it, it makes no sense. Are you really that dim?" I rammed a knee into his groin, failing to control the contempt swelling in my chest.

"I had to risk it," Cline said coughing. "He always went to pay Matiere and Giang the day they arrived. If they didn't get half their cash that day, they'd up the price and delay delivery. We needed product to keep everyone content. Other suppliers are a few months away from meeting demand. My hope was you would actually need fifty-five hours. I didn't know you'd run a fucking marathon to get there and be in the trees."

"Nixon got his accord. We're pulling out of Vietnam. Why kill Giang and Matiere?" Nick asked.

"They were legit targets. Who knew an accord would come so fast or we'd leave so quick? I thought a year or two. Giang and Matiere's price doubled recently because they sensed the sugar tit going dry. Hell, it might have tripled; it is too much to pay. I didn't trust them. If I cut them off cold turkey, they'd talk, and I'd be fucked. They've talked anyway. From day one, I cultivated new sources for the operation. As noted, that production was coming on-line, with a better price, and I didn't need Giang or Matiere. Since you were going to kill Si Duc, I figured why not take out Giang and Matiere. Smooth, huh?"

"The peace accord screwed you anyway."

"I'll take it all to a new assignment," he said. "I don't stop."

"You downed our chopper," Nick said.

Cline shrugged, saying, "The cost of doing business, ace. What were a few lives in the scheme of things? You were supposed to die in that crash. If not, they had agreed to shoot you. The boys I hired double-crossed me; they took you prisoner. Despite any mistreatment, you actually lucked out." He spit blood. "Let me go. You can each have two million. I'll make it happen, today. Money can get us past this. The war is over, let bygones be bygones."

"You set us up, tried to kill us, and we suffered," Nick said.

"We don't want money," I added. "The price is Sing's daughters. I'd bet money you know all about Matiere's fetish."

He suddenly wanted to believe we would let him go.

"They're in a brothel in Hanoi, off Trang Tien Street, not far from the Opera House," he said, giving the name and location.

"I know this street," Sing said.

"Can you get word to them?" Nick asked.

"Yes, if they know I am not disgraced, they come home. I know people to help," Sing added.

"Matiere puts all his used whores there." Cline spat blood.

"My daughters are no whores," Sing said, punching him.

Cline chuckled and said, "If you say so, you little shit."

Those were Cline's last words. After I put a knife in his heart, we buried his body in a shallow grave and drove away. Sing smiled but did not speak.

—

Julia and I were together every day and night for the next two weeks, passionately together. The bond we formed before the mission to Muong Te had crystallized; we were inseparable.

Sometimes, in the many soft moments we shared, I studied Julia's face, as I would a masterpiece. I discovered it changed in the light or with varying angles—always beautiful, always breathtaking, at once a mystery and a certainty. She was remarkably different from any woman I had ever known. She possessed quiet intensity, unyielding confidence, and a rare, often carefree, ebullience. Her deep intelligence anchored every action, thought, and comment.

Her surprise was genuine when I questioned it one night as we lay in her hotel room, not far from the clinic, gazing into the sky searching for shooting stars from a bed near the window.

"Is it obvious?"

"It is to me."

I felt the rise and fall of her breathing as she pressed against me, her back against my chest and my arm around her waist.

"Truly?"

"As sure as the sun rises."

"I didn't realize you noticed."

She was quiet.

"You won't tell me?" I said, squeezing her.

She giggled.

"Tell you what?"

"Your dreams; things you hope for, what you want from life."

"I'm not complicated," Julia said, laughing and facing me.

"Good."

"And, just so you know, it embarrasses me to discuss this."

"Hey, sweetness, it's me."

"I know," she replied and kissed my cheek.

"So, tell me."

"Well, because you insist, I guess I'll open up." She paused and sighed. "I've always believed I could do or have anything I wanted. My father reinforced that each day of my life. He believed the more a person knows, the easier life will be and, you know, he was correct."

"Your dad's a wise man."

"He believes the best minds will win in the end, regardless."

"Regardless of what?"

"Man or woman, king or queen." Again, she giggled. "I dream old-fashioned dreams."

"I like old and I like fashion, like those white lace dresses one sees in second-hand stores."

She poked my ribs.

"You know I didn't say old fashion!"

"I know," I kissed her forehead. Her skin was warm, she smelled lovely.

"Okay, here goes. First, I want to be deeply in love, until the end of my life. I want that feeling daily. Second, I want to be the finest wife and a mother. Third, I want to be the best pediatrician ever."

"Ever, as in for all time?"

"Ever, as in all time," she said, laughing at the way I teased her. "Now, it's your turn, anything beyond writing, tough guy?"

"Only you?"

"That goes without saying."

"I know. Just that I'll write books. When I leave in a few days, I'll begin to write books people will want to read repeatedly, books exploring the human condition, books people will discuss for years. They'll be your only real competition."

"As long as I live I'll have no rivals. You're mine; I'm yours."

"We must make a living, a good one, I hope. You'll be a rich doctor and I'll write great books."

"It's wise to dream the dream of kings."

"Or queens, or the dream of those who want to be the best ever...as in for all time. Neither road will be easy, I suspect."

"Sans doute," she whispered. "But you'll find a way, as will I. I'll be in love everlasting with a famous writer."

She smiled and kissed me. Her mouth was sweet from the dark chocolates we nibbled.

"You'd think it's important?" she asked

"Fame or love everlasting?"

She kissed my chin.

"Your gratitude for my love everlasting is assumed. I meant fame, of course."

"Only if it pleases you," I whispered.

"Would you write a book about me, if I asked?"

"Sure, about the best pediatrician ever?"

"No, silly, about your one and only everlasting love," she replied, pinching the skin on my forearm.

"An easy book to write," I suggested.

"Then, one day you must."

She moved into me and we became one in body and spirit as several shooting stars whipped across the sky. As we made love, Julia felt the earth's power at her fingertips and when she touched my back, she passed that power to me. Hearing her murmur, I leaned and kissed her forehead.

"Will you marry me?"

"I decided that weeks ago, when you first touched my face. Yes and we'll be together 'til the end of time."

Julia's eyes sparkled in the moonlight and I knew we were destined for each other and nothing could destroy us.

However, as she slept in my arms that night, as we laughed and talked, and as we watched sunrises and sunsets—in everything we shared—I was painfully aware of human frailty. I prayed we would grow old together in days not yet known.

Chapter 22
THAT TENDER LIGHT

Sycamore Glen Farm, St Omer, IN
7:12 a.m., Thursday, October 23, 1986

THE NEXT MORNING the farmhouse was quiet and after taking care of Sam, I went into Lily's library, with a cup of coffee in hand. I only had a few pages left to write and I knew it would not take long to complete my story. I reread the pages I wrote after I spoke to Lily the day before and soon I was back in Laos:

Vientiane, Laos
March 1973

The remainder of our two weeks slipped by quickly and before I returned to the States, Julia wanted to have a picnic. She left early for the clinic the morning of my next to last day and, before departing, suggested I meet her at three. She said she would visit a few patients in the afternoon and, afterward, we could picnic on a spot above the Mekong.

"You'll love it, the sunset is breathtaking," she said when I arrived at the clinic that afternoon. She was radiant in a white dress and white sandals.

"How long have you been planning this?"

"A while," she replied, smiling.

A hired driver took us out along the river and, when the car stopped, Julia pointed to the location downriver.

"It's only a few hundred yards away," she said. "I'll walk over after I see my patients. You can get everything ready." She handed me a bottle of red wine. "It's French; I bought it yesterday near the Palace."

I looked at the bottle.

"Is it dry?"

"Of course," she replied, giggling, knowing my preference.

That Tender Light

"When we open the bottle, remember don't judge until your second sip," she said, "The second sip is always sweeter."

"Okay, love," I said, kissing her cheek, "Don't be long."

She told the driver when to return and departed.

—

Before sunset, in the part of day when light lingers and night beckons, I saw Julia walking on the sandy shore.

Tanned, beautiful, and dressed in white. She was my love. Even at a distance, I could see it in her eyes. In a matter of weeks, we would be together, forever.

I smiled when she emerged from trees near a bend in the river. I watched the elegant way she walked and the erotic sway of her hips.

As she moved along the river's edge, I noticed the dancer's bounce in her step. Here and there, she came near the water's edge. Then, as she moved toward me when she neared an eddy some fifty yards away, she removed her sandals, trailing footprints in the wet sand. She waved and smiled.

"I'm here," she yelled. "Sorry, I took longer than expected."

"I took a nap. Are you hungry?"

"Famished," she replied.

"I drank all the wine," I shouted.

"I doubt it."

Clouds blocked the sun and the shadows softened her beauty as her shoulder-length, auburn hair floated like strands of fine silk in late-day breezes.

The wind molded her flowing white dress perfectly against her lithe body.

As she drew nearer, I could see she appeared to be singing and I fell in love with her all over again. As she neared the point where the shoreline curved up to the trees where I stood waiting, a dog barked.

As I turned to find the animal, a burning sensation ignited on my left side. I spun around. As I fell to the ground, Julia screamed and I yelled to her to get down but I was much too late and I knew it.

I felt another burning sensation from a second shot, but managed to turn my head. The front of Julia's white dress was now crimson. She fell to her knees and her body whipped forward as another shot tore into the back of her neck. Before she hit the sand, I knew she was dead.

Another shot grazed my shoulder and, as I rolled over, I whispered Julia's name. Before I lost consciousness, thoughts of payback entered my mind, payback for the lives I had taken.

—

I opened my eyes a week later and saw Nick Kunz sitting beside the bed. I looked at him and started to tremble.

Nick leaned over the bed and hugged me, until my trembling subsided. After a while, I heard aircraft departing.

"Where am I?"

"In Thailand, Udorn Air Base," he replied.

"Why?"

"Jacobs ordered you out, you're going home. He was told it was a random attack, but is skeptical because of Muong Te."

How long have I been here?"

"About a week."

"Julia?"

"I'm sorry," Nick whispered.

I put my face in my hands and sobbed.

"This is so terribly hard...why Julia?"

"I don't know, Jackson." Nick squeezed my hand. He studied my face. He whispered into my ear, "If it's any consolation, I killed the man who shot you and Julia."

I looked at him, surprised, and said, "What?"

"Your driver, Jack, they used the driver; paid him four hundred dollars. I killed him."

"Who?"

"The replacement driver was the shooter, Jack. I've not told a soul and won't. When you came into the hospital, you were semi-conscious and rambling. The doctor told me you mentioned a picnic with Julia. I went to the clinic and found out who drove that day. IASS uses a contract company."

That Tender Light

"Julia's normal driver was out ill," I said, remembering.

"It seemed too convenient for me," Nick said. "I found him and he told me he received a hundred dollars to be ill. Before he died, he told me who his replacement was. I found him and, before he died, he told me Xia Julang paid him to kill you."

"Who's that?" I inquired.

"Cline's man," Nick replied,

"He must have suspected we took out Cline and wanted to cover his ass. How do you know this, Nick? Can you be sure he was responsible?"

"Sing and I followed the piece of shit and caught him in an alley. He confessed and I put a knife through his temple. Nobody knows, except you and Sing. Nobody cares, Jack."

I closed my eyes.

"What we did will haunt me, forever, Nick," I whispered. I turned and looked out the window at the blue sky. "It's my fault," I said. "All of it. I made the deal. I didn't need the mission; the Medal would've taken me home. If I had accepted the Medal earlier, Julia would be alive and none of this would have happened."

"I know it hurts and I know you don't want to live. That is how I felt when my mother died. Whatever you do in life from this day forward, do it for Julia, earn the love she gave you."

"I'll try," I replied. "I'll carry this war with me forever."

"We all will. They used all of us, each day and in every way."

Niagara Falls, New York
February 1975

Winter birds sang and daylight was creeping over the icy treetops. I sat up, found my shoes, and stood up. My feet were cold but otherwise okay. I was lucky I had tucked them under my heavy overcoat. I wiggled my feet into the shoes.

I stooped, picked up my leather portfolio, looked at the river for a few seconds, threw the manuscript into the rapids, turned, and limped away.

It took five minutes to hobble back to my car, parked in a nearby lot. I sat inside, started the engine, and turned on the heater to warm the interior. I placed the portfolio on the seat beside me.

As I warmed myself, I looked in the review window and saw a maintenance man approaching. He knocked on the driver's window and I rolled it down half way.

"Are you okay mister? I saw you come from the river's edge a moment ago. You must be cold, you need help?"

"No," I lied. "I was watching the rapids. I'm a writer."

The man, dressed in a park uniform, looked into the car and saw my portfolio on the seat. He studied my drawn face.

"For some reason, I don't think you were just watching. Stay right here, I have something to help you."

The man ran to his truck and came back with a towel and half a pint of brandy.

"Better rub your hands with the towel to warm 'em up. They look a little frostbit to me."

"They'll be fine."

He gave me the brandy and he motioned toward the river.

"I can't say you weren't watching the rapids, but I've seen jumpers and I'll say one thing, you go in there, mister, you won't live to write another word."

I placed the bottle on the seat next to the portfolio, noticed a few written pages I missed and quickly removed them.

"Are you collecting garbage?"

"Sure."

I gave the pages to him.

"Throw these away and promise me you won't read then."

"I'm not the best reader. Drink the brandy. It'll warm you."

I looked at the bottle.

"Sure, why not." I took a long pull.

"Mister," the man said, "the second sip is always sweeter."

I looked at him and smiled; Julia had said the same thing.

"I hope so," I said, sipping again. I had to fulfill my promise to Julia to write great stories. I owed her that much and more.

CHAPTER 23
THAT TENDER LIGHT

Hoosier Hills, Hannlin, IN
1:07 p.m., Friday, October 24, 1986

LILY WENT BACK to her apartment near the campus. That particular afternoon there was a three-hour break before the final session and she wanted to relax and nap. She was up late the night before and had not slept well.

She took a hot shower, put on her robe, set the alarm clock, and was about to pull the covers back on her bed, when she heard the doorbell chime.

Assuming a work-related delivery, Lily carelessly opened her door without checking the peephole.

As soon as she unlocked the door, Henry Malone barged in, grabbed the collar of her robe, and pushed her hard against the entrance wall.

"So," he said, "The bitch has found a new lover."

She smelled whiskey on his breath.

"Henry you will not do this to me. You're drunk; get the hell out of my apartment."

Her eyes searched the parking lot for someone who might help her, but at midday, most residents were away. She managed to free herself and slapped Malone hard across his angry face.

Her slap enraged him. He closed the door quietly and hit her again. His hand over her mouth stifled her scream.

He punched her twice in the face and when she fell to the floor, he kicked her hard several times in the small of her back. Then, he lifted Lily and threw her against the staircase to the second floor. Suddenly, Lily was in a state of semi-consciousness, with no feeling in her arms and legs. She could barely breathe and she could not speak.

"You should have been nicer to me, Lily. You were never as nice to me as you are to the book writer you're whoring around with. I've been watching you. This will teach you that you should never have left me. Oh, just try to prove I hit you, you stupid slut. I'll skate on this, too."

He kicked her twice and the room spun.

All she remembered thereafter was his insidious laughter, the taste of blood in her mouth, and that she could not feel pain. Something was horribly wrong. Luckily, Malone left the door ajar when he departed.

A RINGING TELEPHONE pulled me away from the press release I was writing for the phone call I intended to make that afternoon to my agent.

"Hello."

"Who is this?" a male voice asked.

"Josiah Taylor."

"I'm sorry to bother you, sir. I'm calling for Margaret Lee. Lily Hall has her listed as next of kin."

The term *next of kin* terrified me and I stood at Lily's desk, scared.

"Margaret Lee is in Chicago; I'm Ms. Hall's future husband. Is something wrong?"

"Sir, my name is Lieutenant Ted Krauss with the Indiana State Police. I am sorry to tell you that someone assaulted Ms. Hall. A maintenance man saw her door ajar, investigated, and found her unconscious.

Her condition is critical. She is en route to Indianapolis as we speak via emergency air evacuation. She is stable. A state trooper will arrive at your location shortly to drive you to the hospital. Sir, do you have a phone number for Margaret Lee?"

CHAPTER 24
THAT TENDER LIGHT

Methodist Hospital, Indianapolis, IN
8:02 pm, Friday, December 5, 1986

I PICKED UP Lily's mail from the nurse's station and was about to enter her room, when I heard her voice. At first, I thought she was with a doctor but soon realized she was with her cousin and dear friend Peter Bender. Good judgment told me not to interrupt the conversation, which had a private tenor. Instead, I leaned against the wall by the door and sorted Lily's mail. I would read the cards and messages to her later, as I always did when we were alone.

After several moments, I distinctly heard Peter say, "If that's what you want, Lily; the outcome is irreversible."

"It's precisely what I want, the sooner the better."

"Lily, these things take preparation...it has to be done in a way that eliminates suspicion. I'll need some time."

"Do what you must, Peter. He'll be at his cabin, that's clearly one option. Stop that bastard or he will continue to hurt women. The law will not touch him; his father is too powerful. Make sure he knows it's by my instruction."

"I'll figure a way," Bender replied.

"Does my request bother you?"

"No, Lily. I considered it the first time and recently, too. He's dirt."

"Good," Lily replied. "Peter, this remains our secret. Neither Jack nor Missy must ever suspect a thing. I fear Jack will do something and he cannot carry another burden, not with what I'll ask him to do."

I wondered what Lily meant. Then, I heard her crying. I fought an urge to rush to her side. If I had, she would have known I overheard the discussion.

"Jack will never know, no one will," Bender said. "I'll make it appear accidental."

I had heard enough! Instinct told me Lily had asked Peter Bender to kill Henry Malone. I succinctly understood her motivation; Malone had destroyed Lily's and my life.

Via a stairway, I went to the floor below where I took an elevator to the ground floor and the cafeteria. I could not risk Lily or her cousin knowing I had overheard their conversation. I sat for a while thinking and then finished a drawing Lily requested. When I saw Peter Bender exit the hospital, I went to Lily's room.

LILY OPENED HER eyes, smiled her wonderfully crooked smile, and whispered, "Hi."

"Hello, sweetheart."

Lily's expression seemed remarkably calm, as if some huge burden had disappeared. I held her cold hand in mine, knowing she could not feel my warmth. As I kissed the back of her hand, a shiver crossed my shoulders. When Lily looked at me, that shiver became a terrifying chill because of her discussion with Peter Bender.

"Have you been here long?"

"About an hour."

"Why didn't you come up?"

"I knew Peter was here; I saw his station wagon in the lot. I figured you needed private time so I had coffee and finished the sketch of you sleeping on the cabin porch."

I had never lied to Lily, not ever, and my guilt felt wrong, hurtful, and unfamiliar.

I showed her the sketch and she smiled as if she had not a care in the world. In the six weeks since her attack, Lily had rarely revealed her frustration, which always swirled just a fraction of an inch below the surface.

"What time is it?"

I glanced at my wristwatch.

"It's 9:17 p.m. I fed Sam, showered, and came back."

"I'm happy you did, I miss you. I knew it was later in the evening," Lily replied. "The hospital's quiet. You get to where you can tell time by the building's mood. Sounds and silences repeat themselves. Did you eat?"

"Half a sandwich in the coffee shop, I wasn't very hungry."

"You know, I don't remember the last time I felt hunger." She glanced at the I.V. perched beside her bed. "It feeds me constantly. You should've awakened me went you entered, why sit alone?"

"I wasn't alone, Lily, I was with you. I love to watch you sleep. In you, I see God's perfection. I wish I'd have known you all my life. My world would've been much warmer."

"Perfection is *not* a word I'd use; besides you only say that because you love me."

"I say it because it's true and, yes, I do love you."

"How's the apartment?"

"It's small but there's enough room. Thankfully, they allow pets, so Sam bunks with me. Missy calls it cozy. We're nearby, which is all that matters."

She smiled again and my heart ached because I was losing her and was unable to do anything about it. I felt desperately alone. I searched her blue eyes for an answer; however, all I saw was the woman I loved slipping away, a second at a time. Her white arms seemed thinner than I remembered; her face terribly pale. I am sure she saw despair in my face each time she looked at me.

Everything I loved and ever wanted, was drying up and would soon scatter in the winds of time, just as it had with Julia Ormandy. Twice in one lifetime seemed unforgiveable.

I glanced away and wiped my tears with my sleeve, grateful Lily could not see them.

I studied her remarkable face. Her smile was a treasure. Lily brought joy at a level I never imagined existed; a joy that permeated every action and thought.

I squeezed her hand, willing her to feel it. Lily did not react. The skin on the back of her hand seemed translucent in the dim light. Her hand in mine was frail, yet familiar and forever.

Through the window, my eyes lingered on the nighttime skyline of Indianapolis and the cold late-autumn rain that soaked the city. The lights reflected milky white on the wet pavement; the city looked as bleak as I felt.

"You received more cards today, mostly from students. I'll read them to you later."

"I'd like that," she replied. "Please, kiss me." Her breathing was labored, her voice a weaker variation from that of just weeks ago.

I sat on the bed. She closed her eyes as I leaned forward and kissed her forehead, her cheek, and her mouth. The tingle never changed; the spark always excited.

"Your whiskers tickle. You need a shave, Hemingway."

"I know. Dr. Stephens said your afternoon was peaceful."

"Peaceful? I cannot feel anything and never will. I have a constant throbbing in the center of my forehead."

"Is it getting worse?"

She hesitated. "Yes."

She looked at me intensely.

"I love your smile. I miss your wrinkled and beautiful face when you're away. Kiss me again."

I hugged her as best I could; her body against mine was like holding heaven. I kissed her tenderly and, for just a moment, her paralysis disappeared.

"Why now," she whispered, fighting back tears, "Just when our lives were flawlessly aligned?"

"You are my love, Lily Veronica."

"I know," she replied, "You are mine, forever! Can you lift me up a bit?"

I pressed a button and the bed moved. I tucked the blanket around her body. I knew Lily watched the gentle movement of my hands. What I did not know was she was garnering strength to send me away. She had reached her decision earlier in the day, after meeting Dr. Wright, the neurologist I invited from St. Jude's in Memphis.

"Did I hear rain earlier?" she asked.

"It's raining now."

She sighed and swallowed hard.

"I love rain; I used to love to watch it as a girl. I wish I could watch it again, with you. More than anything I wish I could feel it dance upon my skin." She paused. "Jack, what was it your grandmother said when it rained?"

I kissed her hand and placed it on the bed.

"You remember?"

"Sure. I remember everything you tell me, everything we've done and experienced. Come on, what did she say?"

I brushed my hand affectionately across her cheek.

"Let's see, when I was a tyke she told me raindrops were angel kisses. As I grew a bit older, she said rain was God's way of washing away all the bad things men do."

Lily giggled and, briefly, her blue eyes glowed.

"You believed her?"

"Sure, at the time. Why do you ask?"

"I've been thinking about us and what's happened, and I want you to do something for me."

"Anything."

"It goes back to that conversation we had our very first night."

"In your bedroom, after we made love?"

"Yes, silly."

"As I recall we discussed endings."

"Yes, we did."
"Okay."
"Do you remember you said you would never leave me?"
"Sure." I kissed her cheek. "What's this about, Lily?"
The sadness in her face and the tears on her cheeks scared me.
"Do you remember what else you said?"
I studied her eyes in the dim light.
"I said I'd only leave if you asked me to go."
Suddenly, I knew!
"Jack, you do love me, don't you?"
Tears formed in my eyes as I said, "To the level of every day's most quiet need, by sun and candlelight."
"Elizabeth Browning. I love her poems," Lily replied.
"I do, too."
"How does it start? Help me. How do…"
"…I love thee, let me count the ways, I love thee…" An eerie feeling gripped my heart and I stopped. A knot formed deep in my gut. "I won't leave, Lily."
She swallowed hard and her eyes found mine.
"Jack, my sweet man, we deserve a good ending. I despise being only a fraction of the woman I was, a woman who cannot respond to the man she loves."
I hated those words the minute she spoke them.
"What must stay in your heart forever is how I've loved you, and the way I looked, felt and breathed when I did."
"Lily, don't ask me this."
She blinked back tears.
"Please, allow me to finish. Jack, the woman I once was is gone, forever. There's no cure. Today, Dr. Wright confirmed what all other specialists have said.
"It destroys me to know when you enter the room and see me and remember how we loved each other that I won't be able to respond.

"I can't feel your touch. I can't reach for you. I can't offer myself to you. I've always responded to you. Even when I didn't know you existed, I sensed you coming toward me. Do you understand?"

"Yes."

"Not to acknowledge you or demonstrate with my body how much I love you hurts more than the beating. It isn't the ending I want."

Her voice was firm, her expression filled with determination. More tears slipped from the corners of her eyes and rolled down her cheeks. Her beauty defied comprehension.

"But, I'll know you, Lily."

"No, you won't. I won't be the same person. It's a matter of choice. It's my choice to say how I want you to remember me. The woman you loved no longer exists. I won't allow you to see me like this, day after day. It detracts from what has been the most beautiful, remarkable, and satisfying moments of my life.

"When you're alone in the coming months, getting through this as you will, I want you to remember how I was when I was a fully functioning woman. Not, the shell I have now become.

"However much it hurts you; it hurts me more. I can't feel your warmth. When I recall the intangibles, the memories consume me.

"I sit in the middle of a collage and everything I admire—your smiles, your kindnesses, your intimate caresses, the familiar glances, the silly jokes, the love you have for the written word, your knack for knowing my thoughts, your handsome face, your beautiful body, and your sexuality—is inches beyond my grasp. You have completed me. It's a pure love. Sadly, I can only respond by looking at you. There is no joy in that."

My world was crumbling around me.

"Jack, I won't be able to reach over and smell your pillow when you leave the room in the morning. I'll miss not being able to adjust your shirt collar after you dress. We'll never again be able to shower together or make love after we swim. I'll hear music but we cannot dance. Never again can I hold your shirt against my cheek to absorb your energy, as I've often done. I can't pick up a book, make dinner, clean myself, or drive a car. I fear I will become bitter. It's already begun. I can't live like this."

"I want to be with you. Regarding Malone, I'll..."

"Shhhh, I'll not hear you say those words. That can never get between us. You won't carry that burden, too. I love you and you will be in my heart, always. Stay with me tonight; hold me with the joy we've known these past months. We'll make love, if we're able. It's the last gift I ask of you. It's the last gift I'll give you. In the morning, I want you to leave."

"Lily," I whispered.

"Get past this as best you can. You are the strongest man I've ever known. Find someone to believe in, find a new life."

"Lily!"

"No, Jack, this is way it must be. Remember me as your lover and your dearest friend. If we end it now, you'll always remember the good because you will never have seen or tasted the bad that will come. I'll know you'll leave understanding how much I love you. I'll know you had the best of me, not the worst. Believe me; I'm on a narrow ledge.

"Go away for a long time. When you've worked it all out, tell the world how much we loved each other, and tell them about the joy we felt. Tell them about Laos and Julia, too, that will soothe your soul and strengthen our bond."

I AWOKE BEFORE sunrise and held Lily's hand, watching her sleep, until the hospital room filled with sunlight.

I stood and wrote a note. It simply stated that I would always love her and there would never be another. I placed the note on the nightstand beside a blue, velvet box.

As I leaned to kiss her goodbye, Lily opened her eyes.

"Please, in the top drawer," she whispered.

There, sitting atop white towels, was a penny and a photo.

"It's the same penny I gave to you when we first met. You took the photo of Sam and me. Missy placed them there for me. A penny for good fortune," she whispered as tears slipped from her eyes. "We'll always be together. We'll always have the best of that tender light that comes with true love. Ours was a gift, a fortune. Our time will always be precious and I will always be but a moment away."

I hugged her and sobbed until she asked me to leave. As I started to pull away forever, Lily placed her lips to my ear.

"Know this, Jack Taylor. You are my love and my joy," she whispered. "I believe when I opened my eyes as an infant I was destined to love you. When I close them forever, I'll be in love with only you. The pleasure you've given me will sustain me through eternity. With every sunrise and every sunset, and in every waking moment between, every fiber of my being will yearn for only you. When I sleep, my love, your sweet smile will comfort my dreams.

THREE WEEKS LATER...

MEMORIES OF LILY lingered like music from another time.

A woman would pass on a sidewalk wearing similar clothing and suddenly Lily would be in my arms with her warmth and presence so thick around me that I could hardly breathe.

Sometimes, in a crowd, I would turn toward soft laughter, friendly and intimate, only to stare awkwardly at some unsuspecting stranger.

Occasionally, the sunlight would catch a woman's blue eyes just so and Lily would be standing there and, for an instant, the world stopped turning.

The scent of her perfume came to me when least expected and I remembered sunrises, long nights, and the peppery scent of lovemaking. Along the way, there were thousands of other reminders and memories.

Now, out west, in a four-stool café near Missoula, Montana, on the day after Christmas, a woman entered a restroom. Black hair, like Lily's, held me at the counter, anxiously sipping coffee. Soon, a young mother emerged with a lovely daughter of eight or nine and hope paled again. The woman was pretty but not Lily, no other woman could be!

I found the chain around my neck and briefly held the coin she gave me for good luck. Knowing she touched it brought comfort. Suddenly, I felt foolish for thinking Lily could be in a remote part of Montana. It was not possible and never would be. However, my mind played tricks and at times hope made the illogical turns I tried to take seem more real than reasonable.

Lily! Her name mirrored the beauty of poetry.

I thought hard about Lily that day, praying she found peace. I sat there, my coffee cup a window to the past, and relived every moment we ever shared. I heard her laughter, sensed the stare of her violet-blue eyes, and felt the jab of her subtle humor. I saw her crooked smile and remembered her quick wit and the depth of her magnificent intelligence.

I recalled the books Lily read and the way she looked when we made love in early morning shadows as the world slumbered. I tasted her sweet mouth, saw her silky skin in the moonlight, and listened intently to the easy songs she sang as she consumed her day. Most of all, I remembered her exquisite hands moving gracefully as she spoke.

My fingertips retained the texture of Lily's warm skin.

I imaged her naked body against mine and heard the murmurs, which always followed her sexual release.

Every ounce of her had been mine, but now only memories and indescribable loneliness remained. Nothing I had ever experienced—not the violence of war, not the guilt of killing another human being, not the loss of Julia, not the death of my grandfather—compared to the intense despair that tortured me after Lily. It overwhelmed me. If this were a test, I was failing. If it were fate, it was bitter and shallow, and payback for all the wrongs I ever committed.

"We're closing, handsome," a voice interrupted, pulling me back into the smoky café.

"Excuse me?"

An older woman—pleasant face and hair in a bun—stood nearby smoking a cigarette. She pointed nonchalantly to a sign above the counter. Her wrinkled face retained only a shadow of its youthful beauty.

"We close at six on Fridays, hon. Afternoon has gone. Everybody around here goes over to Nathan's on Route 2 for catfish or trout. No sense stayin' open, I'm goin' there myself. Food's good. You ought to go. Music. Cold beer. A pretty gal or two. A good lookin' fella like you, who knows..."

Her raspy voice dwindled, replaced by a mischievous smile and insightful nod.

I shook my head, indicating no interest.

"I don't think so. I'm due out west in a few days."

The reply was a half-truth; I was moving westward, but had no definite plan or schedule. The white lie allowed me to fade off, a man hidden safely away from an intrusive world.

"How much do I owe?" I reached for my wallet, embarrassed to be the only customer in the café. Minutes had become more than two hours.

"Gee, it's only coffee, mister," the woman replied. "Besides if it calms what's ripping you apart, it's on the house."

I smiled sheepishly.

"That noticeable?"

"Yep, and then some."

I took two biscuits from a nearby tray and placed two fifty-dollar bills on the counter. Tommy would have approved of my generosity.

"Have some fun and a cold pitcher or two on me."

She picked up the bills, quickly folding them. Her spotted hand found a pocket in her red apron. Her smile reflected deep understanding.

"Good luck, mister. She must be something real special."

"Thanks," I replied, thinking *she is*.

I handed the woman a letter.

"Would you mail this for me?"

"Sure. Merry Christmas and Happy New Year; travel well and enjoy the day."

I paused, looking at her oddly. How strange to hear the exact words I once whispered to Lily.

Possibly the old woman was an angel.

"Thanks, I will."

OUTSIDE, NIGHT KICKED afternoon aside. The cold air snapped against my cheeks. I started the jeep, let the engine idle, and ruffled the hair on Sam's head. He had been asleep on the front seat. He looked at me with two big tired eyes and yawned.

"Want some supper, bud?"

I gave him a biscuit, broke the other in half, and took a bite. Sam chewed the food gratefully, licking up every crumb, happy I remembered him.

"We've miles to go," I said, rubbing my dog's chin. Not being hungry, I gave him the remains of my biscuit.

"A long way," I repeated, staring at the horizon. "We need lots of time."

However, I often wondered if I would make it. Only Lily's strength and her final words kept me going. Sam looked at me and then at the cooler on the floor. I removed a bottle of beer, opened it, and allowed him several gulps, in honor of Tommy. I put the bottle back in the cooler.

"You can have the rest later."

Sam whined and then, sensing we were about to leave, sat up to watch traffic. An eighteen-wheeler, heavy with lumber, roared past, its tires humming a symphony on the cold pavement. In the rearview mirror, a wide black sky formed a deep backdrop behind the brightly lighted café.

Nighttime in the Midwest and Lily's day was ending. If only...I blinked hard, choosing not to complete the thought.

In front of me, the horizon blended reds, purples, and oranges. As I drove westward, traffic passed in the opposite direction with headlights ablaze. As they sped by, the drivers and passengers were unaware that every fiber in the body of the man in the old jeep with the yellow dog by his side ached for a woman he would never see again.

Thus, the minutes, hours and days passed. Occasionally, time slipped by and, for a moment or two, everything seemed normal. Then something casual would occur. A glance. A smile. A song. The scent of perfume. The lilt of a female voice. The sight of a man and woman walking.
Something reminiscent of my life with Lily would cross my mind. Then, Lily's absence would hurt like hell. I relied on time, prayer, and the open road because that's all I had.

More than anything, I wanted Lily back in my life. I wanted what Malone took away from me. I wanted everything that cost that man his life.

Lily! I yearned for long walks, smiles from across the room, her hand in mine, and the passion our union created...all that molded two people into one. I wanted to hold Lily through the night to love and protect her.

The words she whispered when I left her that morning sustained me in the darkest moments of my life. Sam studied my face as I choked back tears. His eyes said he would always be there for me.

We passed the semi carrying lumber and sped off into the night, going nowhere fast. My sole purpose was to make it to the next day. I hoped at some point, in the days ahead, the hurt I felt would heal.

My wealth afforded me freedom and independence. I liked independence because I needed to be alone until I worked it all out. My money was now a means to an end. It would help the poor in honor of Lily. It bought privacy and days in which to heal. However, it did not take away the emptiness or longing—longing as wide, and high, and black as the night sky in Montana.

Book Three

August 2010 – January 2011

Come old girl and dance with me one more time.
Hold me in your arms and tell me all the secrets you know,
secrets that will change the world forever!
—D. James Then

One

Sycamore Glen Farms, St. Omer, IN
2 p.m., Friday, August 13, 2010

MARGARET LEE SAT on the front porch glider, rocking in the easy breezes of a warm Indiana afternoon. She wore a simple yellow dress and her ever-present white apron. Gold barrettes clipped her white, shoulder-length hair regally above each ear, giving her patrician features a royal flair. A gold, heart-shaped pendent, edged with diamonds, accented her neckline. Her intelligent blue eyes sparkled in afternoon shadows and grew immediately inquisitive as an automobile crossed the covered bridge not far from the entrance to her farm.

Lockwood McGuire, she thought, drumming her fingers anxiously upon her knees. As a sedan started up the long driveway, Missy thought about forgiveness, broken hearts, changed minds, and her oncologist's assessment: *if luck is ours, you have a year.* His words became her motivation; she would fulfill Jack Taylor's request before it was too late.

Missy did not fear death. She lived a wonderful life, was sorry for her sins, and was ready whenever God called. However, leaving unfinished business behind troubled her.

God knows, like a selfish old fool, I have guarded the story too long, she thought. She needed to feel the elation of doing something truly good just once more before she died.

Missy's intuition said Lockwood McGuire was the right person. The background report confirmed it. Now, all she needed was McGuire's promise and commitment.

She smoothed her apron and considered what she was about to set in motion. THE NEW YORK EPOCH, the world's leading newspaper, had ample resources and Taylor's book would receive broad exposure.

All that remained was to look into McGuire's eyes, take his measure, and receive his promise.

That is how her daddy taught her to conduct commerce and this, above all, would be a business transaction. A great deal of money would be involved...trust, privacy, and commitment, too!

She watched the sedan pass through intermittent patches of sunlight and shadow. She glanced at the Flatrock River, closed her eyes, and said a prayer. She reopened them when car doors slammed. A thin auburn-haired man came up the sidewalk, accompanied by a lovely woman with raven hair.

The man carried a worn leather satchel. She immediately liked his manner and handsome face. His hair was combed neatly, his eyes friendly and sincere. She thought of a young Robert Kennedy. The woman was stunning, like Lily.

"Lockwood McGuire," Missy said, "It is a pleasure to meet you, sir."

"Yes, ma'am, it is a great pleasure for me, too; thank you for inviting me. Please, call me Lock."

"I prefer Mr. McGuire." She turned to Bridgette Hannah. "And who is this lovely child? You are pretty."

Bridgette extended her hand.

"Thank you, I'm Bridgette Hannah, and I work with Lock. Please call me Biddy."

"Biddy...I like that." She shook Bridgette's hand.

Lock placed his satchel near the railing and shook Missy's delicate hand, which felt warm, small, and fragile in his. As the old woman withdrew her hand, she motioned to her guests to sit beside her on a green glider. In the distance, they heard the blare of a passing train.

"It sounds different in daytime," Missy offered. "At night, a train's air horn sounds forlorn. It resonates friendlier in daylight, more an expression of hope. Are you thirsty," she asked, her intelligent eyes replete with anticipation.

"Sure," Biddy replied.

"Me, too," Missy said. "Glasses, ice, and ginger ale are in the cooler beside the glider. Please, pour an old woman a summertime drink. I hope you'll join me, it's impolite for a lady to drink alone."

AS SHE DRANK, Missy closed her eyes and savored the ginger ale's flavor. When she reopened them, Lock thought of pools of warm blue water.

"Ginger contains many antioxidants," Missy said. "I read once where ginger root was first cultivated in southern China, which I think sounds exotic. Have you ever visited China?"

"No ma'am," Lock replied. Biddy shook her head.

"Nor I, a dear friend of mine was there briefly many years ago," Missy continued. After another sip, she said, "You think a woman as old as I would've seen more of our world. I guess our lives fill up with what's important at the time. While we're busy living, life itself slips by virtually unnoticed, like yonder train. We hear a toot now and then, but seldom climb aboard."

She studied her glass, seemingly bemused by minute bubbles floating toward the brim. Her face was fascinating. Despite her age, her delicate skin was flawless and her eyes moved like those of a younger woman hidden in an aged exterior. They seemed to yearn for refuge in a youthful, more beautiful body.

Lock imagined, in days long gone, her beauty beguiled many young men with hints of intimate evenings and impassioned whispers. In those young years, she would have selected her suitors with discretion and the fortunate ones would have experienced pleasures beyond their wildest imaginations. Young men would have fallen in love with Margaret Lee quite easily.

"I've lived in Decatur County for nearly a century," Missy continued, looking first at Lock, then at Bridgette. "I know much of its history—written, whispered, or conjured. I'm probably related to better than a quarter of the native-born residents of Decatur and Ripley Counties; surely more in a ten-mile radius. Do folks where you're from look after one another?"

"In many ways, New York is a city of strangers," Bridgette whispered. "But when it matters, we come together quickly."

"Like the tragedy of September 11?"

"Yes."

"That day nicked us all," she said. "It's hard to believe nine years have passed. I visited New York only once, with my niece Jenny and her husband. We went after another of my nieces, Lily, received her doctorate from Cornell University.

"New York City was busy and I loved the blends of people. I'd never seen a town so alive and vibrant at all hours. I think I saw every nationality on God's earth. I found New York a city of hope and promise; it must offer great inspiration to any writer."

"It's the pull of the raw and refined," Lock concurred. "Actually, what I find here is equally appealing."

"It seems easy to wear," Bridgette added.

Missy tilted her head and smiled, as if hearing a long-forgotten voice.

"Easy to wear," she repeated. Jack Taylor had said something similar when she first met him in Chicago. Perhaps destiny's hand had guided this young couple to her front porch, after all.

"I like your description and yes, as a friend once said, the land wears gentle on the soul. Do you have children, Mr. McGuire?"

"No."
"Do you, Biddy?"
"No, ma'am."
"Why do you ask?" Lock inquired.
"Farms are great places to raise families…just an old lady's interest. Do you fancy our warm weather and low humidity?"
"Yes," Lock replied.
"It's quite comfortable here on your porch," Biddy added.
"It's these big sycamore trees," Missy explained. "They shade the house, which catches westerly winds. It's usually much cooler here, even with higher humidity. The trees buffer the snow in winter."
"Do you get much snow?"
"Sometimes we do."
All three turned when the screen door squeaked behind them. A young woman, perhaps twenty, stood in red shorts, wearing a red and white Indiana University tee shirt. Her features, the shape of her eyes, and the curl of her smile were those of Margaret Lee.
"Sorry to interrupt," the woman shrugged apologetically.
"Tillie, meet my guests. They've come from New York City to research a story. This is Louise Matilda Templar, my niece and quite possibly the only person alive to use my given name, instead of Missy. We call this lovely child Tillie. Tillie say hello to Lockwood McGuire and Bridgette Hannah from THE EPOCH."
"Hello, Tillie," Biddy said. Lock nodded and bowed slightly. With his peripheral vision, he noticed Margaret Lee measuring his deportment, evaluating him in some private way. He wondered if he passed her examination.
Tillie smiled politely and turned to her aunt.
"Aunt Margaret, mom wants to know if your guests will stay for supper."

"We don't want to impose," Lock said. "We'll only need a few hours."

Missy grinned and glanced at the gold watch on her left wrist.

"A few hours," she questioned. "Hardly enough time to shake the dust off. This is Indiana; we Hoosiers move at a slower pace, but when we get there, it has meaning."

She smiled and, as with her eyes, her perfectly formed teeth were incongruous to her aged exterior. They, too, deserved a younger venue.

Surprised, Lock asked, "Why would we need more time?"

"Because, sometimes simple questions require complex answers," Missy replied cryptically.

She touched Lock's arm affectionately and smiled at Bridgette.

"Can you stay longer?"

"We can," he offered, "if you think it's necessary."

The old woman pursed her lips several times. A playful expression filled her splendid face and soon transformed into a teasingly friendly smile.

"Stay for supper," Missy pleaded. "I enjoy guests in the house. We're having country ham, yams, corn, biscuits, homemade applesauce, and blueberry pie. Correct, Tillie?"

"Yes, Aunt Margaret."

"Good," Missy continued. "I'd feel bad if you and Biddy came all the way from Manhattan without sampling our hospitality. Besides, the two of you might find a drive around our farm informative. Our land has a renewing effect. You'll see some of its natural beauty, learn a bit of its history, and feel some of its magic. Tillie, tell your mom we have dinner guests."

"Okay."

The screen door squeaked and Tillie disappeared into the dark interior of the farmhouse. Missy rolled her eyes.

"Damn door squawks at me constantly. I have it fixed and, days later, it yaps again. Has a mind of its own, so I've stopped trying. Sometimes it's better to let things take their course." She laughed heartily and then, turning and looking squarely at Lock, she asked, "Where are you staying and when do you leave?"

"At Bender's B & B...we have a noon flight tomorrow."

"Indianapolis?"

"Cincinnati was less expensive with a better schedule," Bridgette explained.

"I see," Maggie said, "All easily modified?"

"I guess."

"Why do people call you Missy?" asked Bridgette.

"My father called me that and it stuck. Maggie or Margaret works, too. Now, tell me, why the burning interest in Jack Taylor?"

Two

Sycamore Glen Farms, St. Omer, IN
2:22 p.m., Friday, August 13, 2010

H<small>ER DIRECT QUESTION</small> surprised Lock. He appreciated directness and responded in kind.

"You knew him, didn't you, Ms. Lee?"

When she did not reply, he found himself listening to leaves rustling in nearby trees. He looked at Bridgette, who smiled slightly. Her smile touched his heart. After a few awkward moments, Lock placed his satchel on the glider, gathered his thoughts, and explained his assignment.

"The story line isn't new," Missy said as he finished. "As a devotee of Taylor's books, I've read speculative articles about his disappearance. Most are implausible, others bizarre. Few, if any, are informative. For example, a recent story in an Indianapolis newspaper mentioned a possible sighting in Spain. I suspect no real insight. How do people come up with this stuff?"

"Great imaginations," Bridgette stated. "We've read them all and agree with you."

"It's all conjecture," Missy said. "I've read so many theories. Let me think. Once, I read he lived in the Yukon and panned for gold. Another claimed he was in the mountains of Honduras. One columnist speculated he roams the high seas on cargo ships writing under pseudonyms. Who knows?"

"I think you do."

"I like your cheek young man. I don't know where he is and that is truthful. If alive, he could be anywhere. My guess, only a select few know and I suspect only Taylor knows who they are."

"Then, why did you agree to see me?" asked Lock.

"It's coincidental. I must do something," she said guardedly. "Also, you're so cocksure he visited my farm. Perhaps I thought it adventurous. Since sex is no longer in the equation, an old girl needs other forms of adventure to stoke her fires."

Lock smiled. He liked her.

"I don't think adventure has a thing to do with it," he replied. "We've proof he visited your farm. However, what I want to know is why he left and when, is he alive, and, if so, does he still write?"

"Answers to two of your questions would surely be speculative on my part."

Lock studied Missy's eyes. If she lied, she was damned good. "So, you do have some answers?"

She remained silent.

"His status is anyone's guess," Lock continued. "There wasn't much to begin with and, surprisingly, nothing newsworthy has surfaced since he disappeared.

"We've talked to more than a hundred twenty people. Our research has been thorough but insignificant in terms of what caused Taylor to cancel his final book tour. Save for one rare lead, we might've failed."

"We know Taylor enjoyed his privacy," Bridgette explained. "If he's alive, we believe he's changed his identity and people around him don't recognize him or, if they do, they don't..."

"Give a hoot in hell about who he is," Missy finished Bridgette's sentence and smiled.

"Exactly," Lock stated. "When I received the assignment, I didn't consider it much of a story. I mean successful people drop out sometimes. I considered it a high-profile feature story, not my first choice as an investigative reporter."

"You thought it beneath your talents?"

"He didn't think it had legs," Bridgette stated, nodding.

"Now, I can't leave it alone," stated Lock. "Taylor was a respected writer and, as a Medal-of-Honor recipient, a man of rare courage. Taylor worked damned hard to develop his truly remarkable talent. Not typical of a man who turns his back on life."

"Is there a typical profile, Mr. McGuire?"

"Yes, for losers, drunkards, and underachievers. However, it's inconsistent with Taylor's work ethic or his history."

"So, what have you learned?"

"We've learned it's abnormal and completely out of character. We've learned if a man wants to hide, he will, regardless of his standing. After reading hundreds of clippings, after many interviews, after a review of his books, and after studying Taylor's life, his war record, his affection for his grandparents, and his eventual disappearance, the incongruity of it all strikes us as odd.

"He was gifted and lived a dream life. He was wealthy. Then, mysteriously, in the middle of a book tour, without notice, he vanishes—not a wince, whisper, or wave goodbye.

"Here one day and gone the next, to use an over-used cliché. It's common for an average Joe who can't cope with a mortgage, a bad marriage, or the bottom of a bottle. It's astounding when one considers Taylor's background, his accomplishments, and the promise he left behind.

"Something significant forced a radical shift. Until a few weeks ago, we had not a clue and almost conceded defeat. Then, luckily, Biddy found something. It prompted my phone call. It's the reason we're here today."

Missy smiled at Bridgette; her sparkling eyes and a nod encouraged Lock to continue.

"At first, I thought it was because of his grandfather's death. Now, however, I don't think Taylor's disappearance had any connection to Tomas Gomez' demise. In interviews from London, Taylor said he would continue to write.

"He claimed he had many ideas for books, including one about Gomez. Our suspicion is that something else pushed Taylor away, something private and traumatic."

"And we think it happened here at Sycamore Glen," Bridgette added.

As seconds passed, Missy's expression held fast. Margaret Lee was a hell of a poker player.

"The more we've learned," Lock stated, "the more fascinating the possibilities."

"It's difficult to find anyone of note who doesn't consider him a splendid writer," Bridgette continued. "Some say he was in line for a Nobel Prize. Except for his dog, he left everything behind—friends, family, fame, possessions, wealth, royalties, and his property."

"His agent," Lock added, "had power of attorney, sold everything, and placed all profits and residuals in a private trust. The agent's son now controls Taylor's estate.

"I've met with him several times. He doesn't know why Taylor disappeared, where he is or was, or if he's alive. He's protective about the specifics of Taylor's trust, offering vague references to charities. I don't know how the author's money is spent."

"Wouldn't he know if Taylor's dead?" asked Missy.

"I can't say," Lock replied. "A long-time secretary at the firm, who retired recently, swears old man Levy received an envelope from Taylor around the time he disappeared. Although there was no return address, she claims the handwriting was Taylor's and remembers a Missoula, Montana, postmark. She couldn't recall the exact date; however, she says it came a few days after Christmas 1986."

"How would she remember that?" Missy asked.

"She took a New Year's cruise," Bridgette noted, "and remembers placing the envelope on Levy's desk before leaving. We found nothing in Missoula."

"Employees in Levy's firm tell us Taylor's trust is off limits, that it's never discussed," Lock added. "However, one person suspects money passes to Taylor through an intermediary. They can't prove it. Incidentally, we've tried but failed to access IRS records."

He moved to the edge of the glider.

"The story," he said, "Rests with the *why*. I've been on this assignment for nine months. It seems on all of God's good earth, nobody has any understanding about Taylor's status except perhaps you. We find a reference to Indiana and your farm and my instinct says you are the person. Something tragic drove him away and I think you know what that tragedy was."

Missy's eyes narrowed as she smiled slightly.

"I don't know much about Nobel Prizes, Levy's secretary or trusts," she stated. The old woman became thoughtful and, remembering the email she received the previous day, deftly changed the subject, "I understand you've recently stopped smoking. I trust that is working out for you?"

From his expression, Missy knew she had surprised Lockwood McGuire. She liked having an edge. Always had; always would.

"How do you know that?" he asked.

Missy pursed her lips several times.

"Oh come now, Mr. McGuire, you're not the only person who can investigate another. Money buys favor. I never extend an invitation to dance with a man, especially an inquisitive one, unless I know something about him. Had I known Ms. Hannah would visit, I'd know something of her, too. You phoned unexpectedly; I wanted to learn a thing or two before we met. It's the reason I asked you to visit today rather than earlier in the week."

"Go on," Lock replied. He glanced at Bridgette, whose eyebrows raised appreciatively.

"From what I've learned, you're a good and decent man, although you can be stubborn, independent, absent-minded, and temperamental."

Bridgette smiled and nodded; clearly, she agreed with Miss Lee's analysis. Lock blushed slightly.

"No need for embarrassment, Mr. McGuire. Stubborn people have a refined sense of self-worth and are creative and quite principled. I'm bullheaded myself, always have been, always will be. You might be the best investigative reporter in the country. You've won numerous awards, including three Pulitzers.

"You're as modest about your achievements as you are aggressive in your reporting, and you're selective. Humility and an exacting nature are gifts from the Almighty, given to those He favors. Don't ever change. Far too many uncaring and indiscriminate people circle in our midst. I believe the aggregate effect of their selfish narrow-mindedness undermines our culture and our specific way of life."

She paused, sipped ginger ale, and added, "The fact you're a decent man is more important than you can ever know."

Looking at Bridgette, Missy recognized affirmation.

"I suspect there's more?" asked Lock.

"Of course, you're recently divorced. You get along well with most people, despite your penchant for debate. Your sister became ill last year and has been recuperating from the removal of a lung. I take it that's the reason you've stopped smoking."

He nodded and it gave Bridgette a chance to add, "Lock is extremely focused and dedicated to his work."

Missy raised her eyebrows.

"Then," she whispered, "I'll make your trip worthwhile."

Lock studied her elegant face and the way her nose wrinkled slightly as she smiled. He had underestimated Margaret Lee.

She was a tough, ingenious, talented, compassionate, and smart woman.

"We'd like that very much," Lock replied.

Missy adjusted her position.

"So, what is this proof you brought to my farm?"

"Dumb luck combined with a dash of ingenuity. A literary critic in England was the only one to reference a gift Taylor received from a friend in Indiana. It fascinated me because as far as I knew Taylor had never visited the state. I did some digging, checked flights, airports, looked though manifests, and learned he took a flight from Philadelphia. I researched rental car companies. Eventually, I found what we needed.

"I suppose you possess proof," Missy stated.

Lock removed a plastic sleeve from his satchel.

"The distance to your farm from the Cincinnati Airport is what, sixty miles? I assumed he'd need transportation once he arrived."

"What's this?"

"Taylor rented a 1985 Crown Victoria and kept it for several weeks. He held it with a credit card. However, when he returned the car, he paid cash. You're holding a copy of a receipt I obtained from rental company archives in Oklahoma."

"Wouldn't something like this be confidential?"

"Grease a few palms and information slides through. Please see what's written in the space marked destination next to his signature, and please note the phone number."

Missy examined the document.

"Sycamore Glen Farms, St. Omer, Indiana," she said, "My farm, my phone number."

"Yes."

"Well, I'll be goddamned," she whispered. Her hand quickly covered her mouth.

"Yes, Taylor visited your farm."

She looked directly at Lock, then at Bridgette, and smiled. After several moments, she lowered her hand and cleared her throat.

"You're good. Why was this never discovered before?"

"My guess, no one knew about the Indiana connection. Investigative reporting is luck and perseverance. If I didn't know about the Indiana reference or include Philadelphia in my search, I'd have missed it, too. If you don't give up and if you're creative, you usually win."

As he studied her face, the carotid artery on the right side of her neck pulsed like a little blue bellow as blood rushed into her magnificent brain. The heart-shaped pendant she wore sparkled in the afternoon sunlight. Her eyes danced with his.

"The newspaper clipping from London and the rental car receipt are the only new pieces of insight we've uncovered in nine months. Walter Levy postponed Taylor's book tour. Later, he cancelled it completely. The reasons given were fatigue resulting from Taylor's trip abroad and complications from the boat explosion, which took his grandfather's life. Of all the people we've met, no one else has anything new. It comes squarely down to you.

"He was here in September 1986 and possibly October and November, too. I say he disappeared in December, based on Levy's secretary's recollection."

He paused, seeking affirmation in Missy's anxious blue eyes. For just a moment, she appeared innocent and frail. She swallowed hard to collect her composure.

Lock held the receipt and studied Missy's pretty face.

"Someone knows the truth. I believe that's you."

The old woman bit her upper lip and then massaged her temples with the tips of her frail fingers. Clear polish covered her expertly shaped nails.

"Thorough my friends," she replied. She looked at Bridgette and asked, "Did you have a hand in this?"

"We're good at what we do; Lock is the best."

"Levy's son is in the dark," the old woman whispered. "I don't think his father knew all that much, either. Jack was exceptionally private. He rarely discussed his personal life. However, you did miss one important fact."

"Which is?"

"The story begins in August 1986, not September, and it starts in the Virgin Islands."

"Earlier than September?"

"Yes and your intuition is correct, I have many answers. However, I also have a few conditions. I'm only doing this because of something Jack requested. He told me it was my choice and I've decided to comply with his wish; however, I must and will do it in my way."

"I don't understand?"

"You will. Between now and Sunday, you'll know it all."

"Okay."

"However, you must agree to three requests."

"I'm sorry, Missy, what if one is not to write the story?"

"I assure you the story is yours and you'll write it. However, you must trust me. If you do not, we have no deal."

"We'll get the story?"

"You'll get the story and much more. You've my word of honor." She smiled, adding, "You're both about to become famous. If you agree, we will have a deal."

Fame did not interest Lock. He took several deep breaths and calmed himself. He looked at Bridgette for her reaction. A slight nod indicated he should proceed.

"Okay, we have a deal."

"Good choice, son, good choice."

"How so," he asked, seeking more information; he wanted to learn as much as he could.

"In due time," she said. "As an old lady, I've earned the right." She glanced at her watch. "I'd like to rest now. It's nearly 2:30 p.m. I nap during this time of day. We'll meet at four o'clock. Meanwhile, please use your free time for any calls you must make, to amend your schedule, and to check messages."

Given the option, Lock and Bridgette would have preferred to continue talking but Missy had tired visibly.

"As you wish," he replied.

"Rest well Ms. Lee," Bridgette whispered. Her expression indicated that a few more hours made little difference in the scheme of things.

"Thank you; I do enjoy a good snooze. Tillie!"

Seconds later, the porch door squeaked open.

"Yes, Aunt Margaret."

"Help me to my room and show our guests to the library. Point them to the half-bath."

"Sure."

"Tillie, you're a sweetheart. Give each some of your mama's sweet tea, too."

Missy stood, took up her cane, patted Lock's shoulder affectionately, and, guided by her niece, turned toward the screen door. Before entering the house, she paused, smiled at Bridgette, and then cupped Lock's chin in her fragile hand. Her eyes embraced his.

"All things in their time, Mr. McGuire," she whispered. "Yours is nigh. I'm glad you and Biddy can summon great patience; it's virtuous. I suspect Miss Hannah's influence is a guide. The fact you and she are here courts much favor."

Three

Sycamore Glen Farms, St. Omer, IN
3:41 p.m., Friday, August 13, 2010

Lock stood on thick beige carpeting in the library—a quiet and cozy room in the center of Margaret Lee's expansive white farmhouse. A dozen or more original landscapes, he assumed venues of the farm, hung on the wall to his left. Positioned off to one side, on a decorative easel, was a sketch of a rustic cabin where a woman slept on a porch swing, her face hidden by long, black hair. The detail was intricate, the pose alluring.

He slowly rotated and studied the entire room. Except of windows, floor-to-ceiling bookshelves lined the remaining three walls, supporting hundreds of books written mainly by British, Russian, and American authors. It seemed many were first editions.

Although arranged in alphabetical order, Lock read the author's names randomly. Hemingway. Chekhov. Faulkner. Lewis. Steinbeck. Shakespeare. Longfellow. Fitzgerald. Marlowe. Frost. Wordsworth. Burns. Tolstoy. Chesterton. Hawthorne. Lewis. Wilder. Chandler. Dickinson. Thomas. Shelly. Keats. Pope. Hammett. Dostoyevsky. Yeats. Byron. Stevenson. Emerson. Kipling. Browning. St. Vincent Millay. He saw other names, too, recognizing most of them.

He walked over to an antique cherry desk. On one corner, pewter bookends bearing the seal of Hannlin College supported Jack Taylor's eight novels. He lifted a book randomly, opened it, and found a brief, handwritten inscription:

For Missy, with deepest affection, Jack Taylor

That Tender Light

A quick check of the remaining books revealed the identical message.

He opened Taylor's eighth novel—THE LAST CHAMPION AND THE LAST KING—and, thumbing through the pages, immediately recognized the author's penchant for character introspection which, when coupled with his use of symmetry, distinguished Taylor from his contemporaries. Taylor won the Pulitzer Prize for Fiction for this particular novel—a prize the author never collected.

Lock searched for a particular passage, which presented the thoughts of Christian Arnett, the book's main character, an old man who spent most of his life as an African safari guide and a mercenary fighting in many of Africa's struggles for independence. At this point near the story's conclusion, Arnett battles the final days of a terminal illness. Alone and forgotten, he is dying in a Spanish hospital and is trying to comprehend his life choices:

Thus, my mind wanders, uneasy and unsettled, seeking those glorious days from my past; but, sadly, they're gone. For some reason, they have slipped away. I know I lived and breathed in those times; I hunted and fought in them; and I wore them as proudly as some men wear princely garb. However, they have faded from my memory, just as my strength fades from my weakened body. How vibrant I was! How hapless I've become. I feel empty because I no longer sense their presence. Like crumbs of dried bread, they have blown away in the winds of vanished decades. Sadly, everything blurs. Everything! I want to blame God for my misfortune because I have no one to turn to. I'm here in this room, alone. However, in the depths of my soul, I know blame does not rest with the Almighty. It rests in the choices I made in days long spent. Now, I only have this bed, this simple room, and the magnificent Spanish sun. The sun warms my wrinkled body and, in the days I have left, it eases the pain of old age, of glory forgotten, of death to come.

D. James Then

Is the pain of what I've lost God's fault or His plan? Everything we love and cherish eventually fades and passes. Nothing is, as it seems. Not money. Not fame. Not position. Not beauty. Much of life is as fleeting as the spring waters on the Serengeti. I alone am responsible for what has happened to me. I alone forged the iron of my life. They were my choices, not God's!

I should have clung to the woman I loved in Kenya. I remember her face and her lovely name, Maua, which means flowers. I could have fathered her children. I should have tithed for my old age. Men are foolish to think things will work out. They rarely do! We are born and we die, and what happens between is our responsibility. Turn to or fro; those are the only choices.

I do know, regardless of the outcome of one's life, whether diamonds or stones, everything we have crumbles and blows away. Only love endures; it exists to warm and comfort our souls as we journey through eternity.

Love is God's precious gift to humankind. How foolish to waste His lovely gift! I should have loved more and hated less. I should have given more and taken less. I should have sung more and shouted less. Had I done so, I would have Maua's soft brown eyes to comfort me as I die. Sadly, only ashes will remain and I fear my journey through eternity will be somber and dreadfully cold.

He handed the passage to Bridgette Hannah as she entered the library.

"Do you think this passage in any way reflects Taylor's present state of mind?" she asked after reading it.

"It could. What do you think Ms. Lee has up her sleeve?"

"She wants to protect something," Bridgette noted.

She handed the novel to Lock.

"I agree," Lock said. "I wish I knew what. Do we have any issues with our flights or the B & B?"

"No, we're good to go." She explained the new schedule.

Lock nodded, turned the book over, and studied Taylor's photograph, taken in the late 1970s at his home in St. John. His angled face was handsome, his shoulders broad, his green eyes intense but remote, perhaps slightly hard.

Lock tried to envision the same face after nearly thirty years. That image, like the youth of the Taylor's character Christian Arnett, was a blur.

"Why did you leave?" Lock whispered.

The answer, however, remained as silent as the spines of the books in the library, which quickly muted his question.

Lock replaced the book in its slot between the bookends and studied the photograph of a remarkably beautiful woman. Framed in silver, it angled inward toward Taylor's eight novels. The woman's beauty was beguiling. Blue eyes. Freckles. Large dimples. Dark hair with wisps of silver and gold. A sexy and inviting smile. Thin lips. Tanned skin.

Lock lifted the photograph and showed it to Bridgette.

"The niece, Lily?" asked Biddy.

"That's my guess. She definitely is the reason Taylor came to Sycamore Glen."

Bridgette nodded. "The more important question: *is she the reason he left?*"

Lock glanced at the books in the room.

"These books know the story; too bad they can't talk."

JUST THEN, THEY heard movement in the hallway and soon Margaret Lee shuffled into the library, her pink bedroom slippers scraping softly upon the polished hardwood floor. Her knuckles were white where she grasped her cane.

The scrape of her footsteps disappeared when she stepped onto the carpet. Seconds later, she settled into one of three worn leather armchairs directly across from the desk. She smiled and leaned her cane against an armrest.

"Sleep does my wrinkled old body wonders. I love this old chair," she said, settling her backside into it. "It's comfy. It might be as old as I am. I like the way it fits my bottom."

Lock laughed as a shorter, stockier woman, in her late fifties and wearing wire-rimmed glasses entered the room. She carried a ceramic tea service, edged in silver.

The violets on the teapot matched the color of the eyes of the woman in the photograph.

"Mr. McGuire, Miss Hannah," Missy began, "Please say hello to Tillie's mama, Jennifer Hall Templar. Jenny, this is Bridgette Hannah and Lockwood McGuire from THE NEW YORK EPOCH."

As Jennifer Templar placed the tea service on a nearby table, Lock noticed a likeness to the woman in the photograph. Bridgette's wink told him she did, too. Instead of flecks of gold and silver, wisps of gray highlighted Jennifer's hair. Her face was appealing in a rounded way. Her pink dress and white sandals brightened the room.

Lock shook the woman's hand.

"It's a pleasure to meet you," he said.

"Likewise, Ms. Hannah's and your visit has renewed Missy's resilience. Promise and resolve fill her eyes again. They've not sparkled like that for a long time. Clearly, she's enthused and up to something. You're good for her, but watch out."

Jenny glanced affectionately at Missy, who blushed slightly.

"Although," Jenny added, with a chuckle, "Missy's too stubborn to admit anything."

The old woman's sincere expression quickly became a mock frown and she whispered, "Stubborn I am; stubborn I'll remain."

Jenny lifted the teapot and prepared to pour, but she turned to Missy's guests.

That Tender Light

"Mr. McGuire, Ms. Hannah my aunt drinks tea and honey, flavored with peppermint, at this time of day. I thought you might enjoy a cup with her before dinner. We'll eat about five thirty. There are cookies here, too."

"Tea sounds delicious," Bridgette replied.

"Jenny and Tillie come to visit me from Carmel, Indiana, at this time of year when my housekeeper, Ruthie, takes her vacation," Missy explained. "Jenny makes a great cup of tea, better than Ruthie, but if you ever meet Ruth, don't repeat that. I'd have hell to pay."

Jenny filled three cups, added honey and peppermint, stirred briskly, and served her aunt. She handed cups to Lock and Bridgette, smiled, and prepared to leave.

"It smells delicious," Lock offered.

"It is," she replied over her shoulder as she departed.

"I trust you've been able to rearrange your schedule," Missy asked, cooling her tea by whistling her breath across its hot surface. Before Lock or Bridgette could answer, Missy turned quickly, checked the hallway, confirmed her niece's departure, and removed a small silver flask from her apron. She opened it and poured some of its contents neatly into her teacup. For her age, her hand was remarkably steady.

Bridgette smiled at Margaret Lee's mischievous action.

"A few drops of rum blend nicely. Let it remain our secret."

"Absolutely," Lock replied.

"You are a gentleman; somewhere your mother's proud."

He bowed slightly and the old woman's eyes filled with appreciation. The three now shared an innocent secret and, with it, a bond.

"Jenny frowns on drinking," she continued. "She's a teetotaler. I'm not and never will be. If the Lord imbibed, I can, too. An ounce or two is good for one's spirit and heart. A nephew provides the rum."

"Wouldn't Jenny or Ruth notice the rum bottle?"

"Biddy, my nephew fills a ginger ale bottle and slips it to me when he visits. The color's a near-perfect match. If Jenny knows, she doesn't let on and I'm sure Ruthie hasn't a clue. Secrets are fun to keep, especially harmless ones. Don't make 'em if they're not. Please, be seated."

Missy giggled, returned the flask to her apron pocket, and sampled the spiked tea.

"That's much better," she said, winking. "Now tell me, have you revised your plans?"

"Not a problem. We fly out Sunday afternoon."

"Good," Missy said, watching Bridgette sip her tea. "I have more rum, if you want a hit."

"Not for me, thank you."

"Mr. McGuire?"

"No, thank you. This is a comfortable room; the books are magnificent. Have you read them all?"

"Oh, lord, no! I've read some. This was my niece Lily's library. Many of the books are first editions. Lily read them all. This was the dining room in the original farmhouse. After a few modifications and additions, Lily made it her library and study. Her photo's on the desk."

"She's beautiful."

Missy selected a cookie.

"The daughter I never had. She was twelve when her mom died. I raised her. My brother William, Lily's father, needed help. Lily was a professor of literature at Hannlin College, about forty miles away. She often worked in this room, although she kept a studio apartment near campus. She'd stay during the academic year, especially for functions, or if the weather was iffy.

"She spent summers on the farm. After her father died, it became hers and mine jointly. In our family, the land passes from generation to generation.

"After my father died, it went to William, Lily's dad. It's been in our family since before the Civil War. The pencil sketch on the easel is the cabin where it all started—Sycamore Glen's original farmhouse.

"My great grandfather Angus Hall was barely twenty when he came from Scotland with his bride, Elizabeth. He purchased two-hundred acres with gold he inherited from his father."

"Why'd he settle in Indiana?"

"He followed others from Scotland. The hardwood forests attracted him. A carpenter by trade, he dreamed of making furniture. His older brother James migrated with him. He, James, and Elizabeth built the cabin out by the river that first summer. James eventually married a woman from Rushville.

"Lily loved the old cabin. It's quite the spot, out near an orchard. Jenny and I stayed there last night. You'll see it tomorrow. My ancestors built this house in the 1880s. Of course, it was smaller back then. It grew, as the family did.

"Farming wasn't Angus Hall's first calling, that fell to his brother James, who farmed while Angus cut lumber and made furniture. He earned a great deal of money making coffins in the Civil War and then sold his company to a fellow from Batesville. He paid off all his debts, invested some, and purchased three hundred-sixty acres. As fortune goes, Angus was good with a spade, too. They were very successful farmers and continued to sell logs periodically, as I still do. The brothers purchased another two hundred ninety acres in 1904 and paid cash for the parcel. By then, the farm had grown to eight hundred and fifty acres. My father sold two hundred acres to stay afloat during the depression and William sold a hundred more in the 1960s, to cover Lily's education—she attended expensive schools. Today, we have five hundred fifty acres."

She paused, adding, "Jenny and Tillie get the farm next."

She pointed to a collection of photographs on the credenza behind the desk.

"See the picture of four men, the one with the gold frame?"

"Yes."

"My father, James, named for Angus' brother, is on the left. Lily's daddy, my brother William, stands next to him; beside him is my younger brother, Colin, Jenny's daddy. He's deceased, too."

"And the fourth man on the right?" Bridgette said.

Missy paused, holding her cookie thoughtfully, the sparkle in her eyes dimmed.

"Billie Lee, my husband; he died after Normandy, actually inland a bit, on June 9, 1944."

"I'm sorry."

"I never dated much thereafter," she offered. "I never wanted the feel of another man. The photograph is from summer 1943, out near where my flower garden grows today. We had a gazebo back then. It seems a simpler time, but possibly my age and memories make it so.

"Billie's leave ended a few days later and I never saw him again. I have all his letters, though. I read them occasionally—but not often—and wonder what might have been. Many women faced similar experiences. It was part of the times but it still hurts. I truly loved him."

An awkward silence filled the library as Missy relived private memories. Soon, she shook them away and sipped her tea.

"I presume you saw my Taylor collection?" she asked. "I've read all his books."

"I thumbed through several," Lock said, "and noticed a handwritten inscription. Was Taylor collaborating with your niece, Lily, perhaps on a book?"

"In a manner of speaking," Missy replied.

She reached over, squeezed Lock's hand with hers. She stood up, surprisingly agile for a woman of nearly a hundred and led Lock and Bridgette to the large window overlooking a sweeping green lawn and a magnificent flower garden.

She placed her delicate hands atop the windowsill. Looking out, she did not see her farm a decade into a new century but the farm as it appeared in the mid-eighties.

After some introspection, she turned and touched the side of Lock's face affectionately, like a mother caressing her child. Her fingertips were cool on his skin; her breath smelled of peppermint.

"Why did he stop writing? What forced him away?"

"Lockwood, it starts and ends with Lily. You'll need most of a day to understand."

He smiled, realizing she'd used his given name for the first time. They had just crossed an important threshold in their relationship.

"We've all the time you need, Ms. Lee."

"I know," she whispered softly. "From here on, you and Biddy are to call me Missy."

Briefly, she turned back to the window. Then, she looked at each, her blue eyes intense.

"Let's walk before supper. I want to be near my flowers and my memories of Billie."

Four

Sycamore Glen Farms, St. Omer, IN
4:09 p.m., Friday, August 13, 2010

"LILY'S LIGHT BRIGHTENED many lives," Missy said as they walked between two huge butterfly bushes at the east entrance of the expansive flower garden. Bridgette held the old woman's right arm, their footsteps barely audible on a slate path. Lock walked beside them.

"Lily's charm perfected itself naturally and over time. Lily drew people like a flame draws a moth...equal parts warmth, charisma, intelligence, beauty, and self-reliance."

"Sounds remarkably confident," Lock said.

"Yes, and fiercely independent," Missy replied. "She was a tomboy, too. Growing up on the farm did it. For all her refinements, Lily loved tinkering with old cars, driving the farm equipment, and repairing things. She hated pretension and was smart as a whip. She could have been a doctor or lawyer, anything—maybe even a novelist. However, as a girl, she set her mind on teaching. We thought high school. Not Lily! She went to Purdue, Dartmouth, and Cornell, where she earned a Ph.D. in American and English Literature. She earned all A's, perhaps on a rare occasion an A minus. It wasn't conceit; Lily just wanted to be the best. Anything she did looked easy."

Missy paused to let her breathing even after they took a slight incline.

"Lily made one mistake in her life, an ill-fated marriage to Henry Malone, an attorney. He was so nice to her when they were dating, but it turned sour quickly. He couldn't stand Lily's independent streak or the fact that she was not happy anywhere but on the farm; also, she was not as submissive as he would have preferred. He beat her up pretty bad."

"Was he jailed?" Bridgette inquired.

"Not a chance, he was smart, there were no witnesses, and his father vouched for him, giving him an alibi. Because of their influence in the legal community, Henry got off; walked away as if nothing ever happened. He was a real bastard that one." Missy paused and took a deep breath. "Sorry, I get carried away talking about that son of a bitch. Anyway, to understand my Lily, you must know this land," Missy continued. "The two were inseparable. A deep sense of family pride, our pioneer spirit, and Sycamore Glen's beauty and bounty sat in the middle of Lily's heart...at all times. She loved this land and the family who built it."

Missy started walking again, using her cane, and Bridgette's arm for support.

"Lily's willpower pulled us through some tough times," she added. "We almost lost the farm but she never gave up; she would not sell. She made personal sacrifices and never complained. She made it through that bad marriage, too. She did what needed doing—for me, for her parents, for her ancestors, for the future, for herself. A rough go rattled us hard in the late seventies and early eighties. Lily's teaching salary and our combined reserves saved us."

Missy paused, hooked her cane on her arm, and laced her fingers through waist-high Black-eyed Susans.

"My little Susies hold a special place in my heart," she said, lightly touching the edges of yellow-orange petals. "They're actually wildflowers, sisters of the sunflower. I've always been partial to 'em. They've grown in my gardens longer than I can remember, which means close to eighty years. I started growing them after I graduated accounting school. Probably thirty variations exist and I have ten or twelve." The old woman lifted her cane and pointed. "There, there, and over there; see how lovely. They always tilt toward the sun." She paused and asked, "Where was I?"

"Lily saved the farm," Bridgette reminded her.

"Thank you," she said, walking. "I was in my forties when her mama died. Lily was nearly a teenager. I worked as an accountant at a bank in Greensburg when my brother asked me to raise Lily after his wife died. Lily made me young again and changed my life. God, we laughed together."

She admired patches of russet chrysanthemums and, then, looked into Lock's eyes.

"Am I too pokey?"

"You're fine."

"Just a bit, I think. After her doctorate," Missy continued, "Lily taught briefly at a college in New York and, when a position opened at Hannlin, she came home. The college is not far away. She could have taught at any prestigious university, but she chose Hannlin, the farm, and me. She loved teaching and she loved farming."

Missy's voice faded.

"I sense a 'but' coming," Lock offered.

"You've an intuitive feel for the flow of conversation, Lockwood. It makes you good at what you do. Let me phrase this properly. Something changed on Lily's thirty-eighth birthday. For many women forty is the milestone, but not for Lily. Something scared her deep inside. When she turned thirty-eight, she realized some part of her soul was dry; I'm guessing the part that Henry or other men were never able to access. Those are my words, not hers. If you knew where to look and I did, you saw a different resolve in those striking blue eyes of hers."

"Which was?" Lock asked.

"Biddy might understand this better than you, Lockwood. Sometimes a woman needs a man to feel complete. Feminists might say I'm a fool, but I don't give two damns or a checker about what they think. For some women, their nature demands it.

"Jack Taylor happened along at the right moment. Is chance the right word? Maybe. Fortuitous? Possibly. Fate or destiny? Perhaps. Whatever it was, some powerful and consuming force brought Lily and Jack Taylor together. They knew it when they met. They loved each other with unselfish certainty, which is both rare and indefinable."

Using the tip of her cane as a makeshift hoe, she loosened dirt at the base of wispy Russian sage.

"Most of my flowers need direct sunlight. Lily and Jack needed each other just as flowers need the sun. I don't have to tell you they were lovers," she added.

"I assumed as much," Lock replied.

"How did they meet?" Bridgette asked.

Missy winked and squeezed Bridgette's hand.

"That's easy. They met in St. John in August 1986. I said it was chance; Lily disagreed. She alluded to a more profound power. As I said earlier, Lily went to St. John each year. Let me digress. Did either of you go to St. John?"

"Yes," they replied simultaneously.

"And did you visit Sister Teresa's orphanage and school?"

"No, we met at a hospital in Charlotte Amalie, and discussed Taylor and Gomez."

"You should visit her school. Lily and Terri—Sister Teresa—met at Cornell. On visits to the island, Lily tutored Terri's more promising students; she read, tanned, relaxed on the beach, and took long walks—a wonderful way to renew her spirit."

"We missed this, Biddy." Lock's words hinted at self-criticism.

"Don't be hard on yourself. You've done a remarkable job."

"Did Lily meet Jack at the orphanage?"

"No, Biddy, they spoke for the first time the day Jack buried his grandfather. Lily knew the doctor from his service at the orphanage.

"She was leaving for home that day and attended the graveside service before leaving St. John. Jack and Lily's first meeting was moving. For Lily, it was especially important because of her bad marriage and her age, for Jack emotions stirred from his past."

"I don't follow," Lock said.

"You will. Each had a premonition about the other."

"Honestly?"

Missy admired patches of red and bronze blanket flowers.

"Biddy, fate or destiny plays a remarkable role in our lives and few of us ever realize it," Missy added. "We believe things happen by chance; however, after living nearly a hundred years, I don't think chance has much to do with it.

"Strong and unseen forces swirl around us at all times, forces we never truly comprehend, like the force bringing you here today. What is it? If you think it's because of your hard work, I assure you, it's not. Some indefinable force placed the assignment squarely in your lap; that force has put you at my farm. I believe it; I just can't prove it."

She saw questions forming in their eyes.

"You'll get answers," Missy continued. "Lily never told me about Jack until he came to the farm. I asked her why and she said their first meeting was too personal. She feared its value might diminish if she shared it with anyone, even me. Lily said something I thought odd. She said she knew he'd come for her.

"I remember saying many women think similar thoughts. However, she corrected me. She said she knew the instant they met. It seems remarkable to be that adamant on a moment's notice. I never experienced anything as touching!"

"Taylor stopped writing because of Lily, didn't he?"

"I don't know that he stopped writing, do you? As for Lily," Missy paused in mid-sentence and nodded slightly. "We've much to discuss and dinner's close," she whispered.

She noticed Lock's frown and said, "I'm not being sly. Here and now, the story lacks context. Tomorrow promises a better venue. We'll take a drive. I want to show you the farm. To know Lily, you must know something about her land." She paused, adding, "I need your trust on this."

"A deal's a deal," he replied. "They met in August 1986?"

Missy turned in a slow circle, absorbing the beauty of her entire garden, closing her eyes, breathing in the mixed fragrances. When she looked at him, she pointed toward another path lined with pink autumn joy. As they walked, she loosened the dirt around the plants with her cane.

"These little ones need the soil tended to prosper. Yes, they met in mid-August, a few days after her birthday. Lily went for three weeks instead of her usual two that year. She had a sabbatical and, therefore, more time to visit."

"She planned to do research?" Bridgette inquired.

"Some," Missy replied. "She actually took the sabbatical to renovate the old cabin out yonder." She pointed toward the woods with her cane. "Because her ancestors built it and her daddy was born there, Lily wanted it preserved. She was as happy as a kitten with a saucer of cream."

"Her father wasn't born in the farmhouse?"

"One would think but in 1906, my mother, Lily's grandmother was picking apples in the orchard when William decided upon his entry. She delivered him alone on the cabin's front porch and carried him back to the farmhouse. Sweet Jesus, it must have been a sight to see! We'll take a ride tomorrow. Where was I? Oh yes, St. John! Lily took an extra week that year just because she could. Much of the outside work and foundation repairs were finished and Lily needed to get away and relax."

"She did the work herself?"

"No, she hired local carpenters and farmhands helped, too. When she returned, she was rested, and eager to go."

"Did Lily have another man in her life?"

"Before Henry, her share, but after, she chose to go it alone. Although, I truly believe Jack was her only true love. Love came late in Lily's life but with dynamic force."

"We'll discuss this tomorrow?" asked Lock.

"Yes, with detail." Missy added, "He came to the farm because of Lily. He was smitten with her. His face lit up when she entered the room. Lily felt the same about Jack."

Lock removed a pad from his hip pocket.

"You won't need notes; concentrate on what I tell you. I'll make sure you have every detail before you leave." She thought of Jack's request. "I'm committed to it."

"Committed?"

"A promise to an old friend," she replied. "The day he arrived in Cincinnati is the same day he came to Sycamore Glen. See these roses," Missy whispered and pointed to several dozen bushes covered with pink and white buds. "I love roses but they die too quickly after they're clipped from the bush.

"The purest form of love is the same. It seldom lasts long. Because of its intensity, something usually comes along to spoil it. Jack arrived the same day I went to Chicago to visit my sister, Helen. September 20, 1986. Jack surprised her."

"Lily didn't know he was coming?" asked Bridgette.

"Did you assume he was coming here because of some prearrangement?"

"You mentioned she knew," Lock noted.

"She knew in her heart, Lockwood, but not a specific day. He flew into Cincinnati on a whim and drove to the farm with his big, loveable, yellow dog Sam. Lily wasn't here when he arrived. Jack tracked her down over in Batesville."

"How long did Taylor stay?

"Nearly three months."

"Really?"

"Yes, tomorrow, we'll drive to the cabin. I want you to see it. The day should be lovely and we'll spend most of it there. Tomorrow you and your lovely associate will get your answers."

"Did he write while he was here?"

Missy smiled.

"Yes, and I read some of it," she replied. "He took it with him when he left."

The screen door slammed on the back porch.

"Aunt Margaret!"

Tillie ran halfway to the garden.

"What is it, dear?"

"Mom says we'll eat in ten minutes."

Missy looked at Lock and said, "I hope you're hungry?"

"We haven't eaten since breakfast." He clearly thought of something and added, "I need to make a call before supper."

"Sure, Tillie will help me inside."

"Thank you," Lock said. "Bridgette, join me, please."

Missy turned to her niece and said, "Tillie, take my arm."

She watched Lockwood and Bridgette pass her niece and smiled. Missy liked them both. They made a good couple and, whether or not McGuire knew it, she was sure that beautiful young woman was in love with him. Missy looked at the blue sky, watching huge white clouds drift eastward.

"So far so good, Billie," she whispered, "It's not as difficult as I thought." Then, Missy turned her attention to a cluster of golden coreopsis.

"What's not hard, Aunt Margaret?"

The old woman smiled at her niece.

"Oh, nothing, Tillie; I'm just a silly old woman with memories."

Five

Sycamore Glen Farms, St. Omer, IN
5:11 p.m., Friday, August 13, 2010

"LOCK, HAVE YOU finished your call?"
He turned to see Jennifer Templar in the doorway.
"Yes."
"Good, dinner's ready."
He stood up from the desk and nodded at the photograph.
"How well did you know Lily, Jenny?"
"We were exceptionally close, especially as teenagers, even though she was older. We spent summers on the farm. We did not see each other often as adults because life pulls people apart. However, we remained close; we talked often, sometimes daily."
"You knew Taylor?"
"I did."
"Why'd he leave?"
She moved aside and pointed toward the dining room.
"I'm sure Missy will tell you and Miss Hannah."

THEY ATE IN a large dining room. Two picture windows on the west and south walls offered different views of the farm, its fields, woods, and, of course, the Flatrock River.

Missy wore a dark blue dress accented by a strand of pink pearls; her lips bore a wisp of matching pink lipstick. An exquisite diamond bracelet adorned her left wrist and a rectangular, blue-velvet case was next to her dinner plate.

"Biddy and Lockwood enjoy the food," she said, after the blessing. "We don't stand on formalities. We thank the Lord and dig in. We don't account for what people eat either. Please, eat your fill. Men and women as persistent as you are ought to have healthy appetites."

That Tender Light

She served herself ham and vegetables, saying, "I trust everything is fine?"

"Fine?"

"Your phone call?"

She smiled, adding a biscuit to her plate, awaiting his response.

"Yes, we had to attend to business."

Lock filled his plate.

Missy studied Lock's face, as he tasted the ham.

"Do you like it?" she asked, her expression hopeful.

"Very tasty," he said, nodding with deference toward Jennifer.

"It's Missy's recipe, she deserves the credit," Jenny said.

"It's the combination of cloves, honey and cinnamon," Missy acknowledged. "We mix it all together, put a glaze on the ham, and it renders a wonder flavor. How's the wine?"

"Delicious," Bridgette replied. Lock nodded agreement.

"It's a favorite of mine; a California vintage. I buy several cases annually."

Lock glanced at the bottle's label as Missy lifted her wineglass.

"A toast to our guests," she offered cheerfully.

Lock and Bridgette lifted their glasses and Jenny and Tillie held water goblets.

"May God's peace be in our hearts and our lives filled with joy. We ask for happy endings and mysteries solved."

Lock smiled as they all clinked glasses. He sipped his wine.

"Mysteries solved," he repeated. "Thank you."

"Speaking of mysteries," Missy stated, "The box here on the table contains a treasure. I never told anyone I have it. I'm bursting to show you."

She lifted the box with fragile fingers, opened it, and handed it to Lock. His expression filled with surprise.

"What is it Aunt Margaret?" Tillie asked.

"The U.S. Army Medal of Honor," Missy responded, smiling affectionately. "It's given to people who display extraordinary courage. It belonged to a friend of mine."

"I didn't know," Jenny whispered.

Missy smiled and gave a slight nod.

"Yes, indeed!"

Lock held the case so Bridgette could see the Medal and, together, they examined it.

"Tillie," Missy added, "a friend gave it to Lily before you were born."

Lock touched the blue ribbon with a fingertip, feeling the embroidered white stars. He counted thirteen, one for each of the original states. The Medal, a laurel wreath with elegant oak leaves encircling a five-pointed gold star, had a depiction of the Roman Goddess Minerva at its center and the words United States of America. Lock brushed his thumb across the word valor and a surmounted eagle.

"I've seen them," he whispered, "but never held one."

He glanced at Missy.

"We'll know why he left this behind," he said.

"Of course, it's integral to the story."

"I think I know," Jennifer whispered.

"I suspect you do. I've had it since 1986," Missy stated. "Courage comes in many forms, which we'll discuss."

He shrugged. "I'll wait. I'm learning the virtue of patience."

Missy giggled, reached across the table, and touched Lock's hand affectionately.

"It's good you're kind to an old woman; it earns you points in heaven."

"May I see it?" Jenny said.

"Surely."

Lock handed the Medal across the table.

"You never told me you had this, Missy."
Jenny angled it for her daughter's benefit.
"I know. At times, I've been a selfish old fool."
"No, you haven't," Jenny replied.
"When it comes to Lily, I have."
Missy received the Medal from Jenny and placed it beside her dinner plate.
"Lockwood, do you know why he received it?"
Lock sipped his wine and said, "I remember the gist. It was for his heroism during action in Tray Ninh Province, South Vietnam. It was his second time in combat with an army unit. When the unit commander died, Taylor assumed command. He almost single-handedly deterred an attack by nearly several hundred men without regard for his personal well-being."
"He must have been enormously brave," Missy added
"He's unit was out manned ten to one," Lock added. "He improvised, planted mines along a road, used hand grenades, and an M-16. Not one of his men died."
"How old was he at the time?" asked Jennifer.
"Barely twenty-four," Bridgette replied.
"He never discussed it," Missy whispered.
"We've talked to a dozen or so Medal recipients," Lock said, "Each related how some inexplicable force guided his actions. These men didn't focus on their safety, only that of others. To a man, they agreed their actions occurred out-of-body, as if in slow motion. Yet, instinctively they knew what to do. I've no way of knowing if Taylor experienced anything similar."
"Is courage God given?" Missy wondered aloud.
Bridgette answered. "Perhaps at some precise moment it is or possibly it resides in each of us and only a few rare individuals have the ability to make it surface when needed. Either way, it's both atypical and admirable."

"He showed remarkable courage," Lock said, "yet, he never wrote about it."

"He did when he was here," Missy said.

Lock dabbed his mouth with a napkin.

"Do you know this for sure?"

"Yes. As I said earlier, he never told me personally. Lily gave me a few pages to read once when he was away. He took the story with him when he left the farm."

"Do you remember any of it?"

"Passages about the Medal of Honor and detailed descriptions of prison camps," she replied.

"Will we cover this tomorrow?"

"Of course," she replied.

Thereafter, the dining room became quiet, placing undue emphasis on the movement of knives and forks and the soft hiss of air conditioning in the background. After the meal, Lock noticed Missy's pensive mood. She was deep in thought and unaware of the others. Then, she turned toward him.

"I cannot comprehend such bravery," she whispered.

"Nor, I," Lock replied, "Medal recipients told us they had no idea why it happened. None demonstrated that kind of courage previously in their lives, certainly nothing as monumental thereafter."

"Remarkable," Jennifer added.

As is your aunt, Lock thought, as is this day.

"Would you and Bridgette like more wine?" asked Missy. "It'll help you sleep. Remember, we've a busy day tomorrow and you need your rest."

"Perhaps half a glass," he replied, comfortable that Saturday would bring answers to months of questions.

"We have pie for dessert," Jennifer announced. "We usually eat dessert on the porch in the summer. Will you have some? I'll make a fresh pot of coffee."

"Coffee with dessert sounds wonderful," Bridgette stated.

That Tender Light

"Has this day met your expectations?" Missy asked, as they sat together on the front porch.

Missy, Lock, and Bridgette were enjoying their second cups of coffee after eating blueberry pie. The evening air had cooled considerably and the setting sun left a remarkable purple sky in its wake. The sound of cicadas filled the air. Jennifer and Tillie were inside cleaning dishes.

"Yes," Lock replied. "A question, please?"

"Okay."

"Earlier you said courage comes in many forms, you meant Lily, didn't you?"

"I did."

"And tomorrow you'll explain?"

"Tomorrow will be a special day. Can you arrive by eight?"

"Sure," he stifled a yawn. "Lily's the story, isn't she?"

Missy placed her hand on Lock's shoulder, affectionately.

"Lockwood, without Lily, there is no story. You and Bridgette will spend the entire day with me tomorrow. Please, help me up. I like to read before I sleep."

He helped her off the green glider.

"May I ask what you're reading?"

"Poetry these days, tonight Ode on Intimations of Immortality," she replied. "Wordsworth is a favorite of mine. I like the passage near the end...*Thanks to the human heart by which we live, thanks to its tenderness, its joys, and fears, to me the meanest flower which blows can give...*"

"*...thoughts which do often lie too deep for tears,*" Lock finished the line.

She smiled and rested her head briefly on his chest. Then, she lifted her face upwards, took his collar in her hands, pulled him near, and kissed his cheek.

"Sleep well," she said. "I'm pleased you're here. Tomorrow will be a good day." She paused. "If you don't already know, Bridgette's a lovely woman and she loves you."

She called for Tillie and, seconds later, they disappeared.

He watched Tillie hold her great aunt's arm, lending support as they entered the hallway to Missy's suite.

Lock watched her depart and soon Bridgette stood by his side.

"What did she whisper to you?"

"She said she was pleased we were here, told me tomorrow would be a good day, and told me how lovely you were. She said you were in love with me."

"She's incredibly intuitive," Bridgette whispered.

Lock kissed her forehead, then turned and watched night settle comfortably over the farm. He noticed mist feathering above the Flatrock River.

He listened to the rush of rapids, heard crickets in the garden, felt the wind on his face, and reviewed everything Margaret Lee mentioned.

He looked out across the quiet fields, watching thousands of fireflies blinking like miniature neon lights, moving to the rhythm of cicadas.

Jack Taylor spent time at Sycamore Glen. Who knows, he might have stood on the same spot, on a night much like this one. Taylor came to Indiana because of Lily Hall. What pulled them together, what pushed them apart, and was Taylor alive?

Lock smiled at Bridgette.

"You know, Biddy, I was bitterly disappointed when Jake Prescott gave me this assignment."

He pulled her close and kissed her.

"Life places treasures in the most unexpected places, like a quiet farm in rural Indiana."

"A guy just never knows," she whispered. "Let's go back to the room. I want to see if we have an answer to our question."

"And afterward?" asked Lock.

That Tender Light

Bridgette smiled, "Missy is a particularly perceptive woman. Afterward, I'll show you how lovely I can be."

"It's a date."

"I hoped it would be."

He kissed her again, lifted his satchel, escorted Bridgette to the rental car, and drove away leaving the story in the twilight with the crickets, cicadas, fireflies, and the misty fog forming near the Flatrock River.

Six

Sycamore Glen Farms, St. Omer, IN
8:25 a.m., Saturday, August 14, 2010

THE NEXT MORNING, an old Dodge pickup bounced on a dirt road toward a distant patch of woods. Margaret Lee sat between Bridgette Hannah and Jenny, who drove. Lock was jammed in behind the passenger seat. He glanced briefly at the Flatrock River on their right and then out the rear window, where the white farmhouse stood framed against a high blue sky in the middle of rolling fields.

Missy turned to him.

Big difference from what you're used to, huh?"

"Yes, quite a bit actually," he replied.

"The land's in my blood," Missy said, "and was in Lily's, too. You know my great grandfather and his brother helped escaping slaves during the Civil War. Such charity makes a family proud and speaks volumes about human kindness. A natural cave is to the south in distant hills. They hid slaves who were working their way to Cincinnati and points north. Another cave is up ahead.

"If Grandpa Angus' diary is accurate, several Civil War skirmishes occurred here and men died. People think land is just trees and fields, but it's much more—it's life, love, history, and human passion. Believe me; the land knows the secrets of all who pass by. It knows more than any person does. The land witnesses everything, if it could talk what a tale it would tell."

"Shakespeare wrote something similar."

"Well, then, he was a wise man."

After they negotiated a bend in the Flatrock River, they crossed over a single-lane wooden bridge and, after exiting, Jennifer turned sharply left onto a little-used road.

That Tender Light

"There's an old orchard out this way," Jenny said, slowing the pickup. "We're headed there. Biddy, pull your arm in."

The river, now on their left, meandered pleasingly to the eye. The road was nothing more than a wide path through thick woods. Branches scraped against the truck's windows and roof and then, after a quarter mile, the path widened, eased toward the right, and ascended a small rise. They stopped on the edge of a magnificent orchard and Bridgette helped Missy exit. Soon, they stood in a natural, sunny, alcove surrounded by rows of fruit trees heavy with crop. From the nearby river, they heard the sound of rapids and falling water.

"There's a small falls over yonder; just beyond it, a good-sized trestle," Missy said, pointing her cane. "Remember, yesterday's train." Not waiting for a reply, she started up a stone path, which wound through rows of aligned fruit trees.

"Come along," she said. "You need to see a few things; they're elemental to the story. And take my arm, Lockwood, before I land on my bum; sometimes I dizzy out."

In the background, Jenny and Bridgette chuckled. Lock hurriedly took Missy's arm.

Jennifer followed, carrying a large picnic basket while Bridgette carried several blankets.

"Legend says Johnny Appleseed planted these trees," Missy said, smiling mischievously as they walked along.

"Truthfully?"

Missy shook her head slightly.

"Lockwood, I think my relatives did the planting, but who knows. It's fun to pretend Johnny Appleseed."

"Wasn't he from Massachusetts?"

"Yes, but he's buried up near Fort Wayne." Then, smiling, she added, "A wholesome fib does no harm." She looked at him and winked. "Farms are fun places, if you know what to look for. Have you spent much time on a farm?"

"No. I grew up in Utica, in a residential area—big trees; big houses."

"One becomes accustomed to a farm quickly," Missy noted. "However, for it to seep into your blood and sinew, you must live on a farm for years. Then, it never leaves you! It hones character."

The path through the trees abruptly ended in a broad clearing. There, Lock discovered a neatly manicured lawn with yet another magnificent flower garden and a picturesque cabin.

Missy noted his appreciative expression.

"Farmhands tend it for me and replace trees when necessary. They work the orchard, which continues to provide fruit after all these years. We do some canning and bake pies but most of the harvest we give to the poor. An access road's on the other side, but it's not very scenic. My men use it. I prefer the way we came. I came that way as a girl. Lily did, too."

Missy shook her arm free and walked slowly toward the cabin's front porch. She sat on a rocking chair, tilted her head upwards, and let sunshine warm her face. She looked at Lock and Bridgette and pointed to chairs beside her.

"My friends please sit here. God's given us another good day, again low humidity."

"When should I return, Missy?" Jennifer asked, setting the basket down. She put a blanket across her aunt's legs.

"I'll call when we're ready, I think late afternoon, sweetheart." She looked at Lock and Bridgette. "No worry, Jenny has taken care of us proper. Facilities are inside and we have a wonderful lunch. It's a grand day for learning new things. Sound good?"

Lock and Bridgette nodded as Jenny touched the basket.

"There are thermoses of sweet tea and one of hot honeyed tea; cold sodas, too. I've made sandwiches," she said.

"You also have fruit, apple pie, and other odds and ends," she continued. "A cell phone is in the basket in case you need me. Hold in the number two for the farmhouse."

"Thank you, sweetheart. You're a jewel," Missy replied, resting her cane against her leg.

As her niece walked away, Missy waved timidly and watched Jennifer disappear into the trees. Then, with an impish air, she removed the blanket.

"I never get as cold as she thinks I do." Missy listened, waiting for the pickup's sound to fade. When the motor receded, she pointed across the clearing.

"Not far from the cabin is the family plot. Lily's buried next to her parents. Although he's somewhere in France, I placed a stone there for Billie, too. It's where I'll be."

Questions formed in Lock and Bridgette's expressions.

"I have problems with cancer." She shrugged. "Only God knows when I'll go, but soon.

"I've one more job to do in my life and, coincidentally, you have a story to write. It's more than chance we're together. I'd think it's providential."

She saw concern linger in Lock's eyes.

"I'm ready to go; have been for years. I've made peace for the bad I've done in my life,"

"How long were Jack and Lily together?" Bridgette asked, changing the subject.

"Good girl, you get right to it."

Bridgette smiled and glanced quickly at Lock.

"I've learned from the best."

"They were not together long enough," Missy replied. "It happened fast and was very intense. Lily was a beautiful and courageous woman. I held her in my arms the day she was born and she was in my arms the day she died. She loved this spot near the river, which was to have been their home. It's a damn shame how things turn out.

"They spent a great deal of time on the restoration. You know, Lily told me they made love out here." She smiled, nodding approvingly. "I rather like the thought of that, Biddy," she added. She looked upward through the opening in the trees. "Yes, by God, I do. I can see where it would be breathtaking, making love here in twilight with a million stars peeking down, as warm winds rush across naked skin.

"The warmth of afternoon sunshine wouldn't be bad either. When love's involved, I believe it's the only unselfish gift a man and woman can give each other.

"In its purest form, if done right, it dazzles the human spirit. Wraps it up and turns it inside out. I believe they experienced such emotion." She paused, thinking. "Yes, a special gift."

"Missy, in our research we learned something of a contradiction. Jack left here late in 1986, remembering the letter to his agent from Montana. Yet, our research shows that Lily did not die until the spring of 1987. Did they have a falling out?"

"God, no, Lockwood."

"We also learned from a local waitress who recognized Taylor that she didn't see him at Lily's service," Bridgette added. "She said she saw him often at a diner with Lily; however, she didn't see him at Lily's funeral."

"My, you've been busy, which waitress?"

"A woman named Betty."

Missy smiled.

"Oh, Betty...I changed her diapers when she was a baby. Is she well?"

"She seems fine," Lock said.

"I like Betty. Her husband's a musician. Well, she's correct; Jack wasn't there and he had his reasons."

"What were they?"

"In due time," she replied.

That Tender Light

"There's something else," Bridgette said. "The call we made last night concerned Henry Malone. We hoped to find out more background, maybe talk to him. However, we learned he died in a fire in northern Indiana in mid-December, after Jack left."

"I know and I can't think of a happier ending for that bastard." She stood. "I'll be just a moment."

"Do you need help?"

"No, I can manage." She went inside and returned moments later carrying a large manila envelope. She sat and wiped her brow, placing the envelope on her lap.

Bridgette removed a tape recorder from her purse.

"You'll be reading for a while, dear, and won't need that. I'll make sure all your questions are answered," she said. "May I have a glass of sweet tea?"

She rocked easily in her chair, watching Lock handle a thermos. He filled three glasses decorated with butterflies and looked at Missy.

"No spiced rum, today?"

"Stop being a snit," she said, smiling. She handed the package to Bridgette.

"What is it?"

"Jack Taylor's unpublished ninth novel entitled: THAT TENDER LIGHT. Actually, it's two novels in one. One is about his love affair with Lily, the other is an untitled story about his final mission in Southeast Asia, and a woman he loved in Laos named Julia Ormandy. She was a physician.

"It's autobiographical. He wrote it in the first person. I believe it's truthful. I'll go inside to work on a quilt. I'll be there when you finish. However, I must confirm that I have your word that you still agree to my terms. Do we need to put that in writing?"

"We can, if you prefer; however, we'll keep our promise."

"Good, Lockwood, never forget that commitment."

Seven

Sycamore Glen Farms, St. Omer, IN
4:56 p.m., Saturday, August 14, 2010

Missy was sleeping when they entered the cabin. She opened her eyes as she heard movement.

"What time is it?"

"Nearly five o'clock," Lock said.

"I slept four hours," she said. "I was working on my quilt and nodded off." Noting the picnic basket, she said, "I'm starving; let's eat in the kitchen and discuss Jack's book."

After they ate sandwiches, nibbled raw vegetables and fruit, and drank hot tea, Bridgette cut wedges of apple pie. They were well into the pie when Missy broke the silence.

"I'm sure you have questions," she offered, anxiously.

Bridgette spoke first. "Nobody in the Indianapolis hospital knew Jack's identity? That seems unreal."

"He used Josiah and nobody made the connection, not even the specialists. The press hardly covered Lily's misfortune. They would have, had they known Jack was involved but he controlled it. Remember he was reclusive."

"What about payment for the specialists?"

"Jack took care of that, I never asked about it."

"Did Lily actually ask Bender to kill Malone?"

"Yes, she did."

"I have to ask," Bridgette followed, "Did he do it?"

"I'd like to hold my answer for a while, but I will respond."

"Sure," Lock replied, sensing sorrow in Missy's voice. "Jack departed because Lily asked him to go?"

"Yes, he was devastated, Lockwood; he was a broken man with a broken heart. Jack's time with Lily changed him forever and his love for her is the only reason he left. He would have stayed; I believe that in my heart."

"It's a wonderfully written story," Bridgette said. "However, it reveals harsh realities. The book will surely sully his reputation. He killed an agent, he assassinated three men and killed six others indiscriminately, and that doesn't include those Taylor killed escaping or in battle."

"I don't think he gives a hoot about his reputation; I'd say the past twenty or so years prove that. Apparently, he moved on a long time ago."

"Do you know where he is or think you know?" Lock's voice was firm; his eyes steady.

"Truthfully, I do not, Lockwood."

"The authorities will surely question you and Bender about Malone's death."

Missy rubbed her eyes and said, "I know, but what proof do they have...a few words in a book from an overheard conversation? An attorney would have it dismissed as hearsay within minutes. By the way, Peter is deceased."

"Still, speculation will flourish," Lock observed. "It's fairly obvious what Lily asked Bender to do."

Missy sipped tea. "If you believe what Jack wrote," she said. "Again what's the proof? I'm dying. I don't care about speculation. I can take heat; it won't be the first time in my life I've been jammed up. However, I assure you, I have nothing to fear because neither Peter nor I killed Malone. Someone else did. Let them come at me all they want?"

"Missy, if you or Bender hired someone, it's the same as if you did it yourselves," Bridgette noted.

"We didn't, Biddy. I didn't know about Lily and Peter's conversation until I read the manuscript. That's when I learned Jack knew. By then, Henry was already dead."

"Are you saying Malone's death was accidental?"

"That's what I'd say."

"Missy," Bridgette replied, "it sounds too coincidental, and terribly convenient."

"I know...I know." Missy sighed. "I trust anything I tell you in the course of this conversation remains confidential. You won't reveal it, in any way; do I have your word?"

"Yes," Bridgette replied. Lock nodded.

The old woman scratched her chin.

"Peter did not kill Henry Malone," Missy whispered. "At the time Henry died, he was in Margaret Mary Hospital over in Batesville, recovering from a severely broken leg and a concussion. He fell on ice."

"Then who did it, do you know?" Lock asked.

Missy stared at him for several moments, her eyes as cold as death itself. When she spoke, her voice was barely audible.

"I think Jack killed Henry. In fact, I'm sure of it."

"Jack?"

"Yes," Missy replied.

Lock whispered, "How?"

Missy turned to him. "When we were in Chicago at the anniversary party, we were discussing people's quirks and Lily told us that Henry always went to his hunting lodge the day after his birthday and always alone. Surprisingly, Lily mentioned she still had a duplicate key in her dresser on a Notre Dame key-ring, which she never returned."

"When was Malone's birthday?"

"December 9."

Bridgette checked her email and looked at Lock.

"He died on December 10," she whispered.

"And, as I indicated, Peter was in the hospital. He entered on December 8, three days after he spoke with Lily and two days after Jack left. Peter did not leave the hospital until December 13. He did not kill Hank Malone and he never hired anyone to do it."

"Okay, but why were you discussing Malone's lodge at an anniversary party?"

"Hell, Lockwood, you know how conversations go, one person says one thing, which reminds another of something else, and so on. Lily had several drinks and was funny as hell. Anyway, she said Henry liked to get away by himself annually, to clean his guns, and winterize everything and he always went there on that day. She said he was adamant about it from the time he was a young man. She even wished aloud that one of his shotguns would go off. Her statement was both sad and funny, but without intent."

The kitchen was suddenly quiet and the sound of the waterfalls seemed magnified through an open window.

"Is this the reason you didn't published his book?"

"The main reason, yes," she replied. "I assumed the law would come snooping, if they thought Peter had anything to do with Malone's demise.

"Lily obviously wanted him to do it. I am sure that if the authorities learned about Peter's hospitalization, their attention would have turned to Jack or me. I protected Lily and Jack. I didn't want the law sniffing about.

"At one time, I decided never to publish the book and I almost burned it. I don't know what stopped me. Possibly, it was my love for Lily; maybe I wanted some good to come from her ordeal. I just hid it and pushed it out of my mind. You know, let sleeping dogs lie. However, after my oncologist said my time was nigh, I reconsidered. I mean to say, Peter is deceased and what can they do to me?

"I'll probably be gone in a few months. If people want to speculate, let them. I'll see the book published and, then, whatever happens is God's will. Frankly, I hope the book earns millions for charity."

"I never imagined this when we started our journey."

"People get sidetracked, Lockwood. You know, Jack called me once after he left the farm," Missy continued. "He wanted me to know he was safe and getting on with his life.

"He told me I would receive a package that included a book about Lily and him. He said his time with her was the most authentic of his life. He said there could never be another woman."

"Did he say anything about Malone?"

"Not in any direct way, Biddy."

"But he said something," Lock probed.

"When I told him Malone was dead, the way he said *I know* piqued my curiosity. I don't doubt Peter would have killed Henry. In fact, when I questioned him about it, after I read Jack's manuscript, he admitted he was preparing to do so, but then he slipped on ice. Of course, by the time he left the hospital, Malone was dead."

"I still don't understand why you think Jack did it?"

"Biddy, it goes back to his phone call, his manuscript, and that damn key. At the end of his manuscript he writes, *I wanted what Malone took away from me. I wanted everything that cost that man his life.*

"After I read that passage, I went into Lily's room and searched for the key but couldn't find it. I asked Peter if he took it. He did not."

"What was Peter's reaction?"

"He was happy Malone was dead."

"And what did he say about Jack's possible involvement?"

"Peter said, however it happened, Malone's death was justified, for Lily's sake." She paused, thinking. "Lily and Jack were inseparable. They breathed together. Each fearful that any time they spent apart would burst their dream or diminish its value.

"Jack told me he could never replay it chronologically. He said it all blended into one continuous force, as streams form a lake. He thought of it as one thinks of sunlight: warm, bright, penetrating, and nourishing, no one part better or more important than any other part."

"He said he craved the love she gave him, physically and emotionally, and knew Lily felt the same. They were at each other's core each day, in every way."

Bridgette toyed with her fork.

"For a man who suffered from killing so freely," Bridgette whispered, "It's ironic that he killed once more for the woman he loved."

"Life is filled with irony," Missy whispered.

"There are more things you should know. The key on that Notre Dame key-ring was in Malone's curled hand. I think Jack placed it there as a signal to Peter or me."

"We didn't know that," Bridgette said.

"Not widely reported; but, several stories included it."

"Missy, you specifically said *more* things?"

"Yes, there's another reason Lily wanted Malone dead. She carried Jack's baby, but miscarried after the beating. That, too, must never become public. Lily said Jack never knew and, if he's alive, reporting it has no value. She kept their baby a secret and it should remain that way. She was adamant. Lily knew having him leave bordered on the unbearable; losing a child might have ended him."

"Could this be more tangled," Bridgette observed.

Missy nodded, "There is another piece."

When Missy did not continue, Lock said, "Jack asked Lily to marry him. Did they marry?"

"No, that's not it. I was never able to find any legal documents. He never wanted to leave Lily. I believe he would have stayed with her to the end and married her. Of course, once he agreed to Lily's request, marriage was no longer in the equation."

"Did the police ever interview you about Malone's death?"

"They never made the connection. The newspaper reports I read said death was accidental, due to a faulty gas line."

Missy put her head in her hands and cried uncontrollably.

"Henry broke her back and she was a quadriplegic," she said amid sobs. "Jack had specialists in from all over; the prognosis never changed." Missy breathed deeply and dried her eyes. "After weeks of testing and crushed hopes, Lily had enough. Her natural resolve took over. She told Jack to let it be. Those were her exact words. We sat in her hospital room when she said it. He loved her and did what she wanted, although she did see a specialist on their next to last day. Scheduled for weeks, it was Jack's last ray of hope.

"Before he left, he was always in her hospital room. They listened to music, he read books to her, and they talked seemingly without interruption. He sketched or painted all the scenes of the farm you see in my library. She described the images she wanted and he gave her the only things he could, his talent, time, and love.

"When they were alone, I don't honestly know what they did or said. In the book, Jack states she asked him to make love to her one final time. Whether she felt it physically, I cannot say. I know she did emotionally because she told me."

"Lily had grit," Lock whispered.

"More than you know," Missy replied. "She was the one suffering, yet she kept Jack's and my spirits up. She made it her goal to ease his pain and make him laugh as a way to dilute the devastation. Henry Malone was an evil, jealous, controlling son of bitch who deserved to die for what he did.

"Everything Jack feared came true. He loved Lily and lost her. He always feared losing her, said it would be his retribution, a cross to carry for all the bad things he'd done in life."

"Did he feel that way when he departed?"

"Yes...he blamed himself."

"When did he leave?"

"Early December 1986," she replied. "Lily asked him to leave, just as he wrote in the book. Come, walk with me."

Eight

Sycamore Glen Farms, St. Omer, IN
6:07 p.m., Saturday, August 14, 2010

THEY WENT BEHIND the cabin and took a path through a grove of trees

"Lily's obituary said she died as a result of complications from her paralysis."

"So, you knew all along?"

"We read the obituary yesterday," Bridgette whispered. "I wish it had been different."

"Not more than I. It hurts more than you can ever imagine."

Lock watched a blue jay flittering in an apple tree.

"He left because he loved her."

"Yes, think of the sacrifice," Missy replied. "He tried hard to convince Lily to let him to stay. She declined.

"She couldn't stand the thought of him seeing her paralyzed and so reliant. Thus, their life together ended. She wanted him to remember her as a vibrant, loving, passionate woman. They were together only a few months."

"He never came back after he departed?"

"No, he did as she asked and left for good.

"I remember his desolate expression. The last time I saw him was when he drove away with his yellow dog by his side. Lily was still in Indianapolis. We took a lease on a small apartment near the hospital but he and I came back to the farm. He gathered his papers and things, and I transferred the title of an old jeep I owned, and off he went."

"Is that when he took Malone's key?"

"My guess would be yes, Biddy. In the ensuing weeks, Jack apparently drifted trying to find peace, according to his book."

"Lily lived only a few months, thereafter?"

"Suffered is a better choice of words, Lock. She was home by then. One morning I went into her room to check on her and Lily asked me if I thought Jack still loved her. I said I was sure of it. By then she knew of Malone's death and Peter's hospitalization. If you ask me, she knew in her heart Jack killed Malone. I hugged her that day and she told me she could no longer tolerate the emotional sting of losing the only man she truly loved."

Missy entered her family's cemetery and pointed to Lily's headstone. She read the inscription aloud:

The sunshine is a glorious birth;
But yet I know, where'er I go,
That there hath past away
A glory from the earth.

"William Wordsworth," Lock whispered.
"Yes," Missy said, "I chose the words."
"She died here on the farm?"
"Yes, she chose to die where she lived, where they loved each other unequivocally. She chose to be near those memories. Today's her birthday; she would be sixty-two."

Missy bowed her head slightly and wept again.
"Do you know where Jack is?"
"No, Lock, and I don't choose to know." She cried some more and eventually said, "I want to publish THAT TENDER LIGHT and I want you to help me.

"That's why I did a background check. I wanted to deem you worthy and you are. The proceeds will go into a private trust with three purposes: to feed the poor, to fight paralysis and to support St. Teresa's orphanage and others. We will make the arrangements through my attorney, in concert with Jack's literary agency. I have his power of attorney.

"Since he never signed a new contract to write more novels, I control his final book. I have all the legal documents prepared." She reached into her apron pocket and removed a letter. "Here," she offered, "It's from Jack."

Lock and Bridgette read simultaneously:

My life has changed and this is my final book. I have found a new life, something I feel is a fitting turn. I am teaching now and joy and promise fill my days. After many years of struggle and torment, I have learned peace and happiness is ours to embrace, with God's help. He guides us to the proper choices. If we listen and follow, salvation will be ours, regardless of the evil we have done.

I know now I will never write another book. I have tried and I cannot. Fortunately, other forms of creativity provide solace. I will forever be indebted to their counsel and protection.

Please understand the gifts I have sent are songs from my heart. Please fulfill my request; however, because of Lily, the final decision is yours alone. Whatever you decide is fine with me. Included herein is everything you will need to proceed.

Look out toward the Flatrock River in the evenings and, when you do, think of us.

Enjoy your days and God's blessings,
Jack

Lock glanced at Missy.
"He teaches; where?"
"He did teach, that letter was written more than two decades ago, long after he left my farm." She cleared her throat. "I don't know if he's still teaching, or if he's alive."
"What were the gifts he sent?"
"These clips you see in my hair, a silver comb, a vintage bottle of my favorite wine—petite sirah—and his novel."
She paused and seemed suddenly nervous.

"You mentioned another stipulation."

"Yes, Lockwood, I did. Thus far you've promised to protect whatever I asked you to keep confidential."

"We've agreed."

Margaret Lee looked at them with a steeled expression.

"This is something Lily wanted from the day Jack left. Because of her paralysis and the emotional strain, Lily asked me to end her life, which I did. I injected her with enough insulin to stop her heart."

"How did you get insulin?"

"Peter was a diabetic, Lockwood. I stole it from him."

"He never suspected anything was missing?

"No, I snitched two empty vials from his waste basket several weeks before. I filled them with water and broke them intentionally, pretending they were the unused vials. I was in his fridge looking for a ginger ale and said I knocked them to the floor. It was easy. I took one of his old syringes and used that. Peter never knew. I hugged Lily as tightly as I could and told her Jack loved her as did I it. She breathed deeply and died. Jack doesn't know. If alive, he must never know. I recognize killing is wrong; however, in Lily's case, death was justified; in Malone's case more so. There is such a squabble over assisted death. It was her choice; I was a conduit. I have told God the same; my fate's in His hands."

"Why are you telling us? You didn't have to do that."

"I understand Biddy. I want you to know how brave Lily was, how strong until the end. I also needed the catharsis of a confession. I already feel better for having done so."

Thereafter, she shook noticeably and, for a moment, the world seemed to stop, all sound disappeared, and the air felt neither warm nor cold. Lock and Bridgette looked at each other until the blare of a passing train broke the spell.

Lock hugged Margaret Lee tenderly to calm her trembling body. In her ear he whispered, "We'll never tell a soul."

NINE

Prescott Residence, New York, NY
12:17 p.m., Monday, January 17, 2011

T*HAT* T*ENDER* L*IGHT*, hit bookstores on September 20, 2010, exactly twenty-four years after Jack Taylor first arrived at Sycamore Glen and the same day Lock McGuire and Bridgette Hannah's front-page story made news in T*HE* N*EW* Y*ORK* E*POCH*. As of January 17, Taylor's book stood atop bestseller charts everywhere.

In November, Lock and Bridgette completed a series of national interviews. Lock is now an editor and sits in the chair once occupied by Jake Prescott; Bridgette is an investigative reporter. Their story is with the Pulitzer Committee. They were married Thanksgiving weekend.

One night in San Francisco, Lock opened a plummy petite sirah from Hope Vintners of Northern California.

"Isn't this the same wine Missy enjoyed?"

"Indeed." Lock pointed to the label, his eyebrows arching.

"Do you think he's there? How did you figure it out?"

"A hunch...I went on line. In addition to wine, some of the clerics are noted silversmiths, some teach migrant children."

"The comb, the wine, and teachers," she said.

"There's more...the Abbey's vicar general was a green beret and once served in the same unit as Taylor."

"What should we do?"

"We let it go," he replied.

The media and Indiana State Police asked if Bridgette or Lock knew of Taylor's location. They never mentioned their suspicion about Hope Vintners. When asked if Peter Bender killed Henry Malone, they noted Peter's alibi. True to their pledge to Missy, they said Taylor's story was factual and he loved Lily Hall, who sent him away with a broken heart.

Lock and Bridgette visited Missy in late September to present the first copy of Taylor's book. Sadly, Margaret Lee died on New Year's Eve 2010, her ninety-ninth birthday. She, too, had met with police concerning Malone's death; however, lack of evidence negated further investigation.

Sadly, Jake Prescott, Lock's editor, died on January 14, 2011. Until his death, he never missed a chance to remind Lock whose hunch began the ball rolling on the Taylor story.

AFTER PRESCOTT'S FUNERAL, Jake's daughter pulled Lock aside, offered an envelope, and said, "From my dad." Lock smiled, thinking Jake wanted to rib him one last time about the story. Instead, he found a surprise:

Lock, this is why I chose you. Taylor's grandmother Rebecca and I were lovers, despite our ages. She was widowed and lonely; I was alone, too. It happened before I met my wife. Thanks for helping an old friend learn the truth about the grandson of a woman for whom he had deep affection.

In the envelope, Lock found a worn photograph. The caption read LACKAWANNA TRIBUNE'S EDITOR MEETS STAFF. The people identified in the photograph were Prescott, Rebecca Smith Taylor, and young Jack Taylor, her grandson.

Lock chuckled, slipped the photo into his pocket, and turned to Prescott's daughter. "Your dad's the best, an exceptional man. He knew Jack Taylor and never told me. Janet, his note answers a question I had from the start."

"Which was?"

"When he assigned the Taylor story, I fought it. I challenged; your dad persisted. I kept asking the same pointless question, repeatedly. Now, I have my answer."

"What was your question?"

"Why me?"

Epilogue

April 2011

"Of all acts of man, repentance is the most divine. The greatest of all faults is to be conscious of none."
—Thomas Carlyle

Abbey of Hope
Northern California
5:30 p.m., Holy Saturday, April 23, 2011

The eldest cleric, Brother Thespis, heard the dinner bell, which summoned the monks in from the fields for their evening meal. He stood, stretched his tired back, and motioned for his brothers to follow. The clerics gathered in the center of the vineyard and, carrying their tools, started for the Abbey, leaving their labor in the cool afternoon air.

The clerics formed a single line and, as if on cue, their voices became one as they chanted, VICTIMAE PASCHALI LAUDES, in honor of Christ's sacrifice on the cross.

One brother with a thin scar near his temple stood at the end of the queue. Inspired by the brilliant colors of a dying sun and the scent of God's good earth in the air, he sang with the others, his soft tenor on key.

Slowly, they passed the silver shop and entered the barn where they hung their tools.

Their song faded as they entered the Abbey's narthex. Once inside, they washed at communal sinks, drying their faces and hands with clean white towels.

Soon, they sat at a long table in high-backed chairs in a richly paneled dining hall, awaiting their evening meal of vegetables, potatoes, beef, dark bread, and in honor of the Lenten Fast, a very tasty jus de raisin with a particularly robust flavor. As Brother Thespis stood, heads bowed:

Heavenly Father, thank you for the food and drink we share, for this day, for each other's company, for our families and loved ones, for the joy in our lives, and for the pleasure of cultivating the bounty of your good earth. Father, remember us this day in your kingdom. In your wisdom, end all hatred and replace it with love and charity. Amen.

They blessed themselves, filled their plates, and ate in candlelight. Muted conversations, jovial observations, and laughter quickly filled the dining hall. The clerics clearly enjoyed their banter at the dusking of the day.

Afterward, in their free time before Vespers, some clerics wandered back to their rooms, others read, a few chose music, and several wrote letters.

Two brothers sat at a table beside a fireplace to conclude a game of chess begun several days ago. The Abbey's own mineral water stood in glasses beside the game board and orange flames from a crackling fire reflected in the crystal.

Twenty minutes later, footsteps echoed off the Abbey's polished marble floor. Stephen gestured with his forefinger to gain his friend's attention.

"We have a visitor," Stephen said. "From his eyes, I believe Brother Nicholas seeks you."

"I thought it might be the vicar," his opponent whispered. "He has a distinct pause and scrape in every step. An old war wound, I've learned."

"I wonder what he wants."

His opponent shrugged and spotted his queen.

"We shall learn. Checkmate," Brother Josiah smiled. "Let's resume your lesson with a game tomorrow evening."

Stephen scratched his beard, bowed in deference to the more skillful player, and asked, "Where did you learn such a move?"

"In Laos, from an Australian Cistercian; tomorrow I'll show you a move Anatoly Karpov used against Viktor Korchnoi in their tenth game."

"A word, please," Nicholas' voice came into Josiah's ear.

"Surely," Josiah replied. To his opponent, he said, "Let's try again tomorrow night, Stephen. You must remember the importance of defending your monarch's flank."

"Same place, same time," Stephen responded, nodding.

That Tender Light

Josiah stood and smiled at the vicar.

"Is this about the school's mortgage? You should not be angry that it has been paid in full, I must use the money."

"No, a package came for you earlier in the day. You were in the vineyard. Knowing its importance, I placed it in my office safe."

Brother Josiah's expression changed immediately and, in that instant, he was again Jack Taylor.

"Have you told anyone, Nick?"

"Not a soul knows."

"From Sing's daughter in Chicago?" asked Jack.

"Yes."

Nicholas was the only one Jack trusted with the full story, the only man entrusted with the package's significance, the only man who knew Jack was not ordained.

"My God...I'd forgotten she would probably send it," Jack whispered. "Let's go see what we have."

The two men walked down the marbled hallway, their footsteps speaking in echoes behind them. They descended a stairway and entered a brightly lighted office. The fragrance in the room was that of hyacinths. Jack stood aside as his friend opened a safe and withdrew a medium box. As he handed it to Jack, he studied his friend's impassive eyes.

Jack examined the package and recognized its sender immediately. Sing's daughter was the discreet intermediary selected to transfer any missive from Margaret Lee. She had no knowledge of its contents or its ultimate recipient. She simply did what her father asked the day he came from his home in Wisconsin years ago with a special request.

"When I arrived more than twenty years ago, Nick," Jack whispered, "you gave me time and a place to heal. I don't know if I want to reopen old wounds."

"You must," Nick replied. "It will bring symmetry to your life; you've changed for the better."

"Symmetry," Jack repeated. "It once had meaning."

Nick moved beside Jack and said, "You saved our lives in Laos. You sponsored Sing, helped find his daughters, brought his children to this country, and funded their educations. You helped Father Webster's lepers. You've given millions to IASS. Once, I believed we'd never make it. We did and we're better for it. My leg constantly reminds me of the hate we shared in Laos, but it also says I survived. God's miracles are puzzling; only he does the sketch and paints the canvas. We know not the *why* in His scheme. The contents of this box is an example, consider all the good it will do. You've done your penance; now, enjoy your miracle."

Jack studied Nick's eyes and said, "We carry similar scars. Does God truly forgive men like us, Nick?"

"Yes, of course he does."

"For what we've done, for the lives we destroyed?"

"Destroyed on earth but not in heaven...yes, He's delivered us from darkness. We are His instruments. His divine glory is in your repentance, is in the good you do to honor Lily, is in the years of hope you've given the poor to honor Julia. Hate and bitterness were prologue; they had to happen before you knew how to change lives. Take the time you need. Absence at Lauds or Vespers won't be questioned."

Jack placed his hand on Nick's shoulder, squeezed it appreciatively, smiled slightly, and went to his quarters, cradling the package against his chest. Once there, he latched the door. He placed the box on his desk, selected an opera and soon the definitive beauty of Puccini's MADAME BUTTERFLY filled the air.

Jack sat at his desk and his hands shook as he prepared to open the parcel. From its weight, he guessed its contents. He used a penknife to cut away a seal and removed a heavy manila envelope.

Well, he thought, the old girl did really cast the die.

That Tender Light

A smaller, white envelope yellowed by time—an envelope he had personally preaddressed and sent to Missy some twenty-two years ago—was taped and centered onto the manila envelope. He asked her to use it to route correspondence secretly through a P.O. Box controlled by Sing's oldest daughter, now a physician in Illinois. Sing's daughter, per her father's direction, always waited a few months before forwarding anything.

With the penknife, Jack removed the smaller envelope. He soon unfolded a letter written on Sycamore Glen Farms stationery, which he quickly read:

Dear Jack,

I hope you have found peace after all these years. I realize the address you gave to me years ago is not your actual location. Therefore, I do not fear sending your novel, THAT TENDER LIGHT. I am sure a discreet process will protect your location.

Many critics have raved about your book; a few, because of your actions, have not been as kind. However, after all these years, you have another bestseller!

Per my attorney, the money from this book will support charities, as you requested. The proceeds will create an endowment to feed and clothe the poor for years to come.

I think of you and Lily often and pray others will not suffer as Lily did. Jack, I realize I will never see or hear from you again. I do not have long to live and may have passed by the time you receive my package. You are in my thoughts and prayers and I thank you for loving Lily.

With great fondness,
Missy Lee

He reread the letter and placed it in a dog-eared copy of Thomas Merton's SEVEN STORY MOUNTAIN.

He reached for and opened the manila envelope. Within, he found a newly printed hardbound copy of his ninth novel: THAT TENDER LIGHT. The cover design showed a woman in white on a beach at sunset.

He opened the book and savored the scent of fresh ink on new paper. After all the work, that peculiar scent made writing worthwhile. He soon read the book's introduction:

Jack Taylor, one of the foremost writers of the 20th Century, disappeared mysteriously in the autumn of 1986. No one knows if he is alive and, if so, where he lives. We never learned that.

However, through the pages of his book we at last understand why he changed his life forever.

For years, THAT TENDER LIGHT was the possession of Margaret Lee. Ms. Lee is the last known connection to Jack Taylor. She is the aunt of Lily Veronica Hall, a woman who was and, we believe, continues to be the great love of Jack Taylor's life. Their time together moved him deeply.

Taylor chose to share their story as if real life became great fiction. Margaret Lee advises the story is true as written. Taylor has also included an autobiographical account of the love and torment he experienced while serving in Laos in conjunction with the Vietnam War.

It reveals his fears based on the lives he took in war and includes a personal account of his Medal of Honor valor—insight never before presented. Tragically, it reveals he killed a man with cold-blooded revenge, an act many deem heinous.

Proceeds from this book will feed and clothe the poor, provide college educations for the children of Christ-on-the-Cross School in the U.S. Virgin Islands, and fund the fight against human paralysis.

Royalties from his previous books have supported these causes for years. Wherever Taylor is, we thank him for his generosity and this moving story. We hope peace and harmony fill his remaining days.

The reporters, Bridgette Hannah and Lockwood McGuire, worked for THE NEW YORK EPOCH. When Jack read their story on-line, in the Abbey's library, he wondered about a package from Missy but soon it slipped his mind. He never ordered the book himself. Because of vows of poverty and obedience, brothers did not purchase personal items, such as books. They could only accept gifts. If Jack did not follow this practice, questions would arise and he despised attention of any sort.

He reached into a bottom desk drawer and removed a small album, glancing at a few photos he retained. In one of them, he saw himself and Nick Kunz, now Brother Nicholas, who had traveled a tortuous path to this point-in-time. Jack then studied his own face, hardly recognizing the young man he saw staring back, a young man who received the Medal of Honor but who killed with incomprehensible abandon.

He turned a page and studied the photograph of his grandparents, Tomas and Anne Gomez. He touched it, wishing he could have a few minutes to talk to them again.

There was also a picture of him with Rebecca Taylor and Jake Prescott, the young editor of Jack's hometown weekly. Each had encouraged him to write. His photo of Julia Ormandy brought a smile. He saw a photograph of Margaret Lee. She had been wonderfully warm to him and now, thanks to her, many people would receive help. Then, for the first time in two decades, he turned the page and looked at his only photograph of Lily Veronica Hall.

She sat on a swing at Sycamore Glen with Sam, his dog, by her side. Suddenly, as if she were in the room, he smelled Lily's perfume, studied her blue eyes, felt the touch of her lips on his, and heard the mid-western curl in her magnificent voice. After a moment's reflection, he reached inside his cassock and touched Lily's coin.

"A penny for good fortune," he whispered her exact words.

D. James Then

Her penny now hung on an elegant gold chain, encircled in gold, next to a simple crucifix. He smiled as he remembered her humor, her tenderness, and the love she brought into his life. He recalled their last night together and was able to accept the memory without much pain.

Many times since he left Indiana, her spirit had guided him. He never believed he would heal, but he did. Prayer did move mountains as Tommy once advised.

Jack now understood how the ripples of one life touch others, and blend as one story across the pages of time. He knew, no matter what the grievance, God forgives men, if they forgive themselves.

He felt sorrow for all the lives he had taken, except for Henry Malone. For Malone, he felt nothing. He believed his action was justified; however, it would never even the score.

He touched Lily' photograph and said, "I miss you."

He closed the album, turned to the first chapter of his final novel, THAT TENDER LIGHT, and read:

JUST BEFORE SUNSET, in that quiet part of day when light lingers and night beckons, the woman emerged from the pines at the northern sweep of the island. Tanned, mysterious, and dressed in white, she was beautiful, with something elegant and erotic in the sway of her hips.

As she strolled along the secluded beach, she skirted the water's edge with the grace of a dancer. Here and there, she toyed with the surf, as it rushed across her bare feet.

When she reached a tidal pool some fifty yards away from my home, she angled away from the water, leaving a trail of delicate footprints in the wet sand.

"She's returned, Sam...

The End